The Queen of Hearts

by

Wilkie Collins

The Echo Library 2005

Published by

The Echo Library

Paperbackshop Ltd
Cockrup Farm House
Coln St Aldwyns
Cirencester GL7 5AZ

www.echo-library.com

ISBN 1-84637-047-7

LETTER OF DEDICATION.

—

TO
EMILE FORGUES.

—

AT a time when French readers were altogether unaware of the existence of any books of my writing, a critical examination of my novels appeared under your signature in the *Revue des Deux Moudes*. I read that article, at the time of its appearance, with sincere pleasure and sincere gratitude to the writer, and I have honestly done my best to profit by it ever since.

At a later period, when arrangements were made for the publication of my novels in Paris, you kindly undertook, at some sacrifice of your own convenience, to give the first of the series—"The Dead Secret"—the great advantage of being rendered into French by your pen. Your excellent translation of "The Lighthouse" had already taught me how to appreciate the value of your assistance; and when "The Dead Secret" appeared in its French form, although I was sensibly gratified, I was by no means surprised to find my fortunate work of fiction, not translated, in the mechanical sense of the word, but transformed from a novel that I had written in my language to a novel that you might have written in yours.

I am now about to ask you to confer one more literary obligation on me by accepting the dedication of this book, as the earliest acknowledgment which it has been in my power to make of the debt I owe to my critic, to my translator, and to my friend.

The stories which form the principal contents of the following pages are all, more or less, exercises in that art which I have now studied anxiously for some years, and which I still hope to cultivate, to better and better purpose, for many more. Allow me, by inscribing the collection to you, to secure one reader for it at the outset of its progress through the world of letters whose capacity for seeing all a writer's defects may be matched by many other critics, but whose rarer faculty of seeing all a writer's merits is equaled by very few.

WILKIE COLLINS.
THE QUEEN OF HEARTS.

CHAPTER I.

OURSELVES.

WE were three quiet, lonely old men, and SHE was a lively, handsome young woman, and we were at our wits' end what to do with her.

A word about ourselves, first of all—a necessary word, to explain the singular situation of our fair young guest.

We are three brothers; and we live in a barbarous, dismal old house called The Glen Tower. Our place of abode stands in a hilly, lonesome district of South Wales. No such thing as a line of railway runs anywhere near us. No gentleman's seat is within an easy drive of us. We are at an unspeakably inconvenient distance from a town, and the village to which we send for our letters is three miles off.

My eldest brother, Owen, was brought up to the Church. All the prime of his life was passed in a populous London parish. For more years than I now like to reckon up, he worked unremittingly, in defiance of failing health and adverse fortune, amid the multitudinous misery of the London poor; and he would, in all probability, have sacrificed his life to his duty long before the present time if The Glen Tower had not come into his possession through two unexpected deaths in the elder and richer branch of our family. This opening to him of a place of rest and refuge saved his life. No man ever drew breath who better deserved the gifts of fortune; for no man, I sincerely believe, more tender of others, more diffident of himself, more gentle, more generous, and more simple-hearted than Owen, ever walked this earth.

My second brother, Morgan, started in life as a doctor, and learned all that his profession could teach him at home and abroad. He realized a moderate independence by his practice, beginning in one of our large northern towns and ending as a physician in London; but, although he was well known and appreciated among his brethren, he failed to gain that sort of reputation with the public which elevates a man into the position of a great doctor. The ladies never liked him. In the first place, he was ugly (Morgan will excuse me for mentioning this); in the second place, he was an inveterate smoker, and he smelled of tobacco when he felt languid pulses in elegant bedrooms; in the third place, he was the most formidably outspoken teller of the truth as regarded himself, his profession, and his patients, that ever imperiled the social standing of the science of medicine. For these reasons, and for others which it is not necessary to mention, he never pushed his way, as a doctor, into the front ranks, and he never cared to do so. About a year after Owen came into possession of The Glen Tower, Morgan discovered that he had saved as much money for his old age as a sensible man could want; that he was tired of the active pursuit—or, as he termed it, of the dignified quackery of his profession; and that it was only common charity to give his invalid brother a companion who could physic him for nothing, and so prevent him from getting rid of his money in the worst of all possible ways, by wasting it on doctors' bills. In a week after Morgan had arrived at these conclusions, he was settled at The Glen Tower; and from that time, opposite as their characters were, my two elder brothers lived together in their lonely retreat, thoroughly understanding, and, in their very different ways, heartily loving one another.

Many years passed before I, the youngest of the three—christened by the unmelodious name of Griffith—found my way, in my turn, to the dreary old house, and the sheltering quiet of the Welsh hills. My career in life had led me away from my brothers; and even now, when we are all united, I have still ties and interests to connect me with the outer world which neither Owen nor Morgan possess.

I was brought up to the Bar. After my first year's study of the law, I wearied of it, and strayed aside idly into the brighter and more attractive paths of literature. My occasional occupation with my pen was varied by long traveling excursions in all parts of the Continent; year by year my circle of gay friends and acquaintances increased, and I bade fair to sink into the condition of a wandering desultory man, without a fixed purpose in life of any sort, when I was saved by what has saved many another in my situation—an attachment to a good and a sensible woman. By the time I had reached the age of thirty-five, I had done what neither of my brothers had done before me—I had married.

As a single man, my own small independence, aided by what little additions to it I could pick up with my pen, had been sufficient for my wants; but with marriage and its responsibilities came the necessity for serious exertion. I returned to my neglected studies, and grappled resolutely, this time, with the intricate difficulties of the law. I was called to the Bar. My wife's father aided me with his interest, and I started into practice without difficulty and without delay.

For the next twenty years my married life was a scene of happiness and prosperity, on which I now look back with a grateful tenderness that no words of mine can express. The memory of my wife is busy at my heart while I think of those past times. The forgotten tears rise in my eyes again, and trouble the course of my pen while it traces these simple lines.

Let me pass rapidly over the one unspeakable misery of my life; let me try to remember now, as I tried to remember then, that she lived to see our only child—our son, who was so good to her, who is still so good to me—grow up to manhood; that her head lay on my bosom when she died; and that the last frail movement of her hand in this world was the movement that brought it closer to her boy's lips.

I bore the blow—with God's help I bore it, and bear it still. But it struck me away forever from my hold on social life; from the purposes and pursuits, the companions and the pleasures of twenty years, which her presence had sanctioned and made dear to me. If my son George had desired to follow my profession, I should still have struggled against myself, and have kept my place in the world until I had seen h im prosperous and settled. But his choice led him to the army; and before his mother's death he had obtained his commission, and had entered on his path in life. No other responsibility remained to claim from me the sacrifice of myself; my brothers had made my place ready for me by their fireside; my heart yearned, in its desolation, for the friends and companions of the old boyish days; my good, brave son promised that no year should pass, as long as he was in England, without his coming to cheer me; and so it happened that I, in my turn, withdrew from the world, which had once been a bright and a happy world to me, and retired to end my days, peacefully, contentedly, and gratefully, as my brothers are ending theirs, in the solitude of The Glen Tower.

How many years have passed since we have all three been united it is not necessary to relate. It will be more to the purpose if I briefly record that we have never been separated since the day which first saw us assembled together in our hillside retreat; that we have never yet wearied of the time, of the place, or of ourselves; and that the influence of solitude on our hearts and minds has not altered them for the worse, for it has not embittered us toward our fellow-creatures, and it has not dried up in us the sources from which harmless occupations and innocent pleasures may flow refreshingly to the last over the waste places of human life. Thus much for our own story, and for the circumstances which have withdrawn us from the world for the rest of our days.

And now imagine us three lonely old men, tall and lean, and white-headed; dressed, more from past habit than from present association, in customary suits of solemn black: Brother Owen, yielding, gentle, and affectionate in look, voice, and manner; brother Morgan, with a quaint, surface-sourness of address, and a tone of dry sarcasm in his talk, which single him out, on all occasions, as a character in our little circle; brother Griffith forming the link between his two elder companions, capable, at one time, of sympathizing with the quiet, thoughtful tone of Owen's conversation, and ready, at another, to exchange brisk severities on life and manners with Morgan—in short, a pliable, double-sided old lawyer, who stands between the clergyman-brother and the physician-brother with an ear ready for each, and with a heart open to both, share and share together.

Imagine the strange old building in which we live to be really what its name implies—a tower standing in a glen; in past times the fortress of a fighting Welsh chieftain; in present times a dreary land-lighthouse, built up in many stories of two rooms each, with a little modern lean-to of cottage form tacked on quaintly to one of its sides; the great hill, on whose lowest slope it stands, rising precipitously behind it; a dark, swift-flowing stream in the valley below; hills on hills all round, and no way of approach but by one of the loneliest and wildest crossroads in all South Wales.

Imagine such a place of abode as this, and such inhabitants of it as ourselves, and them picture the descent among us—as of a goddess dropping from the clouds—of a lively, handsome, fashionable young lady—a bright, gay, butterfly creature, used to flutter away its existence in the broad sunshine of perpetual gayety—a child of the new generation, with all the modern ideas whirling together in her pretty head, and all the modern accomplishments at the tips of her delicate fingers. Imagine such a light-hearted daughter of Eve as this, the spoiled darling of society, the charming spendthrift of Nature's choicest treasures of beauty and youth, suddenly flashing into the dim life of three weary old men—suddenly dropped into the place, of all others, which is least fit for her—suddenly shut out from the world in the lonely quiet of the loneliest home in England. Realize, if it be possible, all that is most whimsical and most anomalous in such a situation as this, and the startling confession contained in the opening sentence of these pages will no longer excite the faintest emotion of surprise. Who can wonder now, when our bright young goddess really descended on us, that I and my brothers were all three at our wits' end what to do with her!

CHAPTER II.

OUR DILEMMA.

WHO is the young lady? And how did she find her way into The Glen Tower?

Her name (in relation to which I shall have something more to say a little further on) is Jessie Yelverton. She is an orphan and an only child. Her mother died while she was an infant; her father was my dear and valued friend, Major Yelverton. He lived long enough to celebrate his darling's seventh birthday. When he died he intrusted his authority over her and his responsibility toward her to his brother and to me.

When I was summoned to the reading of the major's will, I knew perfectly well that I should hear myself appointed guardian and executor with his brother; and I had been also made acquainted with my lost friend's wishes as to his daughter's education, and with his intentions as to the disposal of all his property in her favor. My own idea, therefore, was, that the reading of the will would inform me of nothing which I had not known in the testator's lifetime. When the day came for hearing it, however, I found that I had been over hasty in arriving at this conclusion. Toward the end of the document there was a clause inserted which took me entirely by surprise.

After providing for the education of Miss Yelverton under the direction of her guardians, and for her residence, under ordinary circumstances, with the major's sister, Lady Westwick, the clause concluded by saddling the child's future inheritance with this curious condition:

From the period of her leaving school to the period of her reaching the age of twenty-one years, Miss Yelverton was to pass not less than six consecutive weeks out of every year under the roof of one of her two guardians. During the lives of both of them, it was left to her own choice to say which of the two she would prefer to live with. In all other respects the condition was imperative. If she forfeited it, excepting, of course, the case of the deaths of both her guardians, she was only to have a life-interest in the property; if she obeyed it, the money itself was to become her own possession on the day when she completed her twenty-first year.

This clause in the will, as I have said, took me at first by surprise. I remembered how devotedly Lady Westwick had soothed her sister-in-law's death-bed sufferings, and how tenderly she had afterward watched over the welfare of the little motherless child—I remembered the innumerable claims she had established in this way on her brother's confidence in her affection for his orphan daughter, and I was, therefore, naturally amazed at the appearance of a condition in his will which seemed to show a positive distrust of Lady Westwick's undivided influence over the character and conduct of her niece.

A few words from my fellow-guardian, Mr. Richard Yelverton, and a little after-consideration of some of my deceased friend's peculiarities of disposition and feeling, to which I had not hitherto attached sufficient importance, were enough to make me understand the motives by which he had been influenced in providing for the future of his child.

Major Yelverton had raised himself to a position of affluence and eminence from a very humble origin. He was the son of a small farmer, and it was his pride never to forget this circumstance, never to be ashamed of it, and never to allow the prejudices of society to influence his own settled opinions on social questions in general.

Acting, in all that related to his intercourse with the world, on such principles as these, the major, it is hardly necessary to say, held some strangely heterodox opinions on the modern education of girls, and on the evil influence of society over the characters of women in general. Out of the strength of those opinions, and out of the certainty of his conviction that his sister did not share them, had grown that condition in his will which removed his daughter from the influence of her aunt for six consec utive weeks in every year. Lady Westwick was the most light-hearted, the most generous, the most impulsive of women; capable, when any serious occasion called it forth, of all that was devoted and self-sacrificing, but, at other and ordinary times, constitutionally restless, frivolous, and eager for perpetual gayety. Distrusting the sort of life which he knew his daughter would lead under her aunt's roof, and at the same time gratefully remembering his sister's affectionate devotion toward his dying wife and her helpless infant, Major Yelverton had attempted to make a compromise, which, while it allowed Lady Westwick the close domestic intercourse with her niece that she had earned by innumerable kind offices, should, at the same time, place the young girl for a fixed period of every year of her minority under the corrective care of two such quiet old-fashioned guardians as his brother and myself. Such is the history of the clause in the will. My friend little thought, when he dictated it, of the extraordinary result to which it was one day to lead.

For some years, however, events ran on smoothly enough. Little Jessie was sent to an excellent school, with strict instructions to the mistress to make a good girl of her, and not a fashionable young lady. Although she was reported to be anything but a pattern pupil in respect of attention to her lessons, she became from the first the chosen favorite of every one about her. The very offenses which she committed against the discipline of the school were of the sort which provoke a smile even on the stern countenance of authority itself. One of these quaint freaks of mischief may not inappropriately be mentioned here, inasmuch as it gained her the pretty nickname under which she will be found to appear occasionally in these pages.

On a certain autumn night shortly after the Midsummer vacation, the mistress of the school fancied she saw a light under the door of the bedroom occupied by Jessie and three other girls. It was then close on midnight; and, fearing that some case of sudden illness might have happened, she hastened into the room. On opening the door, she discovered, to her horror and amazement, that all four girls were out of bed—were dressed in brilliantly-fantastic costumes, representing the four grotesque "Queens" of Hearts, Diamonds, Spades, and Clubs, familiar to us all on the pack of cards—and were dancing a quadrille, in which Jessie sustained the character of The Queen of Hearts. The next morning's investigation disclosed that Miss Yelverton had smuggled the dresses into the school, and had amused herself by giving an impromptu fancy ball to her companions, in imitation of an entertainment of the same kind at which she had figured in a "court-card" quadrille at her aunt's country house.

The dresses were instantly confiscated and the necessary punishment promptly administered; but the remembrance of Jessie's extraordinary outrage on bedroom discipline lasted long enough to become one of the traditions of the school, and she and her sister-culprits were thenceforth hailed as the "queens" of the four "suites" by their class-companions whenever the mistress's back was turned, Whatever might have become of the nicknames thus employed in relation to the other three girls, such a mock title as The Queen of Hearts was too appropriately descriptive of the natural charm of Jessie's character, as well as of the adventure in which she had taken the lead, not to rise naturally to the lips of every one who knew her. It followed her to her aunt's house—it came to be as habitually and familiarly connected with her, among her friends of all ages, as if it had been formally inscribed on her baptismal register; and it has stolen its way into these pages because it falls from my pen naturally and inevitably, exactly as it often falls from my lips in real life.

When Jessie left school the first difficulty presented itself—in other words, the necessity arose of fulfilling the conditions of the will. At that time I was already settled at The Glen Tower, and her living six weeks in our dismal solitude and our humdrum society was, as she herself frankly wrote me word, quite out of the question. Fortunately, she had always got on well with her uncle and his family; so she exerted her liberty of choice, and, much to her own relief and to mine also, passed her regular six weeks of probation, year after year, under Mr. Richard Yelverton's roof.

During this period I heard of her regularly, sometimes from my fellow-guardian, sometimes from my son George, who, whenever his military duties allowed him the opportunity, contrived to see her, now at her aunt's house, and now at Mr. Yelverton's. The particulars of her character and conduct, which I gleaned in this way, more than sufficed to convince me that the poor major's plan for the careful training of his daughter's disposition, though plausible enough in theory, was little better than a total failure in practice. Miss Jessie, to use the expressive common phrase, took after her aunt. She was as generous, as impulsive, as light-hearted, as fond of change, and gayety, and fine clothes—in short, as complete and genuine a woman as Lady Westwick herself. It was impossible to reform the "Queen of Hearts," and equally impossible not to love her. Such, in few words, was my fellow-guardian's report of his experience of our handsome young ward.

So the time passed till the year came of which I am now writing—the ever-memorable year, to England, of the Russian war. It happened that I had heard less than usual at this period, and indeed for many months before it, of Jessie and her proceedings. My son had been ordered out with his regiment to the Crimea in 1854, and had other work in hand now than recording the sayings and doings of a young lady. Mr. Richard Yelverton, who had been hitherto used to write to me with tolerable regularity, seemed now, for some reason that I could not conjecture, to have forgotten my existence. Ultimately I was reminded of my ward by one of George's own letters, in which he asked for news of her; and I wrote at once to Mr. Yelverton. The answer that reached me was written by his wife: he was dangerously ill. The next letter that came informed me of his death. This happened early in the spring of the year 1855.

I am ashamed to confess it, but the change in my own position was the first idea that crossed my mind when I read the news of Mr. Yelverton's death. I was now left sole guardian, and Jessie Yelverton wanted a year still of coming of age.

By the next day's post I wrote to her about the altered state of the relations between us. She was then on the Continent with her aunt, having gone abroad at the very beginning of the year. Consequently, so far as eighteen hundred and fifty-five was concerned, the condition exacted by the will yet remained to be performed. She had still six weeks to pass—her last six weeks, seeing that she was now twenty years old—under the roof of one of her guardians, and I was now the only guardian left.

In due course of time I received my answer, written on rose-colored paper, and expressed throughout in a tone of light, easy, feminine banter, which amused me in spite of myself. Miss Jessie, according to her own account, was hesitating, on receipt of my letter, between two alternatives—the one, of allowing herself to be buried six weeks in The Glen Tower; the other, of breaking the condition, giving up the money, and remaining magnanimously contented with nothing but a life-interest in her father's property. At present she inclined decidedly toward giving up the money and escaping the clutches of "the three horrid old men;" but she would let me know again if she happened to change her mind. And so, with best love, she would beg to remain always affectionately mine, as long as she was well out of my reach.

The summer passed, the autumn came, and I never heard from her again. Under ordinary circumstances, this long silence might have made me feel a little uneasy. But news reached me about this time from the Crimea that my son was wounded—not dangerously, thank God, but still severely enough to be la id up— and all my anxieties were now centered in that direction. By the beginning of September, however, I got better accounts of him, and my mind was made easy enough to let me think of Jessie again. Just as I was considering the necessity of writing once more to my refractory ward, a second letter arrived from her. She had returned at last from abroad, had suddenly changed her mind, suddenly grown sick of society, suddenly become enamored of the pleasures of retirement, and suddenly found out that the three horrid old men were three dear old men, and that six weeks' solitude at The Glen Tower was the luxury, of all others, that she languished for most. As a necessary result of this altered state of things, she would therefore now propose to spend her allotted six weeks with her guardian. We might certainly expect her on the twentieth of September, and she would take the greatest care to fit herself for our society by arriving in the lowest possible spirits, and bringing her own sackcloth and ashes along with her.

The first ordeal to which this alarming letter forced me to submit was the breaking of the news it contained to my two brothers. The disclosure affected them very differently. Poor dear Owen merely turned pale, lifted his weak, thin hands in a panic-stricken manner, and then sat staring at me in speechless and motionless bewilderment. Morgan stood up straight before me, plunged both his hands into his pockets, burst suddenly into the harshest laugh I ever heard from his lips, and told me, with an air of triumph, that it was exactly what he expected.

"What you expected?" I repeated, in astonishment.

"Yes," returned Morgan, with his bitterest emphasis. "It doesn't surprise me in the least. It's the way things go in this world—it's the regular moral see-saw of good and evil—the old story with the old end to it. They were too happy in the garden of Eden—down comes the serpent and turns them out. Solomon was too wise—down comes the Queen of Sheba, and makes a fool of him. We've been too comfortable at The Glen Tower—down comes a woman, and sets us all three by the ears together. All I wonder at is that it hasn't happened before." With those words Morgan resignedly took out his pipe, put on his old felt hat and turned to the door.

"You're not going away before she comes?" exclaimed Owen, piteously. "Don't leave us—please don't leave us!"

"Going!" cried Morgan, with great contempt. "What should I gain by that? When destiny has found a man out, and heated his gridiron for him, he has nothing left to do, that I know of, but to get up and sit on it."

I opened my lips to protest against the implied comparison between a young lady and a hot gridiron, but, before I could speak, Morgan was gone.

"Well," I said to Owen, "we must make the best of it. We must brush up our manners, and set the house tidy, and amuse her as well as we can. The difficulty is where to put her; and, when that is settled, the next puzzle will be, what to order in to make her comfortable. It's a hard thing, brother, to say what will or what will not please a young lady's taste."

Owen looked absently at me, in greater bewilderment than ever—opened his eyes in perplexed consideration—repeated to himself slowly the word "tastes"— and then helped me with this suggestion:

"Hadn't we better begin, Griffith, by getting her a plum-cake?"

"My dear Owen," I remonstrated, "it is a grown young woman who is coming to see us, not a little girl from school."

"Oh!" said Owen, more confused than before. "Yes—I see; we couldn't do wrong, I suppose—could we?—if we got her a little dog, and a lot of new gowns."

There was, evidently, no more help in the way of advice to be expected from Owen than from Morgan himself. As I came to that conclusion, I saw through the window our old housekeeper on her way, with her basket, to the kitchen-garden, and left the room to ascertain if she could assist us.

To my great dismay, the housekeeper took even a more gloomy view than Morgan of the approaching event. When I had explained all the circumstances to her, she carefully put down her basket, crossed her arms, and said to me in slow, deliberate, mysterious tones:

"You want my advice about what's to be done with this young woman? Well, sir, here's my advice: Don't you trouble your head about her. It won't be no use. Mind, I tell you, it won't be no use."

"What do you mean?"

"You look at this place, sir—it's more like a prison than a house, isn't it? You, look at us as lives in it. We've got (saving your presence) a foot apiece in our graves, haven't we? When you was young yourself, sir, what would you have done if they had shut you up for six weeks in such a place as this, among your grandfathers and grandmothers, with their feet in the grave?"

"I really can't say."

"I can, sir. You'd have run away. *She'll* run away. Don't you worry your head about her—she'll save you the trouble. I tell you again, she'll run away."

With those ominous words the housekeeper took up her basket, sighed heavily, and left me.

I sat down under a tree quite helpless. Here was the whole responsibility shifted upon my miserable shoulders. Not a lady in the neighborhood to whom I could apply for assistance, and the nearest shop eight miles distant from us. The toughest case I ever had to conduct, when I was at the Bar, was plain sailing compared with the difficulty of receiving our fair guest.

It was absolutely necessary, however, to decide at once where she was to sleep. All the rooms in the tower were of stone—dark, gloomy, and cold even in the summer-time. Impossible to put her in any one of them. The only other alternative was to lodge her in the little modern lean-to, which I have already described as being tacked on to the side of the old building. It contained three cottage-rooms, and they might be made barely habitable for a young lady. But then those rooms were occupied by Morgan. His books were in one, his bed was in another, his pipes and general lumber were in the third. Could I expect him, after the sour similitudes he had used in reference to our expected visitor, to turn out of his habitation and disarrange all his habits for her convenience? The bare idea of proposing the thing to him seemed ridiculous; and yet inexorable necessity left me no choice but to make the hopeless experiment. I walked back to the tower hastily and desperately, to face the worst that might happen before my courage cooled altogether.

On crossing the threshold of the hall door I was stopped, to my great amazement, by a procession of three of the farm-servants, followed by Morgan, all walking after each other, in Indian file, toward the spiral staircase that led to the top of the tower. The first of the servants carried the materials for making a fire; the second bore an inverted arm-chair on his head; the third tottered under a heavy load of books; while Morgan came last, with his canister of tobacco in his hand, his dressing-gown over his shoulders, and his whole collection of pipes hugged up together in a bundle under his arm.

"What on earth does this mean?" I inquired.

"It means taking Time by the forelock," answered Morgan, looking at me with a smile of sour satisfaction. "I've got the start of your young woman, Griffith, and I'm making the most of it."

"But where, in Heaven's name, are you going?" I asked, as the head man of the procession disappeared with his firing up the staircase.

"How high is this tower?" retorted Morgan.

"Seven stories, to be sure," I replied.

"Very good," said my eccentric brother, setting his foot on the first stair, "I'm going up to the seventh."

"You can't," I shouted.

"*She* can't, you mean," said Morgan, "and that's exactly why I'm going there."

"But the room is not furnished."

"It's out of her reach."

"One of the windows has fallen to pieces."

"It's out of her reach."

"There's a crow's nest in the corner."

"It's out of her reach."

By the time this unanswerable argument had attained its third repetition, Morgan, in his turn, had disappeared up the winding stairs. I knew him too well to attempt any further protest.

Here was my first difficulty smoothed away most unexpectedly; for here were the rooms in the lean-to placed by their owner's free act and deed at my disposal. I wrote on the spot to the one upholsterer of our distant county town to come immediately and survey the premises, and sent off a mounted messenger with the letter. This done, and the necessary order also dispatched to the carpenter and glazier to set them at work on Morgan's sky-parlor in the seventh story, I began to feel, for the first time, as if my scattered wits were coming back to me. By the time the evening had closed in I had hit on no less than three excellent ideas, all providing for the future comfort and amusement of our fair guest. The first idea was to get her a Welsh pony; the second was to hire a piano from the county town; the third was to send for a boxful of novels from London. I must confess I thought these projects for pleasing her very happily conceived, and Owen agreed with me. Morgan, as usual, took the opposite view. He said she would yawn over the novels, turn up her nose at the piano, and fracture her skull with the pony. As for the housekeeper, she stuck to her text as stoutly in the evening as she had stuck to it in the morning. "Pianner or no pianner, story-book or no story-book, pony or no pony, you mark my words, sir—that young woman will run away."

Such were the housekeeper's parting words when she wished me good-night.

When the next morning came, and brought with it that terrible waking time which sets a man's hopes and projects before him, the great as well as the small, stripped bare of every illusion, it is not to be concealed that I felt less sanguine of our success in entertaining the coming guest. So far as external preparations were concerned, there seemed, indeed, but little to improve; but apart from these, what had we to offer, in ourselves and our society, to attract her? There lay the knotty point of the question, and there the grand difficulty of finding an answer.

I fall into serious reflection while I am dressing on the pursuits and occupations with which we three brothers have been accustomed, for years past, to beguile the time. Are they at all likely, in the case of any one of us, to interest or amuse her?

My chief occupation, to begin with the youngest, consists, in acting as steward on Owen's property. The routine of my duties has never lost its sober attraction to my tastes, for it has always employed me in watching the best interests of my brother, and of my son also, who is one day to be his heir. But can I expect our fair guest to sympathize with such family concerns as these? Clearly not.

Morgan's pursuit comes next in order of review—a pursuit of a far more ambitious nature than mine. It was always part of my second brother's whimsical, self-contradictory character to view with the profoundest contempt the learned profession by which he gained his livelihood, and he is now occupying the long leisure hours of his old age in composing a voluminous treatise, intended, one of these days, to eject the whole body corporate of doctors from the position which they have usurped in the estimation of their fellow-creatures. This daring work is entitled "An Examination of the Claims of Medicine on the Gratitude of Mankind. Decided in the Negative by a Retired Physician." So far as I can tell, the book is likely to extend to the dimensions of an Encyclopedia; for it is Morgan's plan to treat his comprehensive subject principally from the historical point of view, and to run down all the doctors of antiquity, one after another, in regular succession, from the first of the tribe. When I last heard of his progress he was hard on the heels of Hippocrates, but had no immediate prospect of tripping up his successor, Is this the sort of occupation (I ask myself) in which a modern young lady is likely to feel the slightest interest? Once again, clearly not.

Owen's favorite employment is, in its way, quite as characteristic as Morgan's, and it has the great additional advantage of appealing to a much larger variety of tastes. My eldest brother—great at drawing and painting when he was a lad, always interested in artists and their works in after life—has resumed, in his declining years, the holiday occupation of his schoolboy days. As an amateur landscape-painter, he works with more satisfaction to himself, uses more color, wears out more brushes, and makes a greater smell of paint in his studio than any artist by profession, native or foreign, whom I ever met with. In look, in manner, and in disposition, the gentlest of mankind, Owen, by some singular anomaly in his character, which he seems to have caught from Morgan, glories placidly in the wildest and most frightful range of subjects which his art is capable of representing. Immeasurable ruins, in howling wildernesses, with blood-red sunsets gleaming over them; thunder-clouds rent with lightning, hovering over splitting trees on the verges of awful precipices; hurricanes, shipwrecks, waves, and whirlpools follow each other on his canvas, without an intervening glimpse of quiet everyday nature to relieve the succession of pictorial horrors. When I see him at his easel, so neat and quiet, so unpretending and modest in himself, with such a composed expression on his attentive face, with such a weak white hand to guide such bold, big brushes, and when I look at the frightful canvasful of terrors which he is serenely aggravating in fierceness and intensity with every successive touch, I find it difficult to realize the connection between my brother and his work, though I see them before me not six inches apart. Will this quaint spectacle possess any humorous attractions for Miss Jessie? Perhaps it may. There is some slight chance that Owen's employment will be lucky enough to interest her.

Thus far my morning cogitations advance doubtfully enough, but they altogether fail in carrying me beyond the narrow circle of The Glen Tower. I try hard, in our visitor's interest, to look into the resources of the little world around us, and I find my efforts rewarded by the prospect of a total blank.

Is there any presentable living soul in the neighborhood whom we can invite to meet her? Not one. There are, as I have already said, no country seats near us; and society in the county town has long since learned to regard us as three misanthropes, strongly suspected, from our monastic way of life and our dismal black costume, of being popish priests in disguise. In other parts of England the clergyman of the parish might help us out of our difficulty; but here in South Wales, and in this latter half of the nineteenth century, we have the old type parson of the days of Fielding still in a state of perfect preservation. Our local clergyman receives a stipend which is too paltry to bear comparison with the wages of an ordinary mechanic. In dress, manners, and tastes he is about on a level with the upper class of agricultural laborer. When attempts have been made by well-meaning gentlefolks to recognize the claims of his profession by asking him to their houses, he has been known, on more than one occasion, to leave his plowman's pair of shoes in the hall, and enter the drawing-room respectfully in his stockings. Where he preaches, miles and miles away from us and from the poor cottage in which he lives, if he sees any of the company in the squire's pew yawn or fidget in their places, he takes it as a hint that they are tired of listening, and closes his sermon instantly at the end of the sentence. Can we ask this most irreverent and unclerical of men to meet a young lady? I doubt, even if we made the attempt, whether we should succeed, by fair means, in getting him beyond the servants' hall.

Dismissing, therefore, all idea of inviting visitors to entertain our guest, and feeling, at the same time, more than doubtful of her chance of discovering any attraction in the sober society of the inmates of the house, I finish my dressing and go down to breakfast, secretly veering round to the housekeeper's opinion that Miss Jessie will really bring matters to an abrupt conclusion by running away. I find Morgan as bitterly resigned to his destiny as ever, and Owen so affectionately anxious to make himself of some use, and so lamentably ignorant of how to begin, that I am driven to disembarrass myself of him at the outset by a stratagem.

I suggest to him that our visitor is sure to be interested in pictures, and that it would be a pretty attention, on his part, to paint her a landscape to hang up in her room. Owen brightens directly, informs me in his softest tones that he is then at work on the Earthquake at Lisbon, and inquires whether I think she would like that subject. I preserve my gravity sufficiently to answer in the affirmative, and my brother retires meekly to his studio, to depict the engulfing of a city and the destruction of a population. Morgan withdraws in his turn to the top of the tower, threatening, when our guest comes, to draw all his meals up to his new residence by means of a basket and string. I am left alone for an hour, and then the upholsterer arrives from the county town.

This worthy man, on being informed of our emergency, sees his way, apparently, to a good stroke of business, and thereupon wins my lasting gratitude by taking, in opposition to every one else, a bright and hopeful view of existing circumstances.

"You'll excuse me, sir," he says, confidentially, when I show him the rooms in the lean-to, "but this is a matter of experience. I'm a family man myself, with grown-up daughters of my own, and the natures of young women are well known to me. Make their rooms comfortable, and you make 'em happy. Surround their lives, sir, with a suitable atmosphere of furniture, and you never hear a word of complaint drop from their lips. Now, with regard to these rooms, for example, sir—you put a neat French bedstead in that corner, with curtains conformable— say a tasty chintz; you put on that bedstead what I will term a sufficiency of bedding; and you top up with a sweet little eider-down quilt, as light as roses, and similar the same in color. You do that, and what follows? You please her eye when she lies down at night, and you please her eye when she gets up in the morning—and you're all right so far, and so is she. I will not dwell, sir, on the toilet-table, nor will I seek to detain you about the glass to show her figure, and the other glass to show her face, because I have the articles in stock, and will be myself answerable for their effect on a lady's mind and person."

He led the way into the next room as he spoke, and arranged its future fittings, and decorations, as he had already planned out the bedroom, with the strictest reference to the connection which experience had shown him to exist between comfortable furniture and female happiness.

Thus far, in my helpless state of mind, the man's confidence had impressed me in spite of myself, and I had listened to him in superstitious silence. But as he continued to rise, by regular gradations, from one climax of upholstery to another, warning visions of his bill disclosed themselves in the remote background of the scene of luxury and magnificence which my friend was conjuring up. Certain sharp professional instincts of bygone times resumed their influence over me; I began to start doubts and ask questions; and as a necessary consequence the interview between us soon assumed something like a practical form.

Having ascertained what the probable expense of furnishing would amount to and having discovered that the process of transforming the lean-to (allowing for the time required to procure certain articles of rarity from Bristol) would occupy nearly a fortnight, I dismissed the upholsterer with the understanding that I should take a day or two for consideration, and let him know the result. It was then the fifth of September, and our Queen of Hearts was to arrive on the twentieth. The work, therefore, if it was begun on the seventh or eighth, would be begun in time.

In making all my calculations with a reference to the twentieth of September, I relied implicitly, it will be observed, on a young lady's punctuality in keeping an appointment which she had herself made. I can only account for such extraordinary simplicity on my part on the supposition that my wits had become sadly rusted by long seclusion from society. Whether it was referable to this cause or not, my innocent trustfulness was at any rate destined to be practically rebuked before long in the most surprising manner. Little did I suspect, when I parted from the upholsterer on the fifth of the month, what the tenth of the month had in store for me.

On the seventh I made up my mind to have the bedroom furnished at once, and to postpone the question of the sitting-room for a few days longer. Having dispatched the necessary order to that effect, I next wrote to hire the piano and to order the box of novels. This done, I congratulated myself on the forward state of the preparations, and sat down to repose in the atmosphere of my own happy delusions.

On the ninth the wagon arrived with the furniture, and the men set to work on the bedroom. From this moment Morgan retired definitely to the top of the tower, and Owen became too nervous to lay the necessary amount of paint on the Earthquake at Lisbon.

On the tenth the work was proceeding bravely. Toward noon Owen and I strolled to the door to enjoy the fine autumn sunshine. We were sitting lazily on our favorite bench in front of the tower when we were startled by a shout from above us. Looking up directly, we saw Morgan half in and half out of his narrow window In the seventh story, gesticulating violently with the stem of his long meerschaum pipe in the direction of the road below us.

We gazed eagerly in the quarter thus indicated, but our low position prevented us for some time from seeing anything. At last we both discerned an old yellow post-chaise distinctly and indisputably approaching us.

Owen and I looked at one another in panic-stricken silence. It was coming to us—and what did it contain? Do pianos travel in chaises? Are boxes of novels conveyed to their destination by a postilion? We expected the piano and expected the novels, but nothing else—unquestionably nothing else.

The chaise took the turn in the road, passed through the gateless gap in our rough inclosure-wall of loose stone, and rapidly approached us. A bonnet appeared at the window and a hand gayly waved a white handkerchief.

Powers of caprice, confusion, and dismay! It was Jessie Yelverton herself— arriving, without a word of warning, exactly ten days before her time.

CHAPTER III.

OUR QUEEN OF' HEARTS.

THE chaise stopped in front of us, and before we had recovered from our bewilderment the gardener had opened the door and let down the steps.

A bright, laughing face, prettily framed round by a black veil passed over the head and tied under the chin—a traveling-dress of a nankeen color, studded with blue buttons and trimmed with white braid—a light brown cloak over it—little neatly-gloved hands, which seized in an instant on one of mine and on one of Owen's—two dark blue eyes, which seemed to look us both through and through in a moment—a clear, full, merrily confident voice—a look and manner gayly and gracefully self-possessed—such were the characteristics of our fair guest which first struck me at the moment when she left the postchaise and possessed herself of my hand.

"Don't begin by scolding me," she said, before I could utter a word of welcome. "There will be time enough for that in the course of the next six weeks. I beg pardon, with all possible humility, for the offense of coming ten days before my time. Don't ask me to account for it, please; if you do, I shall be obliged to confess the truth. My dear sir, the fact is, this is an act of impulse."

She paused, and looked us both in the face with a bright confidence in her own flow of nonsense that was perfectly irresistible.

"I must tell you all about it," she ran on, leading the way to the bench, and inviting us, by a little mock gesture of supplication, to seat ourselves on either side of her. "I feel so guilty till I've told you. Dear me! how nice this is! Here I am quite at home already. Isn't it odd? Well, and how do you think it happene d? The morning before yesterday Matilda—there is Matilda, picking up my bonnet from the bottom of that remarkably musty carriage—Matilda came and woke me as usual, and I hadn't an idea in my head, I assure you, till she began to brush my hair. Can you account for it?—I can't—but she seemed, somehow, to brush a sudden fancy for coming here into my head. When I went down to breakfast, I said to my aunt, 'Darling, I have an irresistible impulse to go to Wales at once, instead of waiting till the twentieth.' She made all the necessary objections, poor dear, and my impulse got stronger and stronger with every one of them. 'I'm quite certain,' I said, 'I shall never go at all if I don't go now.' 'In that case,' says my aunt, 'ring the bell, and have your trunks packed. Your whole future depends on your going; and you terrify me so inexpressibly that I shall be glad to get rid of you.' You may not think it, to look at her—but Matilda is a treasure; and in three hours more I was on the Great Western Railway. I have not the least idea how I got here—except that the men helped me everywhere. They are always such delightful creatures! I have been casting myself, and my maid, and my trunks on their tender mercies at every point in the journey, and their polite attentions exceed all belief. I slept at your horrid little county town last night; and the night before I missed a steamer or a train, I forget which, and slept at Bristol; and that's how I got here. And, now I am here, I ought to give my guardian a kiss—oughtn't

I? Shall I call you papa? I think I will. And shall I call *you* uncle, sir, and give you a kiss too? We shall come to it sooner or later—shan't we?—and we may as well begin at once, I suppose."

Her fresh young lips touched my old withered cheek first, and then Owen's; a soft, momentary shadow of tenderness, that was very pretty and becoming, passing quickly over the sunshine and gayety of her face as she saluted us. The next moment she was on her feet again, inquiring "who the wonderful man was who built The Glen Tower," and wanting to go all over it immediately from top to bottom.

As we took her into the house, I made the necessary apologies for the miserable condition of the lean-to, and assured her that, ten days later, she would have found it perfectly ready to receive her. She whisked into the rooms—looked all round them—whisked out again—declared she had come to live in the old Tower, and not in any modern addition to it, and flatly declined to inhabit the lean-to on any terms whatever. I opened my lips to state certain objections, but she slipped away in an instant and made straight for the Tower staircase.

"Who lives here?" she asked, calling down to us, eagerly, from the first-floor landing.

"I do," said Owen; "but, if you would like me to move out--"

She was away up the second flight before he could say any more. The next sound we heard, as we slowly followed her, was a peremptory drumming against the room door of the second story.

"Anybody here?" we heard her ask through the door.

I called up to her that, under ordinary circumstances, I was there; but that, like Owen, I should be happy to move out—

My polite offer was cut short as my brother's had been. We heard more drumming at the door of the third story. There were two rooms here also—one perfectly empty, the other stocked with odds and ends of dismal, old-fashioned furniture for which we had no use, and grimly ornamented by a life-size basket figure supporting a complete suit of armor in a sadly rusty condition. When Owen and I got to the third-floor landing, the door was open; Miss Jessie had taken possession of the rooms; and we found her on a chair, dusting the man in armor with her cambric pocket-handkerchief.

"I shall live here," she said, looking round at us briskly over her shoulder.

We both remonstrated, but it was quite in vain. She told us that she had an impulse to live with the man in armor, and that she would have her way, or go back immediately in the post-chaise, which we pleased. Finding it impossible to move her, we bargained that she should, at least, allow the new bed and the rest of the comfortable furniture in the lean-to to be moved up into the empty room for her sleeping accommodation. She consented to this condition, protesting, however, to the last against being compelled to sleep in a bed, because it was a modern conventionality, out of all harmony with her place of residence and her friend in armor.

Fortunately for the repose of Morgan, who, under other circumstances, would have discovered on the very first day that his airy retreat was by no means high enough to place him out of Jessie's reach, the idea of settling herself instantly in her new habitation excluded every other idea from the mind of our fair guest. She pinned up the nankeen-colored traveling dress in festoons all round her on the spot; informed us that we were now about to make acquaintance with her in the new character of a woman of business; and darted downstairs in mad high spirits, screaming for Matilda and the trunks like a child for a set of new toys. The wholesome protest of Nature against the artificial restraints of modern life expressed itself in all that she said and in all that she did. She had never known what it was to be happy before, because she had never been allowed, until now, to do anything for herself. She was down on her knees at one moment, blowing the fire, and telling us that she felt like Cinderella; she was up on a table the next, attacking the cobwebs with a long broom, and wishing she had been born a housemaid. As for my unfortunate friend, the upholsterer, he was leveled to the ranks at the first effort he made to assume the command of the domestic forces in the furniture department. She laughed at him, pushed him about, disputed all his conclusions, altered all his arrangements, and ended by ordering half his bedroom furniture to be taken back again, for the one unanswerable reason that she meant to do without it.

As evening approached, the scene presented by the two rooms became eccentric to a pitch of absurdity which is quite indescribable. The grim, ancient walls of the bedroom had the liveliest modern dressing-gowns and morning-wrappers hanging all about them. The man in armor had a collection of smart little boots and shoes dangling by laces and ribbons round his iron legs. A worm-eaten, steel-clasped casket, dragged out of a corner, frowned on the upholsterer's brand-new toilet-table, and held a miscellaneous assortment of combs, hairpins, and brushes. Here stood a gloomy antique chair, the patriarch of its tribe, whose arms of blackened oak embraced a pair of pert, new deal bonnet-boxes not a fortnight old. There, thrown down lightly on a rugged tapestry table-cover, the long labor of centuries past, lay the brief, delicate work of a week ago in the shape of silk and muslin dresses turned inside out. In the midst of all these confusions and contradictions, Miss Jessie ranged to and fro, the active center of the whole scene of disorder, now singing at the top of her voice, and now declaring in her lighthearted way that one of us must make up his mind to marry her immediately, as she was determined to settle for the rest of her life at The Glen Tower.

She followed up that announcement, when we met at dinner, by inquiring if we quite understood by this time that she had left her "company manners" in London, and that she meant to govern us all at her absolute will and pleasure, throughout the whole period of her stay. Having thus provided at the outset for the due recognition of her authority by the household generally and individually having briskly planned out all her own forthcoming occupations and amusements over the wine and fruit at dessert, and having positively settled, between her first and second cups of tea, where our connection with them was to begin and where it was to end, she had actually succeeded, when the time came to separate for the night, in setting us as much at our ease, and in making herself as completely a necessary part of our household as if she had lived among us for years and years past.

Such was our first day's experience of the formidable guest whose anticipated visit had so sorely and so absurdly discomposed us all. I could hardly believe that I had actually wasted hours of precious time in worrying myself and everybody else in the house about the best means of laboriously entertaining a lively, high-spirited girl, who was perfectly capable, without an effort on her own part or on ours, of entertaining herself.

Having upset every one of our calculations on the first day of her arrival, she next falsified all our predictions before she had been with us a week. Instead of fracturing her skull with the pony, as Morgan had prophesied, she sat the sturdy, sure-footed, mischievous little brute as if she were part and parcel of himself. With an old water-proof cloak of mine on her shoulders, with a broad-flapped Spanish hat of Owen's on her head, with a wild imp of a Welsh boy following her as guide and groom on a bare-backed pony, and with one of the largest and ugliest cur-dogs in England (which she had picked up, lost and starved by the wayside) barking at her heels, she scoured the country in all directions, and came back to dinner, as she herself expressed it, "with the manners of an Amazon, the complexion of a dairy-maid, and the appetite of a wolf."

On days when incessant rain kept her indoors, she amused herself with a new freak. Making friends everywhere, as became The Queen of Hearts, she even ingratiated herself with the sour old housekeeper, who had predicted so obstinately that she was certain to run away. To the amazement of everybody in the house, she spent hours in the kitchen, learning to make puddings and pies, and trying all sorts of recipes with very varying success, from an antiquated cookery book which she had discovered at the back of my bookshelves. At other times, when I expected her to be upstairs, languidly examining her finery, and idly polishing her trinkets, I heard of her in the stables, feeding the rabbits, and talking to the raven, or found her in the conservatory, fumigating the plants, and half suffocating the gardener, who was trying to moderate her enthusiasm in the production of smoke.

Instead of finding amusement, as we had expected, in Owen's studio, she puckered up her pretty face in grimaces of disgust at the smell of paint in the room, and declared that the horrors of the Earthquake at Lisbon made her feel hysterical. Instead of showing a total want of interest in my business occupations on the estate, she destroyed my dignity as steward by joining me in my rounds on her pony, with her vagabond retinue at her heels. Instead of devouring the novels I had ordered for her, she left them in the box, and put her feet on it when she felt sleepy after a hard day's riding. Instead of practicing for hours every evening at the piano, which I had hired with such a firm conviction of her using it, she showed us tricks on the cards, taught us new games, initiated us into the mystics of dominoes, challenged us with riddles, an even attempted to stimulate us into acting charades—in short, tried every evening amusement in the whole category except the amusement of music. Every new aspect of her character was a new surprise to us, and every fresh occupation that she chose was a fresh contradiction to our previous expectations. The value of experience as a guide is unquestionable in many of the most important affairs of life; but, speaking for myself personally, I never understood the utter futility of it, where a woman is concerned, until I was brought into habits of daily communication with our fair guest.

In her domestic relations with ourselves she showed that exquisite nicety of discrimination in studying our characters, habits and tastes which comes by instinct with women, and which even the longest practice rarely teaches in similar perfection to men. She saw at a glance all the underlying tenderness and generosity concealed beneath Owen's external shyness, irresolution, and occasional reserve; and, from first to last, even in her gayest moments, there was always a certain quietly-implied consideration—an easy, graceful, delicate deference—in her manner toward my eldest brother, which won upon me and upon him every hour in the day.

With me she was freer in her talk, quicker in her actions, readier and bolder in all the thousand little familiarities of our daily intercourse. When we met in the morning she always took Owen's hand, and waited till he kissed her on the forehead. In my case she put both her hands on my shoulders, raised herself on tiptoe, and saluted me briskly on both checks in the foreign way. She never differed in opinion with Owen without propitiating him first by some little artful compliment in the way of excuse. She argued boldly with me on every subject under the sun, law and politics included; and, when I got the better of her, never hesitated to stop me by putting her hand on my lips, or by dragging me out into the garden in the middle of a sentence.

As for Morgan, she abandoned all restraint in his case on the second day of her sojourn among us. She had asked after him as soon as she was settled in her two rooms on the third story; had insisted on knowing why he lived at the top of the tower, and why he had not appeared to welcome her at the door; had entrapped us into all sorts of damaging admissions, and had thereupon discovered the true state of the case in less than five minutes.

From that time my unfortunate second brother became the victim of all that was mischievous and reckless in her disposition. She forced him downstairs by a series of maneuvers which rendered his refuge uninhabitable, and then pretended to fall violently in love with him. She slipped little pink three-cornered notes under his door, entreating him to make appointments with her, or tenderly inquiring how he would like to see her hair dressed at dinner on that day. She followed him into the garden, sometimes to ask for the privilege of smelling his tobacco-smoke, sometimes to beg for a lock of his hair, or a fragment of his ragged old dressing-gown, to put among her keepsakes. She sighed at him when he was in a passion, and put her handkerchief to her eyes when he was sulky. In short, she tormented Morgan, whenever she could catch him, with such ingenious and such relentless malice, that he actually threatened to go back to London, and prey once more, in the unscrupulous character of a doctor, on the credulity of mankind.

Thus situated in her relations toward ourselves, and thus occupied by country diversions of her own choosing, Miss Jessie passed her time at The Glen Tower, excepting now and then a dull hour in the long evenings, to her guardian's satisfaction—and, all things considered, not without pleasure to herself. Day followed day in calm and smooth succession, and five quiet weeks had elapsed out of the six during which her stay was to last without any remarkable occurrence to distinguish them, when an event happened which personally affected me in a very serious manner, and which suddenly caused our handsome Queen of Hearts to become the object of my deepest anxiety in the present, and of my dearest hopes for the future.

CHAPTER IV.

OUR GRAND PROJECT.

AT the end of the fifth week of our guest's stay, among the letters which the morning's post brought to The Glen Tower there was one for me, from my son George, in the Crimea.

The effect which this letter produced in our little circle renders it necessary that I should present it here, to speak for itself.

This is what I read alone in my own room:

"MY DEAREST FATHER—After the great public news of the fall of Sebastopol, have you any ears left for small items of private intelligence from insignificant subaltern officers? Prepare, if you have, for a sudden and a startling announcement. How shall I write the words? How shall I tell you that I am really coming home?

"I have a private opportunity of sending this letter, and only a short time to write it in; so I must put many things, if I can, into few words. The doctor has reported me fit to travel at last, and I leave, thanks to the privilege of a wounded man, by the next ship. The name of the vessel and the time of starting are on the list which I inclose. I have made all my calculations, and, allowing for every possible delay, I find that I shall be with you, at the latest, on the first of November—perhaps some days earlier.

"I am far too full of my return, and of something else connected with it which is equally dear to me, to say anything about public affairs, more especially as I know that the newspapers must, by this time, have given you plenty of information. Let me fill the rest of this paper with a subject which is very near to my heart—nearer, I am almost ashamed to say, than the great triumph of my countrymen, in which my disabled condition has prevented me from taking any share.

"I gathered from your last letter that Miss Yelverton was to pay you a visit this autumn, in your capacity of her guardian. If she is already with you, pray move heaven and earth to keep her at The Glen Tower till I come back. Do you anticipate my confession from this entreaty? My dear, dear father, all my hopes rest on that one darling treasure which you are guarding perhaps, at this moment, under your own roof—all my happiness depends on making Jessie Yelverton my wife.

"If I did not sincerely believe that you will heartily approve of my choice, I should hardly have ventured on this abrupt confession. Now that I have made it, let me go on and tell you why I have kept my attachment up to this time a secret from every one—even from Jessie herself. (You see I call her by her Christian name already!)

"I should have risked everything, father, and have laid my whole heart open before her more than a year ago, but for the order which sent our regiment out to take its share in this great struggle of the Russian war. No ordinary change in my life would have silenced me on the subject of all others of which I was most anxious to speak; but this change made me think seriously of the future; and out of those thoughts came the resolution which I have kept until this time. For her sake, and for her sake only, I constrained myself to leave the words unspoken which might have made her my promised wife. I resolved to spare her the dreadful suspense of waiting for her betrothed husband till the perils of war might, or might not, give him back to her. I resolved to save her from the bitter grief of my death if a bullet laid me low. I resolved to preserve her from the wretched sacrifice of herself if I came back, as many a brave man will come back from this war, invalided for life. Leaving her untrammeled by any engagement, unsuspicious perhaps of my real feelings toward her, I might die, and know that, by keeping silence, I had spared a pang to the heart that was dearest to me. This was the thought that stayed the words on my lips when I left England, uncertain whether I should ever come back. If I had loved her less dearly, if her happiness had been less precious to me, I might have given way under the hard restraint I imposed on myself, and might have spoken selfishly at the last moment.

"And now the time of trial is past; the war is over; and, although I still walk a little lame, I am, thank God, in as good health and in much better spirits than when I left home. Oh, father, if I should lose her now—if I should get no reward for sparing her but the bitterest of all disappointments! Sometimes I am vain enough to think that I made some little impression on her; sometimes I doubt if she has a suspicion of my love. She lives in a gay world—she is the center of perpetual admiration—men with all the qualities to win a woman's heart are perpetually about her—can I, dare I hope? Yes, I must! Only keep her, I entreat you, at The Glen Tower. In that quiet world, in that freedom from frivolities and temptations, she will listen to me as she might listen nowhere else. Keep her, my dearest, kindest father—and, above all things, breathe not a word to her of this letter. I have surely earned the privilege of being the first to open her eyes to the truth. She must know nothing, now that I am coming home, till she knows all from my own lips."

Here the writing hurriedly broke off. I am only giving myself credit for common feeling, I trust, when I confess that what I read deeply affected me. I think I never felt so fond of my boy, and so proud of him, as at the moment when I laid down his letter.

As soon as I could control my spirits, I began to calculate the question of time with a trembling eagerness, which brought back to my mind my own young days of love and hope. My son was to come back, at the latest, on the first of November, and Jessie's allotted six weeks would expire on the twenty-second of October. Ten days too soon! But for the caprice which had brought her to us exactly that number of days before her time she would have been in the house, as a matter of necessity, on George's return.

I searched back in my memory for a conversation that I had held with her a week since on her future plans. Toward the middle of November, her aunt, Lady Westwick, had arranged to go to her house in Paris, and Jessie was, of course, to accompany her—to accompany her into that very circle of the best English and the best French society which contained in it the elements most adverse to

George's hopes. Between this time and that she had no special engagement, and she had only settled to write and warn her aunt of her return to London a day or two before she left The Glen Tower.

Under these circumstances, the first, the all-important necessity was to prevail on her to prolong her stay beyond the allotted six weeks by ten days. After the caution to be silent impressed on me (and most naturally, poor boy) in George's letter, I felt that I could only appeal to her on the ordinary ground of hospitality. Would this be sufficient to effect the object?

I was sure that the hours of the morning and the afternoon had, thus far, been fully and happily occupied by her various amusements indoors and out. She was no more weary of her days now than she had been when she first came among us. But I was by no means so certain that she was not tired of her evenings. I had latterly noticed symptoms of weariness after the lamps were lit, and a suspicious regularity in retiring to bed the moment the clock struck ten. If I could provide her with a new amusement for the long evenings, I might leave the days to take care of themselves, and might then make sure (seeing that she had no special engagement in London until the middle of November) of her being sincerely thankful and ready to prolong her stay.

How was this to be done? The piano and the novels had both failed to attract her. What other amusement was there to offer?

It was useless, at present, to ask myself such questions as these. I was too much agitated to think collectedly on the most trifling subjects. I was even too restless to stay in my own room. My son's letter had given me so fresh an interest in Jessie that I was now as impatient to see her as if we were about to meet for the first time. I wanted to look at her with my new eyes, to listen to her with my new ears, to study her secretly with my new purposes, and my new hopes and fears. To my dismay (for I wanted the very weather itself to favor George's interests), it was raining heavily that morning. I knew, therefore, that I should probably find her in her own sitting-room. When I knocked at her door, with George's letter crumpled up in my hand, with George's hopes in full possession of my heart, it is no exaggeration to say that my nerves were almost as much fluttered, and my ideas almost as much confused, as they were on a certain memorable day in the far past, when I rose, in brand-new wig and gown, to set my future prospects at the bar on the hazard of my first speech.

When I entered the room I found Jessie leaning back languidly in her largest arm-chair, watching the raindrops dripping down the window-pane. The unfortunate box of novels was open by her side, and the books were lying, for the most part, strewed about on the ground at her feet. One volume lay open, back upward, on her lap, and her hands were crossed over it listlessly. To my great dismay, she was yawning—palpably and widely yawning—when I came in.

No sooner did I find myself in her presence than an irresistible anxiety to make some secret discovery of the real state of her feelings toward George took possession of me. After the customary condolences on the imprisonment to which she was subjected by the weather, I said, in as careless a manner as it was possible to assume:

"I have heard from my son this morning. He talks of being ordered home, and tells me I may expect to see him before the end of the year."

I was too cautious to mention the exact date of his return, for in that case she might have detected my motive for asking her to prolong her visit.

"Oh, indeed?" she said. "How very nice. How glad you must be."

I watched her narrowly. The clear, dark blue eyes met mine as openly as ever. The smooth, round cheeks kept their fresh color quite unchanged. The full, good-humored, smiling lips never trembled or altered their expression in the slightest degree. Her light checked silk dress, with its pretty trimming of cherry-colored ribbon, lay quite still over the bosom beneath it. For all the information I could get from her look and manner, we might as well have been a hundred miles apart from each other. Is the best woman in the world little better than a fathomless abyss of duplicity on certain occasions, and where certain feelings of her own are concerned? I would rather not think that; and yet I don't know how to account otherwise for the masterly manner in which Miss Jessie contrived to baffle me.

I was afraid—literally afraid—to broach the subject of prolonging her sojourn with us on a rainy day, so I changed the topic, in despair, to the novels that were scattered about her.

"Can you find nothing there," I asked, "to amuse you this wet morning?"

"There are two or three good novels," she said, carelessly, "but I read them before I left London."

"And the others won't even do for a dull day in the country?" I went on.

"They might do for some people," she answered, "but not for me. I'm rather peculiar, perhaps, in my tastes. I'm sick to death of novels with an earnest purpose. I'm sick to death of outbursts of eloquence, and large-minded philanthropy, and graphic descriptions, and unsparing anatomy of the human heart, and all that sort of thing. Good gracious me! isn't it the original intention or purpose, or whatever you call it, of a work of fiction, to set out distinctly by telling a story? And how many of these books, I should like to know, do that? Why, so far as telling a story is concerned, the greater part of them might as well be sermons as novels. Oh, dear me! what I want is something that seizes hold of my interest, and makes me forget when it is time to dress for dinner—something that keeps me reading, reading, reading, in a breathless state to find out the end. You know what I mean—at least you ought. Why, there was that little chance story you told me yesterday in the garden—don't you remember?—about your strange client, whom you never saw again: I declare it was much more interesting than half these novels, *because* it was a story. Tell me another about your young days, when you were seeing the world, and meeting with all sorts of remarkable people. Or, no—don't tell it now—keep it till the evening, when we all want something to stir us up. You old people might amuse us young ones out of your own resources oftener than you do. It was very kind of you to get me these books; but, with all respect to them, I would rather have the rummaging of your memory than the rummaging of this box. What's the matter? Are you afraid I have found out the window in your bosom already?"

I had half risen from my chair at her last words, and I felt that my face must have flushed at the same moment. She had started an idea in my mind—the very idea of which I had been in search when I was pondering over the best means of amusing her in the long autumn evenings.

I parried her questions by the best excuses I could offer; changed the conversation for the next five minutes, and then, making a sudden remembrance of business my apology for leaving her, hastily withdrew to devote myself to the new idea in the solitude of my own room.

A little quiet thinking convinced me that I had discovered a means not only of occupying her idle time, but of decoying her into staying on with us, evening by evening, until my son's return. The new project which she had herself unconsciously suggested involved nothing less than acting forthwith on her own chance hint, and appealing to her interest and curiosity by the recital of incidents and adventures drawn from my own personal experience and (if I could get them to help me) from the experience of my brothers as well. Strange people and startling events had connected themselves with Owen's past life as a clergyman, with Morgan's past life as a doctor, and with my past life as a lawyer, which offered elements of interest of a strong and striking kind ready to our hands. If these narratives were written plainly and unpretendingly; if one of them was read every evening, under circumstances that should pique the curiosity and impress the imagination of our young guest, the very occupation was found for her weary hours which would gratify her tastes, appeal to her natural interest in the early lives of my brothers and myself, and lure her insensibly into prolonging her visit by ten days without exciting a suspicion of our real motive for detaining her.

I sat down at my desk; I hid my face in my hands to keep out all impressions of external and present things; and I searched back through the mysterious labyrinth of the Past, through the dun, ever-deepening twilight of the years that were gone.

Slowly, out of the awful shadows, the Ghosts of Memory rose about me. The dead population of a vanished world came back to life round me, a living man. Men and women whose earthly pilgrimage had ended long since, returned upon me from the unknown spheres, and fond, familiar voices burst their way back to my ears through the heavy silence of the grave. Moving by me in the nameless inner light, which no eye saw but mine, the dead procession of immaterial scenes and beings unrolled its silent length. I saw once more the pleading face of a friend of early days, with the haunting vision that had tortured him through life by his side again—with the long-forgotten despair in his eyes which had once touched my heart, and bound me to him, till I had tracked his destiny through its darkest windings to the end. I saw the figure of an innocent woman passing to and fro in an ancient country house, with the shadow of a strange suspicion stealing after her wherever she went. I saw a man worn by hardship and old age, stretched dreaming on the straw of a stable, and muttering in his dream the terrible secret of his life.

Other scenes and persons followed these, less vivid in their revival, but still always recognizable and distinct; a young girl alone by night, and in peril of her life, in a cottage on a dreary moor—an upper chamber of an inn, with two beds in it; the curtains of one bed closed, and a man standing by them, waiting, yet dreading to draw them back—a husband secretly following the first traces of a mystery which his wife's anxious love had fatally hidden from him since the day when they first met; these, and other visions like them, shadowy reflections of the living beings and the real events that had been once, peopled the solitude and the emptiness around me. They haunted me still when I tried to break the chain of thought which my own efforts had wound about my mind; they followed me to and fro in the room; and they came out with me when I left it. I had lifted the veil from the Past for myself, and I was now to rest no more till I had lifted it for others.

I went at once to my eldest brother and showed him my son's letter, and told him all that I have written here. His kind heart was touched as mine had been. He felt for my suspense; he shared my anxiety; he laid aside his own occupation on the spot.

"Only tell me," he said, "how I can help, and I will give every h our in the day to you and to George."

I had come to him with my mind almost as full of his past life as of my own; I recalled to his memory events in his experience as a working clergyman in London; I set him looking among papers which he had preserved for half his lifetime, and the very existence of which he had forgotten long since; I recalled to him the names of persons to whose necessities he had ministered in his sacred office, and whose stories he had heard from their own lips or received under their own handwriting. When we parted he was certain of what he was wanted to do, and was resolute on that very day to begin the work.

I went to Morgan next, and appealed to him as I had already appealed to Owen. It was only part of his odd character to start all sorts of eccentric objections in reply; to affect a cynical indifference, which he was far from really and truly feeling; and to indulge in plenty of quaint sarcasm on the subject of Jessie and his nephew George. I waited till these little surface-ebullitions had all expended themselves, and then pressed my point again with the earnestness and anxiety that I really felt.

Evidently touched by the manner of my appeal to him even more than by the language in which it was expressed, Morgan took refuge in his customary abruptness, spread out his paper violently on the table, seized his pen and ink, and told me quite fiercely to give him his work and let him tackle it at once.

I set myself to recall to his memory some very remarkable experiences of his own in his professional days, but he stopped me before I had half done.

"I understand," he said, taking a savage dip at the ink, "I'm to make her flesh creep, and to frighten her out of her wits. I'll do it with a vengeance!"

Reserving to myself privately an editorial right of supervision over Morgan's contributions, I returned to my own room to begin my share—by far the largest one—of the task before us. The stimulus applied to my mind by my son's letter must have been a strong one indeed, for I had hardly been more than an hour at my desk before I found the old literary facility of my youthful days, when I was a writer for the magazines, returning to me as if by magic. I worked on unremittingly till dinner-time, and then resumed the pen after we had all separated for the night. At two o'clock the next morning I found myself—God help me!—masquerading, as it were, in my own long-lost character of a hard-writing young man, with the old familiar cup of strong tea by my side, and the old familiar wet towel tied round my head.

My review of the progress I had made, when I looked back at my pages of manuscript, yielded all the encouragement I wanted to drive me on. It is only just, however, to add to the record of this first day's attempt, that the literary labor which it involved was by no means of the most trying kind. The great strain on the intellect—the strain of invention—was spared me by my having real characters and events ready to my hand. If I had been called on to create, I should, in all probability, have suffered severely by contrast with the very worst of those unfortunate novelists whom Jessie had so rashly and so thoughtlessly condemned. It is not wonderful that the public should rarely know how to estimate the vast service which is done to them by the production of a good book, seeing that they are, for the most part, utterly ignorant of the immense difficulty of writing even a bad one.

The next day was fine, to my great relief; and our visitor, while we were at work, enjoyed her customary scamper on the pony, and her customary rambles afterward in the neighborhood of the house. Although I had interruptions to contend with on the part of Owen and Morgan, neither of whom possessed my experience in the production of what heavy people call "light literature," and both of whom consequently wanted assistance, still I made great progress, and earned my hours of repose on the evening of the second day.

On that evening I risked the worst, and opened my negotiations for the future with "The Queen of Hearts."

About an hour after the tea had been removed, and when I happened to be left alone in the room with her, I noticed that she rose suddenly and went to the writing-table. My suspicions were aroused directly, and I entered on the dangerous subject by inquiring if she intended to write to her aunt.

"Yes," she said. "I promised to write when the last week came. If you had paid me the compliment of asking me to stay a little longer, I should have returned it by telling you I was sorry to go. As it is, I mean to be sulky and say nothing."

With those words she took up her pen to begin the letter.

"Wait a minute," I remonstrated. "I was just on the point of begging you to stay when I spoke."

"Were you, indeed?" she returned. "I never believed in coincidences of that sort before, but now, of course, I put the most unlimited faith in them!"

"Will you believe in plain proofs?" I asked, adopting her humor. "How do you think I and my brothers have been employing ourselves all day to-day and all day yesterday? Guess what we have been about."

"Congratulating yourselves in secret on my approaching departure," she answered, tapping her chin saucily with the feather-end of her pen.

I seized the opportunity of astonishing her, and forthwith told her the truth. She started up from the table, and approached me with the eagerness of a child, her eyes sparkling, and her cheeks flushed.

"Do you really mean it?" she said.

I assured her that I was in earnest. She thereupon not only expressed an interest in our undertaking, which was evidently sincere, but, with characteristic impatience, wanted to begin the first evening's reading on that very night. I disappointed her sadly by explaining that we required time to prepare ourselves, and by assuring her that we should not be ready for the next five days. On the sixth day, I added, we should be able to begin, and to go on, without missing an evening, for probably ten days more.

"The next five days?" she replied. "Why, that will just bring us to the end of my six weeks' visit. I suppose you are not setting a trap to catch me? This is not a trick of you three cunning old gentlemen to make me stay on, is it?"

I quailed inwardly as that dangerously close guess at the truth passed her lips.

"You forget," I said, "that the idea only occurred to me after what you said yesterday. If it had struck me earlier, we should have been ready earlier, and then where would your suspicions have been?"

"I am ashamed of having felt them," she said, in her frank, hearty way. "I retract the word 'trap,' and I beg pardon for calling you 'three cunning old gentlemen.' But what am I to say to my aunt?"

She moved back to the writing-table as she spoke.

"Say nothing," I replied, "till you have heard the first story. Shut up the paper-case till that time, and then decide when you will open it again to write to your aunt."

She hesitated and smiled. That terribly close guess of hers was not out of her mind yet.

"I rather fancy," she said, slyly, "that the story will turn out to be the best of the whole series."

"Wrong again," I retorted. "I have a plan for letting chance decide which of the stories the first one shall be. They shall be all numbered as they are done; corresponding numbers shall be written inside folded pieces of card and well mixed together; you shall pick out any one card you like; you shall declare the number written within; and, good or bad, the story that answers to that number shall be the story that is read. Is that fair?"

"Fair!" she exclaimed; "it's better than fair; it makes *me* of some importance; and I must be more or less than woman not to appreciate that."

"Then you consent to wait patiently for the next five days?"

"As patiently as I can."

"And you engage to decide nothing about writing to your aunt until you have heard the first story?"

"I do," she said, returning to the writing-table. "Behold the proof of it." She raised her hand with theatrical solemnity, and closed the paper-case with an impressive bang.

I leaned back in my chair with my mind at ease for the first time since the receipt of my son's letter.

"Only let George return by the first of November," I thought to myself, "and all the aunts in Christendom shall not prevent Jessie Yelverton from being here to meet him."

THE TEN DAYS.

THE FIRST DAY.

SHOWERY and unsettled. In spite of the weather, Jessie put on my Mackintosh cloak and rode off over the hills to one of Owen's outlying farms. She was already too impatient to wait quietly for the evening's reading in the house, or to enjoy any amusement less exhilarating than a gallop in the open air.

I was, on my side, as anxious and as uneasy as our guest. Now that the six weeks of her stay had expired—now that the day had really arrived, on the evening of which the first story was to be read, I began to calculate the chances of failure as well as the chances of success. What if my own estimate of the interest of the stories turned out to be a false one? What if some unforeseen accident occurred to delay my son's return beyond ten days?

The arrival of the newspaper had already become an event of the deepest importance to me. Unreasonable as it was to expect any tidings of George at so early a date, I began, nevertheless, on this first of our days of suspense, to look for the name of his ship in the columns of telegraphic news. The mere mechanical act of looking was some relief to my overstrained feelings, although I might have known, and did know, that the search, for the present, could lead to no satisfactory result.

Toward noon I shut myself up with my collection of manuscripts to revise them for the last time. Our exertions had thus far produced but six of the necessary ten stories. As they were only, however, to be read, one by one, on six successive evenings, and as we could therefore count on plenty of leisure in the daytime, I was in no fear of our failing to finish the little series.

Of the six completed stories I had written two, and had found a third in the form of a collection of letters among my papers. Morgan had only written one, and this solitary contribution of his had given me more trouble than both my own put together, in consequence of the perpetual intrusion of my brother's eccentricities in every part of his narrative. The process of removing these quaint turns and frisks of Morgan's humor—which, however amusing they might have been in an essay, were utterly out of place in a story appealing to suspended interest for its effect—certainly tried my patience and my critical faculty (such as it is) more severely than any other part of our literary enterprise which had fallen my share.

Owen's investigations among his papers had supplied us with the two remaining narratives. One was contained in a letter, and the other in the form of a diary, and both had been received by him directly from the writers. Besides these contributions, he had undertaken to help us by some work of his own, and had been engaged for the last four days in molding certain events which had happened within his personal knowledge into the form of a story. His extreme fastidiousness as a writer interfered, however, so seriously with his progress that he was still sadly behindhand, and was likely, though less heavily burdened than Morgan or myself, to be the last to complete his allotted task.

Such was our position, and such the resources at our command, when the first of the Ten Days dawned upon us. Shortly after four in the afternoon I completed my work of revision, numbered the manuscripts from one to six exactly as they happened to lie under my hand, and inclosed them all in a portfolio, covered with purple morocco, which became known from that time by the imposing title of The Purple Volume.

Miss Jessie returned from her expedition just as I was tying the strings of the portfolio, and, womanlike, instantly asked leave to peep inside, which favor I, manlike, positively declined to grant.

As soon as dinner was over our guest retired to array herself in magnificent evening costume. It had been arranged that the readings were to take place in her own sitting-room; and she was so enthusiastically desirous to do honor to the occasion, that she regretted not having brought with her from London the dress in which she had been presented at court the year before, and not having borrowed certain materials for additional splendor which she briefly described as "aunt's diamonds."

Toward eight o'clock we assembled in the sitting-room, and a strangely assorted company we were. At the head of the table, radiant in silk and jewelry, flowers and furbelows, sat The Queen of Hearts, looking so handsome and so happy that I secretly congratulated my absent son on the excellent taste he had shown in falling in love with her. Round this bright young creature (Owen, at the foot of the table, and Morgan and I on either side) sat her three wrinkled, gray-headed, dingily-attired hosts, and just behind her, in still more inappropriate companionship, towered the spectral figure of the man in armor, which had so unaccountably attracted her on her arrival. This strange scene was lighted up by candles in high and heavy brass sconces. Before Jessie stood a mighty china punch-bowl of the olden time, containing the folded pieces of card, inside which were written the numbers to be drawn, and before Owen reposed the Purple Volume from which one of us was to read. The walls of the room were hung all round with faded tapestry; the clumsy furniture was black with age; and, in spite of the light from the sconces, the lofty ceiling was almost lost in gloom. If Rembrandt could have painted our background, Reynolds our guest, and Hogarth ourselves, the picture of the scene would have been complete.

When the old clock over the tower gateway had chimed eight, I rose to inaugurate the proceedings by requesting Jessie to take one of the pieces of card out of the punch-bowl, and to declare the number.

She laughed; then suddenly became frightened and serious; then looked at me, and said, "It was dreadfully like business;" and then entreated Morgan not to stare at her, or, in the present state of her nerves, she should upset the punch-bowl. At last she summoned resolution enough to take out one of the pieces of card and to unfold it.

"Declare the number, my dear," said Owen.

"Number Four," answered Jessie, making a magnificent courtesy, and beginning to look like herself again.

Owen opened the Purple Volume, searched through the manuscripts, and suddenly changed color. The cause of his discomposure was soon explained. Malicious fate had assigned to the most diffident individual in the company the trying responsibility of leading the way. Number Four was one of the two narratives which Owen had found among his own papers.

"I am almost sorry," began my eldest brother, confusedly, "that it has fallen to my turn to read first. I hardly know which I distrust most, myself or my story."

"Try and fancy you are in the pulpit again," said Morgan, sarcastically. "Gentlemen of your cloth, Owen, seldom seem to distrust themselves or their manuscripts when they get into that position."

"The fact is," continued Owen, mildly impenetrable to his brother's cynical remark, "that the little thing I am going to try and read is hardly a story at all. I am afraid it is only an anecdote. I became possessed of the letter which contains my narrative under these circumstances. At the time when I was a clergyman in London, my church was attended for some months by a lady who was the wife of a large farmer in the country. She had been obliged to come to town, and to remain there for the sake of one of her children, a little boy, who required the best medical advice."

At the words "medical advice" Morgan shook his head and growled to himself contemptuously. Owen went on:

"While she was attending in this way to one child, his share in her love was unexpectedly disputed by another, who came into the world rather before his time. I baptized the baby, and was asked to the little christening party afterward. This was my first introduction to the lady, and I was very favorably impressed by her; not so much on account of her personal appearance, for she was but a little wo man and had no pretensions to beauty, as on account of a certain simplicity, and hearty, downright kindness in her manner, as well as of an excellent frankness and good sense in her conversation. One of the guests present, who saw how she had interested me, and who spoke of her in the highest terms, surprised me by inquiring if I should ever have supposed that quiet, good-humored little woman to be capable of performing an act of courage which would have tried the nerves of the boldest man in England? I naturally enough begged for an explanation; but my neighbor at the table only smiled and said, 'If you can find an opportunity, ask her what happened at The Black Cottage, and you will hear something that will astonish you.' I acted on the hint as soon as I had an opportunity of speaking to her privately. The lady answered that it was too long a story to tell then, and explained, on my suggesting that she should relate it on some future day, that she was about to start for her country home the next morning. 'But,' she was good enough to add, 'as I have been under great obligations to you for many Sundays past, and as you seem interested in this matter, I will employ my first leisure time after my return in telling you by writing, instead of by word of mouth, what really happened to me on one memorable night of my life in The Black Cottage.'

"She faithfully performed her promise. In a fortnight afterward I received from her the narrative which I am now about to read."

BROTHER OWEN'S STORY

OF

THE SIEGE OF THE BLACK COTTAGE.

To begin at the beginning, I must take you back to the time after my mother's death, when my only brother had gone to sea, when my sister was out at service, and when I lived alone with my father in the midst of a moor in the west of England.

The moor was covered with great limestone rocks, and intersected here and there by streamlets. The nearest habitation to ours was situated about a mile and a half off, where a strip of the fertile land stretched out into the waste like a tongue. Here the outbuildings of the great Moor Farm, then in the possession of my husband's father, began. The farm-lands stretched down gently into a beautiful rich valley, lying nicely sheltered by the high platform of the moor. When the ground began to rise again, miles and miles away, it led up to a country house called Holme Manor, belonging to a gentleman named Knifton. Mr. Knifton had lately married a young lady whom my mother had nursed, and whose kindness and friendship for me, her foster-sister, I shall remember gratefully to the last day of my life. These and other slight particulars it is necessary to my story that I should tell you, and it is also necessary that you should be especially careful to bear them well in mind.

My father was by trade a stone-mason. His cottage stood a mile and a half from the nearest habitation. In all other directions we were four or five times that distance from neighbors. Being very poor people, this lonely situation had one great attraction for us—we lived rent free on it. In addition to that advantage, the stones, by shaping which my father gained his livelihood, lay all about him at his very door, so that he thought his position, solitary as it was, quite an enviable one. I can hardly say that I agreed with him, though I never complained. I was very fond of my father, and managed to make the best of my loneliness with the thought of being useful to him. Mrs. Knifton wished to take me into her service when she married, but I declined, unwillingly enough, for my father's sake. If I had gone away, he would have had nobody to live with him; and my mother made me promise on her death-bed that he should never be left to pine away alone in the midst of the bleak moor.

Our cottage, small as it was, was stoutly and snugly built, with stone from the moor as a matter of course. The walls were lined inside and fenced outside with wood, the gift of Mr. Knifton's father to my father. This double covering of cracks and crevices, which would have been superfluous in a sheltered position, was absolutely necessary, in our exposed situation, to keep out the cold winds which, excepting just the summer months, swept over us continually all the year round. The outside boards, covering our roughly-built stone walls, my father protected against the wet with pitch and tar. This gave to our little abode a curiously dark, dingy look, especially when it was seen from a distance; and so it had come to be called in the neighborhood, even before I was born, The Black Cottage.

I have now related the preliminary particulars which it is desirable that you should know, and may proceed at once to the pleasanter task of telling you my story.

One cloudy autumn day, when I was rather more than eighteen years old, a herdsman walked over from Moor Farm with a letter which had been left there for my father. It came from a builder living at our county town, half a day's journey off, and it invited my father to come to him and give his judgment about an estimate for some stonework on a very large scale. My father's expenses for loss of time were to be paid, and he was to have his share of employment afterwards in preparing the stone. He was only too glad, therefore, to obey the directions which the letter contained, and to prepare at once for his long walk to the county town.

Considering the time at which he received the letter, and the necessity of resting before he attempted to return, it was impossible for him to avoid being away from home for one night, at least. He proposed to me, in case I disliked being left alone in the Black Cottage, to lock the door and to take me to Moor Farm to sleep with any one of the milkmaids who would give me a share of her bed. I by no means liked the notion of sleeping with a girl whom I did not know, and I saw no reason to feel afraid of being left alone for only one night; so I declined. No thieves had ever come near us; our poverty was sufficient protection against them; and of other dangers there were none that even the most timid person could apprehend. Accordingly, I got my father's dinner, laughing at the notion of my taking refuge under the protection of a milkmaid at Moor Farm. He started for his walk as soon as he had done, saying he should try and be back by dinner-time the next day, and leaving me and my cat Polly to take care of the house.

I had cleared the table and brightened up the fire, and had sat down to my work with the cat dozing at my feet, when I heard the trampling of horses, and, running to the door, saw Mr. and Mrs. Knifton, with their groom behind them, riding up to the Black Cottage. It was part of the young lady's kindness never to neglect an opportunity of coming to pay me a friendly visit, and her husband was generally willing to accompany her for his wife's sake. I made my best courtesy, therefore, with a great deal of pleasure, but with no particular surprise at seeing them. They dismounted and entered the cottage, laughing and talking in great spirits. I soon heard that they were riding to the same county town for which my father was bound and that they intended to stay with some friends there for a few days, and to return home on horseback, as they went out.

I heard this, and I also discovered that they had been having an argument, in jest, about money-matters, as they rode along to our cottage. Mrs. Knifton had accused her husband of inveterate extravagance, and of never being able to go out with money in his pocket without spending it all, if he possibly could, before he got home again. Mr. Knifton had laughingly defended himself by declaring that all his pocket-money went in presents for his wife, and that, if he spent it lavishly, it was under her sole influence and superintendence.

"We are going to Cliverton now," he said to Mrs. Knifton, naming the county town, and warming himself at our poor fire just as pleasantly as if he had been standing on his own grand hearth. "You will stop to admire every pretty thing in every one of the Cliverton shop-windows; I shall hand you the purse, and you will go in and buy. When we have reached home again, and you have h ad time to get tired of your purchases, you will clasp your hands in amazement, and declare that you are quite shocked at my habits of inveterate extravagance. I am only the banker who keeps the money; you, my love, are the spendthrift who throws it all away!"

"Am I, sir?" said Mrs. Knifton, with a look of mock indignation. "We will see if I am to be misrepresented in this way with impunity. Bessie, my dear" (turning to me), "you shall judge how far I deserve the character which that unscrupulous man has just given to me. *I* am the spendthrift, am I? And you are only the banker? Very well. Banker, give me my money at once, if you please!"

Mr. Knifton laughed, and took some gold and silver from his waistcoat pocket.

"No, no," said Mrs. Knifton, "you may want what you have got there for necessary expenses. Is that all the money you have about you? What do I feel here?" and she tapped her husband on the chest, just over the breast-pocket of his coat.

Mr. Knifton laughed again, and produced his pocketbook. His wife snatched it out of his hand, opened it, and drew out some bank-notes, put them back again immediately, and, closing the pocketbook, stepped across the room to my poor mother's little walnut-wood book-case, the only bit of valuable furniture we had in the house.

"What are you going to do there?" asked Mr. Knifton, following his wife.

Mrs. Knifton opened the glass door of the book-case, put the pocketbook in a vacant place on one of the lower shelves, closed and locked the door again, and gave me the key.

"You called me a spendthrift just now," she said. "There is my answer. Not one farthing of that money shall you spend at Cliverton on *me*. Keep the key in your pocket, Bessie, and, whatever Mr. Knifton may say, on no account let him have it until we call again on our way back. No, sir, I won't trust you with that money in your pocket in the town of Cliverton. I will make sure of your taking it all home again, by leaving it here in more trustworthy hands than yours until we ride back. Bessie, my dear, what do you say to that as a lesson in economy inflicted on a prudent husband by a spendthrift wife?"

She took Mr. Knifton's arm while she spoke, and drew him away to the door. He protested and made some resistance, but she easily carried her point, for he was far too fond of her to have a will of his own in any trifling matter between them. Whatever the men might say, Mr. Knifton was a model husband in the estimation of all the women who knew him.

"You will see us as we come back, Bessie. Till then, you are our banker, and the pocketbook is yours," cried Mrs. Knifton, gayly, at the door. Her husband lifted her into the saddle, mounted himself, and away they both galloped over the moor as wild and happy as a couple of children.

Although my being trusted with money by Mrs. Knifton was no novelty (in her maiden days she always employed me to pay her dress-maker's bills), I did not feel quite easy at having a pocketbook full of bank-notes left by her in my charge. I had no positive apprehensions about the safety of the deposit placed in my hands, but it was one of the odd points in my character then (and I think it is still) to feel an unreasonably strong objection to charging myself with money responsibilities of any kind, even to suit the convenience of my dearest friends. As soon as I was left alone, the very sight of the pocketbook behind the glass door of the book-case began to worry me, and instead of returning to my work, I puzzled my brains about finding a place to lock it up in, where it would not be exposed to the view of any chance passers-by who might stray into the Black Cottage.

This was not an easy matter to compass in a poor house like ours, where we had nothing valuable to put under lock and key. After running over various hiding-places in my mind, I thought of my tea-caddy, a present from Mrs. Knifton, which I always kept out of harm's way in my own bedroom. Most unluckily—as it afterward turned out—instead of taking the pocketbook to the tea-caddy, I went into my room first to take the tea-caddy to the pocketbook. I only acted in this roundabout way from sheer thoughtlessness, and severely enough I was punished for it, as you will acknowledge yourself when you have read a page or two more of my story.

I was just getting the unlucky tea-caddy out of my cupboard, when I heard footsteps in the passage, and, running out immediately, saw two men walk into the kitchen—the room in which I had received Mr. and Mrs. Knifton. I inquired what they wanted sharply enough, and one of them answered immediately that they wanted my father. He turned toward me, of course, as he spoke, and I recognized him as a stone-mason, going among his comrades by the name of Shifty Dick. He bore a very bad character for everything but wrestling, a sport for which the working men of our parts were famous all through the county. Shifty Dick was champion, and he had got his name from some tricks of wrestling, for which he was celebrated. He was a tall, heavy man, with a lowering, scarred face, and huge hairy hands—the last visitor in the whole world that I should have been glad to see under any circumstances. His companion was a stranger, whom he addressed by the name of Jerry—a quick, dapper, wicked-looking man, who took off his cap to me with mock politeness, and showed, in so doing, a very bald head, with some very ugly-looking knobs on it. I distrusted him worse than I did Shifty Dick, and managed to get between his leering eyes and the book-case, as I told the two that my father was gone out, and that I did not expect him back till the next day.

The words were hardly out of my mouth before I repented that my anxiety to get rid of my unwelcome visitors had made me incautious enough to acknowledge that my father would be away from home for the whole night.

Shifty Dick and his companion looked at each other when I unwisely let out the truth, but made no remark except to ask me if I would give them a drop of cider. I answered sharply that I had no cider in the house, having no fear of the consequences of refusing them drink, because I knew that plenty of men were at work within hail, in a neighboring quarry. The two looked at each other again when I denied having any cider to give them; and Jerry (as I am obliged to call him, knowing no other name by which to distinguish the fellow) took off his cap to me once more, and, with a kind of blackguard gentility upon him, said they would have the pleasure of calling the next day, when my father was at home. I said good-afternoon as ungraciously as possible, and, to my great relief, they both left the cottage immediately afterward.

As soon as they were well away, I watched them from the door. They trudged off in the direction of Moor Farm; and, as it was beginning to get dusk, I soon lost sight of them.

Half an hour afterward I looked out again.

The wind had lulled with the sunset, but the mist was rising, and a heavy rain was beginning to fall. Never did the lonely prospect of the moor look so dreary as it looked to my eyes that evening. Never did I regret any slight thing more sincerely than I then regretted the leaving of Mr. Knifton's pocketbook in my charge. I cannot say that I suffered under any actual alarm, for I felt next to certain that neither Shifty Dick nor Jerry had got a chance of setting eyes on so small a thing as the pocketbook while they were in the kitchen; but there was a kind of vague distrust troubling me—a suspicion of the night—a dislike of being left by myself, which I never remember having experienced before. This feeling so increased after I had closed the door and gone back to the kitchen, that, when I heard the voices of the quarrymen as they passed our cottage on their way home to the village in the valley below Moor Farm, I stepped out into the passage with a momentary notion of telling them how I was situated, and asking them for advice and protection.

I had hardly formed this idea, however, before I dismissed it. None of the quarrymen were intimate friends of mine. I had a nodding acquaintance with them, and believed them to be honest men, as times went. But my own common sense told me that what little knowledge of their characters I had was by no means sufficient to warrant me in admitting them into my confidence in the matter of the pocketbook. I had seen enough of poverty and poor men to know what a terrible temptation a large sum of money is to those whose whole lives are passed in scraping up sixpences by weary hard work. It is one thing to write fine sentiments in books about incorruptible honesty, and another thing to put those sentiments in practice when one day's work is all that a man has to set up in the way of an obstacle between starvation and his own fireside.

The only resource that remained was to carry the pocketbook with me to Moor Farm, and ask permission to pass the night there. But I could not persuade myself that there was any real necessity for taking such a course as this; and, if the truth must be told, my pride revolted at the idea of presenting myself in the character of a coward before the people at the farm. Timidity is thought rather a graceful attraction among ladies, but among poor women it is something to be laughed at. A woman with less spirit of her own than I had, and always shall have, would have considered twice in my situation before she made up her mind to encounter the jokes of plowmen and the jeers of milkmaids. As for me, I had hardly considered about going to the farm before I despised myself for entertaining any such notion. "No, no," thought I, "I am not the woman to walk a mile and a half through rain, and mist, and darkness to tell a whole kitchenful of people that I am afraid. Come what may, here I stop till father gets back."

Having arrived at that valiant resolution, the first thing I did was to lock and bolt the back and front doors, and see to the security of every shutter in the house.

That duty performed, I made a blazing fire, lighted my candle, and sat down to tea, as snug and comfortable as possible. I could hardly believe now, with the light in the room, and the sense of security inspired by the closed doors and shutters, that I had ever felt even the slightest apprehension earlier in the day. I sang as I washed up the tea-things; and even the cat seemed to catch the infection of my good spirits. I never knew the pretty creature so playful as she was that evening.

The tea-things put by, I took up my knitting, and worked away at it so long that I began at last to get drowsy. The fire was so bright and comforting that I could not muster resolution enough to leave it and go to bed. I sat staring lazily into the blaze, with my knitting on my lap—sat till the splashing of the rain outside and the fitful, sullen sobbing of the wind grew fainter and fainter on my ear. The last sounds I heard before I fairly dozed off to sleep were the cheerful crackling of the fire and the steady purring of the cat, as she basked luxuriously in the warm light on the hearth. Those were the last sounds before I fell asleep. The sound that woke me was one loud bang at the front door.

I started up, with my heart (as the saying is) in my mouth, with a frightful momentary shuddering at the roots of my hair—I started up breathless, cold and motionless, waiting in the silence I hardly knew for what, doubtful at first whether I had dreamed about the bang at the door, or whether the blow had really been struck on it.

In a minute or less there came a second bang, louder than the first. I ran out into the passage.

"Who's there?"

"Let us in," answered a voice, which I recognised immediately as the voice of Shifty Dick.

"Wait a bit, my dear, and let me explain," said a second voice, in the low, oily, jeering tones of Dick's companion—the wickedly clever little man whom he called Jerry. "You are alone in the house, my pretty little dear. You may crack your sweet voice with screeching, and there's nobody near to hear you. Listen to reason, my love, and let us in. We don't want cider this time—we only want a very neat-looking pocketbook which you happen to have, and your late excellent mother's four silver teaspoons, which you keep so nice and clean on the chimney-piece. If you let us in we won't hurt a hair of your head, my cherub, and we promise to go away the moment we have got what we want, unless you particularly wish us to stop to tea. If you keep us out, we shall be obliged to break into the house and then—"

"And then," burst in Shifty Dick, "we'll *mash* you!"

"Yes," said Jerry, "we'll mash you, my beauty. But you won't drive us to doing that, will you? You will let us in?"

This long parley gave me time to recover from the effect which the first bang at the door had produced on my nerves. The threats of the two villains would have terrified some women out of their senses, but the only result they produced on *me* was violent indignation. I had, thank God, a strong spirit of my own, and the cool, contemptuous insolence of the man Jerry effectually roused it.

"You cowardly villains!" I screamed at them through the door. "You think you can frighten me because I am only a poor girl left alone in the house. You ragamuffin thieves, I defy you both! Our bolts are strong, our shutters are thick. I am here to keep my father's house safe, and keep it I will against an army of you!"

You may imagine what a passion I was in when I vapored and blustered in that way. I heard Jerry laugh and Shifty Dick swear a whole mouthful of oaths. Then there was a dead silence for a minute or two, and then the two ruffians attacked the door.

I rushed into the kitchen and seized the poker, and then heaped wood on the fire, and lighted all the candles I could find; for I felt as though I could keep up my courage better if I had plenty of light. Strange and improbable as it may appear, the next thing that attracted my attention was my poor pussy, crouched up, panic-stricken, in a corner. I was so fond of the little creature that I took her up in my arms and carried her into my bedroom and put her inside my bed. A comical thing to do in a situation of deadly peril, was it not? But it seemed quite natural and proper at the time.

All this while the blows were falling faster and faster on the door. They were dealt, as I conjectured, with heavy stones picked up from the ground outside. Jerry sang at his wicked work, and Shifty Dick swore. As I left the bedroom after putting the cat under cover, I heard the lower panel of the door begin to crack.

I ran into the kitchen and huddled our four silver spoons into my pocket; then took the unlucky book with the bank-notes and put it in the bosom of my dress. I was determined to defend the property confided to my care with my life. Just as I had secured the pocketbook I heard the door splintering, and rushed into the passage again with my heavy kitchen poker lifted in both hands.

I was in time to see the bald head of Jerry, with the ugly-looking knobs on it, pushed into the passage through a great rent in one of the lower panels of the door.

"Get out, you villain, or I'll brain you on the spot!" I screeched, threatening him with the poker.

Mr. Jerry took his head out again much faster than he put it in.

The next thing that came through the rent was a long pitchfork, which they darted at me from the outside, to move me from the door. I struck at it with all my might, and the blow must have jarred the hand of Shifty Dick up to his very shoulder, for I heard him give a roar of rage and pain. Before he could catch at the fork with his other hand I had drawn it inside. By this time even Jerry lost his temper and swore more awfully than Dick himself.

Then there came another minute of respite. I suspected they had gone to get bigger stones, and I dreaded the giving way of the whole door.

Running into the bedroom as this fear beset me, I laid hold of my chest of drawers, dragged it into the passage, and threw it down against the door. On the top of that I heaped my father's big tool chest, three chairs, and a scuttleful of coals; and last, I dragged out the kitchen table and rammed it as hard as I could against the whole barricade. They heard me as they were coming up to the door with fresh stones. Jerry said: "Stop a bit!" and t hen the two consulted together in whispers. I listened eagerly, and just caught these words:

"Let's try it the other way."

Nothing more was said, but I heard their footsteps retreating from the door.

Were they going to besiege the back door now?

I had hardly asked myself that question when I heard their voices at the other side of the house. The back door was smaller than the front, but it had this advantage in the way of strength—it was made of two solid oak boards joined lengthwise, and strengthened inside by heavy cross pieces. It had no bolts like the front door, but was fastened by a bar of iron running across it in a slanting direction, and fitting at either end into the wall.

"They must have the whole cottage down before they can break in at that door!" I thought to myself. And they soon found out as much for themselves. After five minutes of banging at the back door they gave up any further attack in that direction and cast their heavy stones down with curses of fury awful to hear.

I went into the kitchen and dropped on the window-seat to rest for a moment. Suspense and excitement together were beginning to tell upon me. The perspiration broke out thick on my forehead, and I began to feel the bruises I had inflicted on my hands in making the barricade against the front door. I had not lost a particle of my resolution, but I was beginning to lose strength. There was a bottle of rum in the cupboard, which my brother the sailor had left with us the last time he was ashore. I drank a drop of it. Never before or since have I put anything down my throat that did me half so much good as that precious mouthful of rum!

I was still sitting in the window-seat drying my face, when I suddenly heard their voices close behind me.

They were feeling the outside of the window against which I was sitting. It was protected, like all the other windows in the cottage, by iron bars. I listened in dreadful suspense for the sound of filing, but nothing of the sort was audible. They had evidently reckoned on frightening me easily into letting them in, and had come unprovided with house-breaking tools of any kind. A fresh burst of oaths informed me that they had recognized the obstacle of the iron bars. I listened breathlessly for some warning of what they were going to do next, but their voices seemed to die away in the distance. They were retreating from the window. Were they also retreating from the house altogether? Had they given up the idea of effecting an entrance in despair?

A long silence followed—a silence which tried my courage even more severely than the tumult of their first attack on the cottage.

Dreadful suspicions now beset me of their being able to accomplish by treachery what they had failed to effect by force. Well as I knew the cottage, I began to doubt whether there might not be ways of cunningly and silently entering it against which I was not provided. The ticking of the clock annoyed me; the crackling of the fire startled me. I looked out twenty times in a minute into the dark corners of the passage, straining my eyes, holding my breath, anticipating the most unlikely events, the most impossible dangers. Had they really gone, or were they still prowling about the house? Oh, what a sum of money I would have given only to have known what they were about in that interval of silence!

I was startled at last out of my suspense in the most awful manner. A shout from one of them reached my ears on a sudden down the kitchen chimney. It was so unexpected and so horrible in the stillness that I screamed for the first time since the attack on the house. My worst forebodings had never suggested to me that the two villains might mount upon the roof.

"Let us in, you she-devil!" roared a voice down the chimney.

There was another pause. The smoke from the wood fire, thin and light as it was in the red state of the embers at that moment, had evidently obliged the man to take his face from the mouth of the chimney. I counted the seconds while he was, as I conjectured, getting his breath again. In less than half a minute there came another shout:

"Let us in, or we'll burn the place down over your head!"

Burn it? Burn what? There was nothing easily combustible but the thatch on the roof; and that had been well soaked by the heavy rain which had now fallen incessantly for more than six hours. Burn the place over my head? How?

While I was still casting about wildly in my mind to discover what possible danger there could be of fire, one of the heavy stones placed on the thatch to keep it from being torn up by high winds came thundering down the chimney. It scattered the live embers on the hearth all over the room. A richly-furnished place, with knickknacks and fine muslin about it, would have been set on fire immediately. Even our bare floor and rough furniture gave out a smell of burning at the first shower of embers which the first stone scattered.

For an instant I stood quite horror-struck before this new proof of the devilish ingenuity of the villains outside. But the dreadful danger I was now in recalled me to my senses immediately. There was a large canful of water in my bedroom, and I ran in at once to fetch it. Before I could get back to the kitchen a second stone had been thrown down the chimney, and the floor was smoldering in several places.

I had wit enough to let the smoldering go on for a moment or two more, and to pour the whole of my canful of water over the fire before the third stone came down the chimney. The live embers on the floor I easily disposed of after that.

The man on the roof must have heard the hissing of the fire as I put it out, and have felt the change produced in the air at the mouth of the chimney, for after the third stone had descended no more followed it. As for either of the ruffians themselves dropping down by the same road along which the stones had come, that was not to be dreaded. The chimney, as I well knew by our experience in cleaning it, was too narrow to give passage to any one above the size of a small boy.

I looked upward as that comforting reflection crossed my mind—I looked up, and saw, as plainly as I see the paper I am now writing on, the point of a knife coming through the inside of the roof just over my head. Our cottage had no upper story, and our rooms had no ceilings. Slowly and wickedly the knife wriggled its way through the dry inside thatch between the rafters. It stopped for a while, and there came a sound of tearing. That, in its turn, stopped too; there was a great fall of dry thatch on the floor; and I saw the heavy, hairy hand of Shifty Dick, armed with the knife, come through after the fallen fragments. He tapped at the rafters with the back of the knife, as if to test their strength. Thank God, they were substantial and close together! Nothing lighter than a hatchet would have sufficed to remove any part of them.

The murderous hand was still tapping with the knife when I heard a shout from the man Jerry, coming from the neighborhood of my father's stone-shed in the back yard. The hand and knife disappeared instantly. I went to the back door and put my ear to it, and listened.

Both men were now in the shed. I made the most desperate efforts to call to mind what tools and other things were left in it which might be used against me. But my agitation confused me. I could remember nothing except my father's big stone-saw, which was far too heavy and unwieldy to be used on the roof of the cottage. I was still puzzling my brains, and making my head swim to no purpose, when I heard the men dragging something out of the shed. At the same instant that the noise caught my ear, the remembrance flashed across me like lightning of some beams of wood which had lain in the shed for years past. I had hardly time to feel certain that they were removing one of these beams before I heard Shifty Dick say to Jerry.

"Which door?"

"The front," was the answer. "We've cracked it already; we'll have it down now in no time."

Senses less sharpened by danger than mine would have understood but too easily, from these words, that they were about to use the beam as a battering-ram against the door. When that conviction overcame me, I lost courage at last. I felt that the door must come down. No such barricade as I had constructed could support it for more than a few minutes against such shocks as it was now to receive.

"I can do no more to keep the house against them," I said to myself, with my knees knocking together, and the tears at last beginning to wet my cheeks. "I must trust to the night and the thick darkness, and save my life by running for it while there is yet time."

I huddled on my cloak and hood, and had my hand on the bar of the back door, when a piteous mew from the bedroom reminded me of the existence of poor Pussy. I ran in, and huddled the creature up in my apron. Before I was out in the passage again, the first shock from the beam fell on the door.

The upper hinge gave way. The chairs and coal-scuttle, forming the top of my barricade, were hurled, rattling, on to the floor, but the lower hinge of the door, and the chest of drawers and the tool-chest still kept their places.

"One more!" I heard the villains cry—"one more run with the beam, and down it comes!"

Just as they must have been starting for that "one more run," I opened the back door and fled into the night, with the bookful of banknotes in my bosom, the silver spoons in my pocket, and the cat in my arms. I threaded my way easily enough through the familiar obstacles in the backyard, and was out in the pitch darkness of the moor before I heard the second shock, and the crash which told me that the whole door had given way.

In a few minutes they must have discovered the fact of my flight with the pocketbook, for I heard shouts in the distance as if they were running out to pursue me. I kept on at the top of my speed, and the noise soon died away. It was so dark that twenty thieves instead of two would have found it useless to follow me.

How long it was before I reached the farmhouse—the nearest place to which I could fly for refuge—I cannot tell you. I remember that I had just sense enough to keep the wind at my back (having observed in the beginning of the evening that it blew toward Moor Farm), and to go on resolutely through the darkness. In all other respects I was by this time half crazed by what I had gone through. If it had so happened that the wind had changed after I had observed its direction early in the evening, I should have gone astray, and have probably perished of fatigue and exposure on the moor. Providentially, it still blew steadily as it had blown for hours past, and I reached the farmhouse with my clothes wet through, and my brain in a high fever. When I made my alarm at the door, they had all gone to bed but the farmer's eldest son, who was sitting up late over his pipe and newspaper. I just mustered strength enough to gasp out a few words, telling him what was the matter, and then fell down at his feet, for the first time in my life in a dead swoon.

That swoon was followed by a severe illness. When I got strong enough to look about me again, I found myself in one of the farmhouse beds—my father, Mrs. Knifton, and the doctor were all in the room—my cat was asleep at my feet, and the pocketbook that I had saved lay on the table by my side.

There was plenty of news for me to hear as soon as I was fit to listen to it. Shifty Dick and the other rascal had been caught, and were in prison, waiting their trial at the next assizes. Mr. and Mrs. Knifton had been so shocked at the danger I had run—for which they blamed their own want of thoughtfulness in leaving the pocketbook in my care—that they had insisted on my father's removing from our lonely home to a cottage on their land, which we were to inhabit rent free. The bank-notes that I had saved were given to me to buy furniture with, in place of the things that the thieves had broken. These pleasant tidings assisted so greatly in promoting my recovery, that I was soon able to relate to my friends at the farmhouse the particulars that I have written here. They were all surprised and interested, but no one, as I thought, listened to me with such breathless attention as the farmer's eldest son. Mrs. Knifton noticed this too, and began to make jokes about it, in her light-hearted way, as soon as we were alone. I thought little of her jesting at the time; but when I got well, and we went to live at our new home, "the young farmer," as he was called in our parts, constantly came to see us, and constantly managed to meet me out of doors. I had my share of vanity, like other young women, and I began to think of Mrs. Knifton's jokes with some attention. To be brief, the young farmer managed one Sunday—I never could tell how—to lose his way with me in returning from church, and before we found out the right road home again he had asked me to be his wife.

His relations did all they could to keep us asunder and break off the match, thinking a poor stonemason's daughter no fit wife for a prosperous yeoman. But the farmer was too obstinate for them. He had one form of answer to all their objections. "A man, if he is worth the name, marries according to his own notions, and to please himself," he used to say. "My notion is, that when I take a wife I am placing my character and my happiness—the most precious things I have to trust—in one woman's care. The woman I mean to marry had a small charge confided to her care, and showed herself worthy of it at the risk of her life. That is proof enough for me that she is worthy of the greatest charge I can put into her hands. Rank and riches are fine things, but the certainty of getting a good wife is something better still. I'm of age, I know my own mind, and I mean to marry the stone-mason's daughter."

And he did marry me. Whether I proved myself worthy or not of his good opinion is a question which I must leave you to ask my husband. All that I had to relate about myself and my doings is now told. Whatever interest my perilous adventure may excite, ends, I am well aware, with my escape to the farmhouse. I have only ventured on writing these few additional sentences because my marriage is the moral of my story. It has brought me the choicest blessings of happiness and prosperity, and I owe them all to my night-adventure in *The Black Cottage*.

THE SECOND DAY.

A CLEAR, cloudless, bracing autumn morning. I rose gayly, with the pleasant conviction on my mind that our experiment had thus far been successful beyond our hopes.

Short and slight as the first story had been, the result of it on Jessie's mind had proved conclusive. Before I could put the question to her, she declared of her own accord, and with her customary exaggeration, that she had definitely abandoned all idea of writing to her aunt until our collection of narratives was exhausted.

"I am in a fever of curiosity about what is to come," she said, when we all parted for the night; "and, even if I wanted to leave you, I could not possibly go away now, without hearing the stories to the end."

So far, so good. All my anxieties from this time were for George's return. Again to-day I searched the newspapers, and again there were no tidings of the ship.

Miss Jessie occupied the second day by a drive to our county town to make some little purchases. Owen, and Morgan, and I were all hard at work, during her absence, on the stories that still remained to be completed. Owen desponded about ever getting done; Morgan grumbled at what he called the absurd difficulty of writing nonsense. I worked on smoothly and contentedly, stimulated by the success of the first night.

We assembled as before in our guest's sitting-room. As the clock struck eight she drew out the second card. It was Number Two. The lot had fallen on me to read next.

"Although my story is told in the first person," I said, addressing Jessie, "you must not suppose that the events related in this particular case happened to me. They happened to a friend of mine, who naturally described them to me from his own personal point of view. In producing my narrative from the recollection of what he told me some years since, I have supposed myself to be listening to him again, and have therefore written in his character, and, w henever my memory would help me, as nearly as possible in his language also. By this means I hope I have succeeded in giving an air of reality to a story which has truth, at any rate, to recommend it. I must ask you to excuse me if I enter into no details in offering this short explanation. Although the persons concerned in my narrative have ceased to exist, it is necessary to observe all due delicacy toward their memories. Who they were, and how I became acquainted with them, are matters of no moment. The interest of the story, such as it is, stands in no need, in this instance, of any assistance from personal explanations."

With those words I addressed myself to my task, and read as follows:

BROTHER GRIFFITH'S STORY

OF

THE FAMILY SECRET.

CHAPTER I.

WAS it an Englishman or a Frenchman who first remarked that every family had a skeleton in its cupboard? I am not learned enough to know, but I reverence the observation, whoever made it. It speaks a startling truth through an appropriately grim metaphor—a truth which I have discovered by practical experience. Our family had a skeleton in the cupboard, and the name of it was Uncle George.

I arrived at the knowledge that this skeleton existed, and I traced it to the particular cupboard in which it was hidden, by slow degrees. I was a child when I first began to suspect that there was such a thing, and a grown man when I at last discovered that my suspicions were true.

My father was a doctor, having an excellent practice in a large country town. I have heard that he married against the wishes of his family. They could not object to my mother on the score of birth, breeding, or character—they only disliked her heartily. My grandfather, grandmother, uncles, and aunts all declared that she was a heartless, deceitful woman; all disliked her manners, her opinions, and even the expression of her face—all, with the exception of my father's youngest brother, George.

George was the unlucky member of our family. The rest were all clever; he was slow in capacity. The rest were all remarkably handsome; he was the sort of man that no woman ever looks at twice. The rest succeeded in life; he failed. His profession was the same as my father's, but he never got on when he started in practice for himself. The sick poor, who could not choose, employed him, and liked him. The sick rich, who could—especially the ladies—declined to call him in when they could get anybody else. In experience he gained greatly by his profession; in money and reputation he gained nothing.

There are very few of us, however dull and unattractive we may be to outward appearance, who have not some strong passion, some germ of what is called romance, hidden more or less deeply in our natures. All the passion and romance in the nature of my Uncle George lay in his love and admiration for my father.

He sincerely worshipped his eldest brother as one of the noblest of human beings. When my father was engaged to be married, and when the rest of the family, as I have already mentioned, did not hesitate to express their unfavorable opinion of the disposition of his chosen wife, Uncle George, who had never ventured on differing with anyone before, to the amazement of everybody, undertook the defense of his future sister-in-law in the most vehement and positive manner. In his estimation, his brother's choice was something sacred and indisputable. The lady might, and did, treat him with unconcealed contempt, laugh at his awkwardness, grow impatient at his stammering—it made no difference to Uncle George. She was to be his brother's wife, and, in virtue of that one great fact, she became, in the estimation of the poor surgeon, a very queen, who, by the laws of the domestic constitution, could do no wrong.

When my father had been married a little while, he took his youngest brother to live with him as his assistant.

If Uncle George had been made president of the College of Surgeons, he could not have been prouder and happier than he was in his new position. I am afraid my father never understood the depth of his brother's affection for him. All the hard work fell to George's share: the long journeys at night, the physicking of wearisome poor people, the drunken cases, the revolting cases—all the drudging, dirty business of the surgery, in short, was turned over to him; and day after day, month after month, he struggled through it without a murmur. When his brother and his sister-in-law went out to dine with the county gentry, it never entered his head to feel disappointed at being left unnoticed at home. When the return dinners were given, and he was asked to come in at tea-time, and left to sit unregarded in a corner, it never occurred to him to imagine that he was treated with any want of consideration or respect. He was part of the furniture of the house, and it was the business as well as the pleasure of his life to turn himself to any use to which his brother might please to put him.

So much for what I have heard from others on the subject of my Uncle George. My own personal experience of him is limited to what I remember as a mere child. Let me say something, however, first about my parents, my sister and myself.

My sister was the eldest born and the best loved. I did not come into the world till four years after her birth, and no other child followed me. Caroline, from her earliest days, was the perfection of beauty and health. I was small, weakly, and, if the truth must be told, almost as plain-featured as Uncle George himself. It would be ungracious and undutiful in me to presume to decide whether there was any foundation or not for the dislike that my father's family always felt for my mother. All I can venture to say is, that her children never had any cause to complain of her.

Her passionate affection for my sister, her pride in the child's beauty, I remember well, as also her uniform kindness and indulgence toward me. My personal defects must have been a sore trial to her in secret, but neither she nor my father ever showed me that they perceived any difference between Caroline and myself. When presents were made to my sister, presents were made to me. When my father and mother caught my sister up in their arms and kissed her they scrupulously gave me my turn afterward. My childish instinct told me that there was a difference in their smiles when they looked at me and looked at her; that the kisses given to Caroline were warmer than the kisses given to me; that the hands which dried her tears in our childish griefs, touched her more gently than the hands which dried mine. But these, and other small signs of preference like them, were such as no parents could be expected to control. I noticed them at the time rather with wonder than with repining. I recall them now without a harsh thought either toward my father or my mother. Both loved me, and both did their duty by me. If I seem to speak constrainedly of them here, it is not on my own account. I can honestly say that, with all my heart and soul.

Even Uncle George, fond as he was of me, was fonder of my beautiful child-sister.

When I used mischievously to pull at his lank, scanty hair, he would gently and laughingly take it out of my hands, but he would let Caroline tug at it till his dim, wandering gray eyes winked and watered again with pain. He used to plunge perilously about the garden, in awkward imitation of the cantering of a horse, while I sat on his shoulders; but he would never proceed at any pace beyond a slow and safe walk when Caroline had a ride in her turn. When he took us out walking, Caroline was always on the side next the wall. When we interrupted him over his dirty work in the surgery, he used to tell me to go and play until he was ready for me; but he would put down his bottles, and clean his clumsy fingers on his coarse apron, and lead Caroline out again, as if she had been the greatest lady in the land. Ah! how he loved her! and, let me be honest and grateful, and add, how he loved me, too!

When I was eight years old and Caroline was twelve, I was separated from home for some time. I had been ailing for many months previously; had got benefit from being taken to the sea-side, and had shown symptoms of relapsing on being brought home again to the midland county in which we resided. After much consultation, it was at last resolved that I should be sent to live, until my constitution got stronger, with a maiden sister of my mother's, who had a house at a watering-place on the south coast.

I left home, I remember, loaded with presents, rejoicing over the prospect of looking at the sea again, as careless of the future and as happy in the present as any boy could be. Uncle George petitioned for a holiday to take me to the seaside, but he could not be spared from the surgery. He consoled himself and me by promising to make me a magnificent model of a ship.

I have that model before my eyes now while I write. It is dusty with age; the paint on it is cracked; the ropes are tangled; the sails are moth-eaten and yellow. The hull is all out of proportion, and the rig has been smiled at by every nautical friend of mine who has ever looked at it. Yet, worn-out and faulty as it is— inferior to the cheapest miniature vessel nowadays in any toy-shop window—I hardly know a possession of mine in this world that I would not sooner part with than Uncle George's ship.

My life at the sea-side was a very happy one. I remained with my aunt more than a year. My mother often came to see how I was going on, and at first always brought my sister with her; but during the last eight months of my stay Caroline never once appeared. I noticed also, at the same period, a change in my mother's manner. She looked paler and more anxious at each succeeding visit, and always had long conferences in private with my aunt. At last she ceased to come and see us altogether, and only wrote to know how my health was getting on. My father, too, who had at the earlier periods of my absence from home traveled to the sea-side to watch the progress of my recovery as often as his professional engagements would permit, now kept away like my mother. Even Uncle George, who had never been allowed a holiday to come and see me, but who had hitherto often written and begged me to write to him, broke off our correspondence.

I was naturally perplexed and amazed by these changes, and persecuted my aunt to tell me the reason of them. At first she tried to put me off with excuses; then she admitted that there was trouble in our house; and finally she confessed that the trouble was caused by the illness of my sister. When I inquired what that illness was, my aunt said it was useless to attempt to explain it to me. I next applied to the servants. One of them was less cautious than my aunt, and answered my question, but in terms that I could not comprehend. After much explanation, I was made to understand that "something was growing on my sister's neck that would spoil her beauty forever, and perhaps kill her, if it could not be got rid of." How well I remember the shudder of horror that ran through me at the vague idea of this deadly "something"! A fearful, awe-struck curiosity to see what Caroline's illness was with my own eyes troubled my inmost heart, and I begged to be allowed to go home and help to nurse her. The request was, it is almost needless to say, refused.

Weeks passed away, and still I heard nothing, except that my sister continued to be ill. One day I privately wrote a letter to Uncle George, asking him, in my childish way, to come and tell me about Caroline's illness.

I knew where the post-office was, and slipped out in the morning unobserved and dropped my letter in the box. I stole home again by the garden, and climbed in at the window of a back parlor on the ground floor. The room above was my aunt's bedchamber, and the moment I was inside the house I heard moans and loud convulsive sobs proceeding from it. My aunt was a singularly quiet, composed woman. I could not imagine that the loud sobbing and moaning came from her, and I ran down terrified into the kitchen to ask the servants who was crying so violently in my aunt's room.

I found the housemaid and the cook talking together in whispers with serious faces. They started when they saw me as if I had been a grown-up master who had caught them neglecting their work.

"He's too young to feel it much," I heard one say to the other. "So far as he is concerned, it seems like a mercy that it happened no later."

In a few minutes they had told me the worst. It was indeed my aunt who had been crying in the bedroom. Caroline was dead.

I felt the blow more severely than the servants or anyone else about me supposed. Still I was a child in years, and I had the blessed elasticity of a child's nature. If I had been older I might have been too much absorbed in grief to observe my aunt so closely as I did, when she was composed enough to see me later in the day.

I was not surprised by the swollen state of her eyes, the paleness of her cheeks, or the fresh burst of tears that came from her when she took me in her arms at meeting. But I was both amazed and perplexed by the look of terror that I detected in her face. It was natural enough that she should grieve and weep over my sister's death, but why should she have that frightened look as if some other catastrophe had happened?

I asked if there was any more dreadful news from home besides the news of Caroline's death.

My aunt, said No in a strange, stifled voice, and suddenly turned her face from me. Was my father dead? No. My mother? No. Uncle George? My aunt trembled all over as she said No to that also, and bade me cease asking any more questions. She was not fit to bear them yet she said, and signed to the servant to lead me out of the room.

The next day I was told that I was to go home after the funeral, and was taken out toward evening by the housemaid, partly for a walk, partly to be measured for my mourning clothes. After we had left the tailor's, I persuaded the girl to extend our walk for some distance along the sea-beach, telling her, as we went, every little anecdote connected with my lost sister that came tenderly back to my memory in those first days of sorrow. She was so interested in hearing and I in speaking that we let the sun go down before we thought of turning back.

The evening was cloudy, and it got on from dusk to dark by the time we approached the town again. The housemaid was rather nervous at finding herself alone with me on the beach, and once or twice looked behind her distrustfully as we went on. Suddenly she squeezed my hand hard, and said:

"Let's get up on the cliff as fast as we can."

The words were hardly out of her mouth before I heard footsteps behind me—a man came round quickly to my side, snatched me away from the girl, and, catching me up in his arms without a word, covered my face with kisses. I knew he was crying, because my cheeks were instantly wet with his tears; but it was too dark for me to see who he was, or even how he was dressed. He did not, I should think, hold me half a minute in his arms. The housemaid screamed for help. I was put down gently on the sand, and the strange man instantly disappeared in the darkness.

When this extraordinary adventure was related to my aunt, she seemed at first merely bewildered at hearing of it; but in a moment more there came a change over her face, as if she had suddenly recollected or thought of something. She turned deadly pale, and said, in a hurried way, very unusual with her:

"Never mind; don't talk about it any more. It was only a mischievous trick to frighten you, I dare say. Forget all about it, my dear—forget all about it."

It was easier to give this advice than to make me follow it. For many nights after, I thought of nothing but the strange man who had kissed me and cried over me.

Who could he be? Somebody who loved me very much, and who was very sorry. My childish logic carried me to that length. But when I tried to think over all the grown-up gentlemen who loved me very much, I could never get on, to my own satisfaction, beyond my father and my Uncle George.

CHAPTER II.

I was taken home on the appointed day to suffer the trial—a hard one even at my tender years—of witnessing my mother's passionate grief and my father's mute despair. I remember that the scene of our first meeting after Caroline's death was wisely and considerately shortened by my aunt, who took me out of the room. She seemed to have a confused desire to keep me from leaving her after the door had closed behind us; but I broke away and ran downstairs to the surgery, to go and cry for my lost playmate with the sharer of all our games, Uncle George.

I opened the surgery door and could see nobody. I dried my tears and looked all round the room—it was empty. I ran upstairs again to Uncle George's garret bedroom—he was not there; his cheap hairbrush and old cast-off razor-case that had belonged to my grandfather were not on the dressing-table. Had he got some other bedroom? I went out on the landing and called softly, with an unaccountable terror and sinking at my heart:

"Uncle George!"

Nobody answered; but my aunt came hastily up the garret stairs.

"Hush!" she said. "You must never call that name out here again!"

She stopped suddenly, and looked as if her own words had frightened her.

"Is Uncle George dead?" I asked. My aunt turned red and pale, and stammered.

I did not wait to hear what she said. I brushed past her, down the stairs. My heart was bursting—my flesh felt cold. I ran breathlessly and recklessly into the room where my father and mother had received me. They were both sitting there still. I ran up to them, wringing my hands, and crying out in a passion of tears:

"Is Uncle George dead?"

My mother gave a scream that terrified me into instant silence and stillness. My father looked at her for a moment, rang the bell that summoned the maid, then seized me roughly by the arm and dragged me out of the room.

He took me down into the study, seated himself in his accustomed chair, and put me before him between his knees. His lips were awfully white, and I felt his two hands, as they grasped my shoulders, shaking violently.

"You are never to mention the name of Uncle George again," he said, in a quick, angry, trembling whisper. "Never to me, never to your mother, never to your aunt, never to anybody in this world! Never—never—never!"

The repetition of the word terrified me even more than the suppressed vehemence with which he spoke. He saw that I was frightened, and softened his manner a little before he went on.

"You will never see Uncle George again," he said. "Your mother and I love you dearly; but if you forget what I have told you, you will be sent away from home. Never speak that name again—mind, never! Now kiss me, and go away."

How his lips trembled—and oh, how cold they felt on mine!

I shrunk out of the room the moment he had kissed me, and went and hid myself in the garden.

"Uncle George is gone. I am never to see him any more; I am never to speak of him again"—those were the words I repeated to myself, with indescribable terror and confusion, the moment I was alone. There was something unspeakably horrible to my young mind in this mystery which I was commanded always to respect, and which, so far as I then knew, I could never hope to see revealed. My father, my mother, my aunt, all appeared to be separated from me now by some impassable barrier. Home seemed home no longer with Caroline dead, Uncle George gone, and a forbidden subject of talk perpetually and mysteriously interposing between my parents and me.

Though I never infringed the command my father had given me in his study (his words and looks, and that dreadful scream of my mother's, which seemed to be still ringing in my ears, were more than enough to insure my obedience), I also never lost the secret desire to penetrate the darkness which clouded over the fate of Uncle George.

For two years I remained at home and discovered nothing. If I asked the servants about my uncle, they could only tell me that one morning he disappeared from the house. Of the members of my father's family I could make no inquiries. They lived far away, and never came to see us; and the idea of writing to them, at my age and in my position, was out of the question. My aunt was as unapproachably silent as my father and mother; but I never forgot how her face had altered when she reflected for a moment after hearing of my extraordinary adventure while going home with the servant over the sands at night. The more I thought of that change of countenance in connection with what had occurred on my return to my father's house, the more certain I felt that the stranger who had kissed me and wept over me must have been no other than Uncle George.

At the end of my two years at home I was sent to sea in the merchant navy by my own earnest desire. I had always determined to be a sailor from the time when I first went to stay with my aunt at the sea-side, and I persisted long enough in my resolution to make my parents recognize the necessity of acceding to my wishes.

My new life delighted me, and I remained away on foreign stations more than four years. When I at length returned home, it was to find a new affliction darkening our fireside. My father had died on the very day when I sailed for my return voyage to England.

Absence and change of scene had in no respect weakened my desire to penetrate the mystery of Uncle George's disappearance. My mother's health was so delicate that I hesitated for some time to approach the forbidden subject in her presence. When I at last ventured to refer to it, suggesting to her that any prudent reserve which might have been necessary while I was a child, need no longer be persisted in now that I was growing to be a young man, she fell into a violent fit of trembling, and commanded me to say no more. It had been my father's will, she said, that the reserve to which I referred should be always adopted toward me; he had not authorized her, before he died, to speak more openly; and, now that he was gone, she would not so much as think of acting on her own unaided judgment. My aunt said the same thing in effect when I appealed to her. Determined not to be discouraged even yet, I undertook a journey, ostensibly to pay my respects to my father's family, but with the secret intention of trying what I could learn in that quarter on the subject of Uncle George.

My investigations led to some results, though they were by no means satisfactory. George had always been looked upon with something like contempt by his handsome sisters and his prosperous brothers, and he had not improved his position in the family by his warm advocacy of his brother's cause at the time of my father's marriage. I found that my uncle's surviving relatives now spoke of him slightingly and carelessly. They assured me that they had never heard from him, and that they knew nothing about him, except that he had gone away to settle, as they supposed, in some foreign place, after having behaved very basely and badly to my father. He had been traced to London, where he had sold out of the funds the small share of money which he had inherited after his father's death, and he had been seen on the deck of a packet bound for France later on the same day. Beyond this nothing was known about him. In what the alleged baseness of his behavior had consisted none of his brothers and sisters could tell me. My father had refused to pain them by going into particulars, not only at the time of his brother's disappearance, but afterward, whenever the subject was mentioned. George had always been the black sheep of the flock, and he must have been conscious of his own baseness, or he would certainly have written to explain and to justify himself.

Such were the particulars which I gleaned during my visit to my father's family. To my mind, they tended rather to deepen than to reveal the mystery. That such a gentle, docile, affectionate creature as Uncle George should have injured the brother he loved by word or deed at any period of their intercourse, seemed incredible; but that he should have been guilty of an act of baseness at the very time when my sister was dying was simply and plainly impossible. And yet there was the incomprehensible fact staring me in the face that the death of Caroline and the disappearance of Uncle George had taken plac e in the same week! Never did I feel more daunted and bewildered by the family secret than after I had heard all the particulars in connection with it that my father's relatives had to tell me.

I may pass over the events of the next few years of my life briefly enough.

My nautical pursuits filled up all my time, and took me far away from my country and my friends. But, whatever I did, and wherever I went, the memory of Uncle George, and the desire to penetrate the mystery of his disappearance, haunted me like familiar spirits. Often, in the lonely watches of the night at sea, did I recall the dark evening on the beach, the strange man's hurried embrace, the startling sensation of feeling his tears on my cheeks, the disappearance of him before I had breath or self-possession enough to say a word. Often did I think over the inexplicable events that followed, when I had returned, after my sister's funeral, to my father's house; and oftener still did I puzzle my brains vainly, in the attempt to form some plan for inducing my mother or my aunt to disclose the secret which they had hitherto kept from me so perseveringly. My only chance of knowing what had really happened to Uncle George, my only hope of seeing him again, rested with those two near and dear relatives. I despaired of ever getting my mother to speak on the forbidden subject after what had passed between us, but I felt more sanguine about my prospects of ultimately inducing my aunt to relax in her discretion. My anticipations, however, in this direction were not destined to be fulfilled. On my next visit to England I found my aunt prostrated by a paralytic attack, which deprived her of the power of speech. She died soon afterward in my arms, leaving me her sole heir. I searched anxiously among her papers for some reference to the family mystery, but found no clew to guide me. All my mother's letters to her sister at the time of Caroline's illness and death had been destroyed.

CHAPTER III.

MORE years passed; my mother followed my aunt to the grave, and still I was as far as ever from making any discoveries in relation to Uncle George. Shortly after the period of this last affliction my health gave way, and I departed, by my doctor's advice, to try some baths in the south of France.

I traveled slowly to my destination, turning aside from the direct road, and stopping wherever I pleased. One evening, when I was not more than two or three days' journey from the baths to which I was bound, I was struck by the picturesque situation of a little town placed on the brow of a hill at some distance from the main road, and resolved to have a nearer look at the place, with a view to stopping there for the night, if it pleased me. I found the principal inn clean and quiet—ordered my bed there—and, after dinner, strolled out to look at the church. No thought of Uncle George was in my mind when I entered the building; and yet, at that very moment, chance was leading me to the discovery which, for so many years past, I had vainly endeavored to make—the discovery which I had given up as hopeless since the day of my mother's death.

I found nothing worth notice in the church, and was about to leave it again, when I caught a glimpse of a pretty view through a side door, and stopped to admire it.

The churchyard formed the foreground, and below it the hill-side sloped away gently into the plain, over which the sun was setting in full glory. The cure of the church was reading his breviary, walking up and down a gravel-path that parted the rows of graves. In the course of my wanderings I had learned to speak French as fluently as most Englishmen, and when the priest came near me I said a few words in praise of the view, and complimented him on the neatness and prettiness of the churchyard. He answered with great politeness, and we got into conversation together immediately.

As we strolled along the gravel-walk, my attention was attracted by one of the graves standing apart from the rest. The cross at the head of it differed remarkably, in some points of appearance, from the crosses on the other graves. While all the rest had garlands hung on them, this one cross was quite bare; and, more extraordinary still, no name was inscribed on it.

The priest, observing that I stopped to look at the grave, shook his head and sighed.

"A countryman of yours is buried there," he said. "I was present at his death. He had borne the burden of a great sorrow among us, in this town, for many weary years, and his conduct had taught us to respect and pity him with all our hearts."

"How is it that his name is not inscribed over his grave?" I inquired.

"It was suppressed by his own desire," answered the priest, with some little hesitation. "He confessed to me in his last moments that he had lived here under an assumed name. I asked his real name, and he told it to me, with the particulars of his sad story. He had reasons for desiring to be forgotten after his death. Almost the last words he spoke were, 'Let my name die with me.' Almost the last request he made was that I would keep that name a secret from all the world excepting only one person."

"Some relative, I suppose?" said I.

"Yes—a nephew," said the priest.

The moment the last word was out of his mouth, my heart gave a strange answering bound. I suppose I must have changed color also, for the cure looked at me with sudden attention and interest.

"A nephew," the priest went on, "whom he had loved like his own child. He told me that if this nephew ever traced him to his burial-place, and asked about him, I was free in that case to disclose all I knew. 'I should like my little Charley to know the truth,' he said. 'In spite of the difference in our ages, Charley and I were playmates years ago.' "

My heart beat faster, and I felt a choking sensation at the throat the moment I heard the priest unconsciously mention my Christian name in mentioning the dying man's last words.

As soon as I could steady my voice and feel certain of my self-possession, I communicated my family name to the cure, and asked him if that was not part of the secret that he had been requested to preserve.

He started back several steps, and clasped his hands amazedly.

"Can it be?" he said, in low tones, gazing at me earnestly, with something like dread in his face.

I gave him my passport, and looked away toward the grave. The tears came into my eyes as the recollections of past days crowded back on me. Hardly knowing what I did, I knelt down by the grave, and smoothed the grass over it with my hand. Oh, Uncle George, why not have told your secret to your old playmate? Why leave him to find you *here?*

The priest raised me gently, and begged me to go with him into his own house. On our way there, I mentioned persons and places that I thought my uncle might have spoken of, in order to satisfy my companion that I was really the person I represented myself to be. By the time we had entered his little parlor, and had sat down alone in it, we were almost like old friends together.

I thought it best that I should begin by telling all that I have related here on the subject of Uncle George, and his disappearance from home. My host listened with a very sad face, and said, when I had done:

"I can understand your anxiety to know what I am authorized to tell you, but pardon me if I say first that there are circumstances in your uncle's story which it may pain you to hear—" He stopped suddenly.

"Which it may pain me to hear as a nephew?" I asked.

"No," said the priest, looking away from me, "as a son."

I gratefully expressed my sense of the delicacy and kindness which had prompted my companion's warning, but I begged him, at the same time, to keep me no longer in suspense and to tell me the stern truth, no matter how painfully it might affect me as a listener.

"In telling me all you knew about what you term the Family Secret," said the priest, "you have mentioned as a strange coincidence that your sister's death and your uncle's disappearance took place at the same time. Did you ever suspect what cause it was that occasioned your sister's death?"

"I only knew what my father told me, an d what all our friends believed—that she had a tumor in the neck, or, as I sometimes heard it stated, from the effect on her constitution of a tumor in the neck."

"She died under an operation for the removal of that tumor," said the priest, in low tones; "and the operator was your Uncle George."

In those few words all the truth burst upon me.

"Console yourself with the thought that the long martyrdom of his life is over," the priest went on. "He rests; he is at peace. He and his little darling understand each other, and are happy now. That thought bore him up to the last on his death-bed. He always spoke of your sister as his 'little darling.' He firmly believed that she was waiting to forgive and console him in the other world—and who shall say he was deceived in that belief?"

Not I! Not anyone who has ever loved and suffered, surely!

"It was out of the depths of his self-sacrificing love for the child that he drew the fatal courage to undertake the operation," continued the priest. "Your father naturally shrank from attempting it. His medical brethren whom he consulted all doubted the propriety of taking any measures for the removal of the tumor, in the particular condition and situation of it when they were called in. Your uncle alone differed with them. He was too modest a man to say so, but your mother found it out. The deformity of her beautiful child horrified her. She was desperate enough to catch at the faintest hope of remedying it that anyone might hold out to her; and she persuaded your uncle to put his opinion to the proof. Her horror at the deformity of the child, and her despair at the prospect of its lasting for life, seem to have utterly blinded her to all natural sense of the danger of the operation. It is hard to know how to say it to you, her son, but it must be told, nevertheless, that one day, when your father was out, she untruly informed your uncle that his brother had consented to the performance of the operation, and that he had gone purposely out of the house because he had not nerve enough to stay and witness it. After that, your uncle no longer hesitated. He had no fear of results, provided he could be certain of his own courage. All he dreaded was the effect on him of his love for the child when he first found himself face to face with the dreadful necessity of touching her skin with the knife."

I tried hard to control myself, but I could not repress a shudder at those words.

"It is useless to shock you by going into particulars," said the priest, considerately. "Let it be enough if I say that your uncle's fortitude failed to support him when he wanted it most. His love for the child shook the firm hand which had never trembled before. In a word, the operation failed. Your father returned, and found his child dying. The frenzy of his despair when the truth was told him carried him to excesses which it shocks me to mention—excesses which began in his degrading his brother by a blow, which ended in his binding himself by an oath to make that brother suffer public punishment for his fatal rashness in a court of law. Your uncle was too heartbroken by what had happened to feel

those outrages as some men might have felt them. He looked for one moment at
his sister-in-law (I do not like to say your mother, considering what I have now to
tell you), to see if she would acknowledge that she had encouraged him to attempt
the operation, and that she had deceived him in saying that he had his brother's
permission to try it. She was silent, and when she spoke, it was to join her
husband in denouncing him as the murderer of their child. Whether fear of your
father's anger, or revengeful indignation against your uncle most actuated her, I
cannot presume to inquire in your presence. I can only state facts."

The priest paused and looked at me anxiously. I could not speak to him at
that moment—I could only encourage him to proceed by pressing his hand.

He resumed in these terms:

"Meanwhile, your uncle turned to your father, and spoke the last words he
was ever to address to his eldest brother in this world. He said, 'I have deserved
the worst your anger can inflict on me, but I will spare you the scandal of bringing
me to justice in open court. The law, if it found me guilty, could at the worst but
banish me from my country and my friends. I will go of my own accord. God is
my witness that I honestly believed I could save the child from deformity and
suffering. I have risked all and lost all. My heart and spirit are broken. I am fit for
nothing but to go and hide myself, and my shame and misery, from all eyes that
have ever looked on me. I shall never come back, never expect your pity or
forgiveness. If you think less harshly of me when I am gone, keep secret what has
happened; let no other lips say of me what yours and your wife's have said. I shall
think that forbearance atonement enough—atonement greater than I have
deserved. Forget me in this world. May we meet in another, where the secrets of
all hearts are opened, and where the child who is gone before may make peace
between us!' He said those words and went out. Your father never saw him or
heard from him again."

I knew the reason now why my father had never confided the truth to
anyone, his own family included. My mother had evidently confessed all to her
sister under the seal of secrecy, and there the dreadful disclosure had been
arrested.

"Your uncle told me," the priest continued, "that before he left England he
took leave of you by stealth, in a place you were staying at by the sea-side. Tie had
not the heart to quit his country and his friends forever without kissing you for
the last time. He followed you in the dark, and caught you up in his arms, and left
you again before you had a chance of discovering him. The next day he quitted
England."

"For this place?" I asked.

"Yes. He had spent a week here once with a student friend at the time when
he was a pupil in the Hotel Dieu, and to this place he returned to hide, to suffer,
and to die. We all saw that he was a man crushed and broken by some great
sorrow, and we respected him and his affliction. He lived alone, and only came
out of doors toward evening, when he used to sit on the brow of the hill yonder,
with his head on his hand, looking toward England. That place seemed a favorite
with him, and he is buried close by it. He revealed the story of his past life to no

living soul here but me, and to me he only spoke when his last hour was approaching. What he had suffered during his long exile no man can presume to say. I, who saw more of him than anyone, never heard a word of complaint fall from his lips. He had the courage of the martyrs while he lived, and the resignation of the saints when he died. Just at the last his mind wandered. He said he saw his little darling waiting by the bedside to lead him away, and he died with a smile on his face—the first I had ever seen there."

The priest ceased, and we went out together in the mournful twilight, and stood for a little while on the brow of the hill where Uncle George used to sit, with his face turned toward England. How my heart ached for him as I thought of what he must have suffered in the silence and solitude of his long exile! Was it well for me that I had discovered the Family Secret at last? I have sometimes thought not. I have sometimes wished that the darkness had never been cleared away which once hid from me the fate of Uncle George.

THE THIRD DAY.

FINE again. Our guest rode out, with her ragged little groom, as usual. There was no news yet in the paper—that is to say, no news of George or his ship.

On this day Morgan completed his second story, and in two or three days more I expected to finish the last of my own contributions. Owen was still behindhand and still despondent.

The lot drawing to-night was Five. This proved to be the number of the first of Morgan's stories, which he had completed before we began the readings. His second story, finished this day, being still uncorrected by me, could not yet be added to the common stock.

On being informed that it had come to his turn to occupy the attention of the company, Morga n startled us by immediately objecting to the trouble of reading his own composition, and by coolly handing it over to me, on the ground that my numerous corrections had made it, to all intents and purposes, my story.

Owen and I both remonstrated; and Jessie, mischievously persisting in her favorite jest at Morgan's expense, entreated that he would read, if it was only for her sake. Finding that we were all determined, and all against him, he declared that, rather than hear our voices any longer, he would submit to the minor inconvenience of listening to his own. Accordingly, he took his manuscript back again, and, with an air of surly resignation, spread it open before him.

"I don't think you will like this story, miss," he began, addressing Jessie, "but I shall read it, nevertheless, with the greatest pleasure. It begins in a stable—it gropes its way through a dream—it keeps company with a hostler—and it stops without an end. What do you think of that?"

After favoring his audience with this promising preface, Morgan indulged himself in a chuckle of supreme satisfaction, and then began to read, without wasting another preliminary word on any one of us.

BROTHER MORGAN'S STORY

OF

THE DREAM-WOMAN.

CHAPTER I.

I HAD not been settled much more than six weeks in my country practice when I was sent for to a neighboring town, to consult with the resident medical man there on a case of very dangerous illness.

My horse had come down with me at the end of a long ride the night before, and had hurt himself, luckily, much more than he had hurt his master. Being deprived of the animal's services, I started for my destination by the coach (there were no railways at that time), and I hoped to get back again, toward the afternoon, in the same way.

After the consultation was over, I went to the principal inn of the town to wait for the coach. When it came up it was full inside and out. There was no resource left me but to get home as cheaply as I could by hiring a gig. The price asked for this accommodation struck me as being so extortionate, that I determined to look out for an inn of inferior pretensions, and to try if I could not make a better bargain with a less prosperous establishment.

I soon found a likely-looking house, dingy and quiet, with an old-fashioned sign, that had evidently not been repainted for many years past. The landlord, in this case, was not above making a small profit, and as soon as we came to terms he rang the yard-bell to order the gig.

"Has Robert not come back from that errand?" asked the landlord, appealing to the waiter who answered the bell.

"No, sir, he hasn't."

"Well, then, you must wake up Isaac."

"Wake up Isaac!" I repeated; "that sounds rather odd. Do your hostlers go to bed in the daytime?"

"This one does," said the landlord, smiling to himself in rather a strange way.

"And dreams too," added the waiter; "I shan't forget the turn it gave me the first time I heard him."

"Never you mind about that," retorted the proprietor; "you go and rouse Isaac up. The gentleman's waiting for his gig."

The landlord's manner and the waiter's manner expressed a great deal more than they either of them said. I began to suspect that I might be on the trace of something professionally interesting to me as a medical man, and I thought I should like to look at the hostler before the waiter awakened him.

"Stop a minute," I interposed; "I have rather a fancy for seeing this man before you wake him up. I'm a doctor; and if this queer sleeping and dreaming of his comes from anything wrong in his brain, I may be able to tell you what to do with him."

"I rather think you will find his complaint past all doctoring, sir," said the landlord; "but, if you would like to see him, you're welcome, I'm sure."

He led the way across a yard and down a passage to the stables, opened one of the doors, and, waiting outside himself, told me to look in.

I found myself in a two-stall stable. In one of the stalls a horse was munching his corn; in the other an old man was lying asleep on the litter.

I stooped and looked at him attentively. It was a withered, woe-begone face. The eyebrows were painfully contracted; the mouth was fast set, and drawn down at the corners.

The hollow wrinkled cheeks, and the scanty grizzled hair, told their own tale of some past sorrow or suffering. He was drawing his breath convulsively when I first looked at him, and in a moment more he began to talk in his sleep.

"Wake up!" I heard him say, in a quick whisper, through his clinched teeth. "Wake up there! Murder!"

He moved one lean arm slowly till it rested over his throat, shuddered a little, and turned on his straw. Then the arm left his throat, the hand stretched itself out, and clutched at the side toward which he had turned, as if he fancied himself to be grasping at the edge of something. I saw his lips move, and bent lower over him. He was still talking in his sleep.

"Light gray eyes," he murmured, "and a droop in the left eyelid; flaxen hair, with a gold-yellow streak in it—all right, mother—fair white arms, with a down on them—little lady's hand, with a reddish look under the finger nails. The knife—always the cursed knife—first on one side, then on the other. Aha! you she-devil, where's the knife?"

At the last word his voice rose, and he grew restless on a sudden. I saw him shudder on the straw; his withered face became distorted, and he threw up both his hands with a quick hysterical gasp. They struck against the bottom of the manger under which he lay, and the blow awakened him. I had just time to slip through the door and close it before his eyes were fairly open, and his senses his own again.

"Do you know anything about that man's past life?" I said to the landlord.

"Yes, sir, I know pretty well all about it," was the answer, "and an uncommon queer story it is. Most people don't believe it. It's true, though, for all that. Why, just look at him," continued the landlord, opening the stable door again. "Poor devil! he's so worn out with his restless nights that he's dropped back into his sleep already."

"Don't wake him," I said; "I'm in no hurry for the gig. Wait till the other man comes back from his errand; and, in the meantime, suppose I have some lunch and a bottle of sherry, and suppose you come and help me to get through it?"

The heart of mine host, as I had anticipated, warmed to me over his own wine. He soon became communicative on the subject of the man asleep in the stable, and by little and little I drew the whole story out of him. Extravagant and incredible as the events must appear to everybody, they are related here just as I heard them and just as they happened.

CHAPTER II.

SOME years ago there lived in the suburbs of a large seaport town on the west coast of England a man in humble circumstances, by name Isaac Scatchard. His means of subsistence were derived from any employment that he could get as an hostler, and occasionally, when times went well with him, from temporary engagements in service as stable-helper in private houses. Though a faithful, steady, and honest man, he got on badly in his calling. His ill luck was proverbial among his neighbors. He was always missing good opportunities by no fault of his own, and always living longest in service with amiable people who were not punctual payers of wages. "Unlucky Isaac" was his nickname in his own neighborhood, and no one could say that he did not richly deserve it.

With far more than one man's fair share of adversity to endure, Isaac had but one consolation to support him, and that was of the dreariest and most negative kind. He had no wife and children to increase his anxieties and add to the bitterness of his various failures in life. It might have been from mere insensibility, or it might have been from generous unwillingness to involve another in his own unlucky destiny, but the fact undoubtedly was, that he had arrived at the middle term of life without marrying, and, what is much more remarkable, without once exposing himself, from eighteen to eight-and-thirty, to the genial imputation of ever having had a sweetheart.

When he was out of service he lived alone with his widowed mother. Mrs. Scatchard was a woman above the average in her lowly station as to capacity and manners. She had seen better days, as the phrase is, but she never referred to them in the presence of curious visitors; and, though perfectly polite to every one who approached her, never cultivated any intimacies among her neighbors. She contrived to provide, hardly enough, for her simple wants by doing rough work for the tailors, and always managed to keep a decent home for her son to return to whenever his ill luck drove him out helpless into the world.

One bleak autumn when Isaac was getting on fast toward forty and when he was as usual out of place through no fault of his own, he set forth, from his mother's cottage on a long walk inland to a gentleman's seat where he had heard that a stable-helper was required.

It wanted then but two days of his birthday; and Mrs. Scatchard, with her usual fondness, made him promise, before he started, that he would be back in time to keep that anniversary with her, in as festive a way as their poor means would allow. It was easy for him to comply with this request, even supposing he slept a night each way on the road.

He was to start from home on Monday morning, and, whether he got the new place or not, he was to be back for his birthday dinner on Wednesday at two o'clock.

Arriving at his destination too late on the Monday night to make application for the stablehelper's place, he slept at the village inn, and in good time on the Tuesday morning presented himself at the gentleman's house to fill the vacant situation. Here again his ill luck pursued him as inexorably as ever. The excellent written testimonials to his character which he was able to produce availed him nothing; his long walk had been taken in vain: only the day before the stable-helper's place had been given to another man.

Isaac accepted this new disappointment resignedly and as a matter of course. Naturally slow in capacity, he had the bluntness of sensibility and phlegmatic patience of disposition which frequently distinguish men with sluggishly-working mental powers. He thanked the gentleman's steward with his usual quiet civility for granting him an interview, and took his departure with no appearance of unusual depression in his face or manner.

Before starting on his homeward walk he made some inquiries at the inn, and ascertained that he might save a few miles on his return by following the new road. Furnished with full instructions, several times repeated, as to the various turnings he was to take, he set forth on his homeward journey and walked on all day with only one stoppage for bread and cheese. Just as it was getting toward dark, the rain came on and the wind began to rise, and he found himself, to make matters worse, in a part of the country with which he was entirely unacquainted, though he knew himself to be some fifteen miles from home. The first house he found to inquire at was a lonely roadside inn, standing on the outskirts of a thick wood. Solitary as the place looked, it was welcome to a lost man who was also hungry, thirsty, footsore and wet. The landlord was civil and respectable-looking, and the price he asked for a bed was reasonable enough. Isaac therefore decided on stopping comfortably at the inn for that night.

He was constitutionally a temperate man.

His supper consisted of two rashers of bacon, a slice of home-made bread and a pint of ale. He did not go to bed immediately after this moderate meal, but sat up with the landlord, talking about his bad prospects and his long run of ill-luck, and diverging from these topics to the subjects of horse-flesh and racing. Nothing was said either by himself, his host, or the few laborers who strayed into the tap-room, which could, in the slightest degree, excite the very small and very dull imaginative faculty which Isaac Scatchard possessed.

At a little after eleven the house was closed. Isaac went round with the landlord and held the candle while the doors and lower windows were being secured. He noticed with surprise the strength of the bolts and bars, and iron-sheathed shutters.

"You see, we are rather lonely here," said the landlord. "We never have had any attempts made to break in yet, but it's always as well to be on the safe side. When nobody is sleeping here, I am the only man in the house. My wife and daughter are timid, and the servant-girl takes after her missuses. Another glass of ale before you turn in? No! Well, how such a sober man as you comes to be out of place is more than I can make out, for one. Here's where you're to sleep. You're our only lodger to-night, and I think you'll say my missus has done her best to make you comfortable. You're quite sure you won't have another glass of ale? Very well. Good-night."

It was half-past eleven by the clock in the passage as they went upstairs to the bedroom, the window of which looked on to the wood at the back of the house.

Isaac locked the door, set his candle on the chest of drawers, and wearily got ready for bed.

The bleak autumn wind was still blowing, and the solemn, monotonous, surging moan of it in the wood was dreary and awful to hear through the night-silence. Isaac felt strangely wakeful.

He resolved, as he lay down in bed, to keep the candle alight until he began to grow sleepy, for there was something unendurably depressing in the bare idea of lying awake in the darkness, listening to the dismal, ceaseless moaning of the wind in the wood.

Sleep stole on him before he was aware of it. His eyes closed, and he fell off insensibly to rest without having so much as thought of extinguishing the candle.

The first sensation of which he was conscious after sinking into slumber was a strange shivering that ran through him suddenly from head to foot, and a dreadful sinking pain at the heart, such as he had never felt before. The shivering only disturbed his slumbers; the pain woke him instantly. In one moment he passed from a state of sleep to a state of wakefulness—his eyes wide open—his mental perceptions cleared on a sudden, as if by a miracle.

The candle had burned down nearly to the last morsel of tallow, but the top of the unsnuffed wick had just fallen off, and the light in the little room was, for the moment, fair and full.

Between the foot of his bed and the closed door there stood a woman with a knife in her hand, looking at him.

He was stricken speechless with terror, but he did not lose the preternatural clearness of his faculties, and he never took his eyes off the woman. She said not a word as they stared each other in the face, but she began to move slowly toward the left-hand side of the bed.

His eyes followed her. She was a fair, fine woman, with yellowish flaxen hair and light gray eyes, with a droop in the left eyelid. He noticed those things and fixed them on his mind before she was round at the side of the bed. Speechless, with no expression in her face, with no noise following her footfall, she came closer and closer—stopped—and slowly raised the knife. He laid his right arm over his throat to save it; but, as he saw the knife coming down, threw his hand across the bed to the right side, and jerked his body over that way just as the knife descended on the mattress within an inch of his shoulder.

His eyes fixed on her arm and hand as she slowly drew her knife out of the bed: a white, well-shaped arm, with a pretty down lying lightly over the fair skin—a delicate lady's hand, with the crowning beauty of a pink flush under and round the finger-nails.

She drew the knife out, and passed back again slowly to the foot of the bed; stopped there for a moment looking at him; then came on—still speechless, still with no expression on the blank, beautiful face, still with no sound following the stealthy footfalls—came on to the right side of the bed, where he now lay.

As she approached, she raised the knife again, and he drew himself away to the left side. She struck, as before, right into the mattress, with a deliberate, perpendicularly downward action of the arm. This time his eyes wandered from her to the knife. It was like the large cla sp-knives which he had often seen laboring men use to cut their bread and bacon with. Her delicate little fingers did not conceal more than two-thirds of the handle: he noticed that it was made of buck-horn, clean and shining as the blade was, and looking like new.

For the second time she drew the knife out, concealed it in the wide sleeve of her gown, then stopped by the bedside, watching him. For an instant he saw her standing in that position, then the wick of the spent candle fell over into the socket; the flame diminished to a little blue point, and the room grew dark.

A moment, or less, if possible, passed so, and then the wick flamed up, smokingly, for the last time. His eyes were still looking eagerly over the right-hand side of the bed when the final flash of light came, but they discovered nothing. The fair woman with the knife was gone.

The conviction that he was alone again weakened the hold of the terror that had struck him dumb up to this time. The preternatural sharpness which the very intensity of his panic had mysteriously imparted to his faculties left them suddenly. His brain grew confused—his heart beat wildly—his ears opened for the first time since the appearance of the woman to a sense of the woeful ceaseless moaning of the wind among the trees. With the dreadful conviction of the reality of what he had seen still strong within him, he leaped out of bed, and screaming "Murder! Wake up, there! wake up!" dashed headlong through the darkness to the door.

It was fast locked, exactly as he had left it on going to bed.

His cries on starting up had alarmed the house. He heard the terrified, confused exclamations of women; he saw the master of the house approaching along the passage with his burning rush-candle in one hand and his gun in the other.

"What is it?" asked the landlord, breathlessly. Isaac could only answer in a whisper. "A woman, with a knife in her hand," he gasped out. "In my room—a fair, yellow-haired woman; she jobbed at me with the knife twice over."

The landlord's pale cheeks grew paler. He looked at Isaac eagerly by the flickering light of his candle, and his face began to get red again; his voice altered, too, as well as his complexion.

"She seems to have missed you twice," he said.

"I dodged the knife as it came down," Isaac went on, in the same scared whisper. "It struck the bed each time."

The landlord took his candle into the bedroom immediately. In less than a minute he came out again into the passage in a violent passion.

"The devil fly away with you and your woman with the knife! There isn't a mark in the bedclothes anywhere. What do you mean by coming into a man's place and frightening his family out of their wits about a dream?"

"I'll leave your house," said Isaac, faintly. "Better out on the road, in rain and dark, on my road home, than back again in that room, after what I've seen in it. Lend me a light to get my clothes by, and tell me what I'm to pay."

"Pay!" cried the landlord, leading the way with his light sulkily into the bedroom. "You'll find your score on the slate when you go downstairs. I wouldn't have taken you in for all the money you've got about you if I'd known your dreaming, screeching ways beforehand. Look at the bed. Where's the cut of a knife in it? Look at the window—is the lock bursted? Look at the door (which I heard you fasten yourself)—is it broke in? A murdering woman with a knife in my house! You ought to be ashamed of yourself!"

Isaac answered not a word. He huddled on his clothes, and then they went downstairs together.

"Nigh on twenty minutes past two!" said the landlord, as they passed the clock. "A nice time in the morning to frighten honest people out of their wits!"

Isaac paid his bill, and the landlord let him out at the front door, asking, with a grin of contempt, as he undid the strong fastenings, whether "the murdering woman got in that way."

They parted without a word on either side. The rain had ceased, but the night was dark, and the wind bleaker than ever. Little did the darkness, or the cold, or the uncertainty about the way home matter to Isaac. If he had been turned out into a wilderness in a thunder-storm it would have been a relief after what he had suffered in the bedroom of the inn.

What was the fair woman with the knife? The creature of a dream, or that other creature from the unknown world called among men by the name of ghost? He could make nothing of the mystery—had made nothing of it, even when it was midday on Wednesday, and when he stood, at last, after many times missing his road, once more on the doorstep of home.

CHAPTER III.

His mother came out eagerly to receive him.

His face told her in a moment that something was wrong.

"I've lost the place; but that's my luck. I dreamed an ill dream last night, mother—or maybe I saw a ghost. Take it either way, it scared me out of my senses, and I'm not my own man again yet."

"Isaac, your face frightens me. Come in to the fire—come in, and tell mother all about it."

He was as anxious to tell as she was to hear; for it had been his hope, all the way home, that his mother, with her quicker capacity and superior knowledge, might be able to throw some light on the mystery which he could not clear up for himself. His memory of the dream was still mechanically vivid, though his thoughts were entirely confused by it.

His mother's face grew paler and paler as he went on. She never interrupted him by so much as a single word; but when he had done, she moved her chair close to his, put her arm round his neck, and said to him:

"Isaac, you dreamed your ill dream on this Wednesday morning. What time was it when you saw the fair woman with the knife in her hand?" Isaac reflected on what the landlord had said when they had passed by the clock on his leaving the inn; allowed as nearly as he could for the time that must have elapsed between the unlocking of his bedroom door and the paying of his bill just before going away, and answered:

"Somewhere about two o'clock in the morning."

His mother suddenly quitted her hold of his neck, and struck her hands together with a gesture of despair.

"This Wednesday is your birthday, Isaac, and two o'clock in the morning was the time when you were born."

Isaac's capacities were not quick enough to catch the infection of his mother's superstitious dread. He was amazed, and a little startled, also, when she suddenly rose from her chair, opened her old writing-desk, took pen, ink and paper, and then said to him:

"Your memory is but a poor one, Isaac, and, now I'm an old woman, mine's not much better. I want all about this dream of yours to be as well known to both of us, years hence, as it is now. Tell me over again all you told me a minute ago, when you spoke of what the woman with the knife looked like."

Isaac obeyed, and marveled much as he saw his mother carefully set down on paper the very words that he was saying.

"Light gray eyes," she wrote, as they came to the descriptive part, "with a droop in the left eyelid; flaxen hair, with a gold-yellow streak in it; white arms, with a down upon them; little lady's hand, with a reddish look about the finger nails; clasp-knife with a buck-horn handle, that seemed as good as new." To these particulars Mrs. Scatchard added the year, month, day of the week, and time in the morning when the woman of the dream appeared to her son. She then locked up the paper carefully in her writing-desk.

Neither on that day nor on any day after could her son induce her to return to the matter of the dream. She obstinately kept her thoughts about it to herself, and even refused to refer again to the paper in her writing-desk. Ere long Isaac grew weary of attempting to make her break her resolute silence; and time, which sooner or later wears out all things, gradually wore out the impression produced on him by the dream. He began by thinking of it carelessly, and he ended by not thinking of it at all.

The result was the more easily brought about by the advent of some important changes for the better in his prospects which commenced not long after his terrible night's experience at the inn. He reaped at last th e reward of his long and patient suffering under adversity by getting an excellent place, keeping it for seven years, and leaving it, on the death of his master, not only with an excellent character, but also with a comfortable annuity bequeathed to him as a reward for saving his mistress's life in a carriage accident. Thus it happened that Isaac Scatchard returned to his old mother, seven years after the time of the dream at the inn, with an annual sum of money at his disposal sufficient to keep them both in ease and independence for the rest of their lives.

The mother, whose health had been bad of late years, profited so much by the care bestowed on her and by freedom from money anxieties, that when Isaac's birthday came round she was able to sit up comfortably at table and dine with him.

On that day, as the evening drew on, Mrs. Scatchard discovered that a bottle of tonic medicine which she was accustomed to take, and in which she had fancied that a dose or more was still left, happened to be empty. Isaac immediately volunteered to go to the chemist's and get it filled again. It was as rainy and bleak an autumn night as on the memorable past occasion when he lost his way and slept at the road-side inn.

On going into the chemist's shop he was passed hurriedly by a poorly-dressed woman coming out of it. The glimpse he had of her face struck him, and he looked back after her as she descended the door-steps.

"You're noticing that woman?" said the chemist's apprentice behind the counter. "It's my opinion there's something wrong with her. She's been asking for laudanum to put to a bad tooth. Master's out for half an hour, and I told her I wasn't allowed to sell poison to strangers in his absence. She laughed in a queer way, and said she would come back in half an hour. If she expects master to serve her, I think she'll be disappointed. It's a case of suicide, sir, if ever there was one yet."

These words added immeasurably to the sudden interest in the woman which Isaac had felt at the first sight of her face. After he had got the medicine-bottle filled, he looked about anxiously for her as soon as he was out in the street. She was walking slowly up and down on the opposite side of the road. With his heart, very much to his own surprise, beating fast, Isaac crossed over and spoke to her.

He asked if she was in any distress. She pointed to her torn shawl, her scanty dress, her crushed, dirty bonnet; then moved under a lamp so as to let the light fall on her stern, pale, but still most beautiful face.

"I look like a comfortable, happy woman, don't I?" she said, with a bitter laugh.

She spoke with a purity of intonation which Isaac had never heard before from other than ladies' lips. Her slightest actions seemed to have the easy, negligent grace of a thoroughbred woman. Her skin, for all its poverty-stricken paleness, was as delicate as if her life had been passed in the enjoyment of every social comfort that wealth can purchase. Even her small, finely-shaped hands, gloveless as they were, had not lost their whiteness.

Little by little, in answer to his questions, the sad story of the woman came out. There is no need to relate it here; it is told over and over again in police reports and paragraphs about attempted suicides.

"My name is Rebecca Murdoch," said the woman, as she ended. "I have nine-pence left, and I thought of spending it at the chemist's over the way in securing a passage to the other world. Whatever it is, it can't be worse to me than this, so why should I stop here?"

Besides the natural compassion and sadness moved in his heart by what he heard, Isaac felt within him some mysterious influence at work all the time the woman was speaking which utterly confused his ideas and almost deprived him of his powers of speech. All that he could say in answer to her last reckless words was that he would prevent her from attempting her own life, if he followed her about all night to do it. His rough, trembling earnestness seemed to impress her.

"I won't occasion you that trouble," she answered, when he repeated his threat. "You have given me a fancy for living by speaking kindly to me. No need for the mockery of protestations and promises. You may believe me without them. Come to Fuller's Meadow to-morrow at twelve, and you will find me alive, to answer for myself—No !—no money. My ninepence will do to get me as good a night's lodging as I want."

She nodded and left him. He made no attempt to follow—he felt no suspicion that she was deceiving him.

"It's strange, but I can't help believing her," he said to himself, and walked away, bewildered, toward home.

On entering the house, his mind was still so completely absorbed by its new subject of interest that he took no notice of what his mother was doing when he came in with the bottle of medicine. She had opened her old writing-desk in his absence, and was now reading a paper attentively that lay inside it. On every birthday of Isaac's since she had written down the particulars of his dream from his own lips, she had been accustomed to read that same paper, and ponder over it in private.

The next day he went to Fuller's Meadow.

He had done only right in believing her so implicitly. She was there, punctual to a minute, to answer for herself. The last-left faint defenses in Isaac's heart against the fascination which a word or look from her began inscrutably to exercise over him sank down and vanished before her forever on that memorable morning.

When a man, previously insensible to the influence of women, forms an attachment in middle life, the instances are rare indeed, let the warning circumstances be what they may, in which he is found capable of freeing himself from the tyranny of the new ruling passion. The charm of being spoken to familiarly, fondly, and gratefully by a woman whose language and manners still retained enough of their early refinement to hint at the high social station that she had lost, would have been a dangerous luxury to a man of Isaac's rank at the age of twenty. But it was far more than that—it was certain ruin to him—now that his heart was opening unworthily to a new influence at that middle time of life when strong feelings of all kinds, once implanted, strike root most stubbornly in a man's moral nature. A few more stolen interviews after that first morning in Fuller's Meadow completed his infatuation. In less than a month from the time when he first met her, Isaac Scatchard had consented to give Rebecca Murdoch a new interest in existence, and a chance of recovering the character she had lost by promising to make her his wife.

She had taken possession, not of his passions only, but of his faculties as well. All the mind he had he put into her keeping. She directed him on every point—even instructing him how to break the news of his approaching marriage in the safest manner to his mother.

"If you tell her how you met me and who I am at first," said the cunning woman, "she will move heaven and earth to prevent our marriage. Say l am the sister of one of your fellow-servants—ask her to see me before you go into any more particulars—and leave it to me to do the rest. I mean to make her love me next best to you, Isaac, before she knows anything of who I really am." The motive of the deceit was sufficient to sanctify it to Isaac. The stratagem proposed relieved him of his one great anxiety, and quieted his uneasy conscience on the subject of his mother. Still, there was something wanting to perfect his happiness, something that he could not realize, something mysteriously untraceable, and yet something that perpetually made itself felt; not when he was absent from Rebecca Murdoch, but, strange to say, when he was actually in her presence! She was kindness itself with him. She never made him feel his inferior capacities and inferior manners. She showed the sweetest anxiety to please him in the smallest trifles; but, in spite of all these attractions, he never could feel quite at his ease with her. At their first meeting, there had mingled with his admiration, when he looked in her face, a faint, involuntary feeling of doubt whether that face was entirely strange to him. No after familiarity had the slightest effect on this inexplicable, wearisome uncertainty.

Concealing the truth as he had been directed, he announced his marriage engagement precipitately and confusedly to his mother on the day when he contracted it. Poor Mrs. Scatchard showed her perfect confidence in her son by flinging her arms round his neck, and giving him joy of having found at last, in the sister of one of his fellow-servants, a woman to comfort and care for him after his mother was gone. She was all eagerness to see the woman of her son's choice, and the next day was fixed for the introduction.

It was a bright sunny morning, and the little cottage parlor was full of light as Mrs. Scatchard, happy and expectant, dressed for the occasion in her Sunday gown, sat waiting for her son and her future daughter-in-law.

Punctual to the appointed time, Isaac hurriedly and nervously led his promised wife into the room. His mother rose to receive her—advanced a few steps, smiling—looked Rebecca full in the eyes, and suddenly stopped. Her face, which had been flushed the moment before, turned white in an instant; her eyes lost their expression of softness and kindness, and assumed a blank look of terror; her outstretched hands fell to her sides, and she staggered back a few steps with a low cry to her son.

"Isaac," she whispered, clutching him fast by the arm when he asked alarmedly if she was taken ill, "Isaac, does that woman's face remind you of nothing?"

Before he could answer—before he could look round to where Rebecca stood, astonished and angered by her reception, at the lower end of the room, his mother pointed impatiently to her writing-desk, and gave him the key.

"Open it," she said, in a quick breathless whisper.

"What does this mean? Why am I treated as if I had no business here? Does your mother want to insult me?" asked Rebecca, angrily.

"Open it, and give me the paper in the left-hand drawer. Quick! quick, for Heaven's sake!" said Mrs. Scatchard, shrinking further back in terror.

Isaac gave her the paper. She looked it over eagerly for a moment, then followed Rebecca, who was now turning away haughtily to leave the room, and caught her by the shoulder—abruptly raised the long, loose sleeve of her gown, and glanced at her hand and arm. Something like fear began to steal over the angry expression of Rebecca's face as she shook herself free from the old woman's grasp. "Mad!" she said to herself; "and Isaac never told me." With these few words she left the room.

Isaac was hastening after her when his mother turned and stopped his further progress. It wrung his heart to see the misery and terror in her face as she looked at him.

"Light gray eyes," she said, in low, mournful, awe-struck tones, pointing toward the open door; "a droop in the left eyelid; flaxen hair, with a gold-yellow streak in it; white arms, with a down upon them; little lady's hand, with a reddish look under the finger nails—The Dream- Woman, Isaac, the Dream-Woman!"

That faint cleaving doubt which he had never been able to shake off in Rebecca Murdoch's presence was fatally set at rest forever. He had seen her face, then, before—seven years before, on his birthday, in the bedroom of the lonely inn.

"Be warned! oh, my son, be warned! Isaac, Isaac, let her go, and do you stop with me!"

Something darkened the parlor window as those words were said. A sudden chill ran through him, and he glanced sidelong at the shadow. Rebecca Murdoch had come back. She was peering in curiously at them over the low window-blind.

"I have promised to marry, mother," he said, "and marry I must."

The tears came into his eyes as he spoke and dimmed his sight, but he could just discern the fatal face outside moving away again from the window.

His mother's head sank lower.

"Are you faint?" he whispered.

"Broken-hearted, Isaac."

He stooped down and kissed her. The shadow, as he did so, returned to the window, and the fatal face peered in curiously once more.

CHAPTER IV.

THREE weeks after that day Isaac and Rebecca were man and wife. All that was hopelessly dogged and stubborn in the man's moral nature seemed to have closed round his fatal passion, and to have fixed it unassailably in his heart.

After that first interview in the cottage parlor no consideration would induce Mrs. Scatchard to see her son's wife again or even to talk of her when Isaac tried hard to plead her cause after their marriage.

This course of conduct was not in any degree occasioned by a discovery of the degradation in which Rebecca had lived. There was no question of that between mother and son. There was no question of anything but the fearfully-exact resemblance between the living, breathing woman and the specter-woman of Isaac's dream.

Rebecca on her side neither felt nor expressed the slightest sorrow at the estrangement between herself and her mother-in-law. Isaac, for the sake of peace, had never contradicted her first idea that age and long illness had affected Mrs. Scatchard's mind. He even allowed his wife to upbraid him for not having confessed this to her at the time of their marriage engagement, rather than risk anything by hinting at the truth. The sacrifice of his integrity before his one all-mastering delusion seemed but a small thing, and cost his conscience but little after the sacrifices he had already made.

The time of waking from this delusion—the cruel and the rueful time—was not far off. After some quiet months of married life, as the summer was ending, and the year was getting on toward the month of his birthday, Isaac found his wife altering toward him. She grew sullen and contemptuous; she formed acquaintances of the most dangerous kind in defiance of his objections, his entreaties, and his commands; and, worst of all, she learned, ere long, after every fresh difference with her husband, to seek the deadly self-oblivion of drink. Little by little, after the first miserable discovery that his wife was keeping company with drunkards, the shocking certainty forced itself on Isaac that she had grown to be a drunkard herself.

He had been in a sadly desponding state for some time before the occurrence of these domestic calamities. His mother's health, as he could but too plainly discern every time he went to see her at the cottage, was failing fast, and he upbraided himself in secret as the cause of the bodily and mental suffering she endured. When to his remorse on his mother's account was added the shame and misery occasioned by the discovery of his wife's degradation, he sank under the double trial—his face began to alter fast, and he looked what he was, a spirit-broken man.

His mother, still struggling bravely against the illness that was hurrying her to the grave, was the first to notice the sad alteration in him, and the first to hear of his last worst trouble with his wife. She could only weep bitterly on the day when he made his humiliating confession, but on the next occasion when he went to see her she had taken a resolution in reference to his domestic afflictions which astonished and even alarmed him. He found her dressed to go out, and on asking the reason received this answer:

"I am not long for this world, Isaac," she said, "and I shall not feel easy on my death-bed unless I have done my best to the last to make my son happy. I mean to put my own fears and my own feelings out of the question, and to go with you to your wife, and try what I can do to reclaim her. Give me your arm, Isaac, and let me do the last thing I can in this world to help my son before it is too late."

He could not disobey her, and they walked together slowly toward his miserable home.

It was only one o'clock in the afternoon when they reached the cottage where he lived. It was their dinner-hour, and Rebecca was in the kitchen. He was thus able to take his mother quietly into the parlor, and then prepare his wife for the interview. She had fortunately drunk but little at that early hour, and she was less sullen and capricious than usual.

He returned to his mother with his mind tolerably at ease. His wife soon followed him into the parlor, and the m eeting between her and Mrs. Scatchard passed off better than he had ventured to anticipate, though he observed with secret apprehension that his mother, resolutely as she controlled herself in other respects, could not look his wife in the face when she spoke to her. It was a relief to him, therefore, when Rebecca began to lay the cloth.

She laid the cloth, brought in the bread-tray, and cut a slice from the loaf for her husband, then returned to the kitchen. At that moment, Isaac, still anxiously watching his mother, was startled by seeing the same ghastly change pass over her face which had altered it so awfully on the morning when Rebecca and she first met. Before he could say a word, she whispered, with a look of horror:

"Take me back—home, home again, Isaac. Come with me, and never go back again."

He was afraid to ask for an explanation; he could only sign to her to be silent, and help her quickly to the door. As they passed the breadtray on the table she stopped and pointed to it.

"Did you see what your wife cut your bread with?" she asked, in a low whisper.

"No, mother—I was not noticing—what was it?"

"Look!"

He did look. A new clasp-knife with a buckhorn handle lay with the loaf in the bread-tray. He stretched out his hand shudderingly to possess himself of it; but, at the same time, there was a noise in the kitchen, and his mother caught at his arm.

"The knife of the dream! Isaac, I'm faint with fear. Take me away before she comes back."

He was hardly able to support her. The visible, tangible reality of the knife struck him with a panic, and utterly destroyed any faint doubts that he might have entertained up to this time in relation to the mysterious dream-warning of nearly eight years before. By a last desperate effort, he summoned self-possession enough to help his mother out of the house—so quietly that the "Dream-woman" (he thought of her by that name now) did not hear them departing from the kitchen.

"Don't go back, Isaac—don't go back!" implored Mrs. Scatchard, as he turned to go away, after seeing her safely seated again in her own room.

"I must get the knife," he answered, under his breath. His mother tried to stop him again, but he hurried out without another word.

On his return he found that his wife had discovered their secret departure from the house. She had been drinking, and was in a fury of passion. The dinner in the kitchen was flung under the grate; the cloth was off the parlor table. Where was the knife?

Unwisely, he asked for it. She was only too glad of the opportunity of irritating him which the request afforded her. "He wanted the knife, did he? Could he give her a reason why? No! Then he should not have it—not if he went down on his knees to ask for it." Further recriminations elicited the fact that she had bought it a bargain, and that she considered it her own especial property. Isaac saw the uselessness of attempting to get the knife by fair means, and determined to search for it, later in the day, in secret. The search was unsuccessful. Night came on, and he left the house to walk about the streets. He was afraid now to sleep in the same room with her.

Three weeks passed. Still sullenly enraged with him, she would not give up the knife; and still that fear of sleeping in the same room with her possessed him. He walked about at night, or dozed in the parlor, or sat watching by his mother's bedside. Before the expiration of the first week in the new month his mother died. It wanted then but ten days of her son's birthday. She had longed to live till that anniversary. Isaac was present at her death, and her last words in this world were addressed to him:

"Don't go back, my son, don't go back!" He was obliged to go back, if it were only to watch his wife. Exasperated to the last degree by his distrust of her, she had revengefully sought to add a sting to his grief, during the last days of his mother's illness, by declaring that she would assert her right to attend the funeral. In spite of any thing he could do or say, she held with wicked pertinacity to her word, and on the day appointed for the burial forced herself—inflamed and shameless with drink—into her husband's presence, and declared that she would walk in the funeral procession to his mother's grave.

This last worst outrage, accompanied by all that was most insulting in word and look, maddened him for the moment. He struck her.

The instant the blow was dealt he repented it. She crouched down, silent, in a corner of the room, and eyed him steadily; it was a look that cooled his hot blood and made him tremble. But there was no time now to think of a means of making atonement. Nothing remained but to risk the worst till the funeral was over. There was but one way of making sure of her. He locked her into her bedroom.

When he came back some hours after, he found her sitting, very much altered in look and bearing, by the bedside, with a bundle on her lap. She rose, and faced him quietly, and spoke with a strange stillness in her voice, a strange repose in her eyes, a strange composure in her manner.

"No man has ever struck me twice," she said, "and my husband shall have no second opportunity. Set the door open and let me go. From this day forth we see each other no more."

Before he could answer she passed him and left the room. He saw her walk away up the street.

Would she return?

All that night he watched and waited, but no footstep came near the house. The next night, overpowered by fatigue, he lay down in bed in his clothes, with the door locked, the key on the table, and the candle burning. His slumber was not disturbed. The third night, the fourth, the fifth, the sixth passed, and nothing happened.

He lay down on the seventh, still in his clothes, still with the door locked, the key on the table, and the candle burning, but easier in his mind.

Easier in his mind, and in perfect health of body when he fell off to sleep. But his rest was disturbed. He woke twice without any sensation of uneasiness. But the third time it was that never-to-be-forgotten shivering of the night at the lonely inn, that dreadful sinking pain at the heart, which once more aroused him in an instant.

His eyes opened toward the left-hand side of the bed, and there stood—The Dream-Woman again? No! His wife; the living reality, with the dream-specter's face, in the dream-specter's attitude; the fair arm up, the knife clasped in the delicate white hand.

He sprang upon her almost at the instant of seeing her, and yet not quickly enough to prevent her from hiding the knife. Without a word from him—without a cry from her—he pinioned her in a chair. With one hand he felt up her sleeve, and there, where the Dream-Woman had hidden the knife, his wife had hidden it—the knife with the buckhorn handle, that looked like new.

In the despair of that fearful moment his brain was steady, his heart was calm. He looked at her fixedly with the knife in his hand, and said these last words:

"You told me we should see each other no more, and you have come back. It is my turn now to go, and to go forever. I say that we shall see each other no more, and my word shall not be broken."

He left her, and set forth into the night. There was a bleak wind abroad, and the smell of recent rain was in the air. The distant church-clocks chimed the quarter as he walked rapidly beyond the last houses in the suburb. He asked the first policeman he met what hour that was of which the quarter past had just struck.

The man referred sleepily to his watch, and answered, "Two o'clock." Two in the morning. What day of the month was this day that had just begun? He reckoned it up from the date of his mother's funeral. The fatal parallel was complete: it was his birthday!

Had he escaped the mortal peril which his dream foretold? or had he only received a second warning?

As that ominous doubt forced itself on his mind, he stopped, reflected, and turned back again toward the city. He was still resolute to hold to his word, and never to let her see him more; but there was a thought now in his mind of having her watched and followed. The knife was in his possession; the world was b efore him; but a new distrust of her—a vague, unspeakable, superstitious dread had overcome him.

"I must know where she goes, now she thinks I have left her," he said to himself, as he stole back wearily to the precincts of his house.

It was still dark. He had left the candle burning in the bedchamber; but when he looked up to the window of the room now there was no light in it. He crept cautiously to the house door. On going away, he remembered to have closed it; on trying it now, he found it open.

He waited outside, never losing sight of the house, till daylight. Then he ventured indoors—listened, and heard nothing—looked into kitchen, scullery, parlor and found nothing; went up at last into the bedroom—it was empty. A picklock lay on the floor betraying how she had gained entrance in the night, and that was the only trace of her.

Whither had she gone? That no mortal tongue could tell him. The darkness had covered her flight; and when the day broke, no man could say where the light found her.

Before leaving the house and the town forever, he gave instructions to a friend and neighbor to sell his furniture for anything that it would fetch, and apply the proceeds to employing the police to trace her. The directions were honestly followed, and the money was all spent, but the inquiries led to nothing. The picklock on the bedroom floor remained the one last useless trace of the Dream-Woman.

At this point of the narrative the landlord paused, and, turning toward the window of the room in which we were sitting, looked in the direction of the stable-yard.

"So far," he said, "I tell you what was told to me. The little that remains to be added lies within my own experience. Between two and three months after the events I have just been relating, Isaac Scatchard came to me, withered and old-looking before his time, just as you saw him to-day. He had his testimonials to character with him, and he asked for employment here. Knowing that my wife and he were distantly related, I gave him a trial in consideration of that relationship, and liked him in spite of his queer habits. He is as sober, honest, and willing a man as there is in England. As for his restlessness at night, and his sleeping away his leisure time in the day, who can wonder at it after hearing his story? Besides, he never objects to being roused up when he's wanted, so there's not much inconvenience to complain of, after all."

"I suppose he is afraid of a return of that dreadful dream, and of waking out of it in the dark?" said I.

"No," returned the landlord. "The dream comes back to him so often that he has got to bear with it by this time resignedly enough. It's his wife keeps him waking at night as he has often told me."

"What! Has she never been heard of yet?"

"Never. Isaac himself has the one perpetual thought about her, that she is alive and looking for him. I believe he wouldn't let himself drop off to sleep toward two in the morning for a king's ransom. Two in the morning, he says, is the time she will find him, one of these days. Two in the morning is the time all the year round when he likes to be most certain that he has got that clasp-knife safe about him. He does not mind being alone as long as he is awake, except on the night before his birthday, when he firmly believes himself to be in peril of his life. The birthday has only come round once since he has been here, and then he sat up along with the night-porter. 'She's looking for me,' is all he says when anybody speaks to him about the one anxiety of his life; 'she's looking for me.' He may be right. She may be looking for him. Who can tell?"

"Who can tell?" said I.

THE FOURTH DAY.

THE sky once more cloudy and threatening. No news of George. I corrected Morgan's second story to-day; numbered it Seven, and added it to our stock.

Undeterred by the weather, Miss Jessie set off this morning on the longest ride she had yet undertaken. She had heard—through one of my brother's laborers, I believe—of the actual existence, in this nineteenth century, of no less a personage than a Welsh Bard, who was to be found at a distant farmhouse far beyond the limits of Owen's property. The prospect of discovering this remarkable relic of past times hurried her off, under the guidance of her ragged groom, in a high state of excitement, to see and hear the venerable man. She was away the whole day, and for the first time since her visit she kept us waiting more than half an hour for dinner. The moment we all sat down to table, she informed us, to Morgan's great delight, that the bard was a rank impostor.

"Why, what did you expect to see?" I asked.

"A Welsh patriarch, to be sure, with a long white beard, flowing robes, and a harp to match," answered Miss Jessie.

"And what did you find?"

"A highly-respectable middle-aged rustic; a smiling, smoothly-shaven, obliging man, dressed in a blue swallow-tailed coat, with brass buttons, and exhibiting his bardic legs in a pair of extremely stout. and comfortable corduroy trousers."

"But he sang old Welsh songs, surely?"

"Sang! I'll tell you what he did. He sat down on a Windsor chair, without a harp; he put his hands in his pockets, cleared his throat, looked up at the ceiling, and suddenly burst into a series of the shrillest falsetto screeches I ever heard in my life. My own private opinion is that he was suffering from hydrophobia. I have lost all belief, henceforth and forever, in bards—all belief in everything, in short, except your very delightful stories and this remarkably good dinner."

Ending with that smart double fire of compliments to her hosts, the Queen of Hearts honored us all three with a smile of approval, and transferred her attention to her knife and fork.

The number drawn to-night was One. On examination of the Purple Volume, it proved to be my turn to read again.

"Our story to-night," I said, "contains the narrative of a very remarkable adventure which really befell me when I was a young man. At the time of my life when these events happened I was dabbling in literature when I ought to have been studying law, and traveling on the Continent when I ought to have been keeping my terms at Lincoln's Inn. At the outset of the story, you will find that I refer to the county in which I lived in my youth, and to a neighboring family possessing a large estate in it. That county is situated in a part of England far away from The Glen Tower, and that family is therefore not to be associated with any present or former neighbors of ours in this part of the world."

After saying these necessary words of explanation, I opened the first page, and began the story of my Own Adventure. I observed that my audience started a little as I read the title, which I must add, in my own defense, had been almost forced on my choice by the peculiar character of the narrative. It was "MAD MONKTON."

BROTHER GRIFFITH'S STORY

of

MAD MONKTON

CHAPTER I.

THE Monktons of Wincot Abbey bore a sad character for want of sociability in our county. They never went to other people's houses, and, excepting my father, and a lady and her daughter living near them, never received anybody under their own roof.

Proud as they all certainly were, it was not pride, but dread, which kept them thus apart from their neighbors. The family had suffered for generations past from the horrible affliction of hereditary insanity, and the members of it shrank from exposing their calamity to others, as they must have exposed it if they had mingled with the busy little world around them. There is a frightful story of a crime committed in past times by two of the Monktons, near relatives, from which the first appearance of the insanity was always supposed to date, but it is needless for me to shock any one by repeating it. It is enough to say that at intervals almost every form of madness appeared in the family, monomania being the most frequent manifestation of the affliction among them. I have these particulars, and one or two yet to be related, from my father.

At the period of my youth but three of the Monktons were left at the Abbey—Mr. and Mrs. Monkton and their only child Alfred, heir to the prope rty. The one other member of this, the elder branch of the family, who was then alive, was Mr. Monkton's younger brother, Stephen. He was an unmarried man, possessing a fine estate in Scotland; but he lived almost entirely on the Continent, and bore the reputation of being a shameless profligate. The family at Wincot held almost as little communication with him as with their neighbors.

I have already mentioned my father, and a lady and her daughter, as the only privileged people who were admitted into Wincot Abbey.

My father had been an old school and college friend of Mr. Monkton, and accident had brought them so much together in later life that their continued intimacy at Wincot was quite intelligible. I am not so well able to account for the friendly terms on which Mrs. Elmslie (the lady to whom I have alluded) lived with the Monktons. Her late husband had been distantly related to Mrs. Monkton, and my father was her daughter's guardian. But even these claims to friendship and regard never seemed to me strong enough to explain the intimacy between Mrs. Elmslie and the inhabitants of the Abbey. Intimate, however, they certainly were, and one result of the constant interchange of visits between the two families in due time declared itself: Mr. Monkton's son and Mrs. Elmslie's daughter became attached to each other.

I had no opportunities of seeing much of the young lady; I only remember her at that time as a delicate, gentle, lovable girl, the very opposite in appearance, and apparently in character also, to Alfred Monkton. But perhaps that was one reason why they fell in love with each other. The attachment was soon discovered, and was far from being disapproved by the parents on either side. In all essential points except that of wealth, the Elmslies were nearly the equals of the Monktons, and want of money in a bride was of no consequence to the heir of Wincot. Alfred, it was well known, would succeed to thirty thousand a year on his father's death.

Thus, though the parents on both sides thought the young people not old enough to be married at once, they saw no reason why Ada and Alfred should not be engaged to each other, with the understanding that they should be united when young Monkton came of age, in two years' time. The person to be consulted in the matter, after the parents, was my father, in his capacity of Ada's guardian. He knew that the family misery had shown itself many years ago in Mrs. Monkton, who was her husband's cousin. The *illness*, as it was significantly called, had been palliated by careful treatment, and was reported to have passed away. But my father was not to be deceived. He knew where the hereditary taint still lurked; he viewed with horror the bare possibility of its reappearing one day in the children of his friend's only daughter; and he positively refused his consent to the marriage engagement.

The result was that the doors of the Abbey and the doors of Mrs. Elmslie's house were closed to him. This suspension of friendly intercourse had lasted but a very short time when Mrs. Monkton died. Her husband, who was fondly attached to her, caught a violent cold while attending her funeral. The cold was neglected, and settled on his lungs. In a few months' time he followed his wife to the grave, and Alfred was left master of the grand old Abbey and the fair lands that spread all around it.

At this period Mrs. Elmslie had the indelicacy to endeavor a second time to procure my father's consent to the marriage engagement. He refused it again more positively than before. More than a year passed away. The time was approaching fast when Alfred would be of age. I returned from college to spend the long vacation at home, and made some advances toward bettering my acquaintance with young Monkton. They were evaded—certainly with perfect politeness, but still in such a way as to prevent me from offering my friendship to him again. Any mortification I might have felt at this petty repulse under ordinary circumstances was dismissed from my mind by the occurrence of a real misfortune in our household. For some months past my father's health had been failing, and, just at the time of which I am now writing, his sons had to mourn the irreparable calamity of his death.

This event, through some informality or error in the late Mr. Elmslie's will, left the future of Ada's life entirely at her mother's disposal. The consequence was the immediate ratification of the marriage engagement to which my father had so steadily refused his consent. As soon as the fact was publicly announced, some of Mrs. Elmslie's more intimate friends, who were acquainted with the reports affecting the Monkton family, ventured to mingle with their formal congratulations one or two significant references to the late Mrs. Monkton and some searching inquiries as to the disposition of her son.

Mrs. Elmslie always met these polite hints with one bold form of answer. She first admitted the existence of these reports about the Monktons which her friends were unwilling to specify distinctly, and then declared that they were infamous calumnies. The hereditary taint had died out of the family generations back. Alfred was the best, the kindest, the sanest of human beings. He loved study and retirement; Ada sympathized with his tastes, and had made her choice unbiased; if any more hints were dropped about sacrificing her by her marriage, those hints would be viewed as so many insults to her mother, whose affection for her it was monstrous to call in question. This way of talking silenced people, but did not convince them. They began to suspect, what was indeed the actual truth, that Mrs. Elmslie was a selfish, worldly, grasping woman, who wanted to get her daughter well married, and cared nothing for consequences as long as she saw Ada mistress of the greatest establishment in the whole county.

It seemed, however, as if there was some fatality at work to prevent the attainment of Mrs. Elmslie's great object in life. Hardly was one obstacle to the ill-omened marriage removed by my father's death before another succeeded it in the shape of anxieties and difficulties caused by the delicate state of Ada's health. Doctors were consulted in all directions, and the result of their advice was that the marriage must be deferred, and that Miss Elmslie must leave England for a certain time, to reside in a warmer climate—the south of France, if I remember rightly. Thus it happened that just before Alfred came of age Ada and her mother departed for the Continent, and the union of the two young people was understood to be indefinitely postponed. Some curiosity was felt in the neighborhood as to what Alfred Monkton would do under these circumstances. Would he follow his lady-love? would he go yachting? would he throw open the doors of the old Abbey at last, and endeavor to forget the absence of Ada and the postponement of his marriage in a round of gayeties? He did none of these things. He simply remained at Wincot, living as suspiciously strange and solitary a life as his father had lived before him. Literally, there was now no companion for him at the Abbey but the old priest—the Monktons, I should have mentioned before, were Roman Catholics—who had held the office of tutor to Alfred from his earliest years. He came of age, and there was not even so much as a private dinner-party at Wincot to celebrate the event. Families in the neighborhood determined to forget the offense which his father's reserve had given them, and invited him to their houses. The invitations were politely declined. Civil visitors called resolutely at the Abbey, and were as resolutely bowed away from the doors as soon as they had left their cards. Under this combination of sinister and aggravating circumstances people in all directions took to shaking their heads mysteriously when the name of Mr. Alfred Monkton was mentioned, hinting at the family calamity, and wondering peevishly or sadly, as their tempers inclined them, what he could possibly do to occupy himself month after month in the lonely old house.

The right answer to this question was not easy to find. It was quite useless, for ex ample, to apply to the priest for it. He was a very quiet, polite old gentleman; his replies were always excessively ready and civil, and appeared at the time to convey an immense quantity of information; but when they came to be reflected on, it was universally observed that nothing tangible could ever be got out of them. The housekeeper, a weird old woman, with a very abrupt and repelling manner, was too fierce and taciturn to be safely approached. The few indoor servants had all been long enough in the family to have learned to hold their tongues in public as a regular habit. It was only from the farm-servants who supplied the table at the Abbey that any information could be obtained, and vague enough it was when they came to communicate it.

Some of them had observed the "young master" walking about the library with heaps of dusty papers in his hands. Others had heard odd noises in the uninhabited parts of the Abbey, had looked up, and had seen him forcing open the old windows, as if to let light and air into the rooms supposed to have been shut close for years and years, or had discovered him standing on the perilous summit of one of the crumbling turrets, never ascended before within their memories, and popularly considered to be inhabited by the ghosts of the monks who had once possessed the building. The result of these observations and discoveries, when they were communicated to others, was of course to impress every one with a firm belief that "poor young Monkton was going the way that the rest of the family had gone before him," which opinion always appeared to be immensely strengthened in the popular mind by a conviction—founded on no particle of evidence—that the priest was at the bottom of all the mischief.

Thus far I have spoken from hearsay evidence mostly. What I have next to tell will be the result of my own personal experience.

CHAPTER II.

ABOUT five months after Alfred Monkton came of age I left college, and resolved to amuse and instruct myself a little by traveling abroad.

At the time when I quitted England young Monkton was still leading his secluded life at the Abbey, and was, in the opinion of everybody, sinking rapidly, if he had not already succumbed, under the hereditary curse of his family. As to the Elmslies, report said that Ada had benefited by her sojourn abroad, and that mother and daughter were on their way back to England to resume their old relations with the heir of Wincot. Before they returned I was away on my travels, and wandered half over Europe, hardly ever planning whither I should shape my course beforehand. Chance, which thus led me everywhere, led me at last to Naples. There I met with an old school friend, who was one of the *attaches* at the English embassy, and there began the extraordinary events in connection with Alfred Monkton which form the main interest of the story I am now relating.

I was idling away the time one morning with my friend the *attache* in the garden of the Villa Reale, when we were passed by a young man, walking alone, who exchanged bows with my friend.

I thought I recognized the dark, eager eyes, the colorless cheeks, the strangely-vigilant, anxious expression which I remembered in past times as characteristic of Alfred Monkton's face, and was about to question my friend on the subject, when he gave me unasked the information of which I was in search.

"That is Alfred Monkton," said he; "he comes from your part of England. You ought to know him."

"I do know a little of him," I answered; "he was engaged to Miss Elmslie when I was last in the neighborhood of Wincot. Is he married to her yet?"

"No, and he never ought to be. He has gone the way of the rest of the family—or, in plainer words, he has gone mad."

"Mad! But I ought not to be surprised at hearing that, after the reports about him in England."

"I speak from no reports; I speak from what he has said and done before me, and before hundreds of other people. Surely you must have heard of it?"

"Never. I have been out of the way of news from Naples or England for months past."

"Then I have a very extraordinary story to tell you. You know, of course, that Alfred had an uncle, Stephen Monkton. Well, some time ago this uncle fought a duel in the Roman States with a Frenchman, who shot him dead. The seconds and the Frenchman (who was unhurt) took to flight in different directions, as it is supposed. We heard nothing here of the details of the duel till a month after it happened, when one of the French journals published an account of it, taken from the papers left by Monkton's second, who died at Paris of consumption. These papers stated the manner in which the duel was fought, and how it terminated, but nothing more. The surviving second and the Frenchman have never been traced from that time to this. All that anybody knows, therefore, of the duel is that Stephen Monkton was shot; an event which nobody can regret, for a greater scoundrel never existed. The exact place where he died, and what was done with the body are still mysteries not to be penetrated."

"But what has all this to do with Alfred?"

"Wait a moment, and you will hear. Soon after the news of his uncle's death reached England, what do you think Alfred did? He actually put off his marriage with Miss Elmslie, which was then about to be celebrated, to come out here in search of the burial-place of his wretched scamp of an uncle; and no power on earth will now induce him to return to England and to Miss Elmslie until he has found the body, and can take it back with him, to be buried with all the other dead Monktons in the vault under Wincot Abbey Chapel. He has squandered his money, pestered the police, and exposed himself to the ridicule of the men and the indignation of the women for the last three months in trying to achieve his insane purpose, and is now as far from it as ever. He will not assign to anybody the smallest motive for his conduct. You can't laugh him out of it or reason him out of it. When we met him just now, I happen to know that he was on his way to the office of the police minister, to send out fresh agents to search and inquire through the Roman States for the place where his uncle was shot. And, mind, all this time he professes to be passionately in love with Miss Elmslie, and to be miserable at his separation from her. Just think of that! And then think of his self-imposed absence from her here, to hunt after the remains of a wretch who was a disgrace to the family, and whom he never saw but once or twice in his life. Of all the 'Mad Monktons,' as they used to call them in England, Alfred is the maddest. He is actually our principal excitement in this dull opera season; though, for my own part, when I think of the poor girl in England, I am a great deal more ready to despise him than to laugh at him."

"You know the Elmslies then?"

"Intimately. The other day my mother wrote to me from England, after having seen Ada. This escapade of Monkton's has outraged all her friends. They have been entreating her to break off the match, which it seems she could do if she liked. Even her mother, sordid and selfish as she is, has been obliged at last, in common decency, to side with the rest of the family; but the good, faithful girl won't give Monkton up. She humors his insanity; declares he gave her a good reason in secret for going away; says she could always make him happy when they were together in the old Abbey, and can make him still happier when they are married; in short, she loves him dearly, and will therefore believe in him to the last. Nothing shakes her. She has made up her mind to throw away her life on him, and she will do it."

"I hope not. Mad as his conduct looks to us, he may have some sensible reason for it that we cannot imagine. Does his mind seem at all disordered when he talks on ordinary topics?"

"Not in the least. When you can get him to say anything, which is not often, he talks like a sensible, well-educated man. Keep silence about his precious errand here, and you would fancy him the gentlest and most temperate of human beings; but touch the subject of his vagabond of an uncle, and the Monkton madness comes out directly. The other night a lady asked him, jestingly of course, whether he had ever seen his uncle's ghost. He scowled at her like a perfect fiend, and said that he and his uncle would answer her question together some day, if they came from hell to do it. We laughed at his words, but the lady fainted at his looks, and we had a scene of hysterics and hartshorn in consequence. Any other man would have been kicked out of the room for nearly frightening a pretty woman to death in that way; but 'Mad Monkton,' as we have christened him, is a privileged lunatic in Neapolitan society, because he is English, good-looking, and worth thirty thousand a year. He goes out everywhere under the impression that he may meet with somebody who has been let into the secret of the place where the mysterious duel was fought. If you are introduced to him he is sure to ask you whether you know anything about it; but beware of following up the subject after you have answered him, unless you want to make sure that he is out of his senses. In that case, only talk of his uncle, and the result will rather more than satisfy you."

A day or two after this conversation with my friend the *attache,* I met Monkton at an evening party.

The moment he heard my name mentioned, his face flushed up; he drew me away into a corner, and referring to his cool reception of my advance years ago toward making his acquaintance, asked my pardon for what he termed his inexcusable ingratitude with an earnestness and an agitation which utterly astonished me. His next proceeding was to question me, as my friend had said he would, about the place of the mysterious duel.

An extraordinary change came over him while he interrogated me on this point. Instead of looking into my face as they had looked hitherto, his eyes wandered away, and fixed themselves intensely, almost fiercely, either on the perfectly empty wall at our side, or on the vacant space between the wall and ourselves, it was impossible to say which. I had come to Naples from Spain by sea, and briefly told him so, as the best way of satisfying him that I could not assist his inquiries. He pursued them no further; and, mindful of my friend's warning, I took care to lead the conversation to general topics. He looked back at me directly, and, as long as we stood in our corner, his eyes never wandered away again to the empty wall or the vacant space at our side.

Though more ready to listen than to speak, his conversation, when he did talk, had no trace of anything the least like insanity about it. He had evidently read, not generally only, but deeply as well, and could apply his reading with singular felicity to the illustration of almost any subject under discussion, neither obtruding his knowledge absurdly, nor concealing it affectedly. His manner was in itself a standing protest against such a nickname as "Mad Monkton." He was so shy, so quiet, so composed and gentle in all his actions, that at times I should have been almost inclined to call him effeminate. We had a long talk together on the first evening of our meeting; we often saw each other afterward, and never lost a single opportunity of bettering our acquaintance. I felt that he had taken a liking to me, and, in spite of what I had heard about his behavior to Miss Elmslie, in spite of the suspicions which the history of his family and his own conduct had arrayed against him, I began to like "Mad Monkton" as much as he liked me. We took many a quiet ride together in the country, and sailed often along the shores of the Bay on either side. But for two eccentricities in his conduct, which I could not at all understand, I should soon have felt as much at my ease in his society as if he had been my own brother.

The first of these eccentricities consisted in the reappearance on several occasions of the odd expression in his eyes which I had first seen when he asked me whether I knew anything about the duel. No matter what we were talking about, or where we happened to be, there were times when he would suddenly look away from my face, now on one side of me, now on the other, but always where there was nothing to see, and always with the same intensity and fierceness in his eyes. This looked so like madness—or hypochondria at the least—that I felt afraid to ask him about it, and always pretended not to observe him.

The second peculiarity in his conduct was that he never referred, while in my company, to the reports about his errand at Naples, and never once spoke of Miss Elmslie, or of his life at Wincot Abbey. This not only astonished me, but amazed those who had noticed our intimacy, and who had made sure that I must be the depositary of all his secrets. But the time was near at hand when this mystery, and some other mysteries of which I had no suspicion at that period, were all to be revealed.

I met him one night at a large ball, given by a Russian nobleman, whose name I could not pronounce then, and cannot remember now. I had wandered away from reception-room, ballroom, and cardroom, to a small apartment at one extremity of the palace, which was half conservatory, half boudoir, and which had been prettily illuminated for the occasion with Chinese lanterns. Nobody was in the room when I got there. The view over the Mediterranean, bathed in the bright softness of Italian moonlight, was so lovely that I remained for a long time at the window, looking out, and listening to the dance-music which faintly reached me from the ballroom. My thoughts were far away with the relations I had left in England, when I was startled out of them by hearing my name softly pronounced.

I looked round directly, and saw Monkton standing in the room. A livid paleness overspread his face, and his eyes were turned away from me with the same extraordinary expression in them to which I have already alluded.

"Do you mind leaving the ball early to-night?" he asked, still not looking at me.

"Not at all," said I. "Can I do anything for you? Are you ill?"

"No—at least nothing to speak of. Will you come to my rooms?"

"At once, if you like."

"No, not at once. *I* must go home directly; but don't you come to me for half an hour yet. You have not been at my rooms before, I know, but you will easily find them out; they are close by. There is a card with my address. I *must* speak to you to-night; my life depends on it. Pray come! for God's sake, come when the half hour is up!"

I promised to be punctual, and he left me directly.

Most people will be easily able to imagine the state of nervous impatience and vague expectation in which I passed the allotted period of delay, after hearing such words as those Monkton had spoken to me. Before the half hour had quite expired I began to make my way out through the ballroom.

At the head of the staircase my friend, the *attache*, met me.

"What! going away already?" Said he.

"Yes; and on a very curious expedition. I am going to Monkton's rooms, by his own invitation."

"You don't mean it! Upon my honor, you're a bold fellow to trust yourself alone with 'Mad Monkton' when the moon is at the full."

"He is ill, poor fellow. Besides, I don't think him half as mad as you do."

"We won't dispute about that; but mark my words, he has not asked you to go where no visitor has ever been admitted before without a special purpose. I predict that you will see or hear something to-night which you will remember for the rest of your life."

We parted. When I knocked at the courtyard gate of the house where Monkton lived, my friend's last words on the palace staircase recurred to me, and, though I had laughed at him when he spoke them, I began to suspect even then that his prediction would be fulfilled.

CHAPTER III.

THE porter who let me into the house where Monkton lived directed me to the floor on which his rooms were situated. On getting upstairs, I found his door on the landing ajar. He heard my footsteps, I suppose, for he called to me to come in before I could knock.

I entered, and found him sitting by the table, with some loose letters in his hand, which he was just tying together into a packet. I noticed, as he asked me to sit down, that his express ion looked more composed, though the paleness had not yet left his face. He thanked me for coming; repeated that he had something very important to say to me; and then stopped short, apparently too much embarrassed to proceed. I tried to set him at his ease by assuring him that, if my assistance or advice could be of any use, I was ready to place myself and my time heartily and unreservedly at his service.

As I said this I saw his eyes beginning to wander away from my face—to wander slowly, inch by inch, as it were, until they stopped at a certain point, with the same fixed stare into vacancy which had so often startled me on former occasions. The whole expression of his face altered as I had never yet seen it alter; he sat before me looking like a man in a death-trance.

"You are very kind," he said, slowly and faintly, speaking, not to me, but in the direction in which his eyes were still fixed. "I know you can help me; but—"

He stopped; his face whitened horribly, and the perspiration broke out all over it. He tried to continue—said a word or two—then stopped again. Seriously alarmed about him, I rose from my chair with the intention of getting him some water from a jug which I saw standing on a side-table.

He sprang up at the same moment. All the suspicions I had ever heard whispered against his sanity flashed over my mind in an instant, and I involuntarily stepped back a pace or two.

"Stop," he said, seating himself again; "don't mind me; and don't leave your chair. I want—I wish, if you please, to make a little alteration, before we say anything more. Do you mind sitting in a strong light?"

"Not in the least."

I had hitherto been seated in the shade of his reading-lamp, the only light in the room.

As I answered him he rose again, and, going into another apartment, returned with a large lamp in his hand; then took two candles from the side-table, and two others from the chimney piece; placed them all, to my amazement, together, so as to stand exactly between us, and then tried to light them. His hand trembled so that he was obliged to give up the attempt, and allow me to come to his assistance. By his direction, I took the shade off the reading-lamp after I had lit the other lamp and the four candles. When we sat down again, with this concentration of light between us, his better and gentler manner began to return, and while he now addressed me he spoke without the slightest hesitation.

"It is useless to ask whether you have heard the reports about me," he said; "I know that you have. My purpose to-night is to give you some reasonable explanation of the conduct which has produced those reports. My secret has been hitherto confided to one person only; I am now about to trust it to your keeping, with a special object which will appear as I go on. First, however, I must begin by telling you exactly what the great difficulty is which obliges me to be still absent from England. I want your advice and your help; and, to conceal nothing from you, I want also to test your forbearance and your friendly sympathy, before I can venture on thrusting my miserable secret into your keeping. Will you pardon this apparent distrust of your frank and open character—this apparent ingratitude for your kindness toward me ever since we first met?"

I begged him not to speak of these things, but to go on.

"You know," he proceeded, "that I am here to recover the body of my Uncle Stephen, and to carry it back with me to our family burial-place in England, and you must also be aware that I have not yet succeeded in discovering his remains. Try to pass over, for the present, whatever may seem extraordinary and incomprehensible in such a purpose as mine is, and read this newspaper article where the ink-line is traced. It is the only evidence hitherto obtained on the subject of the fatal duel in which my uncle fell, and I want to hear what course of proceeding the perusal of it may suggest to you as likely to be best on my part."

He handed me an old French newspaper. The substance of what I read there is still so firmly impressed on my memory that I am certain of being able to repeat correctly at this distance of time all the facts which it is necessary for me to communicate to the reader.

The article began, I remember, with editorial remarks on the great curiosity then felt in regard to the fatal duel between the Count St. Lo and Mr. Stephen Monkton, an English gentleman. The writer proceeded to dwell at great length on the extraordinary secrecy in which the whole affair had been involved from first to last, and to express a hope that the publication of a certain manuscript, to which his introductory observations referred, might lead to the production of fresh evidence from other and better-informed quarters. The manuscript had been found among the papers of Monsieur Foulon, Mr. Monkton's second, who had died at Paris of a rapid decline shortly after returning to his home in that city from the scene of the duel. The document was unfinished, having been left incomplete at the very place where the reader would most wish to find it continued. No reason could be discovered for this, and no second manuscript bearing on the all-important subject had been found, after the strictest search among the papers left by the deceased.

The document itself then followed.

It purported to be an agreement privately drawn up between Mr. Monkton's second, Monsieur Foulon, and the Count St. Lo's second, Monsieur Dalville, and contained a statement of all the arrangements for conducting the duel. The paper was dated "Naples, February 22d," and was divided into some seven or eight clauses. The first clause described the origin and nature of the quarrel—a very disgraceful affair on both sides, worth neither remembering nor repeating. The second clause stated that, the challenged man having chosen the pistol as his weapon, and the challenger (an excellent swordsman), having, on his side, thereupon insisted that the duel should be fought in such a manner as to make the first fire decisive in its results, the seconds, seeing that fatal consequences must inevitably follow the hostile meeting, determined, first of all, that the duel should be kept a profound secret from everybody, and that the place where it was to be fought should not be made known beforehand, even to the principals themselves. It was added that this excess of precaution had been rendered absolutely necessary in consequence of a recent address from the Pope to the ruling powers in Italy commenting on the scandalous frequency of the practice of dueling, and urgently desiring that the laws against duelists should be enforced for the future with the utmost rigor.

The third clause detailed the manner in which it had been arranged that the duel should be fought.

The pistols having been loaded by the seconds on the ground, the combatants were to be placed thirty paces apart, and were to toss up for the first fire. The man who won was to advance ten paces marked out for him beforehand—and was then to discharge his pistol. If he missed, or failed to disable his opponent, the latter was free to advance, if he chose, the whole remaining twenty paces before he fired in his turn. This arrangement insured the decisive termination of the duel at the first discharge of the pistols, and both principals and seconds pledged themselves on either side to abide by it.

The fourth clause stated that the seconds had agreed that the duel should be fought out of the Neapolitan States, but left themselves to be guided by circumstances as to the exact locality in which it should take place. The remaining clauses, so far as I remember them, were devoted to detailing the different precautions to be adopted for avoiding discovery. The duelists and their seconds were to leave Naples in separate parties; were to change carriages several times; were to meet at a certain town, or, failing that, at a certain post-house on the high road from Naples to Rome; were to carry drawing-books, color boxes, and camp-stools, as if they had been artists out on a sketching-tour; and were to proceed to the place of the duel on foot, employing no gui des, for fear of treachery. Such general arrangements as these, and others for facilitating the flight of the survivors after the affair was over, formed the conclusion of this extraordinary document, which was signed, in initials only, by both the seconds.

Just below the initials appeared the beginning of a narrative, dated "Paris," and evidently intended to describe the duel itself with extreme minuteness. The hand-writing was that of the deceased second.

Monsieur Foulon, tire gentleman in question, stated his belief that circumstances might transpire which would render an account by an eyewitness of the hostile meeting between St. Lo and Mr. Monkton an important document. He proposed, therefore, as one of the seconds, to testify that the duel had been fought in exact accordance with the terms of the agreement, both the principals conducting themselves like men of gallantry and honor (!). And he further announced that, in order not to compromise any one, he should place the paper containing his testimony in safe hands, with strict directions that it was on no account to be opened except in a case of the last emergency.

After thus preamble, Monsieur Foulon related that the duel had been fought two days after the drawing up of the agreement, in a locality to which accident had conducted the dueling party. (The name of the place was not mentioned, nor even the neighborhood in which it was situated.) The men having been placed according to previous arrangement, the Count St. Lo had won the toss for the first fire, had advanced his ten paces, and had shot his opponent in the body. Mr. Monkton did not immediately fall, but staggered forward some six or seven paces, discharged his pistol ineffectually at the count, and dropped to the ground a dead man. Monsieur Foulon then stated that he tore a leaf from his pocketbook, wrote on it a brief description of the manner in which Mr. Monkton had died, and pinned the paper to his clothes; this proceeding having been rendered necessary by the peculiar nature of the plan organized on the spot for safely disposing of the dead body. What this plan was, or what was done with the corpse, did not appear, for at this important point the narrative abruptly broke off.

A foot-note in the newspaper merely stated the manner in which the document had been obtained for publication, and repeated the announcement contained in the editor's introductory remarks, that no continuation had been found by the persons intrusted with the care of Monsieur Foulon's papers. I have now given the whole substance of what I read, and have mentioned all that was then known of Mr. Stephen Monkton's death.

When I gave the newspaper back to Alfred he was too much agitated to speak, but he reminded me by a sign that he was anxiously waiting to hear what I had to say. My position was a very trying and a very painful one. I could hardly tell what consequences might not follow any want of caution on my part, and could think at first of no safer plan than questioning him carefully before I committed myself either one way or the other.

"Will you excuse me if I ask you a question or two before I give you my advice?" said I.

He nodded impatiently.

"Yes, yes—any questions you like."

"Were you at any time in the habit of seeing your uncle frequently?"

"I never saw him more than twice in my life—on each occasion when I was a mere child."

"Then you could have had no very strong personal regard for him?"

'Regard for him! I should have been ashamed to feel any regard for him. He disgraced us wherever he went."

"May I ask if any family motive is involved in your anxiety to recover his remains?"

"Family motives may enter into it among others—but why do you ask?"

"Because, having heard that you employ the police to assist your search, I was anxious to know whether you had stimulated their superiors to make them do their best in your service by giving some strong personal reasons at headquarters for the very unusual project which has brought you here."

"I give no reasons. I pay for the work I want done, and, in return for my liberality, I am treated with the most infamous indifference on all sides. A stranger in the country, and badly acquainted with the language, I can do nothing to help myself. The authorities, both at Rome and in this place, pretend to assist me, pretend to search and inquire as I would have them search and inquire, and do nothing more. I am insulted, laughed at, almost to my face."

"Do you not think it possible—mind, I have no wish to excuse the misconduct of the authorities, and do not share in any such opinion myself—but do you not think it likely that the police may doubt whether you are in earnest?"

"Not in earnest!" he cried, starting up and confronting me fiercely, with wild eyes and quickened breath. "Not in earnest! *You* think I'm not in earnest too. I know you think it, though you tell me you don't. Stop; before we say another word, your own eyes shall convince you. Come here—only for a minute—only for one minute!"

I followed him into his bedroom, which opened out of the sitting-room. At one side of his bed stood a large packing-case of plain wood, upward of seven feet in length.

"Open the lid and look in," he said, "while I hold the candle so that you can see."

I obeyed his directions, and discovered to my astonishment that the packing-case contained a leaden coffin, magnificently emblazoned with the arms of the Monkton family, and inscribed in old-fashioned letters with the name of "Stephen Monkton," his age and the manner of his death being added underneath.

"I keep his coffin ready for him," whispered Alfred, close at my ear. "Does that look like earnest?"

It looked more like insanity—so like that I shrank from answering him.

"Yes! yes! I see you are convinced," he continued quickly; "we may go back into the next room, and may talk without restraint on either side now."

On returning to our places, I mechanically moved my chair away from the table. My mind was by this time in such a state of confusion and uncertainty about what it would be best for me to say or do next, that I forgot for the moment the position he had assigned to me when we lit the candles. He reminded me of this directly.

"Don't move away," he said, very earnestly; "keep on sitting in the light; pray do! I'll soon tell you why I am so particular about that. But first give me your advice; help me in my great distress and suspense. Remember, you promised me you would."

I made an effort to collect my thoughts, and succeeded. It was useless to treat the affair otherwise than seriously in his presence; it would have been cruel not to have advised him as I best could.

"You know," I said, "that two days after the drawing up of the agreement at Naples, the duel was fought out of the Neapolitan States. This fact has of course led you to the conclusion that all inquiries about localities had better be confined to the Roman territory?"

"Certainly; the search, such as it is, has been made there, and there only. If I can believe the police, they and their agents have inquired for the place where the duel was fought (offering a large reward in my name to the person who can discover it) all along the high road from Naples to Rome. They have also circulated—at least so they tell me—descriptions of the duelists and their seconds; have left an agent to superintend investigations at the post-house, and another at the town mentioned as meeting-points in the agreement; and have endeavored, by correspondence with foreign authorities, to trace the Count St. Lo and Monsieur Dalville to their place or places of refuge. All these efforts, supposing them to have been really made, have hitherto proved utterly fruitless."

"My impression is," said I, after a moment's consideration, "that all inquiries made along the high road, or anywhere near Rome, are likely to be made in vain. As to the discovery of your uncle's remains, that is, I think, identical with the discovery of the place where he was shot; for those engaged in the duel would certainly not risk detection by carrying a corpse any distance with them in their flight. The place, then, is all that we want to find out. Now let us consider for a moment. The dueling-party changed carriages; traveled separately, two and two; doubtless took roundabout roads; stopped at the post-house and the town as a blind; walked, perhaps, a considerable distance unguided. Depend upon it, such precautions as these (which we know they must have employed) left them very little time out of the two days—though they might start at sunrise and not stop at night-fall—for straightforward traveling. My belief therefore is, that the duel was fought somewhere near the Neapolitan frontier; and, if I had been the police agent who conducted the search, I should only have pursued it parallel with the frontier, starting from west to east till I got up among the lonely places in the mountains. That is my idea; do you think it worth anything?"

His face flushed all over in an instant. "I think it an inspiration!" he cried. "Not a day is to be lost in carrying out our plan. The police are not to be trusted with it. I must start myself to-morrow morning; and you—"

He stopped; his face grew suddenly pale; he sighed heavily; his eyes wandered once more into the fixed look at vacancy; and the rigid, deathly expression fastened again upon all his features.

"I must tell you my secret before I talk of to-morrow," he proceeded, faintly. "If I hesitated any longer at confessing everything, I should be unworthy of your past kindness, unworthy of the help which it is my last hope that you will gladly give me when you have heard all."

I begged him to wait until he was more composed, until he was better able to speak; but he did not appear to notice what I said. Slowly, and struggling as it seemed against himself, he turned a little away from me, and, bending his head over the table, supported it on his hand. The packet of letters with which I had seen him occupied when I came in lay just beneath his eyes. He looked down on it steadfastly when he next spoke to me.

CHAPTER IV.

"You were born, I believe, in our county," he said; "perhaps, therefore, you may have heard at some time of a curious old prophecy about our family, which is still preserved among the traditions of Wincot Abbey?"

"I have heard of such a prophecy," I answered, "but I never knew in what terms it was expressed. It professed to predict the extinction of your family, or something of that sort, did it not?"

"No inquiries," he went on, "have traced back that prophecy to the time when it was first made; none of our family records tell us anything of its origin. Old servants and old tenants of ours remember to have heard it from their fathers and grandfathers. The monks, whom we succeeded in the Abbey in Henry the Eighth's time, got knowledge of it in some way, for I myself discovered the rhymes, in which we know the prophecy to have been preserved from a very remote period, written on a blank leaf of one of the Abbey manuscripts. These are the verses, if verses they deserve to be called:

When in Wincot vault a place Waits for one of Monkton's race— When that one forlorn shall lie Graveless under open sky, Beggared of six feet of earth, Though lord of acres from his birth— That shall be a certain sign Of the end of Monkton's line. Dwindling ever faster, faster, Dwindling to the last-left master; From mortal ken, from light of day, Monkton's race shall pass away."

"The prediction seems almost vague enough to have been uttered by an ancient oracle," said I, observing that he waited, after repeating the verses, as if expecting me to say something.

"Vague or not, it is being accomplished," he returned. "I am now the 'last-left master'—the last of that elder line of our family at which the prediction points; and the corpse of Stephen Monkton is not in the vaults of Wincot Abbey. Wait before you exclaim against me. I have more to say about this. Long before the Abbey was ours, when we lived in the ancient manor-house near it (the very ruins of which have long since disappeared), the family burying-place was in the vault under the Abbey chapel. Whether in those remote times the prediction against us was known and dreaded or not, this much is certain: every one of the Monktons (whether living at the Abbey or on the smaller estate in Scotland) was buried in Wincot vault, no matter at what risk or what sacrifice. In the fierce fighting days of the olden time, the bodies of my ancestors who fell in foreign places were recovered and brought back to Wincot, though it often cost not heavy ransom only, but desperate bloodshed as well, to obtain them. This superstition, if you please to call it so, has never died out of the family from that time to the present day; for centuries the succession of the dead in the vault at the Abbey has been unbroken—absolutely unbroken—until now. The place mentioned in the prediction as waiting to be filled is Stephen Monkton's place; the voice that cries vainly to the earth for shelter is the spirit-voice of the dead. As surely as if I saw it, I know that they have left him unburied on the ground where he fell!"

He stopped me before I could utter a word in remonstrance by slowly rising to his feet, and pointing in the same direction toward which his eyes had wandered a short time since.

"I can guess what you want to ask me," he exclaimed, sternly and loudly; "you want to ask me how I can be mad enough to believe in a doggerel prophecy uttered in an age of superstition to awe the most ignorant hearers. I answer" (at those words his voice sank suddenly to a whisper), "I answer, because *Stephen Monkton himself stands there at this moment confirming me in my belief.*"

Whether it was the awe and horror that looked out ghastly from his face as he confronted me, whether it was that I had never hitherto fairly believed in the reports about his madness, and that the conviction of their truth now forced itself upon me on a sudden, I know not, but I felt my blood curdling as he spoke, and I knew in my own heart, as I sat there speechless, that I dare not turn round and look where he was still pointing close at my side.

"I see there," he went on, in the same whispering voice, "the figure of a dark-complexioned man standing up with his head uncovered. One of his hands, still clutching a pistol, has fallen to his side; the other presses a bloody handkerchief over his mouth. The spasm of mortal agony convulses his features; but I know them for the features of a swarthy man who twice frightened me by taking me up in his arms when I was a child at Wincot Abbey. I asked the nurses at the time who that man was, and they told me it was my uncle, Stephen Monkton. Plainly, as if he stood there living, I see him now at your side, with the death-glare in his great black eyes; and so have I ever seen him, since the moment when he was shot; at home and abroad, waking or sleeping, day and night, we are always together, wherever I go!"

His whispering tones sank into almost inaudible murmuring as he pronounced these last words. From the direction and expression of his eyes, I suspected that he was speaking to the apparition. If I had beheld it myself at that moment, it would have been, I think, a less horrible sight to witness than to see him, as I saw him now, muttering inarticulately at vacancy. My own nerves were more shaken than I could have thought possible by what had passed. A vague dread of being near him in his present mood came over me, and I moved back a step or two.

He noticed the action instantly.

"Don't go! pray—pray don't go! Have I alarmed you? Don't you believe me? Do the lights make your eyes ache? I only asked you to sit in the glare of the candles because I could not bear to see the light that always shines from the phantom there at dusk shining over you as you sat in the shadow. Don't go—don't leave me yet!"

There was an utter forlornness, an unspeakable misery in his face as he spoke these words, which gave me back my self-possession by the simple process of first moving me to pity. I resumed my chair, and said that I would stay with him as long as he wished.

"Thank you a thousand times. You are patience and kindness itself," he said, going back to his former place and resuming his former gentleness of manner.

"Now that I have got over my first confession of the misery that follows me in secret wherever I go, I think I can tell you calmly all that remains to be told. You see, as I said, my Uncle Stephen" he turned away his head quickly, and looked down at the table as the name passed his lips—"my Uncle Stephen came twice to Wincot while I was a child, and on both occasions frightened me dreadfully. He only took me up in his arms and spoke to me—very kindly, as I afterward heard, for *him*—but he terrified me, nevertheless. Perhaps I was frightened at his great stature, his swarthy complexion, and his thick black hair and mustache, as other children might have been; perhaps the mere sight of him had some strange influence on me which I could not then understand and cannot now explain. However it was, I used to dream of him long after he had gone away, and to fancy that he was stealing on me to catch me up in his arms whenever I was left in the dark. The servants who took care of me found this out, and used to threaten me with my Uncle Stephen whenever I was perverse and difficult to manage. As I grew up, I still retained my vague dread and abhorrence of our absent relative. I always listened intently, yet without knowing why, whenever his name was mentioned by my father or my mother—listened with an unaccountable presentiment that something terrible had happened to him, or was about to happen to me. This feeling only changed when I was left alone in the Abbey; and then it seemed to merge into the eager curiosity which had begun to grow on me, rather before that time, about the origin of the ancient prophecy predicting the extinction of our race. Are you following me?"

"I follow every word with the closest attention."

"You must know, then, that I had first found out some fragments of the old rhyme in which the prophecy occurs quoted as a curiosity in an antiquarian book in the library. On the page opposite this quotation had been pasted a rude old wood-cut, representing a dark-haired man, whose face was so strangely like what I remembered of my Uncle Stephen that the portrait absolutely startled me. When I asked my father about this—it was then just before his death—he either knew, or pretended to know, nothing of it; and when I afterward mentioned the prediction he fretfully changed the subject. It was just the same with our chaplain when I spoke to him. He said the portrait had been done centuries before my uncle was born, and called the prophecy doggerel and nonsense. I used to argue with him on the latter point, asking why we Catholics, who believed that the gift of working miracles had never departed from certain favored persons, might not just as well believe that the gift of prophecy had never departed, either? He would not dispute with me; he would only say that I must not waste time in thinking of such trifles; that I had more imagination than was good for me, and must suppress instead of exciting it. Such advice as this only irritated my curiosity. I determined secretly to search throughout the oldest uninhabited part of the Abbey, and to try if I could not find out from forgotten family records what the portrait was, and when the prophecy had been first written or uttered. Did you ever pass a day alone in the long-deserted chambers of an ancient house?"

"Never! such solitude as that is not at all to my taste."

"Ah! what a life it was when I began my search. I should like to live it over again. Such tempting suspense, such strange discoveries, such wild fancies, such inthralling terrors, all belonged to that life. Only think of breaking open the door of a room which no living soul had entered before you for nearly a hundred years; think of the first step forward into a region of airless, awful stillness, where the light falls faint and sickly through closed windows and rotting curtains; think of the ghostly creaking of the old floor that cries out on you for treading on it, step as softly as you will; think of arms, helmets, weird tapestries of by-gone days, that seem to be moving out on you from the walls as you first walk up to them in the dim light; think of prying into great cabinets and iron-clasped chests, not knowing what horrors may appear when you tear them open; of poring over their contents till twilight stole on you and darkness grew terrible in the lonely place; of trying to leave it, and not being able to go, as if something held you; of wind wailing at you outside; of shadows darkening round you, and closing you up in obscurity within—only think of these things, and you may imagine the fascination of suspense and terror in such a life as mine was in those past days."

(I shrank from imagining that life: it was bad enough to see its results, as I saw them before me now.)

"Well, my search lasted months and months; then it was suspended a little; then resumed. In whatever direction I pursued it I always found something to lure me on. Terrible confessions of past crimes, shocking proofs of secret wickedness that had been hidden securely from all eyes but mine, came to light. Sometimes these discoveries were associated with particular parts of the Abbey, which have had a horrible interest of their own for me ever since; sometimes with certain old portraits in the picture-gallery, which I actually dreaded to look at after what I had found out. There were periods when the results of this search of mine so horrified me that I determined to give it up entirely; but I never could persevere in my resolution; the temptation to go on seemed at certain intervals to get too strong for me, and then I yielded to it again and again. At last I found the book that had belonged to the monks with the whole of the prophecy written in the blank leaf. This first success encouraged me to get back further yet in the family records. I had discovered nothing hitherto of the identity of the mysterious portrait; but the same intuitive conviction which had assured me of its extraordinary resemblance to my Uncle Stephen seemed also to assure me that he must be more closely connected with the prophecy, and must know more of it than any one else. I had no means of holding any communication with him, no means of satisfying myself whether this strange idea of mine were right or wrong, until the day when my doubts were settled forever by the same terrible proof which is now present to me in this very room."

He paused for a moment, and looked at me intently and suspiciously; then asked if I believed all he had said to me so far. My instant reply in the affirmative seemed to satisfy his doubts, and he went on.

"On a fine evening in February I was standing alone in one of the deserted rooms of the western turret at the Abbey, looking at the sunset. Just before the sun went down I felt a sensation stealing over me which it is impossible to explain. I saw nothing, heard nothing, knew nothing. This utter self-oblivion came suddenly; it was not fainting, for I did not fall to the ground, did not move an inch from my place. If such a thing could be, I should say it was the temporary separation of soul and body without death; but all description of my situation at that time is impossible. Call my state what you will, trance or catalepsy, I know that I remained standing by the window utterly unconscious—dead, mind and body—until the sun had set. Then I came to my senses again; and then, when I opened my eyes, there was the apparition of Stephen Monkton standing opposite to me, faintly luminous, just as it stands opposite me at this very moment by your side."

Was this before the news of the duel reached England?" I asked.

"*Two weeks before* the news of it reached us at Wincot. And even when we heard of the duel, we did not hear of the day on which it was fought. I only found that out when the document which you have read was published in the French newspaper. The date of that document, you will remember, is February 22d, and it is stated that the duel was fought two days afterward. I wrote down in my pocketbook, on the evening when I saw the phantom, the day of the month on which it first appeared to me . That day was the 24th of February.

He paused again, as if expecting me to say something. After the words he had just spoken, what could I say? what could I think?

"Even in the first horror of first seeing the apparition," he went on, "the prophecy against our house came to my mind, and with it the conviction that I beheld before me, in that spectral presence, the warning of my own doom. As soon as I recovered a little, I determined, nevertheless, to test the reality of what I saw; to find out whether I was the dupe of my own diseased fancy or not. I left the turret; the phantom left it with me. I made an excuse to have the drawing-room at the Abbey brilliantly lighted up; the figure was still opposite me. I walked out into the park; it was there in the clear starlight. I went away from home, and traveled many miles to the sea-side; still the tall dark man in his death agony was with me. After this I strove against the fatality no more. I returned to the Abbey, and tried to resign myself to my misery. But this was not to be. I had a hope that was dearer to me than my own life; I had one treasure belonging to me that I shuddered at the prospect of losing; and when the phantom presence stood a warning obstacle between me and this one treasure, this dearest hope, then my misery grew heavier than I could bear. You must know what I am alluding to; you must have heard often that I was engaged to be married?"

"Yes, often. I have some acquaintance myself with Miss Elmslie."

"You never can know all that she has sacrificed for me—never can imagine what I have felt for years and years past"—his voice trembled, and the tears came into his eyes—"but I dare not trust myself to speak of that; the thought of the old happy days in the Abbey almost breaks my heart now. Let me get back to the other subject. I must tell you that I kept the frightful vision which pursued me, at all times and in all places, a secret from everybody, knowing the vile reports about my having inherited madness from my family, and fearing that an unfair advantage would be taken of any confession that I might make. Though the phantom always stood opposite to me, and therefore always appeared either before or by the side of any person to whom I spoke, I soon schooled myself to hide from others that I was looking at it except on rare occasions, when I have perhaps betrayed myself to you. But my self-possession availed me nothing with Ada. The day of our marriage was approaching."

He stopped and shuddered. I waited in silence till he had controlled himself.

"Think," he went on, "think of what I must have suffered at looking always on that hideous vision whenever I looked on my betrothed wife! Think of my taking her hand, and seeming to take it through the figure of the apparition! Think of the calm angel-face and the tortured specter-face being always together whenever my eyes met hers! Think of this, and you will not wonder that I betrayed my secret to her. She eagerly entreated to know the worst—nay, more, she insisted on knowing it. At her bidding I told all, and then left her free to break our engagement. The thought of death was in my heart as I spoke the parting words—death by my own act, if life still held out after our separation. She suspected that thought; she knew it, and never left me till her good influence had destroyed it forever. But for her I should not have been alive now; but for her I should never have attempted the project which has brought me here."

"Do you mean that it was at Miss Elmslie's suggestion that you came to Naples?" I asked, in amazement.

"I mean that what she said suggested the design which has brought me to Naples," he answered. "While I believed that the phantom had appeared to me as the fatal messenger of death, there was no comfort—there was misery, rather, in hearing her say that no power on earth should make her desert me, and that she would live for me, and for me only, through every trial. But it was far different when we afterward reasoned together about the purpose which the apparition had come to fulfill—far different when she showed me that its mission might be for good instead of for evil, and that the warning it was sent to give might be to my profit instead of to my loss. At those words, the new idea which gave the new hope of life came to me in an instant. I believed then, what I believe now, that I have a supernatural warrant for my errand here. In that faith I live; without it I should die. *She* never ridiculed it, never scorned it as insanity. Mark what I say! The spirit that appeared to me in the Abbey—that has never left me since—that stands there now by your side, warns me to escape from the fatality which hangs over our race, and commands me, if I would avoid it, to bury the unburied dead. Mortal loves and mortal interests must bow to that awful bidding. The specter-presence will never leave me till I have sheltered the corpse that cries to the earth to cover it! I dare not return—I dare not marry till I have filled the place that is empty in Wincot vault."

His eyes flashed and dilated—his voice deepened—a fanatic ecstasy shone in his expression as he uttered these words. Shocked and grieved as I was, I made no attempt to remonstrate or to reason with him. It would have been useless to have referred to any of the usual commonplaces about optical delusions or diseased imaginations—worse than useless to have attempted to account by natural causes for any of the extraordinary coincidences and events of which he had spoken.

Briefly as he had referred to Miss Elmslie, he had said enough to show me that the only hope of the poor girl who loved him best and had known him longest of any one was in humoring his delusions to the last. How faithfully she still clung to the belief that she could restore him! How resolutely was she sacrificing herself to his morbid fancies, in the hope of a happy future that might never come! Little as I knew of Miss Elmslie, the mere thought of her situation, as I now reflected on it, made me feel sick at heart.

"They call me Mad Monkton!" he exclaimed, suddenly breaking the silence between us during the last few minutes, "Here and in England everybody believes I am out of my senses except Ada and you. She has been my salvation, and you will be my salvation too. Something told me that when I first met you walking in the Villa Peale. I struggled against the strong desire that was in me to trust my secret to you, but I could resist it no longer when I saw you to-night at the ball; the phantom seemed to draw me on to you as you stood alone in the quiet room. Tell me more of that idea of yours about finding the place where the duel was fought. If I set out to-morrow to seek for it myself, where must I go to first? where?" He stopped; his strength was evidently becoming exhausted, and his mind was growing confused. "What am I to do? I can't remember. You know everything—will you not help me? My misery has made me unable to help myself."

He stopped, murmured something about failing if he went to the frontier alone, and spoke confusedly of delays that might be fatal, then tried to utter the name of "Ada"; but, in pronouncing the first letter, his voice faltered, and, turning abruptly from me, he burst into tears.

My pity for him got the better of my prudence at that moment, and without thinking of responsibilities, I promised at once to do for him whatever he asked. The wild triumph in his expression as he started up and seized my hand showed me that I had better have been more cautious; but it was too late now to retract what I had said. The next best thing to do was to try if I could not induce him to compose himself a little, and then to go away and think coolly over the whole affair by myself.

"Yes, yes," he rejoined, in answer to the few words I now spoke to try and calm him, "don't be afraid about me. After what you have said, I'll answer for my own coolness and composure under all emergencies. I have been so long used to the apparition that I hardly feel its presence at all except on rare occasions. Besides, I have here in this little packet of letters the medicine for every m alady of the sick heart. They are Ada's letters; I read them to calm me whenever my misfortune seems to get the better of my endurance. I wanted that half hour to read them in to-night before you came, to make myself fit to see you, and I shall go through them again after you are gone; so, once more, don't be afraid about me. I know I shall succeed with your help, and Ada shall thank you as you deserve to be thanked when we get back to England. If you hear the fools at Naples talk about my being mad, don't trouble yourself to contradict them; the scandal is so contemptible that it must end by contradicting itself."

I left him, promising to return early the next day.

When I got back to my hotel, I felt that any idea of sleeping after all that I had seen and heard was out of the question; so I lit my pipe, and, sitting by the window—how it refreshed my mind just then to look at the calm moonlight!—tried to think what it would be best to do. In the first place, any appeal to doctors or to Alfred's friends in England was out of the question. I could not persuade myself that his intellect was sufficiently disordered to justify me, under existing circumstances, in disclosing the secret which he had intrusted to my keeping. In the second place, all attempts on my part to induce him to abandon the idea of searching out his uncle's remains would be utterly useless after what I had incautiously said to him. Having settled these two conclusions, the only really great difficulty which remained to perplex me was whether I was justified in aiding him to execute his extraordinary purpose.

Supposing that, with my help, he found Mr. Monkton's body, and took it back with him to England, was it right in me thus to lend myself to promoting the marriage which would most likely follow these events—a marriage which it might be the duty of every one to prevent at all hazards? This set me thinking about the extent of his madness, or to speak more mildly and more correctly, of his delusion. Sane he certainly was on all ordinary subjects; nay, in all the narrative parts of what he had said to me on this very evening he had spoken clearly and connectedly. As for the story of the apparition, other men, with intellects as clear as the intellects of their neighbors had fancied themselves pursued by a phantom, and had even written about it in a high strain of philosophical speculation. It was plain that the real hallucination in the case now before me lay in Monkton's conviction of the truth of the old prophecy, and in his idea that the fancied apparition was a supernatural warning to him to evade its denunciations; and it was equally clear that both delusions had been produced, in the first instance, by the lonely life he had led acting on a naturally excitable temperament, which was rendered further liable to moral disease by an hereditary taint of insanity.

Was this curable? Miss Elmslie, who knew him far better than I did, seemed by her conduct to think so. Had I any reason or right to determine offhand that she was mistaken? Supposing I refused to go to the frontier with him, he would then most certainly depart by himself, to commit all sorts of errors, and perhaps to meet with all sorts of accidents; while I, an idle man, with my time entirely at my own disposal, was stopping at Naples, and leaving him to his fate after I had suggested the plan of his expedition, and had encouraged him to confide in me. In this way I kept turning the subject over and over again in my mind, being quite free, let me add, from looking at it in any other than a practical point of view. I firmly believed, as a derider of all ghost stories, that Alfred was deceiving himself in fancying that he had seen the apparition of his uncle before the news of Mr. Monkton's death reached England, and I was on this account, therefore, uninfluenced by the slightest infection of my unhappy friend's delusions when I at last fairly decided to accompany him in his extraordinary search. Possibly my harum-scarum fondness for excitement at that time biased me a little in forming my resolution; but I must add, in common justice to myself, that I also acted from motives of real sympathy for Monkton, and from a sincere wish to allay, if I could, the anxiety of the poor girl who was still so faithfully waiting and hoping for him far away in England.

Certain arrangements preliminary to our departure, which I found myself obliged to make after a second interview with Alfred, betrayed the object of our journey to most of our Neapolitan friends. The astonishment of everybody was of course unbounded, and the nearly universal suspicion that I must be as mad in my way as Monkton himself showed itself pretty plainly in my presence. Some people actually tried to combat my resolution by telling me what a shameless profligate Stephen Monkton had been—as if I had a strong personal interest in hunting out his remains! Ridicule moved me as little as any arguments of this sort; my mind was made up, and I was as obstinate then as I am now.

In two days' time I had got everything ready, and had ordered the traveling carriage to the door some hours earlier than we had originally settled. We were jovially threatened with "a parting cheer" by all our English acquaintances, and I thought it desirable to avoid this on my friend's account; for he had been more excited, as it was, by the preparations for the journey than I at all liked. Accordingly, soon after sunrise, without a soul in the street to stare at us, we privately left Naples.

Nobody will wonder, I think, that I experienced some difficulty in realizing my own position, and shrank instinctively from looking forward a single day into the future, when I now found myself starting, in company with "Mad Monkton," to hunt for the body of a dead duelist all along the frontier line of the Roman States!

CHAPTER V.

I HAD settled it in my own mind that we had better make the town of Fondi, close on the frontier, our headquarters, to begin with, and I had arranged, with the assistance of the embassy, that the leaden coffin should follow us so far, securely nailed up in its packing-case. Besides our passports, we were well furnished with letters of introduction to the local authorities at most of the important frontier towns, and, to crown all, we had money enough at our command (thanks to Monkton's vast fortune) to make sure of the services of any one whom we wanted to assist us all along our line of search. These various resources insured us every facility for action, provided always that we succeeded in discovering the body of the dead duelist. But, in the very probable event of our failing to do this, our future prospects—more especially after the responsibility I had undertaken—were of anything but an agreeable nature to contemplate. I confess I felt uneasy, almost hopeless, as we posted, in the dazzling Italian sunshine, along the road to Fondi.

We made an easy two days' journey of it; for I had insisted, on Monkton's account, that we should travel slowly.

On the first day the excessive agitation of my companion a little alarmed me; he showed, in many ways, more symptoms of a disordered mind than I had yet observed in him. On the second day, however, he seemed to get accustomed to contemplate calmly the new idea of the search on which we were bent, and, except on one point, he was cheerful and composed enough. Whenever his dead uncle formed the subject of conversation, he still persisted—on the strength of the old prophecy, and under the influence of the apparition which he saw, or thought he saw always—in asserting that the corpse of Stephen Monkton, wherever it was, lay yet unburied. On every other topic he deferred to me with the utmost readiness and docility; on this he maintained his strange opinion with an obstinacy which set reason and persuasion alike at defiance.

On the third day we rested at Fondi. The packing-case, with the coffin in it, reached us, and was deposited in a safe place under lock and key. We engaged some mules, and found a man to act as guide who knew the country thoroughly. It occurred to me that we had better begin by confiding th e real object of our journey only to the most trustworthy people we could find among the better-educated classes. For this reason we followed, in one respect, the example of the fatal dueling-party, by starting, early on the morning of the fourth day, with sketch-books and color-boxes, as if we were only artists in search of the picturesque.

After traveling some hours in a northerly direction within the Roman frontier, we halted to rest ourselves and our mules at a wild little village far out of the track of tourists in general.

The only person of the smallest importance in the place was the priest, and to him I addressed my first inquiries, leaving Monkton to await my return with the guide. I spoke Italian quite fluently, and correctly enough for my purpose, and was extremely polite and cautious in introducing my business, but in spite of all the pains I took, I only succeeded in frightening and bewildering the poor priest more and more with every fresh word I said to him. The idea of a dueling-party and a dead man seemed to scare him out of his senses. He bowed, fidgeted, cast his eyes up to heaven, and piteously shrugging his shoulders, told me, with rapid Italian circumlocution, that he had not the faintest idea of what I was talking about. This was my first failure. I confess I was weak enough to feel a little dispirited when I rejoined Monkton and the guide.

After the heat of the day was over we resumed our journey.

About three miles from the village, the road, or rather cart-track, branched off in two directions. The path to the right, our guide informed us, led up among the mountains to a convent about six miles off. If we penetrated beyond the convent we should soon reach the Neapolitan frontier. The path to the left led far inward on the Roman territory, and would conduct us to a small town where we could sleep for the night. Now the Roman territory presented the first and fittest field for our search, and the convent was always within reach, supposing we returned to Fondi unsuccessful. Besides, the path to the left led over the widest part of the country we were starting to explore, and I was always for vanquishing the greatest difficulty first; so we decided manfully on turning to the left. The expedition in which this resolution involved us lasted a whole week, and produced no results. We discovered absolutely nothing, and returned to our headquarters at Fondi so completely baffled that we did not know whither to turn our steps next.

I was made much more uneasy by the effect of our failure on Monkton than by the failure itself. His resolution appeared to break down altogether as soon as we began to retrace our steps.

He became first fretful and capricious, then silent and desponding. Finally, he sank into a lethargy of body and mind that seriously alarmed me. On the morning after our return to Fondi he showed a strange tendency to sleep incessantly, which made me suspect the existence of some physical malady in his brain. The whole day he hardly exchanged a word with me, and seemed to be never fairly awake. Early the next morning I went into his room, and found him as silent and lethargic as ever. His servant, who was with us, informed me that Alfred had once or twice before exhibited such physical symptoms of mental exhaustion as we were now observing during his father's lifetime at Wincot Abbey. This piece of information made me feel easier, and left my mind free to return to the consideration of the errand which had brought us to Fondi.

I resolved to occupy the time until my companion got better in prosecuting our search by myself. That path to the right hand which led to the convent had not yet been explored. If I set off to trace it, I need not be away from Monkton more than one night, and I should at least be able, on my return, to give him the satisfaction of knowing that one more uncertainty regarding the place of the duel had been cleared up. These considerations decided me. I left a message for my friend in case he asked where I had gone, and set out once more for the village at which we had halted when starting on our first expedition.

Intending to walk to the convent, I parted company with the guide and the mules where the track branched off, leaving them to go back to the village and await my return.

For the first four miles the path gently ascended through an open country, then became abruptly much steeper, and led me deeper and deeper among thickets and endless woods. By the time my watch informed me that I must have nearly walked my appointed distance, the view was bounded on all sides and the sky was shut out overhead by an impervious screen of leaves and branches. I still followed my only guide, the steep path; and in ten minutes, emerging suddenly on a plot of tolerably clear and level ground, I saw the convent before me.

It was a dark, low, sinister-looking place. Not a sign of life or movement was visible anywhere about it. Green stains streaked the once white facade of the chapel in all directions. Moss clustered thick in every crevice of the heavy scowling wall that surrounded the convent. Long lank weeds grew out of the fissures of roof and parapet, and, drooping far downward, waved wearily in and out of the barred dormitory windows. The very cross opposite the entrance-gate, with a shocking life-sized figure in wood nailed to it, was so beset at the base with crawling creatures, and looked so slimy, green, and rotten all the way up, that I absolutely shrank from it.

A bell-rope with a broken handle hung by the gate. I approached it— hesitated, I hardly knew why—looked up at the convent again, and then walked round to the back of the building, partly to gain time to consider what I had better do next, partly from an unaccountable curiosity that urged me, strangely to myself, to see all I could of the outside of the place before I attempted to gain admission at the gate.

At the back of the convent I found an outhouse, built on to the wall—a clumsy, decayed building, with the greater part of the roof fallen in, and with a jagged hole in one of its sides, where in all probability a window had once been. Behind the outhouse the trees grew thicker than ever. As I looked toward them I could not determine whether the ground beyond me rose or fell—whether it was grassy, or earthy, or rocky. I could see nothing but the all-pervading leaves, brambles, ferns, and long grass.

Not a sound broke the oppressive stillness. No bird's note rose from the leafy wilderness around me; no voices spoke in the convent garden behind the scowling wall; no clock struck in the chapel-tower; no dog barked in the ruined outhouse. The dead silence deepened the solitude of the place inexpressibly. I began to feel it weighing on my spirits—the more, because woods were never favorite places with me to walk in. The sort of pastoral happiness which poets often represent when they sing of life in the woods never, to my mind, has half the charm of life on the mountain or in the plain. When I am in a wood, I miss the boundless loveliness of the sky, and the delicious softness that distance gives to the earthly view beneath. I feel oppressively the change which the free air suffers when it gets imprisoned among leaves, and I am always awed, rather than pleased, by that mysterious still light which shines with such a strange dim luster in deep places among trees. It may convict me of want of taste and absence of due feeling for the marvelous beauties of vegetation, but I must frankly own that I never penetrate far into a wood without finding that the getting out of it again is the pleasantest part of my walk—the getting out on to the barest down, the wildest hill-side, the bleakest mountain top—the getting out anywhere, so that I can see the sky over me and the view before me as far as my eye can reach.

After such a confession as I have now made, it will appear surprising to no one that I should have felt the strongest possible inclination, while I stood by the ruined outhouse, to retrace my steps at once, and make the best of my way out of the wood. I had, indeed, actually turned to depart, when the remembrance of the er rand which had brought me to the convent suddenly stayed my feet. It seemed doubtful whether I should be admitted into the building if I rang the bell; and more than doubtful, if I were let in, whether the inhabitants would be able to afford me any clew to the information of which I was in search. However, it was my duty to Monkton to leave no means of helping him in his desperate object untried; so I resolved to go round to the front of the convent again, and ring at the gate-bell at all hazards.

By the merest chance I looked up as I passed the side of the outhouse where the jagged hole was, and noticed that it was pierced rather high in the wall.

As I stopped to observe this, the closeness of the atmosphere in the wood seemed to be affecting me more unpleasantly than ever.

I waited a minute and untied my cravat.

Closeness? surely it was something more than that. The air was even more distasteful to my nostrils than to my lungs. There was some faint, indescribable smell loading it—some smell of which I had never had any previous experience— some smell which I thought (now that my attention was directed to it) grew more and more certainly traceable to its source the nearer I advanced to the outhouse,

By the time I had tried the experiment two or three times, and had made myself sure of this fact, my curiosity became excited. There were plenty of fragments of stone and brick lying about me. I gathered some of them together, and piled them up below the hole, then mounted to the top, and, feeling rather ashamed of what I was doing, peeped into the outhouse.

The sight of horror that met my eyes the instant I looked through the hole is as present to my memory now as if I had beheld it yesterday. I can hardly write of it at this distance of time without a thrill of the old terror running through me again to the heart.

The first impression conveyed to me, as I looked in, was of a long, recumbent object, tinged with a lightish blue color all over, extended on trestles, and bearing a certain hideous, half-formed resemblance to the human face and figure. I looked again, and felt certain of it. There were the prominences of the forehead, nose, and chin, dimly shown as under a veil—there, the round outline of the chest and the hollow below it—there, the points of the knees, and the stiff, ghastly, upturned feet. I looked again, yet more attentively. My eyes got accustomed to the dim light streaming in through the broken roof, and I satisfied myself, judging by the great length of the body from head to foot, that I was looking at the corpse of a man—a corpse that had apparently once had a sheet spread over it, and that had lain rotting on the trestles under the open sky long enough for the linen to take the livid, light-blue tinge of mildew and decay which now covered it.

How long I remained with my eyes fixed on that dread sight of death, on that tombless, terrible wreck of humanity, poisoning the still air, and seeming even to stain the faint descending light that disclosed it, I know not. I remember a dull, distant sound among the trees, as if the breeze were rising—the slow creeping on of the sound to near the place where I stood—the noiseless whirling fall of a dead leaf on the corpse below me, through the gap in the outhouse roof—and the effect of awakening my energies, of relaxing the heavy strain on my mind, which even the slight change wrought in the scene I beheld by the falling leaf produced in me immediately. I descended to the ground, and, sitting down on the heap of stones, wiped away the thick perspiration which covered my face, and which I now became aware of for the first time. It was something more than the hideous spectacle unexpectedly offered to my eyes which had shaken my nerves as I felt that they were shaken now. Monkton's prediction that, if we succeeded in discovering his uncle's body, we should find it unburied, recurred to me the instant I saw the trestles and their ghastly burden. I felt assured on the instant that I had found the dead man—the old prophecy recurred to my memory—a strange yearning sorrow, a vague foreboding of ill, an inexplicable terror, as I thought of the poor lad who was awaiting my return in the distant town, struck through me with a chill of superstitious dread, robbed me of my judgment and resolution, and left me when I had at last recovered myself, weak and dizzy, as if I had just suffered under some pang of overpowering physical pain.

I hastened round to the convent gate and rang impatiently at the bell—waited a little while and rang again—then heard footsteps.

In the middle of the gate, just opposite my face, there was a small sliding panel, not more than a few inches long; this was presently pushed aside from within. I saw, through a bit of iron grating, two dull, light gray eyes staring vacantly at me, and heard a feeble husky voice saying:

"What may you please to want?'

"I am a traveler—" I began.

"We live in a miserable place. We have nothing to show travelers here."

"I don't come to see anything. I have an important question to ask, which I believe some one in this convent will be able to answer. If you are not willing to let me in, at least come out and speak to me here."

"Are you alone?"

"Quite alone."

"Are there no women with you?"

"None."

The gate was slowly unbarred, and an old Capuchin, very infirm, very suspicious, and very dirty, stood before me. I was far too excited and impatient to waste any time in prefatory phrases; so, telling the monk at once how I had looked through the hole in the outhouse, and what I had seen inside, I asked him, in plain terms, who the man had been whose corpse I had beheld, and why the body was left unburied?

The old Capuchin listened to me with watery eyes that twinkled suspiciously. He had a battered tin snuff-box in his hand, and his finger and thumb slowly chased a few scattered grains of snuff round and round the inside of the box all the time I was speaking. When I had done, he shook his head and said: "That was certainly an ugly sight in their outhouse; one of the ugliest sights, he felt sure, that ever I had seen in all my life!"

"I don't want to talk of the sight," I rejoined, impatiently; "I want to know who the man was, how he died, and why he is not decently buried. Can you tell me?"

The monk's finger and thumb having captured three or four grains of snuff at last, he slowly drew them into his nostrils, holding the box open under his nose the while, to prevent the possibility of wasting even one grain, sniffed once or twice luxuriously—closed the box—then looked at me again with his eyes watering and twinkling more suspiciously than before.

"Yes," said the monk, "that's an ugly sight in our outhouse—a very ugly sight, certainly!"

I never had more difficulty in keeping my temper in my life than at that moment. I succeeded, however, in repressing a very disrespectful expression on the subject of monks in general, which was on the tip of my tongue, and made another attempt to conquer the old man's exasperating reserve. Fortunately for my chances of succeeding with him, I was a snuff-taker myself, and I had a box full of excellent English snuff in my pocket, which I now produced as a bribe. It was my last resource.

"I thought your box seemed empty just now," said I; "will you try a pinch out of mine?"

The offer was accepted with an almost youthful alacrity of gesture. The Capuchin took the largest pinch I ever saw held between any man's finger and thumb—inhaled it slowly without spilling a single grain—half closed his eyes—and, wagging his head gently, patted me paternally on the back.

"Oh, my son," said the monk, "what delectable snuff! Oh, my son and amiable traveler, give the spiritual father who loves you yet another tiny, tiny pinch!"

"Let me fill your box for you. I shall have plenty left for myself."

The battered tin snuff-box was given to me before I had done speaking; the paternal hand patted my back more approvingly than ever; the feeble, husky voice grew glib and eloquent in my praise. I had evidently found out the weak side of the old Capuchin, and, on returning him his box, I took instan t advantage of the discovery.

"Excuse my troubling you on the subject again," I said, "but I have particular reasons for wanting to hear all that you can tell me in explanation of that horrible sight in the outhouse."

"Come in," answered the monk.

He drew me inside the gate, closed it, and then leading the way across a grass-grown courtyard, looking out on a weedy kitchen-garden, showed me into a long room with a low ceiling, a dirty dresser, a few rudely-carved stall seats, and one or two grim, mildewed pictures for ornaments. This was the sacristy.

"There's nobody here, and it's nice and cool," said the old Capuchin. It was so damp that I actually shivered. "Would you like to see the church?" said the monk; "a jewel of a church, if we could keep it in repair; but we can't. Ah! malediction and misery, we are too poor to keep our church in repair!"

Here he shook his head and began fumbling with a large bunch of keys.

"Never mind the church now," said I. "Can you, or can you not, tell me what I want to know?"

"Everything, from beginning to end—absolutely everything. Why, I answered the gate-bell—I always answer the gate-bell here," said the Capuchin.

"What, in Heaven's name, has the gate-bell to do with the unburied corpse in your house?"

"Listen, son of mine, and you shall know. Some time ago—some months—ah! me, I'm old; I've lost my memory; I don't know how many months—ah! miserable me, what a very old, old monk I am!" Here he comforted himself with another pinch of snuff.

"Never mind the exact time," said I. "I don't care about that."

"Good," said the Capuchin. "Now I can go on. Well, let us say it is some months ago—we in this convent are all at breakfast—wretched, wretched breakfasts, son of mine, in this convent!—we are at breakfast, and we hear *bang! bang!* twice over. 'Guns,' says I. 'What are they shooting for?' says Brother Jeremy. 'Game,' says Brother Vincent. 'Aha! game,' says Brother Jeremy. 'If I hear more, I shall send out and discover what it means,' says the father superior. We hear no more, and we go on with our wretched breakfasts."

"Where did the report of firearms come from?" I inquired.

"From down below—beyond the big trees at the back of the convent, where there's some clear ground—nice ground, if it wasn't for the pools and puddles. But, ah! misery, how damp we are in these parts! how very, very damp!"

"Well, what happened after the report of firearms?"

"You shall hear. We are still at breakfast, all silent—for what have we to talk about here? What have we but our devotions, our kitchen-garden, and our wretched, wretched bits of breakfasts and dinners? I say we are all silent, when there comes suddenly such a ring at the bell as never was heard before—a very devil of a ring—a ring that caught us all with our bits—our wretched, wretched bits!—in our mouths, and stopped us before we could swallow them. 'Go, brother of mine,' says the father superior to me, 'go; it is your duty—go to the gate.' I am brave—a very lion of a Capuchin. I slip out on tiptoe—I wait—I listen—I pull back our little shutter in the gate—I wait, I listen again—I peep through the hole—nothing, absolutely nothing that I can see. I am brave—I am not to be daunted. What do I do next? I open the gate. Ah! sacred Mother of Heaven, what do I behold lying all along our threshold? A man—dead!—a big man; bigger than you, bigger than me, bigger than anybody in this convent—buttoned up tight in a fine coat, with black eyes, staring, staring up at the sky, and blood soaking through and through the front of his shirt. What do I do? I scream once—I scream twice—and run back to the father superior!"

All the particulars of the fatal duel which I had gleaned from the French newspaper in Monkton's room at Naples recurred vividly to my memory. The suspicion that I had felt when

I looked into the outhouse became a certainty as I listened to the old monk's last words.

"So far I understand," said I. "The corpse I have just seen in the outhouse is the corpse of the man whom you found dead outside your gate. Now tell me why you have not given the remains decent burial."

"Wait—wait—wait," answered the Capuchin. "The father superior hears me scream and comes out; we all run together to the gate; we lift up the big man and look at him close. Dead! dead as this (smacking the dresser with his hand). We look again, and see a bit of paper pinned to the collar of his coat. Aha! son of mine, you start at that. I thought I should make you start at last."

I had started, indeed. That paper was doubtless the leaf mentioned in the second's unfinished narrative as having been torn out of his pocketbook, and inscribed with the statement of how the dead man had lost his life. If proof positive were wanted to identify the dead body, here was such proof found.

"What do you think was written on the bit of paper?" continued the Capuchin "We read and shudder. This dead man has been killed in a duel—he, the desperate, the miserable, has died in the commission of mortal sin; and the men who saw the killing of him ask us Capuchins, holy men, servants of Heaven, children of our lord the Pope—they ask *us* to give him burial! Oh! but we are outraged when we read that; we groan, we wring our hands, we turn away, we tear our beards, we—"

"Wait one moment," said I, seeing that the old man was heating himself with his narrative, and was likely, unless I stopped him, to talk more and more fluently to less and less purpose—"wait a moment. Have you preserved the paper that was pinned to the dead man's coat; and can I look at it?"

The Capuchin seemed on the point of giving me an answer, when he suddenly checked himself. I saw his eyes wander away from my face, and at the same moment heard a door softly opened and closed again behind me.

Looking round immediately, I observed another monk in the sacristy—a tall, lean, black-bearded man, in whose presence my old friend with the snuff-box suddenly became quite decorous and devotional to look at. I suspected I was in the presence of the father superior, and I found that I was right the moment he addressed me.

"I am the father superior of this convent," he said, in quiet, clear tones, and looking me straight in the face while he spoke, with coldly attentive eyes. "I have heard the latter part of your conversation, and I wish to know why you are so particularly anxious to see the piece of paper that was pinned to the dead man's coat?"

The coolness with which he avowed that he had been listening, and the quietly imperative manner in which he put his concluding question, perplexed and startled me. I hardly knew at first what tone I ought to take in answering him. He observed my hesitation, and attributing it to the wrong cause, signed to the old Capuchin to retire. Humbly stroking his long gray beard, and furtively consoling himself with a private pinch of the "delectable snuff," my venerable friend shuffled out of the room, making a profound obeisance at the door just before he disappeared.

"Now," said the father superior, as coldly as ever, "I am waiting, sir, for your reply."

"You shall have it in the fewest possible words," said I, answering him in his own tone. "I find, to my disgust and horror, that there is an unburied corpse in an outhouse attached to your convent. I believe that corpse to be the body of an English gentleman of rank and fortune, who was killed in a duel. I have come into this neighborhood with the nephew and only relation of the slain man, for the express purpose of recovering his remains; and I wish to see the paper found on the body, because I believe that paper will identify it to the satisfaction of the relative to whom I have referred. Do you find my reply sufficiently straightforward? And do you mean to give me permission to look at the paper?"

"I am satisfied with your reply, and see no reason for refusing you a sight of the paper," said the father superior; "but I have something to say first. In speaking of the impression produced on you by beholding the corpse, you used the words 'disgust' and 'horror.' This license of expression in relation to what you have seen in the precincts of a convent proves to me that you are out of the pale of the Holy Catholic Church. You have no right, therefore, to expect any explanation; but I will give you one, nevertheless, as a favor. The slain man died, unabsolved, in the commission of mortal sin. We infer so much from the paper which we found on his body; and we know, by the evidence of our own eyes and ears, that he was killed on the territories of the Church, and in the act of committing direct violation of those special laws against the crime of dueling, the strict enforcement of which the holy father himself has urged on the faithful throughout his dominions by letters signed with his own hand. Inside this convent the ground is consecrated, and we Catholics are not accustomed to bury the outlaws of our religion, the enemies of our holy father, and the violators of our most sacred laws in consecrated ground. Outside this convent we have no rights and no power; and, if we had both, we should remember that we are monks, not grave-diggers, and that the only burial with which *we* can have any concern is burial with the prayers of the Church. That is all the explanation I think it necessary to give. Wait for me here, and you shall see the paper." With those words the father superior left the room as quietly as he had entered it.

I had hardly time to think over this bitter and ungracious explanation, and to feel a little piqued by the language and manner of the person who had given it to me, before the father superior returned with the paper in his hand. He placed it before me on the dresser, and I read, hurriedly traced in pencil, the following lines:

"This paper is attached to the body of the late Mr. Stephen Monkton, an Englishman of distinction. He has been shot in a duel, conducted with perfect gallantry and honor on both sides. His body is placed at the door of this convent, to receive burial at the hands of its inmates, the survivors of the encounter being obliged to separate and secure their safety by immediate flight. I, the second of the slain man, and the writer of this explanation, certify, on my word of honor as a gentleman that the shot which killed my principal on the instant was fired fairly, in the strictest accordance with the rules laid down beforehand for the conduct of the duel.

"(Signed), F."

"F." I recognized easily enough as the initial letter of Monsieur Foulon's name, the second of Mr. Monkton, who had died of consumption at Paris.

The discovery and the identification were now complete. Nothing remained but to break the news to Alfred, and to get permission to remove the remains in the outhouse. I began almost to doubt the evidence of my own senses when I reflected that the apparently impracticable object with which we had left Naples was already, by the merest chance, virtually accomplished.

"The evidence of the paper is decisive," said I, handing it back. "There can be no doubt that the remains in the outhouse are the remains of which we have been in search. May I inquire if any obstacles will be thrown in our way should the late Mr. Monkton's nephew wish to remove his uncle's body to the family burial-place in England?"

"Where is this nephew?" asked the father superior.

"He is now awaiting my return at the town of Fondi."

"Is he in a position to prove his relationship?"

"Certainly; he has papers with him which will place it beyond a doubt."

"Let him satisfy the civil authorities of his claim, and he need expect no obstacle to his wishes from any one here."

I was in no humor for talking a moment longer with my sour-tempered companion than I could help. The day was wearing on me fast; and, whether night overtook me or not, I was resolved never to stop on my return till I got back to Fondi. Accordingly, after telling the father superior that he might expect to hear from me again immediately, I made my bow and hastened out of the sacristy.

At the convent gate stood my old friend with the tin snuff-box, waiting to let me out.

"Bless you, may son," said the venerable recluse, giving me a farewell pat on the shoulder, "come back soon to your spiritual father who loves you, and amiably favor him with another tiny, tiny pinch of the delectable snuff."

CHAPTER VI.

I RETURNED at the top of my speed to the village where I had left the mules, had the animals saddled immediately, and succeeded in getting back to Fondi a little before sunset.

While ascending the stairs of our hotel, I suffered under the most painful uncertainty as to how I should best communicate the news of my discovery to Alfred. If I could not succeed in preparing him properly for my tidings, the results, with such an organization as his, might be fatal. On opening the door of his room, I felt by no means sure of myself; and when I confronted him, his manner of receiving me took me so much by surprise that, for a moment or two, I lost my self-possession altogether.

Every trace of the lethargy in which he was sunk when I had last seen him had disappeared. His eyes were bright, his cheeks deeply flushed. As I entered, he started up, and refused my offered hand.

"You have not treated me like a friend," he said, passionately; "you had no right to continue the search unless I searched with you—you had no right to leave me here alone. I was wrong to trust you; you are no better than all the rest of them."

I had by this time recovered a little from my first astonishment, and was able to reply before he could say anything more. It was quite useless, in his present state, to reason with him or to defend myself. I determined to risk everything, and break my news to him at once.

"You will treat me more justly, Monkton, when you know that I have been doing you good service during my absence," I said. "Unless I am greatly mistaken, the object for which we have left Naples may be nearer attainment by both of us than—"

The flush left his cheeks almost in an instant. Some expression in my face, or some tone in my voice, of which I was not conscious, had revealed to his nervously-quickened perception more than I had intended that he should know at first. His eyes fixed themselves intently on mine; his hand grasped my arm; and he said to me in an eager whisper:

"Tell me the truth at once. Have you found him?"

It was too late to hesitate. I answered in the affirmative.

"Buried or unburied?"

His voice rose abruptly as he put the question, and his unoccupied hand fastened on my other arm.

"Unburied."

I had hardly uttered the word before the blood flew back into his cheeks; his eyes flashed again as they looked into mine, and he burst into a fit of triumphant laughter, which shocked and startled me inexpressibly.

"What did I tell you? What do you say to the old prophecy now?" he cried, dropping his hold on my arms, and pacing backward and forward in the room. "Own you were wrong. Own it, as all Naples shall own it, when once I have got him safe in his coffin!"

His laughter grew more and mere violent. I tried to quiet him in vain. His servant and the landlord of the inn entered the room, but they only added fuel to the fire, and I made them go out again. As I shut the door on them, I observed lying on a table near at hand the packet of letters from Miss Elmslie, which my unhappy friend preserved with such care, and read and re-read with such unfailing devotion. Looking toward me just when I passed by the table, the letters caught his eye. The new hope for the future, in connection with the writer of them, which my news was already awakening in his heart, seemed to overwhelm him in an instant at sight of the treasured memorials that reminded him of his betrothed wife. His laughter ceased, his face changed, he ran to the table, caught the letters up in his hand, looked from them to me for one moment with an altered expression which went to my heart, then sank down on his knees at the table, laid his face on the letters, and burst into tears. I let the new emotion have its way uninterruptedly, and quitted the room without saying a word. When I returned after a lapse of some little time, I found him sitting quietly in his chair, reading one of the letters from the pack et which rested on his knee.

His look was kindness itself; his gesture almost womanly in its gentleness as he rose to meet me, and anxiously held out his hand.

He was quite calm enough now to hear in detail all that I had to tell him. I suppressed nothing but the particulars of the state in which I had found the corpse. I assumed no right of direction as to the share he was to take in our future proceedings, with the exception of insisting beforehand that he should leave the absolute superintendence of the removal of the body to me, and that he should be satisfied with a sight of M. Foulon's paper, after receiving my assurance that the remains placed in the coffin were really and truly the remains of which we had been in search.

"Your nerves are not so strong as mine," I said, by way of apology for my apparent dictation, "and for that reason I must beg leave to assume the leadership in all that we have now to do, until I see the leaden coffin soldered down and safe in your possession. After that I shall resign all my functions to you."

"I want words to thank you for your kindness," he answered. "No brother could have borne with me more affectionately, or helped me more patiently than you."

He stopped and grew thoughtful, then occupied himself in tying up slowly and carefully the packet of Miss Elmslie's letters, and then looked suddenly toward the vacant wall behind me with that strange expression the meaning of which I knew so well. Since we had left Naples I had purposely avoided exciting him by talking on the useless and shocking subject of the apparition by which he believed himself to be perpetually followed. Just now, however, he seemed so calm and collected—so little likely to be violently agitated by any allusion to the dangerous topic, that I ventured to speak out boldly.

"Does the phantom still appear to you," I asked, "as it appeared at Naples?"

He looked at me and smiled.

"Did I not tell you that it followed me everywhere?" His eyes wandered back again to the vacant space, and he went on speaking in that direction as if he had been continuing the conversation with some third person in the room. "We shall part," he said, slowly and softly, when the empty place is filled in Wincot vault. Then I shall stand with Ada before the altar in the Abbey chapel, and when my eyes meet hers they will see the tortured face no more."

Saying this, he leaned his head on his hand, sighed, and began repeating softly to himself the lines of the old prophecy:

When in Wincot vault a place Waits for one of Monkton's race— When that one forlorn shall lie Graveless under open sky, Beggared of six feet of earth, Though lord of acres from his birth— That shall he a certain sign Of the end of Monktons line. Dwindling ever faster, faster, Dwindling to the last-left master; From mortal ken, from light of day, Monkton's race shall pass away."

Fancying that he pronounced the last lines a little incoherently, I tried to make him change the subject. He took no notice of what I said, and went on talking to himself.

"Monkton's race shall pass away," he repeated, "but not with *me*. The fatality hangs over *my* head no longer. I shall bury the unburied dead; I shall fill the vacant place in Wincot vault; and then—then the new life, the life with Ada!" That name seemed to recall him to himself. He drew his traveling desk toward him, placed the packet of letters in it, and then took out a sheet of paper. "I am going to write to Ada," he said, turning to me, "and tell her the good news. Her happiness, when she knows it, will be even greater than mine."

Worn out by the events of the day, I left him writing and went to bed. I was, however, either too anxious or too tired to sleep. In this waking condition, my mind naturally occupied itself with the discovery at the convent and with the events to which that discovery would in all probability lead. As I thought on the future, a depression for which I could not account weighed on my spirits. There was not the slightest reason for the vaguely melancholy forebodings that oppressed me. The remains, to the finding of which my unhappy friend attached so much importance, had been traced; they would certainly be placed at his disposal in a few days; he might take them to England by the first merchant vessel that sailed from Naples; and, the gratification of his strange caprice thus accomplished, there was at least some reason to hope that his mind might recover its tone, and that the new life he would lead at Wincot might result in making him a happy man. Such considerations as these were, in themselves, certainly not calculated to exert any melancholy influence over me; and yet, all through the night, the same inconceivable, unaccountable depression weighed heavily on my spirits—heavily through the hours of darkness—heavily, even when I walked out to breathe the first freshness of the early morning air.

With the day came the all-engrossing business of opening negotiations with the authorities.

Only those who have had to deal with Italian officials can imagine how our patience was tried by every one with whom we came in contact. We were bandied about from one authority to the other, were stared at, cross-questioned, mystified—not in the least because the case presented any special difficulties or intricacies, but because it was absolutely necessary that every civil dignitary to whom we applied should assert his own importance by leading us to our object in the most roundabout manner possible. After our first day's experience of official life in Italy, I left the absurd formalities, which we had no choice but to perform, to be accomplished by Alfred alone, and applied myself to the really serious question of how the remains in the convent outhouse were to be safely removed.

The best plan that suggested itself to me was to write to a friend in Rome, where I knew that it was a custom to embalm the bodies of high dignitaries of the Church, and where, I consequently inferred, such chemical assistance as was needed in our emergency might be obtained. I simply stated in my letter that the removal of the body was imperative, then described the condition in which I had found it, and engaged that no expense on our part should be spared if the right person or persons could be found to help us. Here, again, more difficulties interposed themselves, and more useless formalities were to be gone through, but in the end patience, perseverance, and money triumphed, and two men came expressly from Rome to undertake the duties we required of them.

It is unnecessary that I should shock the reader by entering into any detail in this part of my narrative. When I have said that the progress of decay was so far suspended by chemical means as to allow of the remains being placed in the coffin, and to insure their being transported to England with perfect safety and convenience, I have said enough. After ten days had been wasted in useless delays and difficulties, I had the satisfaction of seeing the convent outhouse empty at last; passed through a final ceremony of snuff-taking, or rather, of snuff-giving, with the old Capuchin, and ordered the traveling carriages to be ready at the inn door. Hardly a month had elapsed since our departure ere we entered Naples successful in the achievement of a design which had been ridiculed as wildly impracticable by every friend of ours who had heard of it.

The first object to be accomplished on our return was to obtain the means of carrying the coffin to England—by sea, as a matter of course. All inquiries after a merchant vessel on the point of sailing for any British port led to the most unsatisfactory results. There was only one way of insuring the immediate transportation of the remains to England, and that was to hire a vessel. Impatient to return, and resolved not to lose sight of the coffin till he had seen it placed in Wincot vault, Monkton decided immediately on hiring the first ship that could be obtained. The vessel in port which we were informed could soonest be got ready for sea was a Sicilian brig, and this vessel my friend accordingly engaged. The best dock-yard artisans tha t could be got were set to work, and the smartest captain and crew to be picked up on an emergency in Naples were chosen to navigate the brig.

Monkton, after again expressing in the warmest terms his gratitude for the services I had rendered him, disclaimed any intention of asking me to accompany him on the voyage to England. Greatly to his surprise and delight, however, I offered of my own accord to take passage in the brig. The strange coincidences I had witnessed, the extraordinary discovery I had hit on since our first meeting in Naples, had made his one great interest in life my one great interest for the time being as well. I shared none of his delusions, poor fellow; but it is hardly an exaggeration to say that my eagerness to follow our remarkable adventure to its end was as great as his anxiety to see the coffin laid in Wincot vault. Curiosity influenced me, I am afraid, almost as strongly as friendship, when I offered myself as the companion of his voyage home.

We set sail for England on a calm and lovely afternoon.

For the first time since I had known him, Monkton seemed to be in high spirits. He talked and jested on all sorts of subjects, and laughed at me for allowing my cheerfulness to be affected by the dread of seasickness. I had really no such fear; it was my excuse to my friend for a return of that unaccountable depression under which I had suffered at Fondi. Everything was in our favor; everybody on board the brig was in good spirits. The captain was delighted with the vessel; the crew, Italians and Maltese, were in high glee at the prospect of making a short voyage on high wages in a well-provisioned ship. I alone felt heavy at heart. There was no valid reason that I could assign to myself for the melancholy that oppressed me, and yet I struggled against it in vain.

Late on our first night at sea, I made a discovery which was by no means calculated to restore my spirits to their usual equilibrium. Monkton was in the cabin, on the floor of which had been placed the packing-case containing the coffin, and I was on deck. The wind had fallen almost to a calm, and I was lazily watching the sails of the brig as they flapped from time to time against the masts, when the captain approached, and, drawing me out of hearing of the man at the helm, whispered in my ear:

"There's something wrong among the men forward. Did you observe how suddenly they all became silent just before sunset?"

I had observed it, and told him so.

"There's a Maltese boy on board," pursued the captain, "who is a smart enough lad, but a bad one to deal with. I have found out that he has been telling the men there is a dead body inside that packing-case of your friend's in the cabin."

My heart sank as he spoke. Knowing the superstitious irrationality of sailors—of foreign sailors especially—I had taken care to spread a report on board the brig, before the coffin was shipped, that the packing-case contained a valuable marble statue which Mr. Monkton prized highly, and was unwilling to trust out of his own sight. How could this Maltese boy have discovered that the pretended statue was a human corpse? As I pondered over the question, my suspicions fixed themselves on Monkton's servant, who spoke Italian fluently, and whom I knew to be an incorrigible gossip. The man denied it when I charged him with betraying us, but I have never believed his denial to this day.

"The little imp won't say where he picked up this notion of his about the dead body," continued the captain. "It's not my place to pry into secrets; but I advise you to call the crew aft, and contradict the boy, whether he speaks the truth or not. The men are a parcel of fools who believe in ghosts, and all the rest of it. Some of them say they would never have signed our articles if they had known they were going to sail with a dead man; others only grumble; but I'm afraid we shall have some trouble with them all, in case of rough weather, unless the boy is contradicted by you or the other gentleman. The men say that if either you or your friend tell them on your words of honor that the Maltese is a liar, they will hand him up to be rope's-ended accordingly; but that if you won't, they have made up their minds to believe the boy."

Here the captain paused and awaited my answer. I could give him none. I felt hopeless under our desperate emergency. To get the boy punished by giving my word of honor to support a direct falsehood was not to be thought of even for a moment. What other means of extrication from this miserable dilemma remained? None that I could think of. I thanked the captain for his attention to our interests, told him I would take time to consider what course I should pursue, and begged that he would say nothing to my friend about the discovery he had made. He promised to be silent, sulkily enough, and walked away from me.

We had expected the breeze to spring up with the morning, but no breeze came. As it wore on toward noon the atmosphere became insufferably sultry, and the sea looked as smooth as glass. I saw the captain's eye turn often and anxiously to windward. Far away in that direction, and alone in the blue heaven, I observed a little black cloud, and asked if it would bring us any wind.

"More than we want," the captain replied, shortly; and then, to my astonishment, ordered the crew aloft to take in sail. The execution of this maneuver showed but too plainly the temper of the men; they did their work sulkily and slowly, grumbling and murmuring among themselves. The captain's manner, as he urged them on with oaths and threats, convinced me we were in danger. I looked again to windward. The one little cloud had enlarged to a great bank of murky vapor, and the sea at the horizon had changed in color.

"The squall will be on us before we know where we are," said the captain. "Go below; you will be only in the way here."

I descended to the cabin, and prepared Monkton for what was coming. He was still questioning me about what I had observed on deck when the storm burst on us. We felt the little brig strain for an instant as if she would part in two, then she seemed to be swinging round with us, then to be quite still for a moment, trembling in every timber. Last came a shock which hurled us from our seats, a deafening crash, and a flood of water pouring into the cabin. We clambered, half drowned, to the deck. The brig had, in the nautical phrase, "broached to," and she now lay on her beam-ends.

Before I could make out anything distinctly in the horrible confusion except the one tremendous certainty that we were entirely at the mercy of the sea, I heard a voice from the fore part of the ship which stilled the clamoring and shouting of the rest of the crew in an instant. The words were in Italian, but I understood their fatal meaning only too easily. We had sprung a leak, and the sea was pouring into the ship's hold like the race of a mill-stream. The captain did not lose his presence of mind in this fresh emergency. He called for his ax to cut away the foremast, and, ordering some of the crew to help him, directed the others to rig out the pumps.

The words had hardly passed his lips before the men broke into open mutiny. With a savage look at me, their ringleader declared that the passengers might do as they pleased, but that he and his messmates were determined to take to the boat, and leave the accursed ship, and *the dead man in her,* to go to the bottom together. As he spoke there was a shout among the sailors, and I observed some of them pointing derisively behind me. Looking round, I saw Monkton, who had hitherto kept close at my side, making his way back to the cabin. I followed him directly, but the water and confusion on deck, and the impossibility, from the position of the brig, of moving the feet without the slow assistance of the hands, so impeded my progress that it was impossible for me to overtake him. When I had got below he was crouched upon the coffin, with the water on the cabin floor whirling and splashing about him as the ship heaved and plunged. I saw a warning brightness in his eyes, a warning flush on his cheek, as I approached and said to him:

"There is nothing left for it, Alfred, but to bow to our misfortune, and do the best we can to save our lives."

"Save yours," he cried, waving his hand to me, "for *you* have a future before you. Mine is gone when this coffin goes to the bottom. If the ship sinks, I shall know that the fatality is accomplished, and shall sink with her."

I saw that he was in no state to be reasoned with or persuaded, and raised myself again to the deck. The men were cutting away all obstacles so as to launch the longboat placed amidships over the depressed bulwark of the brig as she lay on her side, and the captain, after having made a last vain exertion to restore his authority, was looking on at them in silence. The violence of the squall seemed already to be spending itself, and I asked whether there was really no chance for us if we remained by the ship. The captain answered that there might have been the best chance if the men had obeyed his orders, but that now there was none. Knowing that I could place no dependence on the presence of mind of Monkton's servant, I confided to the captain, in the fewest and plainest words, the condition of my unhappy friend, and asked if I might depend on his help. He nodded his head, and we descended together to the cabin. Even at this day it costs me pain to write of the terrible necessity to which the strength and obstinacy of Monkton's delusion reduced us in the last resort. We were compelled to secure his hands, and drag him by main force to the deck. The men were on the point of launching the boat, and refused at first to receive us into it.

"You cowards!" cried the captain, "have we got the dead man with us this time? Isn't he going to the bottom along with the brig? Who are you afraid of when we get into the boat?"

This sort of appeal produced the desired effect; the men became ashamed of themselves, and retracted their refusal.

Just as we pushed off from the sinking ship Alfred made an effort to break from me, but I held him firm, and he never repeated the attempt. He sat by me with drooping head, still and silent, while the sailors rowed away from the vessel; still and silent when, with one accord, they paused at a little distance off, and we all waited and watched to see the brig sink; still and silent, even when that sinking happened, when the laboring hull plunged slowly into a hollow of the sea—

hesitated, as it seemed, for one moment, rose a little again, then sank to rise no more.

Sank with her dead freight—sank, and snatched forever from our power the corpse which we had discovered almost by a miracle—those jealously-preserved remains, on the safe-keeping of which rested so strangely the hopes and the love-destinies of two living beings! As the last signs of the ship in the depths of the waters,

I felt Monkton trembling all over as he sat close at my side, and heard him repeating to himself, sadly, and many times over, the name of "Ada."

I tried to turn his thoughts to another subject, but it was useless. He pointed over the sea to where the brig had once been, and where nothing was left to look at but the rolling waves.

"The empty place will now remain empty forever in Wincot vault."

As he said these words, he fixed his eyes for a moment sadly and earnestly on my face, then looked away, leaned his cheek on his hand, and spoke no more.

We were sighted long before nightfall by a trading vessel, were taken on board, and landed at Cartagena in Spain. Alfred never held up his head, and never once spoke to me of his own accord the whole time we were at sea in the merchantman. I observed, however, with alarm, that he talked often and incoherently to himself—constantly muttering the lines of the old prophecy—constantly referring to the fatal place that was empty in Wincot vault—constantly repeating in broken accents, which it affected me inexpressibly to hear, the name of the poor girl who was awaiting his return to England. Nor were these the only causes for the apprehension that I now felt on his account. Toward the end of our voyage he began to suffer from alternations of fever-fits and shivering-fits, which I ignorantly imagined to be attacks of ague. I was soon undeceived. We had hardly been a day on shore before he became so much worse that I secured the best medical assistance Cartagena could afford. For a day or two the doctors differed, as usual, about the nature of his complaint, but ere long alarming symptoms displayed themselves. The medical men declared that his life was in danger, and told me that his disease was brain fever.

Shocked and grieved as I was, I hardly knew how to act at first under the fresh responsibility now laid upon me. Ultimately I decided on writing to the old priest who had been Alfred's tutor, and who, as I knew, still resided at Wincot Abbey. I told this gentleman all that had happened, begged him to break my melancholy news as gently as possible to Miss Elmslie, and assured him of my resolution to remain with Monkton to the last.

After I had dispatched my letter, and had sent to Gibraltar to secure the best English medical advice that could be obtained, I felt that I had done my best, and that nothing remained but to wait and hope.

Many a sad and anxious hour did I pass by my poor friend's bedside. Many a time did I doubt whether I had done right in giving any encouragement to his delusion. The reasons for doing so which had suggested themselves to me after my first interview with him seemed, however, on reflection, to be valid reasons still. The only way of hastening his return to England and to Miss Elmslie, who was pining for that return, was the way I had taken. It was not my fault that a disaster which no man could foresee had overthrown all his projects and all mine. But, now that the calamity had happened and was irretrievable, how, in the event of his physical recovery, was his moral malady to be combated?

When I reflected on the hereditary taint in his mental organization, on that first childish fright of Stephen Monkton from which he had never recovered, on the perilously-secluded life that he had led at the Abbey, and on his firm persuasion of the reality of the apparition by which he believed himself to be constantly followed, I confess I despaired of shaking his superstitious faith in every word and line of the old family prophecy. If the series of striking coincidences which appeared to attest its truth had made a strong and lasting impression on *me* (and this was assuredly the case), how could I wonder that they had produced the effect of absolute conviction on *his* mind, constituted as it was? If I argued with him, and he answered me, how could I rejoin? If he said, "The prophecy points at the last of the family: *I* am the last of the family. The prophecy mentions an empty place in Wincot vault; there is such an empty place there at this moment. On the faith of the prophecy I told you that Stephen Monkton's body was unburied, and you found that it was unburied"—if he said this, what use would it be for me to reply, "These are only strange coincidences after all?"

The more I thought of the task that lay before me, if he recovered, the more I felt inclined to despond. The oftener the English physician who attended on him said to me, "He may get the better of the fever, but he has a fixed idea, which never leaves him night or day, which has unsettled his reason, and which will end in killing him, unless you or some of his friends can remove it"—the oftener I heard this, the more acutely I felt my own powerlessness, the more I shrank from every idea that was connected with the hopeless future.

I had only expected to receive my answer from Wincot in the shape of a letter. It was consequently a great surprise, as well as a great relief, to be informed one day that two gentlemen wished to speak with me, and to find that of these two gentlemen the first was the old priest, and the second a male relative of Mrs. Elmslie.

Just before their arrival the fever symptoms had disappeared, and Alfred had been pronounced out of danger. Both the priest and his companion were eager to know when the sufferer would be strong enough to travel. The y had come to Cartagena expressly to take him home with them, and felt far more hopeful than I did of the restorative effects of his native air. After all the questions connected with the first important point of the journey to England had been asked and answered, I ventured to make some inquiries after Miss Elmslie. Her relative informed me that she was suffering both in body and in mind from excess of anxiety on Alfred's account. They had been obliged to deceive her as to the dangerous nature of his illness in order to deter her from accompanying the priest and her relation on their mission to Spain.

Slowly and imperfectly, as the weeks wore on, Alfred regained something of his former physical strength, but no alteration appeared in his illness as it affected his mind.

From the very first day of his advance toward recovery, it had been discovered that the brain fever had exercised the strangest influence over his faculties of memory. All recollection of recent events was gone from him. Everything connected with Naples, with me, with his journey to Italy, had dropped in some mysterious manner entirely out of his remembrance. So completely had all late circumstances passed from his memory that, though he recognized the old priest and his own servant easily on the first days of his convalescence, he never recognized me, but regarded me with such a wistful, doubting expression, that I felt inexpressibly pained when I approached his bedside. All his questions were about Miss Elmslie and Wincot Abbey, and all his talk referred to the period when his father was yet alive.

The doctors augured good rather than ill from this loss of memory of recent incidents, saying that it would turn out to be temporary, and that it answered the first great healing purpose of keeping his mind at ease. I tried to believe them— tried to feel as sanguine, when the day came for his departure, as the old friends felt who were taking him home. But the effort was too much for me. A foreboding that I should never see him again oppressed my heart, and the tears came into my eyes as I saw the worn figure of my poor friend half helped, half lifted into the traveling-carriage, and borne away gently on the road toward home.

He had never recognized me, and the doctors had begged that I would give him, for some time to come, as few opportunities as possible of doing so. But for this request I should have accompanied him to England. As it was, nothing better remained for me to do than to change the scene, and recruit as I best could my energies of body and mind, depressed of late by much watching and anxiety. The famous cities of Spain were not new to me, but I visited them again and revived old impressions of the Alhambra and Madrid. Once or twice I thought of making a pilgrimage to the East, but late events had sobered and altered me. That yearning, unsatisfied feeling which we call "homesickness" began to prey upon my heart, and I resolved to return to England.

I went back by way of Paris, having settled with the priest that he should write to me at my banker's there as soon as he could after Alfred had returned to Wincot. If I had gone to the East, the letter would have been forwarded to me. I wrote to prevent this; and, on my arrival at Paris, stopped at the banker's before I went to my hotel.

The moment the letter was put into my hands, the black border on the envelope told me the worst. He was dead.

There was but one consolation—he had died calmly, almost happily, without once referring to those fatal chances which had wrought the fulfillment of the ancient prophecy. "My beloved pupil," the old priest wrote, "seemed to rally a little the first few days after his return, but he gained no real strength, and soon suffered a slight relapse of fever. After this he sank gradually and gently day by day, and so departed from us on the last dread journey. Miss Elmslie (who knows that I am writing this) desires me to express her deep and lasting gratitude for all your kindness to Alfred. She told me when we brought him back that she had waited for him as his promised wife, and that she would nurse him now as a wife should; and she never left him. his face was turned toward her, his hand was clasped in hers when he died. It will console you to know that he never mentioned events at Naples, or the shipwreck that followed them, from the day of his return to the day of his death."

Three days after reading the letter I was at Wincot, and heard all the details of Alfred's last moments from the priest. I felt a shock which it would not be very easy for me to analyze or explain when I heard that he had been buried, at his own desire, in the fatal Abbey vault.

The priest took me down to see the place—a grim, cold, subterranean building, with a low roof, supported on heavy Saxon arches. Narrow niches, with the ends only of coffins visible within them, ran down each side of the vault. The nails and silver ornaments flashed here and there as my companion moved past them with a lamp in his hand. At the lower end of the place he stopped, pointed to a niche, and said, "He lies there, between his father and mother." I looked a little further on, and saw what appeared at first like a long dark tunnel. "That is only an empty niche," said the priest, following me. "If the body of Mr. Stephen Monkton had been brought to Wincot, his coffin would have been placed there."

A chill came over me, and a sense of dread which I am ashamed of having felt now, but which I could not combat then. The blessed light of day was pouring down gayly at the other end of the vault through the open door. I turned my back on the empty niche, and hurried into the sunlight and the fresh air.

As I walked across the grass glade leading down to the vault, I heard the rustle of a woman's dress behind me, and turning round, saw a young lady advancing, clad in deep mourning. Her sweet, sad face, her manner as she held out her hand, told me who it was in an instant.

"I heard that you were here," she said, "and I wished—" Her voice faltered a little. My heart ached as I saw how her lip trembled, but before I could say anything she recovered herself and went on: "I wished to take your hand, and thank you for your brotherly kindness to Alfred; and I wanted to tell you that I am sure in all you did you acted tenderly and considerately for the best. Perhaps you may be soon going away from home again, and we may not meet any more. I shall never, never forget that you were kind to him when he wanted a friend, and that you have the greatest claim of any one on earth to be gratefully remembered in my thoughts as long as I live."

The inexpressible tenderness of her voice, trembling a little all the while she spoke, the pale beauty of her face, the artless candor in her sad, quiet eyes, so affected me that I could not trust myself to answer her at first except by gesture. Before I recovered my voice she had given me her hand once more and had left me.

I never saw her again. The chances and changes of life kept us apart. When I last heard of her, years and years ago, she was faithful to the memory of the dead, and was Ada Elmslie still for Alfred Monkton's sake.

THE FIFTH DAY.

STILL cloudy, but no rain to keep our young lady indoors. The paper, as usual, without interest to *me*.

To-day Owen actually vanquished his difficulties and finished his story. I numbered it Eight, and threw the corresponding number (as I had done the day before in Morgan's case) into the china bowl.

Although I could discover no direct evidence against her, I strongly suspected The Queen of Hearts of tampering with the lots on the fifth evening, to irritate Morgan by making it his turn to read again, after the shortest possible interval of repose. However that might be, the number drawn was certainly Seven, and the story to be read was consequently the story which my brother had finished only two days before.

If I had not known that it was part of Morgan's character always to do exactly the reverse of what might be expected from him, I should have been surprised at the extraordinary docility he exhibited the moment his manuscript was placed i n his hands.

"My turn again?" he said. "How very satisfactory! I was anxious to escape from this absurd position of mine as soon as possible, and here is the opportunity most considerately put into my hands. Look out, all of you! I won't waste another moment. I mean to begin instantly."

"Do tell me," interposed Jessie, mischievously, "shall I be very much interested to-night'?'

"Not you!" retorted Morgan. "You will be very much frightened instead. You hair is uncommonly smooth at the present moment, but it will be all standing on end before I've done. Don't blame me, miss, if you are an object when you go to bed to-night!"

With this curious introductory speech he began to read. I was obliged to interrupt him to say the few words of explanation which the story needed.

"Before my brother begins," I said, "it may be as well to mention that he is himself the doctor who is supposed to relate this narrative. The events happened at a time of his life when he had left London, and had established himself in medical practice in one of our large northern towns."

With that brief explanation, I apologized for interrupting the reader, and Morgan began once more.

BROTHER MORGAN'S STORY

of

THE DEAD HAND

WHEN this present nineteenth century was younger by a good many years than it is now, a certain friend of mine, named Arthur Holliday, happened to arrive in the town of Doncaster exactly in the middle of the race-week, or, in other words, in the middle of the month of September.

He was one of those reckless, rattle-pated, open-hearted, and open-mouthed young gentlemen who possess the gift of familiarity in its highest perfection, and who scramble carelessly along the journey of life, making friends, as the phrase is, wherever they go. His father was a rich manufacturer, and had bought landed property enough in one of the midland counties to make all the born squires in his neighborhood thoroughly envious of him. Arthur was his only son, possessor in prospect of the great estate and the great business after his father's death; well supplied with money, and not too rigidly looked after during his father's lifetime. Report, or scandal, whichever you please, said that the old gentleman had been rather wild in his youthful days, and that, unlike most parents, he was not disposed to be violently indignant when he found that his son took after him. This may be true or not. I myself only knew the elder Mr. Holliday when he was getting on in years, and then he was as quiet and as respectable a gentleman as ever I met with.

Well, one September, as I told you, young Arthur comes to Doncaster, having decided all of a sudden, in his hare-brained way, that he would go to the races. He did not reach the town till toward the close of evening, and he went at once to see about his dinner and bed at the principal hotel. Dinner they were ready enough to give him, but as for a bed, they laughed when he mentioned it. In the race-week at Doncaster it is no uncommon thing for visitors who have not bespoken apartments to pass the night in their carriages at the inn doors. As for the lower sort of strangers, I myself have often seen them, at that full time, sleeping out on the doorsteps for want of a covered place to creep under. Rich as he was, Arthur's chance of getting a night's lodging (seeing that he had not written beforehand to secure one) was more than doubtful. He tried the second hotel, and the third hotel, and two of the inferior inns after that, and was met everywhere with the same form of answer. No accommodation for the night of any sort was left. All the bright golden sovereigns in his pocket would not buy him a bed at Doncaster in the race-week.

To a young fellow of Arthur's temperament, the novelty of being turned away into the street like a penniless vagabond, at every house where he asked for a lodging, presented itself in the light of a new and highly amusing piece of experience. He went on with his carpet-bag in his hand, applying for a bed at every place of entertainment for travelers that he could find in Doncaster, until he wandered into the outskirts of the town.

By this time the last glimmer of twilight had faded out, the moon was rising dimly in a mist, the wind was getting cold, the clouds were gathering heavily, and there was every prospect that it was soon going to rain!

The look of the night had rather a lowering effect on young Holliday's spirits. He began to contemplate the houseless situation in which he was placed from the serious rather than the humorous point of view, and he looked about him for another public house to inquire at with something very like downright anxiety in his mind on the subject of a lodging for the night. The suburban part of the town toward which he had now strayed was hardly lighted at all, and he could see nothing of the houses as he passed them, except that they got progressively smaller and dirtier the further he went. Down the winding road before him shone the dull gleam of an oil lamp, the one faint lonely light that struggled ineffectually with the foggy darkness all round him. He resolved to go on as far as this lamp, and then, if it showed him nothing in the shape of an inn, to return to the central part of the town, and to try if he could not at least secure a chair to sit down on through the night at one of the principal hotels.

As he got near the lamp he heard voices, and, walking close under it, found that it lighted the entrance to a narrow court, on the wall of which was painted a long hand in faded flesh-color, pointing, with a lean forefinger, to this inscription: THE TWO ROBINS.

Arthur turned into the court without hesitation to see what The Two Robins could do for him. Four or five men were standing together round the door of the house, which was at the bottom of the court, facing the entrance from the street. The men were all listening to one other man, better dressed than the rest, who was telling his audience something, in a low voice, in which they were apparently very much interested.

On entering the passage, Arthur was passed by a stranger with a knapsack in his hand, who was evidently leaving the house.

"No," said the traveler with the knapsack, turning round and addressing himself cheerfully to a fat, sly-looking, bald-headed man, with a dirty white apron on, who had followed him down the passage, "no, Mr. Landlord, I am not easily scared by trifles; but I don't mind confessing that I can't quite stand *that.*"

It occurred to young Holliday, the moment he heard these words, that the stranger had been asked an exorbitant price for a bed at The Two Robins, and that he was unable or unwilling to pay it. The moment his back was turned, Arthur, comfortably conscious of his own well-filled pockets, addressed himself in a great hurry, for fear any other benighted traveler should slip in and forestall him, to the sly-looking landlord with the dirty apron and the bald head.

"If you have got a bed to let," he said, "and if that gentleman who has just gone out won't pay your price for it, I will."

The sly landlord looked hard at Arthur. "Will you, sir?" he asked, in a meditative, doubtful way.

"Name your price," said young Holliday, thinking that the landlord's hesitation sprang from some boorish distrust of him. "Name your price, and I'll give you the money at once, if you like."

"Are you game for five shillings?" inquired the landlord, rubbing his stubby double chin and looking up thoughtfully at the ceiling above him.

Arthur nearly laughed in the man's face; but, thinking it prudent to control himself, offered the five shillings as seriously as he could. The sly landlord held out his hand, then suddenly drew it back again.

"You're acting all fair and aboveboard by me," he said, "and, before I take your money, I'll do the same by you. Look here; this is how it stands. You can have a bed all to yourself for five shillings, but you can't have more than a half share of the room it stands in. Do you see what I mean, young gentleman?"

"Of course I do," returned Arthur, a little irritably. "You mean that it is a double-bedded room, and that one of the beds is occupied?"

The land lord nodded his head, and rubbed his double chin harder than ever. Arthur hesitated, and mechanically moved back a step or two toward the door. The idea of sleeping in the same room with a total stranger did not present an attractive prospect to him. He felt more than half inclined to drop his five shillings into his pocket and to go out into the street once more.

"Is it yes or no?" asked the landlord. "Settle it as quick as you can, because there's lots of people wanting a bed at Doncaster to-night besides you."

Arthur looked toward the court and heard the rain falling heavily in the street outside. He thought he would ask a question or two before he rashly decided on leaving the shelter of The Two Robins.

"What sort of man is it who has got the other bed?" he inquired. "Is he a gentleman? I mean, is he a quiet, well-behaved person?"

"The quietest man I ever came across," said the landlord, rubbing his fat hands stealthily one over the other. "As sober as a judge, and as regular as clock-work in his habits. It hasn't struck nine, not ten minutes ago, and he's in his bed already. I don't know whether that comes up to your notion of a quiet man: it goes a long way ahead of mine, I can tell you."

"Is he asleep, do you think?" asked Arthur.

"I know he's asleep," returned the landlord; "and, what's more, he's gone off so fast that I'll warrant you don't wake him. This way, sir," said the landlord, speaking over young Holliday's shoulder, as if he was addressing some new guest who was approaching the house.

"Here you are," said Arthur, determined to be beforehand with the stranger, whoever he might be. "I'll take the bed." And he handed the five shillings to the landlord, who nodded, dropped the money carelessly into his waistcoat pocket, and lighted a candle.

"Come up and see the room," said the host of The Two Robins, leading the way to the staircase quite briskly, considering how fat he was.

They mounted to the second floor of the house. The landlord half opened a door fronting the landing, then stopped, and turned round to Arthur.

"It's a fair bargain, mind, on my side as well as on yours," he said. "You give me five shillings, and I give you in return a clean, comfortable bed; and I warrant, beforehand, that you won't be interfered with, or annoyed in anyway, by the man who sleeps in the same room with you." Saying those words, he looked hard, for a moment, in young Holliday's face, and then led the way into the room.

It was larger and cleaner than Arthur had expected it would be. The two beds stood parallel with each other, a space of about six feet intervening between them. They were both of the same medium size, and both had the same plain white curtains, made to draw, if necessary, all round them.

The occupied bed was the bed nearest the window. The curtains were all drawn round it except the half curtain at the bottom, on the side of the bed furthest from the window. Arthur saw the feet of the sleeping man raising the scanty clothes into a sharp little eminence, as if he was lying flat on his back. He took the candle, and advanced softly to draw the curtain—stopped half way, and listened for a moment—then turned to the landlord.

"He is a very quiet sleeper," said Arthur. "Yes," said the landlord, "very quiet." Young Holliday advanced with the candle, and looked in at the man cautiously.

"How pale he is," said Arthur.

"Yes," returned the landlord, "pale enough, isn't he?"

Arthur looked closer at the man. The bedclothes were drawn up to his chin, and they lay perfectly still over the region of his chest. Surprised and vaguely startled as he noticed this, Arthur stooped down closer over the stranger, looked at his ashy, parted lips, listened breathlessly for an instant, looked again at the strangely still face, and the motionless lips and chest, and turned round suddenly on the landlord with his own cheeks as pale for the moment as the hollow cheeks of the man on the bed.

"Come here," he whispered, under his breath. "Come here, for God's sake! The man's not asleep—he is dead."

"You have found that out sooner than I thought you would," said the landlord, composedly. "Yes, he's dead, sure enough. He died at five o'clock to-day."

"How did he die? Who is he?" asked Arthur, staggered for the moment by the audacious coolness of the answer.

"As to who is he," rejoined the landlord, "I know no more about him than you do. There are his books, and letters, and things all sealed up in that brown paper parcel for the coroner's inquest to open to-morrow or next day. He's been here a week, paying his way fairly enough, and stopping indoors, for the most part, as if he was ailing. My girl brought him up his tea at five to-day, and as he was pouring of it out, he fell down in a faint, or a fit, or a compound of both, for anything I know. We couldn't bring him to, and I said he was dead. And, the doctor couldn't bring him to, and the doctor said he was dead. And there he is. And the coroner's inquest's coming as soon as it can. And that's as much as I know about it."

Arthur held the candle close to the man's lips. The flame still burned straight up as steadily as ever. There was a moment of silence, and the rain pattered drearily through it against the panes of the window.

"If you haven't got nothing more to say to me," continued the landlord, "I suppose I may go. You don't expect your five shillings back, do you? There's the bed I promised you, clean and comfortable. There's the man I warranted not to disturb you, quiet in this world forever. If you're frightened to stop alone with him, that's not my lookout. I've kept my part of the bargain, and I mean to keep the money. I'm not Yorkshire myself, young gentleman, but I've lived long enough in these parts to have my wits sharpened, and I shouldn't wonder if you found out the way to brighten up yours next time you come among us."

With these words the landlord turned toward the door, and laughed to himself softly, in high satisfaction at his own sharpness.

Startled and shocked as he was, Arthur had by this time sufficiently recovered himself to feel indignant at the trick that had been played on him, and at the insolent manner in which the landlord exulted in it.

"Don't laugh," he said sharply, "till you are quite sure you have got the laugh against me. You shan't have the five shillings for nothing, my man. I'll keep the bed."

"Will you?" said the landlord. "Then I wish you a good night's rest." With that brief farewell he went out and shut the door after him.

A good night's rest! The words had hardly been spoken, the door had hardly been closed, before Arthur half repented the hasty words that had just escaped him. Though not naturally over-sensitive, and not wanting in courage of the moral as well as the physical sort, the presence of the dead man had an instantaneously chilling effect on his mind when he found himself alone in the room—alone, and bound by his own rash words to stay there till the next morning. An older man would have thought nothing of those words, and would have acted, without reference to them, as his calmer sense suggested. But Arthur was too young to treat the ridicule even of his inferiors with contempt—too young not to fear the momentary humiliation of falsifying his own foolish boast more than he feared the trial of watching out the long night in the same chamber with the dead.

"It is but a few hours," he thought to himself, "and I can get away the first thing in the morning."

He was looking toward the occupied bed as that idea passed through his mind, and the sharp, angular eminence made in the clothes by the dead man's upturned feet again caught his eye. He advanced and drew the curtains, purposely abstaining, as he did so, from looking at the face of the corpse, lest he might unnerve himself at the outset by fastening some ghastly impression of it on his mind. He drew the curtain very gently, and sighed involuntarily as he closed it.

"Poor fellow," he said, almost as sadly as if he had known the man. "Ah! poor fellow!"

He went next to the window. The night was black, and he could see nothing from it. The rain still pattered heavily agai nst the glass. He inferred, from hearing it, that the window was at the back of the house, remembering that the front was sheltered from the weather by the court and the buildings over it.

While he was still standing at the window—for even the dreary rain was a relief, because of the sound it made; a relief, also, because it moved, and had some faint suggestion, in consequence, of life and companionship in it—while he was standing at the window, and looking vacantly into the black darkness outside, he heard a distant church clock strike ten. Only ten! How was he to pass the time till the house was astir the next morning?

Under any other circumstances he would have gone down to the public-house parlor, would have called for his grog, and would have laughed and talked with the company assembled as familiarly as if he had known them all his life. But the very thought of whiling away the time in this manner was now distasteful to him. The new situation in which he was placed seemed to have altered him to himself already. Thus far his life had been the common, trifling, prosaic, surface-life of a prosperous young man, with no troubles to conquer and no trials to face. He had lost no relation whom he loved, no friend whom he treasured. Till this night, what share he had of the immortal inheritance that is divided among us all had lain dormant within him. Till this night, Death and he had not once met, even in thought.

He took a few turns up and down the room, then stopped. The noise made by his boots on the poorly-carpeted floor jarred on his ear. He hesitated a little, and ended by taking the boots off, and walking backward and forward noiselessly.

All desire to sleep or to rest had left him. The bare thought of lying down on the unoccupied bed instantly drew the picture on his mind of a dreadful mimicry of the position of the dead man. Who was he? What was the story of his past life? Poor he must have been, or he would not have stopped at such a place as the Two Robins Inn; and weakened, probably, by long illness, or he could hardly have died in the manner which the landlord had described. Poor, ill, lonely—dead in a strange place—dead, with nobody but a stranger to pity him. A sad story; truly, on the mere face of it, a very sad story.

While these thoughts were passing through his mind, he had stopped insensibly at the window, close to which stood the foot of the bed with the closed curtains. At first he looked at it absently; then he became conscious that his eyes were fixed on it; and then a perverse desire took possession of him to do the very thing which he had resolved not to do up to this time—to look at the dead man.

He stretched out his hand toward the curtains, but checked himself in the very act of undrawing them, turned his back sharply on the bed, and walked toward the chimney-piece, to see what things were placed on it, and to try if he could keep the dead man out of his mind in that way.

There was a pewter inkstand on the chimney-piece, with some mildewed remains of ink in the bottle. There were two coarse china ornaments of the commonest kind; and there was a square of embossed card, dirty and fly-blown, with a collection of wretched riddles printed on it, in all sorts of zigzag directions, and in variously colored inks. He took the card and went away to read it at the table on which the candle was placed, sitting down with his back resolutely turned to the curtained bed.

He read the first riddle, the second, the third, all in one corner of the card, then turned it round impatiently to look at another. Before he could begin reading the riddles printed here the sound of the church clock stopped him.

Eleven.

He had got through an hour of the time in the room with the dead man.

Once more he looked at the card. It was not easy to make out the letters printed on it in consequence of the dimness of the light which the landlord had left him—a common tallow candle, furnished with a pair of heavy old-fashioned steel snuffers. Up to this time his mind had been too much occupied to think of the light. He had left the wick of the candle unsnuffed till it had risen higher than the flame, and had burned into an odd pent-house shape at the top, from which morsels of the charred cotton fell off from time to time in little flakes. He took up the snuffers now and trimmed the wick. The light brightened directly, and the room became less dismal.

Again he turned to the riddles, reading them doggedly and resolutely, now in one corner of the card, now in another. All his efforts, however, could not fix his attention on them. He pursued his occupation mechanically, deriving no sort of impression from what he was reading. It was as if a shadow from the curtained bed had got between his mind and the gayly printed letters—a shadow that nothing could dispel. At last he gave up the struggle, threw the card from him impatiently, and took to walking softly up and down the room again.

The dead man, the dead man, the *hidden* dead man on the bed!

There was the one persistent idea still haunting him. Hidden! Was it only the body being there, or was it the body being there *concealed,* that was preying on his mind? He stopped at the window with that doubt in him, once more listening to the pattering rain, once more looking out into the black darkness.

Still the dead man!

The darkness forced his mind back upon itself, and set his memory at work, reviving with a painfully vivid distinctness the momentary impression it had received from his first sight of the corpse. Before long the face seemed to be hovering out in the middle of the darkness, confronting him through the window, with the paleness whiter—with the dreadful dull line of light between the imperfectly-closed eyelids broader than he had seen it—with the parted lips slowly dropping further and further away from each other—with the features growing larger and moving closer, till they seemed to fill the window, and to silence the rain, and to shut out the night.

The sound of a voice shouting below stairs woke him suddenly from the dream of his own distempered fancy. He recognized it as the voice of the landlord.

"Shut up at twelve, Ben," he heard it say. "I'm off to bed."

He wiped away the damp that had gathered on his forehead, reasoned with himself for a little while, and resolved to shake his mind free of the ghastly counterfeit which still clung to it by forcing himself to confront, if it was only for a moment, the solemn reality. Without allowing himself an instant to hesitate, he parted the curtains at the foot of the bed, and looked through.

There was the sad, peaceful, white face, with the awful mystery of stillness on it, laid back upon the pillow. No stir, no change there! He only looked at it for a moment before he closed the curtains again, but that moment steadied him, calmed him, restored him—mind and body—to himself. He returned to his old occupation of walking up and down the room, persevering in it this time till the clock struck again.

Twelve.

As the sound of the clock-bell died away, it was succeeded by the confused noise downstairs of the drinkers in the taproom leaving the house. The next sound, after an interval of silence, was caused by the barring of the door and the closing of the shutters at the back of the inn. Then the silence followed again, and was disturbed no more.

He was alone now—absolutely, hopelessly alone with the dead man till the next morning.

The wick of the candle wanted trimming again. He took up the snuffers, but paused suddenly on the very point of using them, and looked attentively at the candle—then back, over his shoulder, at the curtained bed—then again at the candle. It had been lighted for the first time to show him the way upstairs, and three parts of it, at least, were already consumed. In another hour it would be burned out. In another hour, unless he called at once to the man who had shut up the inn for a fresh candle, he would be left in the dark.

Strongly as his mind had been affected since he had entered the room, his unreasonable dread of encountering ridicule and of exposing his courage to suspicion had not altogether lost its influence over him even yet.

He lingered irresolutely by the table, waiting till he could prevail on himself to open the door, and call from the landing, to the man who had shut up the inn. In his present hesitating frame of mind, it was a kind of relief to gain a few moments only by engaging in the trifling occupation of snuffing the candle. His hand trembled a little, and the snuffers were heavy and awkward to use. When he closed them on the wick, he closed them a hair-breadth too low. In an instant the candle was out, and the room was plunged in pitch darkness.

The one impression which the absence of light immediately produced on his mind was distrust of the curtained bed—distrust which shaped itself into no distinct idea, but which was powerful enough, in its very vagueness, to bind him down to his chair, to make his heart beat fast, and to set him listening intently. No sound stirred in the room, but the familiar sound of the rain against the window, louder and sharper now than he had heard it yet.

Still the vague distrust, the inexpressible dread possessed him, and kept him in his chair. He had put his carpet-bag on the table when he first entered the room, and he now took the key from his pocket, reached out his hand softly, opened the bag, and groped in it for his traveling writing-case, in which he knew that there was a small store of matches. When he had got one of the matches he waited before he struck it on the coarse wooden table, and listened intently again without knowing why. Still there was no sound in the room but the steady, ceaseless rattling sound of the rain.

He lighted the candle again without another moment of delay, and, on the instant of its burning up, the first object in the room that his eyes sought for was the curtained bed.

Just before the light had been put out he had looked in that direction, and had seen no change, no disarrangement of any sort in the folds of the closely-drawn curtains.

When he looked at the bed now, he saw hanging over the side of it a long white hand.

It lay perfectly motionless midway on the side of the bed, where the curtain at the head and the curtain at the foot met. Nothing more was visible. The clinging curtains hid everything but the long white hand.

He stood looking at it, unable to stir, unable to call out—feeling nothing, knowing nothing—every faculty he possessed gathered up and lost in the one seeing faculty. How long that first panic held him he never could tell afterward. It might have been only for a moment—it might have been for many minutes together. How he got to the bed—whether he ran to it headlong, or whether he approached it slowly; how he wrought himself up to unclose the curtains and look in, he never has remembered, and never will remember to his dying day. It is enough that he did go to the bed, and that he did look inside the curtains.

The man had moved. One of his arms was outside the clothes; his face was turned a little on the pillow; his eyelids were wide open. Changed as to position and as to one of the features, the face was otherwise fearfully and wonderfully unaltered. The dead paleness and the dead quiet were on it still.

One glance showed Arthur this—one glance before he flew breathlessly to the door and alarmed the house.

The man whom the landlord called "Ben" was the first to appear on the stairs. In three words Arthur told him what had happened, and sent him for the nearest doctor.

I, who tell you this story, was then staying with a medical friend of mine, in practice at Doncaster, taking care of his patients for him during his absence in London; and I, for the time being, was the nearest doctor. They had sent for me from the inn when the stranger was taken ill in the afternoon, but I was not at home, and medical assistance was sought for elsewhere. When the man from The Two Robins rang the night-bell, I was just thinking of going to bed. Naturally enough, I did not believe a word of his story about "a dead man who had come to life again." However, I put on my hat, armed myself with one or two bottles of restorative medicine, and ran to the inn, expecting to find nothing more remarkable, when I got there, than a patient in a fit.

My surprise at finding that the man had spoken the literal truth was almost, if not quite, equaled by my astonishment at finding myself face to face with Arthur Holliday as soon as I entered the bedroom. It was no time then for giving or seeking explanations. We just shook hands amazedly, and then I ordered everybody but Arthur out of the room, and hurried to the man on the bed.

The kitchen fire had not been long out. There was plenty of hot water in the boiler, and plenty of flannel to be had. With these, with my medicines, and with such help as Arthur could render under my direction, I dragged the man literally out of the jaws of death. In less than an hour from the time when I had been called in, he was alive and talking in the bed on which he had been laid out to wait for the coroner's inquest.

You will naturally ask me what had been the matter with him, and I might treat you, in reply, to a long theory, plentifully sprinkled with what the children call hard words. I prefer telling you that, in this case, cause and effect could not be satisfactorily joined together by any theory whatever. There are mysteries in life and the conditions of it which human science has not fathomed yet; and I candidly confess to you that, in bringing that man back to existence, I was, morally speaking, groping haphazard in the dark. I know (from the testimony of the doctor who attended him in the afternoon) that the vital machinery, so far as its action is appreciable by our senses, had, in this case, unquestionably stopped, and I am equally certain (seeing that I recovered him) that the vital principle was not extinct. When I add that he had suffered from a long and complicated illness, and that his whole nervous system was utterly deranged, I have told you all I really know of the physical condition of my dead-alive patient at the Two Robins Inn.

When he "came to," as the phrase goes, he was a startling object to look at, with his colorless face, his sunken cheeks, his wild black eyes, and his long black hair. The first question he asked me about himself when he could speak made me suspect that I had been called in to a man in my own profession. I mentioned to him my surmise, and he told me that I was right.

He said he had come last from Paris, where he had been attached to a hospital; that he had lately returned to England, on his way to Edinburgh, to continue his studies; that he had been taken ill on the journey; and that he had stopped to rest and recover himself at Doncaster. He did not add a word about his name, or who he was, and of course I did not question him on the subject. All I inquired when he ceased speaking was what branch of the profession he intended to follow.

"Any branch," he said, bitterly, "which will put bread into the mouth of a poor man."

At this, Arthur, who had been hitherto watching him in silent curiosity, burst out impetuously in his usual good-humored way:

"My dear fellow" (everybody was "my dear fellow" with Arthur), "now you have come to life again, don't begin by being down-hearted about your prospects. I'll answer for it I can help you to some capital thing in the medical line, or, if I can't, I know my father can."

The medical student looked at him steadily.

"Thank you," he said, coldly; then added, "May I ask who your father is?"

"He's well enough known all about this part of the country," replied Arthur. "He is a great manufacturer, and his name is Holliday."

My hand was on the man's wrist during this brief conversation. The instant the name of Holliday was pronounced I felt the pulse under my fingers flutter, stop, go on suddenly with a bound, and beat afterward for a minute or two at the fever rate.

"How did you come here?" asked the stranger, quickly, excitably, passionately almost.

Arthur related briefly what had happened from the time of his first taking the bed at the inn.

"I am indebted to Mr. Holliday's son, then, for the help that has saved my life," said the medical student, speaking to himself, with a singular sarcasm in his voice. "Come here!"

He held out, as he spoke, his long, white, bony right hand.

"With all my heart," said Arthur, taking his hand cordially. "I may confess it now," he continued, laughing, "upon my honor, you almost frightened me out of my wits."

The stranger did not seem to listen. His wild black eyes were fixed with a look of eager interest on Arthur's face, and his long bony fingers kept tight hold of Arthur's hand. Young Holliday, on his side, returned the gaze, amazed and puzzled by the medical student's odd language and manners. The two faces were close together; I looked at them, and, to my amazement, I was suddenly impressed by the sense of a likeness between them—not in features or complexion, but solely in expression. It must have been a strong likeness, or I should certainly not have found it out, for I am naturally slow at detecting resemblances between faces.

"You have saved my life," said the strange man, still looking hard in Arthur's face, still holding tightly by his hand. "If you had been my own brother, you could not have done more for me than that."

He laid a singularly strong emphasis on those three words "my own brother," and a change passed over his face as he pronounced them—a change that no language of mine is competent to describe.

"I hope I have not done being of service to you yet," said Arthur. "I'll speak to my father as soon as I get home."

"You seem to be fond and proud of your father," said the medical student. "I suppose, in return, he is fond and proud of you?"

"Of course he is," answered Arthur, laughing. "Is there anything wonderful in that? Isn't *your* father fond—"

The stranger suddenly dropped young Holliday's hand and turned his face away.

"I beg your pardon," said Arthur. "I hope I have not unintentionally pained you. I hope you have not lost your father?"

"I can't well lose what I have never had," retorted the medical student, with a harsh mocking laugh.

"What you have never had!"

The strange man suddenly caught Arthur's hand again, suddenly looked once more hard in his face.

"Yes," he said, with a repetition of the bitter laugh. "You have brought a poor devil back into the world who has no business there. Do I astonish you? Well, I have a fancy of my own for telling you what men in my situation generally keep a secret. I have no name and no father. The merciful law of society tells me I am nobody's son! Ask your father if he will be my father too, and help me on in life with the family name."

Arthur looked at me more puzzled than ever.

I signed to him to say nothing, and then laid my fingers again on the man's wrist. No. In spite of the extraordinary speech that he had just made, he was not, as I had been disposed to suspect, beginning to get light-headed. His pulse, by this time, had fallen back to a quiet, slow beat, and his skin was moist and cool. Not a symptom of fever or agitation about him.

Finding that neither of us answered him, he turned to me, and began talking of the extraordinary nature of his case, and asking my advice about the future course of medical treatment to which he ought to subject himself. I said the matter required careful thinking over, and suggested that I should send him a prescription a little later. He told me to write it at once, as he would most likely be leaving Doncaster in the morning before I was up. It was quite useless to represent to him the folly and danger of such a proceeding as this. He heard me politely and patiently, but held to his resolution, without offering any reasons or explanations, and repeated to me that, if I wished to give him a chance of seeing my prescription, I must write it at once.

Hearing this, Arthur volunteered the loan of a traveling writing-case, which he said he had with him, and, bringing it to the bed, shook the note-paper out of the pocket of the case forthwith in his usual careless way. With the paper there fell out on the counterpane of the bed a small packet of sticking-plaster, and a little water-color drawing of a landscape.

The medical student took up the drawing and looked at it. His eye fell on some initials neatly written in cipher in one corner. He started and trembled; his pale face grew whiter than over; his wild black eyes turned on Arthur, and looked through and through him.

"A pretty drawing," he said, in a remarkably quiet tone of voice.

"Ah! and done by such a pretty girl," said Arthur. "Oh, such a pretty girl! I wish it was not a landscape—I wish it was a portrait of her!"

"You admire her very much?"

Arthur, half in jest, half in earnest, kissed his hand for answer.

"Love at first sight," said young Holliday, putting the drawing away again. "But the course of it doesn't run smooth. It's the old story. She's monopolized, as usual; trammeled by a rash engagement to some poor man who is never likely to get money enough to marry her. It was lucky I heard of it in time, or I should certainly have risked a declaration when she gave me that drawing. Here, doctor, here is pen, ink, and paper all ready for you."

"When she gave you that drawing? Gave it? gave it?"

He repeated the words slowly to himself, and suddenly closed his eyes. A momentary distortion passed across his face, and I saw one of his hands clutch up the bedclothes and squeeze them hard. I thought he was going to be ill again, and begged that there might be no more talking. He opened his eyes when I spoke, fixed them once more searchingly on Arthur, and said, slowly and distinctly:

"You like her, and she likes you. The poor man may die out of your way. Who can tell that she may not give you herself as well as her drawing, after all?"

Before young Holliday could answer he turned to me, and said in a whisper: "Now for the prescription." From that time, though he spoke to Arthur again, he never looked at him more.

When I had written the prescription, he examined it, approved of it, and then astonished us both by abruptly wishing us good-night. I offered to sit up with him, and he shook his head. Arthur offered to sit up with him, and he said, shortly, with his face turned away, "No." I insisted on having somebody left to watch him. He gave way when he found I was determined, and said he would accept the services of the waiter at the inn.

"Thank you both," he said, as we rose to go. "I have one last favor to ask— not of you, doctor, for I leave you to exercise your professional discretion, but of Mr. Holliday." His eyes, while he spoke, still rested steadily on me, and never once turned toward Arthur. "I beg that Mr. Holliday will not mention to any one, least of all to his father, the events that have occurred and the words that have passed in this room. I entreat him to bury me in his memory as, but for him, I might have been buried in my grave. I cannot give my reason for making this strange request. I can only implore him to grant it."

His voice faltered for the first time, and he hid his face on the pillow. Arthur, completely bewildered, gave the required pledge. I took young Holliday away with me immediately afterward to the house of my friend, determining to go back to the inn and to see the medical student again before he had left in the morning.

I returned to the inn at eight o'clock, purposely abstaining from waking Arthur, who was sleeping off the past night's excitement on one of my friend's sofas. A suspicion had occurred to me, as soon as I was alone in my bedroom, which made me resolve that Holliday and the stranger whose life he had saved should not meet again, if I could prevent it.

I have already alluded to certain reports or scandals which I knew of relating to the early life of Arthur's father. While I was thinking, in my bed, of what had passed at the inn; of the change in the student's pulse when he heard the name of Holliday; of the resemblance of expression that I had discovered between his face and Arthur's; of the emphasis he had laid on those three words, "my own brother," and of his incomprehensible acknowledgment of his own illegitimacy— while I was thinking of these things, the reports I have me ntioned suddenly flew into my mind, and linked themselves fast to the chain of my previous reflections. Something within me whispered, "It is best that those two young men should not meet again." I felt it before I slept; I felt it when I woke; and I went as I told you, alone to the inn the next morning.

I had missed my only opportunity of seeing my nameless patient again. He had been gone nearly an hour when I inquired for him.

I have now told you everything that I know for certain in relation to the man whom I brought back to life in the double-bedded room of the inn at Doncaster. What I have next to add is matter for inference and surmise, and is not, strictly speaking, matter of fact.

I have to tell you, first, that the medical student turned out to be strangely and unaccountably right in assuming it as more than probable that Arthur Holliday would marry the young lady who had given him the water-color drawing of the landscape. That marriage took place a little more than a year after the events occurred which I have just been relating.

The young couple came to live in the neighborhood in which I was then established in practice. I was present at the wedding, and was rather surprised to find that Arthur was singularly reserved with me, both before and after his marriage, on the subject of the young lady's prior engagement. He only referred to it once when we were alone, merely telling me, on that occasion, that his wife had done all that honor and duty required of her in the matter, and that the engagement had been broken off with the full approval of her parents. I never heard more from him than this. For three years he and his wife lived together happily. At the expiration of that time the symptoms of a serious illness first declared themselves in Mrs. Arthur Holliday. It turned out to be a long, lingering, hopeless malady. I attended her throughout. We had been great friends when she was well, and we became more attached to each other than ever when she was ill. I had many long and interesting conversations with her in the intervals when she suffered least. The result of one of those conversations I may briefly relate, leaving you to draw any inferences from it that you please.

The interview to which I refer occurred shortly before her death.

I called one evening as usual, and found her alone, with a look in her eyes which told me she had been crying. She only informed me at first that she had been depressed in spirits, but by little and little she became more communicative, and confessed to me that she had been looking over some old letters which had been addressed to her, before she had seen Arthur, by a man to whom she had been engaged to be married. I asked her how the engagement came to be broken off. She replied that it had not been broken off, but that it had died out in a very mysterious way. The person to whom she was engaged—her first love, she called him—was very poor, and there was no immediate prospect of their being married. He followed my profession, and went abroad to study. They had corresponded regularly until the time when, as she believed, he had returned to England. From that period she heard no more of him. He was of a fretful, sensitive temperament, and she feared that she might have inadvertently done or said something to offend him. However that might be, he had never written to her again, and after waiting a year she had married Arthur. I asked when the first estrangement had begun, and found that the time at which she ceased to hear anything of her first lover exactly corresponded with the time at which I had been called in to my mysterious patient at The Two Robins Inn.

A fortnight after that conversation she died. In course of time Arthur married again. Of late years he has lived principally in London, and I have seen little or nothing of him.

I have some years to pass over before I can approach to anything like a conclusion of this fragmentary narrative. And even when that later period is reached, the little that I have to say will not occupy your attention for more than a few minutes.

One rainy autumn evening, while I was still practicing as a country doctor, I was sitting alone, thinking over a case then under my charge, which sorely perplexed me, when I heard a low knock at the door of my room.

"Come in," I cried, looking up curiously to see who wanted me.

After a momentary delay, the lock moved, and a long, white, bony hand stole round the door as it opened, gently pushing it over a fold in the carpet which hindered it from working freely on the hinges. The hand was followed by a man whose face instantly struck me with a very strange sensation. There was something familiar to me in the look of him, and yet it was also something that suggested the idea of change.

He quietly introduced himself as "Mr. Lorn," presented to me some excellent professional recommendations, and proposed to fill the place, then vacant, of my assistant. While he was speaking I noticed it as singular that we did not appear to be meeting each other like strangers, and that, while I was certainly startled at seeing him, he did not appear to be at all startled at seeing me.

It was on the tip of my tongue to say that I thought I had met with him before. But there was something in his face, and something in my own recollections—I can hardly say what—which unaccountably restrained me from speaking and which as unaccountably attracted me to him at once, and made me feel ready and glad to accept his proposal.

He took his assistant's place on that very day. We got on together as if we had been old friends from the first; but, throughout the whole time of his residence in my house, he never volunteered any confidences on the subject of his past life, and I never approached the forbidden topic except by hints, which he resolutely refused to understand.

I had long had a notion that my patient at the inn might have been a natural son of the elder Mr. Holliday's, and that he might also have been the man who was engaged to Arthur's first wife. And now another idea occurred to me, that Mr. Lorn was the only person in existence who could, if he chose, enlighten me on both those doubtful points. But he never did choose, and I was never enlightened. He remained with me till I removed to London to try my fortune there as a physician for the second time, and then he went his way and I went mine, and we have never seen one another since.

I can add no more. I may have been right in my suspicion, or I may have been wrong. All I know is that, in those days of my country practice, when I came home late, and found my assistant asleep, and woke him, he used to look, in coming to, wonderfully like the stranger at Doncaster as he raised himself in the bed on that memorable night.

THE SIXTH DAY

AN oppressively mild temperature, and steady, soft, settled rain—dismal weather for idle people in the country. Miss Jessie, after looking longingly out of the window, resigned herself to circumstances, and gave up all hope of a ride. The gardener, the conservatory, the rabbits, the raven, the housekeeper, and, as a last resource, even the neglected piano, were all laid under contribution to help her through the time. It was a long day, but thanks to her own talent for trifling, she contrived to occupy it pleasantly enough.

Still no news of my son. The time was getting on now, and it was surely not unreasonable to look for some tidings of him.

To-day Morgan and I both finished our third and last stories. I corrected my brother's contribution with no very great difficulty on this occasion, and numbered it Nine. My own story came next, and was thus accidentally distinguished as the last of the series—Number Ten. When I dropped the two corresponding cards into the bowl, the thought that there would be now no more to add seemed to quicken my prevailing sense of anxiety on the subject of George's return. A heavy depression hung upon my spirits, and I went out desperately in the rain to shake my mind free of oppressing influences by dint of hard bodily exercise.

The number drawn this evening was Three. On the production of the corresponding man uscript it proved to be my turn to read again.

"I can promise you a little variety to-night," I said, addressing our fair guest, "if I can promise nothing else. This time it is not a story of my own writing that I am about to read, but a copy of a very curious correspondence which I found among my professional papers."

Jessie's countenance fell. "Is there no story in it?" she asked, rather discontentedly.

"Certainly there is a story in it," I replied—"a story of a much lighter kind than any we have yet read, and which may, on that account, prove acceptable, by way of contrast and relief, even if it fails to attract you by other means. I obtained the original correspondence, I must tell you, from the office of the Detective Police of London."

Jessie's face brightened. "That promises something to begin with," she said.

"Some years since," I continued, "there was a desire at headquarters to increase the numbers and efficiency of the Detective Police, and I had the honor of being one of the persons privately consulted on that occasion. The chief obstacle to the plan proposed lay in the difficulty of finding new recruits. The ordinary rank and file of the police of London are sober, trustworthy, and courageous men, but as a body they are sadly wanting in intelligence. Knowing this, the authorities took into consideration a scheme, which looked plausible enough on paper, for availing themselves of the services of that proverbially sharp class of men, the experienced clerks in attorney's offices. Among the persons whose advice was sought on this point, I was the only one who dissented from the arrangement proposed. I felt certain that the really experienced clerks intrusted with conducting private investigations and hunting up lost evidence, were too well paid and too independently situated in their various offices to care about entering the ranks of the Detective Police, and submitting themselves to the rigid discipline of Scotland Yard, and I ventured to predict that the inferior clerks only, whose discretion was not to be trusted, would prove to be the men who volunteered for detective employment. My advice was not taken and the experiment of enlisting the clerks was tried in two or three cases. I was naturally interested in the result, and in due course of time I applied for information in the right quarter. In reply, the originals of the letters of which I am now about to read the copies were sent to me, with an intimation that the correspondence in this particular instance offered a fair specimen of the results of the experiment in the other cases. The letters amused me, and I obtained permission to copy them before I sent them back. You will now hear, therefore, by his own statement, how a certain attorney's clerk succeeded in conducting a very delicate investigation, and how the regular members of the Detective Police contrived to help him through his first experiment."

BROTHER GRIFFITH'S STORY

of

THE BITER BIT.

Extracted from the Correspondence of the London Police.

FROM CHIEF INSPECTOR THEAKSTONE, OF THE DETECTIVE POLICE, TO SERGEANT BULMER, OF THE SAME FORCE.

London, 4th July, 18—.

SERGEANT BULMER—This is to inform you that you are wanted to assist in looking up a case of importance, which will require all the attention of an experienced member of the force. The matter of the robbery on which you are now engaged you will please to shift over to the young man who brings you this letter. You will tell him all the circumstances of the case, just as they stand; you will put him up to the progress you have made (if any) toward detecting the person or persons by whom the money has been stolen; and you will leave him to make the best he can of the matter now in your hands. He is to have the whole responsibility of the case, and the whole credit of his success if he brings it to a proper issue.

So much for the orders that I am desired to communicate to you.

A word in your ear, next, about this new man who is to take your place. His name is Matthew Sharpin, and he is to have the chance given him of dashing into our office at one jump—supposing he turns out strong enough to take it. You will naturally ask me how he comes by this privilege. I can only tell you that he has some uncommonly strong interest to back him in certain high quarters, which you and I had better not mention except under our breaths. He has been a lawyer's clerk, and he is wonderfully conceited in his opinion of himself, as well as mean and underhand, to look at. According to his own account, he leaves his old trade and joins ours of his own free will and preference. You will no more believe that than I do. My notion is, that he has managed to ferret out some private information in connection with the affairs of one of his master's clients, which makes him rather an awkward customer to keep in the office for the future, and which, at the same time, gives him hold enough over his employer to make it dangerous to drive him into a corner by turning him away. I think the giving him this unheard-of chance among us is, in plain words, pretty much like giving him hush money to keep him quiet. However that may be, Mr. Matthew Sharpin is to have the case now in your hands, and if he succeeds with it he pokes his ugly nose into our office as sure as fate. I put you up to this, sergeant, so that you may not stand in your own light by giving the new man any cause to complain of you at headquarters, and remain yours,

FRANCIS THEAKSTONE.

FROM MR. MATTHEW SHARPIN TO CHIEF INSPECTOR THEAKSTONE.

London, 5th July, 18—.

DEAR SIR—Having now been favored with the necessary instructions from Sergeant Bulmer, I beg to remind you of certain directions which I have received relating to the report of my future proceedings which I am to prepare for examination at headquarters.

The object of my writing, and of your examining what I have written before you send it to the higher authorities, is, I am informed, to give me, as an untried hand, the benefit of your advice in case I want it (which I venture to think I shall not) at any stage of my proceedings. As the extraordinary circumstances of the case on which I am now engaged make it impossible for me to absent myself from the place where the robbery was committed until I have made some progress toward discovering the thief, I am necessarily precluded from consulting you personally. Hence the necessity of my writing down the various details, which might perhaps be better communicated by word of mouth. This, if I am not mistaken, is the position in which we are now placed. I state my own impressions on the subject in writing, in order that we may clearly understand each other at the outset; and have the honor to remain your obedient servant,

MATTHEW SHARPIN.

FROM CHIEF INSPECTOR THEAKSTONE TO MR. MATTHEW SHARPIN.

London, 5th July, 18—.

SIR—You have begun by wasting time, ink, and paper. We both of us perfectly well knew the position we stood in toward each other when I sent you with my letter to Sergeant Bulmer. There was not the least need to repeat it in writing. Be so good as to employ your pen in future on the business actually in hand.

You have now three separate matters on which to write me. First, you have to draw up a statement of your instructions received from Sergeant Bulmer, in order to show us that nothing has escaped your memory, and that you are thoroughly acquainted with all the circumstances of the case which has been intrusted to you. Secondly, you are to inform me what it is you propose to do. Thirdly, you are to report every inch of your progress (if you make any) from day to day, and, if need be, from hour to hour as well. This is *your* duty. As to what *my* duty may be, when I want you to remind me of it, I will write and tell you so. In the meantime, I remain yours,

FRANCIS THEAKSTONE.

FROM MR. MATTHEW SHARPIN TO CHIEF INSPECTOR THEAKSTONE.

London, 6th July, 18—.

SIR—You are rather an elderly person, and as such, naturally inclined to be a little jealous of men like me, who are in the prime of their lives and their faculties. Under these circumstances, it is my duty to be considerate toward you, and not to bear too hardly on your small failings. I decline, therefore, altogether to take offense at the tone of your letter; I give you the full benefit of the natural generosity of my nature; I sponge the very existence of your surly communication out of my memory—in short, Chief Inspector Theakstone, I forgive you, and proceed to business.

My first duty is to draw up a full statement of the instructions I have received from Sergeant Bulmer. Here they are at your service, according to my version of them.

At Number Thirteen Rutherford Street, Soho, there is a stationer's shop. It is kept by one Mr. Yatman. He is a married man, but has no family. Besides Mr. and Mrs. Yatman, the other inmates in the house are a lodger, a young single man named Jay, who occupies the front room on the second floor—a shopman, who sleeps in one of the attics, and a servant-of-all-work, whose bed is in the back kitchen. Once a week a charwoman comes to help this servant. These are all the persons who, on ordinary occasions, have means of access to the interior of the house, placed, as a matter of course, at their disposal. Mr. Yatman has been in business for many years, carrying on his affairs prosperously enough to realize a handsome independence for a person in his position. Unfortunately for himself, he endeavored to increase the amount of his property by speculating. He ventured boldly in his investments; luck went against him; and rather less than two years ago he found himself a poor man again. All that was saved out of the wreck of his property was the sum of two hundred pounds.

Although Mr. Yatman did his best to meet his altered circumstances, by giving up many of the luxuries and comforts to which he and his wife had been accustomed, he found it impossible to retrench so far as to allow of putting by any money from the income produced by his shop. The business has been declining of late years, the cheap advertising stationers having done it injury with the public. Consequently, up to the last week, the only surplus property possessed by Mr. Yatman consisted of the two hundred pounds which had been recovered from the wreck of his fortune. This sum was placed as a deposit in a joint-stock bank of the highest possible character.

Eight days ago Mr. Yatman and his lodger, Mr. Jay, held a conversation on the subject of the commercial difficulties which are hampering trade in all directions at the present time. Mr. Jay (who lives by supplying the newspapers with short paragraphs relating to accidents, offenses, and brief records of remarkable occurrences in general—who is, in short, what they call a penny-a-liner) told his landlord that he had been in the city that day and heard unfavorable rumors on the subject of the joint-stock banks. The rumors to which he alluded had already reached the ears of Mr. Yatman from other quarters, and the confirmation of them by his lodger had such an effect on his mind—predisposed as it was to alarm by the experience of his former losses—that he resolved to go at once to the bank and withdraw his deposit. It was then getting on toward the end of the afternoon, and he arrived just in time to receive his money before the bank closed.

He received the deposit in bank-notes of the following amounts: one fifty-pound note, three twenty-pound notes, six ten-pound notes, and six five-pound notes. His object in drawing the money in this form was to have it ready to lay out immediately in trifling loans, on good security, among the small tradespeople of his district, some of whom are sorely pressed for the very means of existence at the present time. Investments of this kind seemed to Mr. Yatman to be the most safe and the most profitable on which he could now venture.

He brought the money back in an envelope placed in his breast pocket, and asked his shopman, on getting home, to look for a small, flat, tin cash-box, which had not been used for years, and which, as Mr. Yatman remembered it, was exactly of the right size to hold the bank-notes. For some time the cash-box was searched for in vain. Mr. Yatman called to his wife to know if she had any idea where it was. The question was overheard by the servant-of-all-work, who was taking up the tea-tray at the time, and by Mr. Jay, who was coming downstairs on his way out to the theater. Ultimately the cash-box was found by the shopman. Mr. Yatman placed the bank-notes in it, secured them by a padlock, and put the box in his coat pocket. It stuck out of the coat pocket a very little, but enough to be seen. Mr. Yatman remained at home, upstairs, all that evening. No visitors called. At eleven o'clock he went to bed, and put the cash-box under his pillow.

When he and his wife woke the next morning the box was gone. Payment of the notes was immediately stopped at the Bank of England, but no news of the money has been heard of since that time.

So far the circumstances of the case are perfectly clear. They point unmistakably to the conclusion that the robbery must have been committed by some person living in the house. Suspicion falls, therefore, upon the servant-of-all-work, upon the shopman, and upon Mr. Jay. The two first knew that the cash-box was being inquired for by their master, but did not know what it was he wanted to put into it. They would assume, of course, that it was money. They both had opportunities (the servant when she took away the tea, and the shopman when he came, after shutting up, to give the keys of the till to his master) of seeing the cash-box in Mr. Yatman's pocket, and of inferring naturally, from its position there, that he intended to take it into his bedroom with him at night.

Mr. Jay, on the other hand, had been told, during the afternoon's conversation on the subject of joint-stock banks, that his landlord had a deposit of two hundred pounds in one of them. He also knew that Mr. Yatman left him with the intention of drawing that money out; and he heard the inquiry for the cash-box afterward, when he was coming downstairs. He must, therefore, have inferred that the money was in the house, and that the cash-box was the receptacle intended to contain it. That he could have had any idea, however, of the place in which Mr. Yatman intended to keep it for the night is impossible, seeing that he went out before the box was found, and did not return till his landlord was in bed. Consequently, if he committed the robbery, he must have gone into the bedroom purely on speculation.

Speaking of the bedroom reminds me of the necessity of noticing the situation of it in the house, and the means that exist of gaining easy access to it at any hour of the night.

The room in question is the back room on the first floor. In consequence of Mrs. Yatman's constitutional nervousness on the subject of fire, which makes her apprehend being burned alive in her room, in case of accident, by the hampering of the lock if the key is turned in it, her husband has never been accustomed to lock the bedroom door. Both he and his wife are, by their own admission, heavy sleepers; consequently, the risk to be run by any evil-disposed persons wishing to plunder the bedroom was of the most trifling kind. They could enter the room by merely turning the handle of the door; and, if they moved with ordinary caution, there was no fear of their waking the sleepers inside. This fact is of importance. It strengthens our conviction that the money must have been taken by one of the inmates of the house, because it tends to show that the robbery, in this case, might have been committed by persons not possessed of the superior vigilance and cunning of the experienced thief.

Such are the circumstances, as they were related to Sergeant Bulmer, when he was first called in to discover the guilty parties, and, if possible, to recover the lost bank-notes. The strictest inquiry which he could institute failed of producing the smallest fragment of evidence against any of the persons on whom suspicion naturally fell. Their language and behavior on being informed of the robbery was perfectly consistent with the language and behavior of innocent people. Sergeant Bulmer felt from the firs t that this was a case for private inquiry and secret observation. He began by recommending Mr. and Mrs. Yatman to affect a feeling of perfect confidence in the innocence of the persons living under their roof, and he then opened the campaign by employing himself in following the goings and comings, and in discovering the friends, the habits, and the secrets of the maid-of-all-work.

Three days and nights of exertion on his own part, and on that of others who were competent to assist his investigations, were enough to satisfy him that there was no sound cause for suspicion against the girl.

He next practiced the same precaution in relation to the shopman. There was more difficulty and uncertainty in privately clearing up this person's character without his knowledge, but the obstacles were at last smoothed away with tolerable success; and, though there is not the same amount of certainty in this case which there was in the case of the girl, there is still fair reason for supposing that the shopman has had nothing to do with the robbery of the cash-box.

As a necessary consequence of these proceedings, the range of suspicion now becomes limited to the lodger, Mr. Jay.

When I presented your letter of introduction to Sergeant Bulmer, he had already made some inquiries on the subject of this young man. The result, so far, has not been at all favorable. Mr. Jay's habits are irregular; he frequents public houses, and seems to be familiarly acquainted with a great many dissolute characters; he is in debt to most of the tradespeople whom he employs; he has not paid his rent to Mr. Yatman for the last month; yesterday evening he came home excited by liquor, and last week he was seen talking to a prize-fighter; in short, though Mr. Jay does call himself a journalist, in virtue of his penny-a-line contributions to the newspapers, he is a young man of low tastes, vulgar manners, and bad habits. Nothing has yet been discovered in relation to him which redounds to his credit in the smallest degree.

I have now reported, down to the very last details, all the particulars communicated to me by Sergeant Bulmer. I believe you will not find an omission anywhere; and I think you will admit, though you are prejudiced against me, that a clearer statement of facts was never laid before you than the statement I have now made. My next duty is to tell you what I propose to do now that the case is confided to my hands.

In the first place, it is clearly my business to take up the case at the point where Sergeant Bulmer has left it. On his authority, I am justified in assuming that I have no need to trouble myself about the maid-of-all-work and the shopman. Their characters are now to be considered as cleared up. What remains to be privately investigated is the question of the guilt or innocence of Mr. Jay. Before we give up the notes for lost, we must make sure, if we can, that he knows nothing about them.

This is the plan that I have adopted, with the full approval of Mr. and Mrs. Yatman, for discovering whether Mr. Jay is or is not the person who has stolen the cash-box:

I propose to-day to present myself at the house in the character of a young man who is looking for lodgings. The back room on the second floor will be shown to me as the room to let, and I shall establish myself there to-night as a person from the country who has come to London to look for a situation in a respectable shop or office.

By this means I shall be living next to the room occupied by Mr. Jay. The partition between us is mere lath and plaster. I shall make a small hole in it, near the cornice, through which I can see what Mr. Jay does in his room, and hear every word that is said when any friend happens to call on him. Whenever he is at home, I shall be at my post of observation; whenever he goes out, I shall be after him. By employing these means of watching him, I believe I may look forward to the discovery of his secret—if he knows anything about the lost bank-notes—as to a dead certainty.

What you may think of my plan of observation I cannot undertake to say. It appears to me to unite the invaluable merits of boldness and simplicity. Fortified by this conviction, I close the present communication with feelings of the most sanguine description in regard to the future, and remain your obedient servant,

MATTHEW SHARPIN.

FROM THE SAME TO THE SAME.

7th July.

SIR—As you have not honored me with any answer to my last communication, I assume that, in spite of your prejudices against me, it has produced the favorable impression on your mind which I ventured to anticipate. Gratified and encouraged beyond measure by the token of approval which your eloquent silence conveys to me, I proceed to report the progress that has been made in the course of the last twenty-four hours.

I am now comfortably established next door to Mr. Jay, and I am delighted to say that I have two holes in the partition instead of one. My natural sense of humor has led me into the pardonable extravagance of giving them both appropriate names. One I call my peep-hole, and the other my pipe-hole. The name of the first explains itself; the name of the second refers to a small tin pipe or tube inserted in the hole, and twisted so that the mouth of it comes close to my ear while I am standing at my post of observation. Thus, while I am looking at Mr. Jay through my peep-hole, I can hear every word that may be spoken in his room through my pipe-hole.

Perfect candor—a virtue which I have possessed from my childhood—compels me to acknowledge, before I go any further, that the ingenious notion of adding a pipe-hole to my proposed peep-hole originated with Mrs. Yatman. This lady—a most intelligent and accomplished person, simple, and yet distinguished in her manners, has entered into all my little plans with an enthusiasm and intelligence which I cannot too highly praise. Mr. Yatman is so cast down by his loss that he is quite incapable of affording me any assistance. Mrs. Yatman, who is evidently most tenderly attached to him, feels her husband's sad condition of mind even more acutely than she feels the loss of the money, and is mainly stimulated to exertion by her desire to assist in raising him from the miserable state of prostration into which he has now fallen.

"The money, Mr. Sharpin," she said to me yesterday evening, with tears in her eyes, "the money may be regained by rigid economy and strict attention to business. It is my husband's wretched state of mind that makes me so anxious for the discovery of the thief. I may be wrong, but I felt hopeful of success as soon as you entered the house; and I believe that, if the wretch who robbed us is to be found, you are the man to discover him." I accepted this gratifying compliment in the spirit in which it was offered, firmly believing that I shall be found, sooner or later, to have thoroughly deserved it.

Let me now return to business—that is to say, to my peep-hole and my pipe-hole.

I have enjoyed some hours of calm observation of Mr. Jay. Though rarely at home, as I understand from Mrs. Yatman, on ordinary occasions, he has been indoors the whole of this day. That is suspicious, to begin with. I have to report, further, that he rose at a late hour this morning (always a bad sign in a young man), and that he lost a great deal of time, after he was up, in yawning and complaining to himself of headache. Like other debauched characters, he ate little or nothing for breakfast. His next proceeding was to smoke a pipe—a dirty clay pipe, which a gentleman would have been ashamed to put between his lips. When he had done smoking he took out pen, ink and paper, and sat down to write with a groan—whether of remorse for having taken the bank-notes, or of disgust at the task before him, I am unable to say. After writing a few lines (too far away from my peep-hole to give me a chance of reading over his shoulder), he leaned back in his chair, and amused himself by humming the tunes of popular songs. I recognized "My Mary Anne," "Bobbin' Around," and "Old Dog Tray," among other melodies. Whether these do or do not represent secret signals by which he communicates with his accomplices remains to be seen. After he had amused himself for some time by humming, he got up and began to walk about the room, occasionally stopping to add a sentence to the paper on his desk. Before long he went to a locked cupboard and opened it. I strained my eyes eagerly, in expectation of making a discovery. I saw him take something carefully out of the cupboard—he turned round—and it was only a pint bottle of brandy! Having drunk some of the liquor, this extremely indolent reprobate lay down on his bed again, and in five minutes was fast asleep.

After hearing him snoring for at least two hours, I was recalled to my peep-hole by a knock at his door. He jumped up and opened it with suspicious activity.

A very small boy, with a very dirty face, walked in, said: "Please, sir, they're waiting for you," sat down on a chair with his legs a long way from the ground, and instantly fell asleep! Mr. Jay swore an oath, tied a wet towel round his head, and, going back to his paper, began to cover it with writing as fast as his fingers could move the pen. Occasionally getting up to dip the towel in water and tie it on again, he continued at this employment for nearly three hours; then folded up the leaves of writing, woke the boy, and gave them to him, with this remarkable expression: "Now, then, young sleepy-head, quick march! If you see the governor, tell him to have the money ready for me when I call for it." The boy grinned and disappeared. I was sorely tempted to follow "sleepy-head," but, on reflection, considered it safest still to keep my eye on the proceedings of Mr. Jay.

In half an hour's time he put on his hat and walked out. Of course I put on my hat and walked out also. As I went downstairs I passed Mrs. Yatman going up. The lady has been kind enough to undertake, by previous arrangement between us, to search Mr. Jay's room while he is out of the way, and while I am necessarily engaged in the pleasing duty of following him wherever he goes. On the occasion to which I now refer, he walked straight to the nearest tavern and ordered a couple of mutton-chops for his dinner. I placed myself in the next box to him, and ordered a couple of mutton-chops for my dinner. Before I had been in the room a minute, a young man of highly suspicious manners and appearance, sitting at a table opposite, took his glass of porter in his hand and joined Mr. Jay. I pretended to be reading the newspaper, and listened, as in duty bound, with all my might.

"Jack has been here inquiring after you," says the young man.

"Did he leave any message?" asks Mr. Jay.

"Yes," says the other. "He told me, if I met with you, to say that he wished very particularly to see you to-night, and that he would give you a look in at Rutherford Street at seven o'clock."

"All right," says Mr. Jay. "I'll get back in time to see him."

Upon this, the suspicious-looking young man finished his porter, and saying that he was rather in a hurry, took leave of his friend (perhaps I should not be wrong if I said his accomplice?), and left the room.

At twenty-five minutes and a half past six—in these serious cases it is important to be particular about time—Mr. Jay finished his chops and paid his bill. At twenty-six minutes and three-quarters I finished my chops and paid mine. In ten minutes more I was inside the house in Rutherford Street, and was received by Mrs. Yatman in the passage. That charming woman's face exhibited an expression of melancholy and disappointment which it quite grieved me to see.

"I am afraid, ma'am," says I, "that you have not hit on any little criminating discovery in the lodger's room?"

She shook her head and sighed. It was a soft, languid, fluttering sigh—and, upon my life, it quite upset me. For the moment I forgot business, and burned with envy of Mr. Yatman.

"Don't despair, ma'am," I said, with an insinuating mildness which seemed to touch her. "I have heard a mysterious conversation—I know of a guilty appointment—and I expect great things from my peep-hole and my pipe-hole to-night. Pray don't be alarmed, but I think we are on the brink of a discovery."

Here my enthusiastic devotion to business got the better part of my tender feelings. I looked—winked—nodded—left her.

When I got back to my observatory, I found Mr. Jay digesting his mutton-chops in an armchair, with his pipe in his mouth. On his table were two tumblers, a jug of water, and the pint bottle of brandy. It was then close upon seven o'clock. As the hour struck the person described as "Jack" walked in.

He looked agitated—I am happy to say he looked violently agitated. The cheerful glow of anticipated success diffused itself (to use a strong expression) all over me, from head to foot. With breathless interest I looked through my peep-hole, and saw the visitor—the "Jack" of this delightful case—sit down, facing me, at the opposite side of the table to Mr. Jay. Making allowance for the difference in expression which their countenances just now happened to exhibit, these two abandoned villains were so much alike in other respects as to lead at once to the conclusion that they were brothers. Jack was the cleaner man and the better dressed of the two. I admit that, at the outset. It is, perhaps, one of my failings to push justice and impartiality to their utmost limits. I am no Pharisee; and where Vice has its redeeming point, I say, let Vice have its due—yes, yes, by all manner of means, let Vice have its due.

"What's the matter now, Jack?" says Mr. Jay.

"Can't you see it in my face?" says Jack. "My dear fellow, delays are dangerous. Let us have done with suspense, and risk it, the day after to-morrow."

"So soon as that?" cries Mr. Jay, looking very much astonished. "Well, I'm ready, if you are. But, I say, Jack, is somebody else ready, too? Are you quite sure of that?"

He smiled as he spoke—a frightful smile—and laid a very strong emphasis on those two words, "Somebody else." There is evidently a third ruffian, a nameless desperado, concerned in the business.

"Meet us to-morrow," says Jack, "and judge for yourself. Be in the Regent's Park at eleven in the morning, and look out for us at the turning that leads to the Avenue Road."

"I'll be there," says Mr. Jay. "Have a drop of brandy-and-water? What are you getting up for? You're not going already?"

"Yes, I am," says Jack. "The fact is, I'm so excited and agitated that I can't sit still anywhere for five minutes together. Ridiculous as it may appear to you, I'm in a perpetual state of nervous flutter. I can't, for the life of me, help fearing that we shall be found out. I fancy that every man who looks twice at me in the street is a spy—"

At these words I thought my legs would have given way under me. Nothing but strength of mind kept me at my peep-hole—nothing else, I give you my word of honor.

"Stuff and nonsense!" cries Mr. Jay, with all the effrontery of a veteran in crime. "We have kept the secret up to this time, and we will manage cleverly to the end. Have a drop of brandy-and-water, and you will feel as certain about it as I do."

Jack steadily refused the brandy-and-water, and steadily persisted in taking his leave.

"I must try if I can't walk it off," he said. "Remember to-morrow morning—eleven o'clock, Avenue Road, side of the Regent's Park."

With those words he went out. His hardened relative laughed desperately and resumed the dirty clay pipe.

I sat down on the side of my bed, actually quivering with excitement.

It is clear to me that no attempt has yet been made to change the stolen bank-notes, and I may add that Sergeant Bulmer was of that opinion also when he left the case in my hands. What is the natural conclusion to draw from the conversation which I have just set down? Evidently that the confederates meet to-morrow to take their respective shares in the stolen money, and to decide on the safest means of getting the notes changed the day after. Mr. Jay is, beyond a doubt, the leading criminal in this business, and he will probably run the chief risk—that of changing the fifty-pound note. I shall, therefore, still make it my business to follow him—attending at the Regent's Par k to-morrow, and doing my best to hear what is said there. If another appointment is made for the day after, I shall, of course, go to it. In the meantime, I shall want the immediate assistance of two competent persons (supposing the rascals separate after their meeting) to follow the two minor criminals. It is only fair to add that, if the rogues all retire together, I shall probably keep my subordinates in reserve. Being naturally ambitious, I desire, if possible, to have the whole credit of discovering this robbery to myself.

8th July.

I have to acknowledge, with thanks, the speedy arrival of my two subordinates—men of very average abilities, I am afraid; but, fortunately, I shall always be on the spot to direct them.

My first business this morning was necessarily to prevent possible mistakes by accounting to Mr. and Mrs. Yatman for the presence of two strangers on the scene. Mr. Yatman (between ourselves, a poor, feeble man) only shook his head and groaned. Mrs. Yatman (that superior woman) favored me with a charming look of intelligence.

"Oh, Mr. Sharpin!" she said, "I am so sorry to see those two men! Your sending for their assistance looks as if you were beginning to be doubtful of success."

I privately winked at her (she is very good in allowing me to do so without taking offense), and told her, in my facetious way, that she labored under a slight mistake.

"It is because I am sure of success, ma'am, that I send for them. I am determined to recover the money, not for my own sake only, but for Mr. Yatman's sake—and for yours."

I laid a considerable amount of stress on those last three words. She said: "Oh, Mr. Sharpin!" again, and blushed of a heavenly red, and looked down at her work. I could go to the world's end with that woman if Mr. Yatman would only die.

I sent off the two subordinates to wait until I wanted them at the Avenue Road gate of the Regent's Park. Half-an-hour afterward I was following the same direction myself at the heels of Mr. Jay.

The two confederates were punctual to the appointed time. I blush to record it, but it is nevertheless necessary to state that the third rogue—the nameless desperado of my report, or, if you prefer it, the mysterious "somebody else" of the conversation between the two brothers—is—a woman! and, what is worse, a young woman! and, what is more lamentable still, a nice-looking woman! I have long resisted a growing conviction that, wherever there is mischief in this world, an individual of the fair sex is inevitably certain to be mixed up in it. After the experience of this morning, I can struggle against that sad conclusion no longer. I give up the sex—excepting Mrs. Yatman, I give up the sex.

The man named "Jack" offered the woman his arm. Mr. Jay placed himself on the other side of her. The three then walked away slowly among the trees. I followed them at a respectful distance. My two subordinates, at a respectful distance, also, followed me.

It was, I deeply regret to say, impossible to get near enough to them to overhear their conversation without running too great a risk of being discovered. I could only infer from their gestures and actions that they were all three talking with extraordinary earnestness on some subject which deeply interested them. After having been engaged in this way a full quarter of an hour, they suddenly turned round to retrace their steps. My presence of mind did not forsake me in this emergency. I signed to the two subordinates to walk on carelessly and pass them, while I myself slipped dexterously behind a tree. As they came by me, I heard "Jack" address these words to Mr. Jay:

"Let us say half-past ten to-morrow morning. And mind you come in a cab. We had better not risk taking one in this neighborhood."

Mr. Jay made some brief reply which I could not overhear. They walked back to the place at which they had met, shaking hands there with an audacious cordiality which it quite sickened me to see. They then separated. I followed Mr. Jay. My subordinates paid the same delicate attention to the other two.

Instead of taking me back to Rutherford Street, Mr. Jay led me to the Strand. He stopped at a dingy, disreputable-looking house, which, according to the inscription over the door, was a newspaper office, but which, in my judgment, had all the external appearance of a place devoted to the reception of stolen goods.

After remaining inside for a few minutes, he came out whistling, with his finger and thumb in his waistcoat pocket. Some men would now have arrested him on the spot. I remembered the necessity of catching the two confederates, and the importance of not interfering with the appointment that had been made for the next morning. Such coolness as this, under trying circumstances, is rarely to be found, I should imagine, in a young beginner, whose reputation as a detective policeman is still to make.

From the house of suspicious appearance Mr. Jay betook himself to a cigar-divan, and read the magazines over a cheroot. From the divan he strolled to the tavern and had his chops. I strolled to the tavern and had my chops. When he had done he went back to his lodging. When I had done I went back to mine. He was overcome with drowsiness early in the evening, and went to bed. As soon as I heard him snoring, I was overcome with drowsiness and went to bed also.

Early in the morning my two subordinates came to make their report.

They had seen the man named "Jack" leave the woman at the gate of an apparently respectable villa residence not far from the Regent's Park. Left to himself, he took a turning to the right, which led to a sort of suburban street, principally inhabited by shopkeepers. He stopped at the private door of one of the houses, and let himself in with his own key—looking about him as he opened the door, and staring suspiciously at my men as they lounged along on the opposite side of the way. These were all the particulars which the subordinates had to communicate. I kept them in my room to attend on me, if needful, and mounted to my peep-hole to have a look at Mr. Jay.

He was occupied in dressing himself, and was taking extraordinary pains to destroy all traces of the natural slovenliness of his appearance. This was precisely what I expected. A vagabond like Mr. Jay knows the importance of giving himself a respectable look when he is going to run the risk of changing a stolen bank-note. At five minutes past ten o'clock he had given the last brush to his shabby hat and the last scouring with bread-crumb to his dirty gloves. At ten minutes past ten he was in the street, on his way to the nearest cab-stand, and I and my subordinates were close on his heels.

He took a cab and we took a cab. I had not overheard them appoint a place of meeting when following them in the Park on the previous day, but I soon found that we were proceeding in the old direction of the Avenue Road gate. The cab in which Mr. Jay was riding turned into the Park slowly. We stopped outside, to avoid exciting suspicion. I got out to follow the cab on foot. Just as I did so, I saw it stop, and detected the two confederates approaching it from among the trees. They got in, and the cab was turned about directly. I ran back to my own cab and told the driver to let them pass him, and then to follow as before.

The man obeyed my directions, but so clumsily as to excite their suspicions. We had been driving after them about three minutes (returning along the road by which we had advanced) when I looked out of the window to see how far they might be ahead of us. As I did this, I saw two hats popped out of the windows of their cab, and two faces looking back at me. I sank into my place in a cold sweat; the expression is coarse, but no other form of words can describe my condition at that trying moment.

"We are found out!" I said, faintly, to my two subordinates. They stared at me in astonishment. My feelings changed instantly from the depth of despair to the height of indignation.

"It is the cabman's fault. Get out, one of you," I said, with dignity—"get out, and punch his head."

Instead of following my directions (I should wish this act of disobedience to be reported at headquarters) they both looked out of the window. Before I could pull them back they both sat down again. Before I could express my just indignation, they both grinned, and said to me: "Please to look out, sir!"

I did look out. Their cab had stopped.

Where?

At a church door!

What effect this discovery might have had upon the ordinary run of men I don't know. Being of a strong religious turn myself, it filled me with horror. I have often read of the unprincipled cunning of criminal persons, but I never before heard of three thieves attempting to double on their pursuers by entering a church! The sacrilegious audacity of that proceeding is, I should think, unparalleled in the annals of crime.

I checked my grinning subordinates by a frown. It was easy to see what was passing in their superficial minds. If I had not been able to look below the surface, I might, on observing two nicely dressed men and one nicely dressed woman enter a church before eleven in the morning on a week day, have come to the same hasty conclusion at which my inferiors had evidently arrived. As it was, appearances had no power to impose on *me*. I got out, and, followed by one of my men, entered the church. The other man I sent round to watch the vestry door. You may catch a weasel asleep, but not your humble servant, Matthew Sharpin!

We stole up the gallery stairs, diverged to the organ-loft, and peered through the curtains in front. There they were, all three, sitting in a pew below—yes, incredible as it may appear, sitting in a pew below!

Before I could determine what to do, a clergyman made his appearance in full canonicals from the vestry door, followed by a clerk. My brain whirled and my eyesight grew dim. Dark remembrances of robberies committed in vestries floated through my mind. I trembled for the excellent man in full canonicals—I even trembled for the clerk.

The clergyman placed himself inside the altar rails. The three desperadoes approached him. He opened his book and began to read. What? you will ask.

I answer, without the slightest hesitation, the first lines of the Marriage Service.

My subordinate had the audacity to look at me, and then to stuff his pocket-handkerchief into his mouth. I scorned to pay any attention to him. After I had discovered that the man "Jack" was the bridegroom, and that the man Jay acted the part of father, and gave away the bride, I left the church, followed by my men, and joined the other subordinate outside the vestry door. Some people in my position would now have felt rather crestfallen, and would have begun to think that they had made a very foolish mistake. Not the faintest misgiving of any kind troubled me. I did not feel in the slightest degree depreciated in my own estimation. And even now, after a lapse of three hours, my mind remains, I am happy to say, in the same calm and hopeful condition.

As soon as I and my subordinates were assembled together outside the church, I intimated my intention of still following the other cab in spite of what had occurred. My reason for deciding on this course will appear presently. The two subordinates appeared to be astonished at my resolution. One of them had the impertinence to say to me:

"If you please, sir, who is it that we are after? A man who has stolen money, or a man who has stolen a wife?"

The other low person encouraged him by laughing. Both have deserved an official reprimand, and both, I sincerely trust, will be sure to get it.

When the marriage ceremony was over, the three got into their cab and once more our vehicle (neatly hidden round the corner of the church, so that they could not suspect it to be near them) started to follow theirs.

We traced them to the terminus of the Southwestern Railway. The newly-married couple took tickets for Richmond, paying their fare with a half sovereign, and so depriving me of the pleasure of arresting them, which I should certainly have done if they had offered a bank-note. They parted from Mr. Jay, saying: "Remember the address—14 Babylon Terrace. You dine with us to-morrow week." Mr. Jay accepted the invitation, and added, jocosely, that he was going home at once to get off his clean clothes, and to be comfortable and dirty again for the rest of the day. I have to report that I saw him home safely, and that he is comfortable and dirty again (to use his own disgraceful language) at the present moment.

Here the affair rests, having by this time reached what I may call its first stage.

I know very well what persons of hasty judgment will be inclined to say of my proceedings thus far. They will assert that I have been deceiving myself all through in the most absurd way; they will declare that the suspicious conversations which I have reported referred solely to the difficulties and dangers of successfully carrying out a runaway match; and they will appeal to the scene in the church as offering undeniable proof of the correctness of their assertions. So let it be. I dispute nothing up to this point. But I ask a question, out of the depths of my own sagacity as a man of the world, which the bitterest of my enemies will not, I think, find it particularly easy to answer.

Granted the fact of the marriage, what proof does it afford me of the innocence of the three persons concerned in that clandestine transaction? It gives me none. On the contrary, it strengthens my suspicions against Mr. Jay and his confederates, because it suggests a distinct motive for their stealing the money. A gentleman who is going to spend his honeymoon at Richmond wants money; and a gentleman who is in debt to all his tradespeople wants money. Is this an unjustifiable imputation of bad motives? In the name of outraged Morality, I deny it. These men have combined together, and have stolen a woman. Why should they not combine together and steal a cash-box? I take my stand on the logic of rigid Virtue, and I defy all the sophistry of Vice to move me an inch out of my position.

Speaking of virtue, I may add that I have put this view of the case to Mr. and Mrs. Yatman. That accomplished and charming woman found it difficult at first to follow the close chain of my reasoning. I am free to confess that she shook her head, and shed tears, and joined her husband in premature lamentation over the loss of the two hundred pounds. But a little careful explanation on my part, and a little attentive listening on hers, ultimately changed her opinion. She now agrees with me that there is nothing in this unexpected circumstance of the clandestine marriage which absolutely tends to divert suspicion from Mr. Jay, or Mr. "Jack," or the runaway lady. "Audacious hussy" was the term my fair friend used in speaking of her; but let that pass. It is more to the purpose to record that Mrs. Yatman has not lost confidence in me, and that Mr. Yatman promises to follow her example, and do his best to look hopefully for future results.

I have now, in the new turn that circumstances have taken, to await advice from your office. I pause for fresh orders with all the composure of a man who has got two strings to his bow. When I traced the three confederates from the church door to the railway terminus, I had two motives for doing so. First, I followed them as a matter of official business, believing them still to have been guilty of the robbery. Secondly, I followed them as a matter of private speculation, with a view of discovering the place of refuge to which the runaway couple intended to retreat, and of making my information a marketable commodity to offer to the young lady's family and friends. Thus, whatever happens, I may congratulate myself beforehand on not having wasted my time. If the office approves of my conduct, I have my plan ready for further proceedings. If the office blames me, I shall take myself off, with my marketable information, to the genteel villa residence in the neighborhood of the Regent's Park. Anyway, the affair puts money into my pocket, and does credit to my penetration as an uncommonly sharp man.

I have only one word more to add, and it is this: If any individual ventures to assert that Mr. Jay and his confederates are innocent o f all share in the stealing of the cash-box, I, in return, defy that individual—though he may even be Chief Inspector Theakstone himself—to tell me who has committed the robbery at Rutherford Street, Soho.

Strong in that conviction, I have the honor to be your very obedient servant,

MATTHEW SHARPIN.

FROM CHIEF INSPECTOR THEAKSTONE TO SERGEANT BULMER.

Birmingham, July 9th.

SERGEANT BULMER—That empty-headed puppy, Mr. Matthew Sharpin, has made a mess of the case at Rutherford Street, exactly as I expected he would. Business keeps me in this town, so I write to you to set the matter straight. I inclose with this the pages of feeble scribble-scrabble which the creature Sharpin calls a report. Look them over; and when you have made your way through all the gabble, I think you will agree with me that the conceited booby has looked for the thief in every direction but the right one. You can lay your hand on the guilty person in five minutes, now. Settle the case at once; forward your report to me at this place, and tell Mr. Sharpin that he is suspended till further notice.

Yours, FRANCIS THEAKSTONE.

FROM SERGEANT BULMER TO CHIEF INSPECTOR THEAKSTONE.

London, July 10th.

INSPECTOR THEAKSTONE—Your letter and inclosure came safe to hand. Wise men, they say, may always learn something even from a fool. By the time I had got through Sharpin's maundering report of his own folly, I saw my way clear enough to the end of the Rutherford Street case, just as you thought I should. In half an hour's time I was at the house. The first person I saw there was Mr. Sharpin himself.

"Have you come to help me?" says he.

"Not exactly," says I. "I've come to tell you that you are suspended till further notice."

"Very good," says he, not taken down by so much as a single peg in his own estimation. "I thought you would be jealous of me. It's very natural and I don't blame you. Walk in, pray, and make yourself at home. I'm off to do a little detective business on my own account, in the neighborhood of the Regent's Park. Ta—ta, sergeant, ta—ta!"

With those words he took himself out of the way, which was exactly what I wanted him to do.

As soon as the maid-servant had shut the door, I told her to inform her master that I wanted to say a word to him in private. She showed me into the parlor behind the shop, and there was Mr. Yatman all alone, reading the newspaper.

"About this matter of the robbery, sir," says I.

He cut me short, peevishly enough, being naturally a poor, weak, womanish sort of man.

"Yes, yes, I know," says he. "You have come to tell me that your wonderfully clever man, who has bored holes in my second floor partition, has made a mistake, and is off the scent of the scoundrel who has stolen my money."

"Yes, sir," says I. "That *is* one of the things I came to tell you. But I have got something else to say besides that."

"Can you tell me who the thief is?" says he, more pettish than ever.

"Yes, sir," says I, "I think I can."

He put down the newspaper, and began to look rather anxious and frightened.

"Not my shopman?" says he. "I hope, for the man's own sake, it's not my shopman."

"Guess again, sir," says I.

"That idle slut, the maid?" says he.

"She is idle, sir," says I, "and she is also a slut; my first inquiries about her proved as much as that. But she's not the thief."

"Then, in the name of Heaven, who is?" says he.

"Will you please to prepare yourself for a very disagreeable surprise, sir?" says I. "And, in case you lose your temper, will you excuse my remarking that I am the stronger man of the two, and that if you allow yourself to lay hands on me, I may unintentionally hurt you, in pure self-defense."

He turned as pale as ashes, and pushed his chair two or three feet away from me.

"You have asked me to tell you, sir, who has taken your money," I went on. "If you insist on my giving you an answer—"

"I do insist," he said, faintly. "Who has taken it?"

"Your wife has taken it," I said, very quietly, and very positively at the same time.

He jumped out of the chair as if I had put a knife into him, and struck his fist on the table so heavily that the wood cracked again.

"Steady, sir," says I. "Flying into a passion won't help you to the truth."

"It's a lie!" says he, with another smack of his fist on the table—"a base, vile, infamous lie! How dare you—"

He stopped, and fell back into the chair again, looked about him in a bewildered way, and ended by bursting out crying.

"When your better sense comes back to you, sir," says I, "I am sure you will be gentleman enough to make an apology for the language you have just used. In the meantime, please to listen, if you can, to a word of explanation. Mr. Sharpin has sent in a report to our inspector of the most irregular and ridiculous kind, setting down not only all his own foolish doings and sayings, but the doings and sayings of Mrs. Yatman as well. In most cases, such a document would have been fit only for the waste paper basket; but in this particular case it so happens that Mr. Sharpin's budget of nonsense leads to a certain conclusion, which the simpleton of a writer has been quite innocent of suspecting from the beginning to the end. Of that conclusion I am so sure that I will forfeit my place if it does not turn out that Mrs. Yatman has been practicing upon the folly and conceit of this young man, and that she has tried to shield herself from discovery by purposely encouraging him to suspect the wrong persons. I tell you that confidently; and I will even go further. I will undertake to give a decided opinion as to why Mrs. Yatman took the money, and what she has done with it, or with a part of it. Nobody can look at that lady, sir, without being struck by the great taste and beauty of her dress—"

As I said those last words, the poor man seemed to find his powers of speech again. He cut me short directly as haughtily as if he had been a duke instead of a stationer.

"Try some other means of justifying your vile calumny against my wife," says he. "Her milliner's bill for the past year is on my file of receipted accounts at this moment."

"Excuse me, sir," says I, "but that proves nothing. Milliners, I must tell you, have a certain rascally custom which comes within the daily experience of our office. A married lady who wishes it can keep two accounts at her dressmaker's; one is the account which her husband sees and pays; the other is the private account, which contains all the extravagant items, and which the wife pays secretly, by installments, whenever she can. According to our usual experience, these installments are mostly squeezed out of the housekeeping money. In your case, I suspect, no installments have been paid; proceedings have been threatened; Mrs. Yatman, knowing your altered circumstances, has felt herself driven into a corner, and she has paid her private account out of your cash-box."

"I won't believe it," says he. "Every word you speak is an abominable insult to me and to my wife."

"Are you man enough, sir," says I, taking him up short, in order to save time and words, "to get that receipted bill you spoke of just now off the file, and come with me at once to the milliner's shop where Mrs. Yatman deals?"

He turned red in the face at that, got the bill directly, and put on his hat. I took out of my pocket-book the list containing the numbers of the lost notes, and we left the house together immediately.

Arrived at the milliner's (one of the expensive West-End houses, as I expected), I asked for a private interview, on important business, with the mistress of the concern. It was not the first time that she and I had met over the same delicate investigation. The moment she set eyes on me she sent for her husband. I mentioned who Mr. Yatman was, and what we wanted.

"This is strictly private?" inquires the husband. I nodded my head.

"And confidential?" says the wife. I nodded again.

"Do you see any objection, dear, to obliging the sergeant with a sight of the books?" says the husband.

"None in the world, love, if you approve of it," says the wife.

All this while poor Mr. Yatman sat looking the picture of astonishment and distress, q uite out of place at our polite conference. The books were brought, and one minute's look at the pages in which Mrs. Yatman's name figured was enough, and more than enough, to prove the truth of every word that I had spoken.

There, in one book, was the husband's account which Mr. Yatman had settled; and there, in the other, was the private account, crossed off also, the date of settlement being the very day after the loss of the cash-box. This said private account amounted to the sum of a hundred and seventy-five pounds, odd shillings, and it extended over a period of three years. Not a single installment had been paid on it. Under the last line was an entry to this effect: "Written to for the third time, June 23d." I pointed to it, and asked the milliner if that meant "last June." Yes, it did mean last June; and she now deeply regretted to say that it had been accompanied by a threat of legal proceedings.

"I thought you gave good customers more than three years' credit?" says I.

The milliner looks at Mr. Yatman, and whispers to me, "Not when a lady's husband gets into difficulties."

She pointed to the account as she spoke. The entries after the time when Mr. Yatman's circumstances became involved were just as extravagant, for a person in his wife's situation, as the entries for the year before that period. If the lady had economized in other things, she had certainly not economized in the matter of dress.

There was nothing left now but to examine the cash-book, for form's sake. The money had been paid in notes, the amounts and numbers of which exactly tallied with the figures set down in my list.

After that, I thought it best to get Mr. Yatman out of the house immediately. He was in such a pitiable condition that I called a cab and accompanied him home in it. At first he cried and raved like a child; but I soon quieted him; and I must add, to his credit, that he made me a most handsome apology for his language as the cab drew up at his house door. In return, I tried to give him some advice about how to set matters right for the future with his wife. He paid very little attention to me, and went upstairs muttering to himself about a separation. Whether Mrs. Yatman will come cleverly out of the scrape or not seems doubtful. I should say myself that she would go into screeching hysterics, and so frighten the poor man into forgiving her. But this is no business of ours. So far as we are concerned, the case is now at an end, and the present report may come to a conclusion along with it.

I remain, accordingly, yours to command,

THOMAS BULMER.

P.S.—I have to add that, on leaving Rutherford Street, I met Mr. Matthew Sharpin coming to pack up his things.

"Only think!" says he, rubbing his hands in great spirits, "I've been to the genteel villa residence, and the moment I mentioned my business they kicked me out directly. There were two witnesses of the assault, and it's worth a hundred pounds to me if it's worth a farthing."

"I wish you joy of your luck," says I.

"Thank you," says he. "When may I pay you the same compliment on finding the thief?"

"Whenever you like," says I, "for the thief is found."

"Just what I expected," says he. "I've done all the work, and now you cut in and claim all the credit—Mr. Jay, of course."

"No," says I.

"Who is it then?" says he.

"Ask Mrs. Yatman," says I. "She's waiting to tell you."

"All right! I'd much rather hear it from that charming woman than from you," says he, and goes into the house in a mighty hurry.

What do you think of that, Inspector Theakstone? Would you like to stand in Mr. Sharpin's shoes? I shouldn't, I can promise you.

FROM CHIEF INSPECTOR THEAKSTONE TO MR. MATTHEW SHARPIN.

July 12th.

SIR—Sergeant Bulmer has already told you to consider yourself suspended until further notice. I have now authority to add that your services as a member of the Detective police are positively declined. You will please to take this letter as notifying officially your dismissal from the force.

I may inform you, privately, that your rejection is not intended to cast any reflections on your character. It merely implies that you are not quite sharp enough for our purposes. If we *are* to have a new recruit among us, we should infinitely prefer Mrs. Yatman.

Your obedient servant,

FRANCIS THEAKSTONE.

NOTE ON THE PRECEDING CORRESPONDENCE, ADDED BY MR. THEAKSTONE.

The inspector is not in a position to append any explanations of importance to the last of the letters. It has been discovered that Mr. Matthew Sharpin left the house in Rutherford Street five minutes after his interview outside of it with Sergeant Bulmer, his manner expressing the liveliest emotions of terror and astonishment, and his left cheek displaying a bright patch of red, which looked as if it might have been the result of what is popularly termed a smart box on the ear. He was also heard by the shopman at Rutherford Street to use a very shocking expression in reference to Mrs. Yatman, and was seen to clinch his fist vindictively as he ran round the corner of the street. Nothing more has been heard of him; and it is conjectured that he has left London with the intention of offering his valuable services to the provincial police.

On the interesting domestic subject of Mr. and Mrs. Yatman still less is known. It has, however, been positively ascertained that the medical attendant of the family was sent for in a great hurry on the day when Mr. Yatman returned from the milliner's shop. The neighboring chemist received, soon afterward, a prescription of a soothing nature to make up for Mrs. Yatman. The day after, Mr. Yatman purchased some smelling-salts at the shop, and afterward appeared at the circulating library to ask for a novel descriptive of high life that would amuse an invalid lady. It has been inferred from these circumstances that he has not thought it desirable to carry out his threat of separating from his wife, at least in the present (presumed) condition of that lady's sensitive nervous system.

THE SEVENTH DAY.

FINE enough for our guest to go out again. Long, feathery lines of white cloud are waving upward in the sky, a sign of coming wind.

There was a steamer telegraphed yesterday from the West Indies. When the next vessel is announced from abroad, will it be George's ship?

I don't know how my brothers feel to-day, but the sudden cessation of my own literary labors has left me still in bad spirits. I tried to occupy my mind by reading, but my attention wandered. I went out into the garden, but it looked dreary; the autumn flowers were few and far between—the lawn was soaked and sodden with yesterday's rain. I wandered into Owen's room. He had returned to his painting, but was not working, as it struck me, with his customary assiduity and his customary sense of enjoyment.

We had a long talk together about George and Jessie and the future. Owen urged me to risk speaking of my son in her presence once more, on the chance of making her betray herself on a second occasion, and I determined to take his advice. But she was in such high spirits when she came home to dinner on this Seventh Day, and seemed so incapable, for the time being, of either feeling or speaking seriously, that I thought it wiser to wait till her variable mood altered again with the next wet day.

The number drawn this evening was Eight, being the number of the story which it had cost Owen so much labor to write. He looked a little fluttered and anxious as he opened the manuscript. This was the first occasion on which his ability as a narrator was to be brought to the test, and I saw him glance nervously at Jessie's attentive face.

"I need not trouble you with much in the way of preface," he said. "This is the story of a very remarkable event in the life of one of my brother clergymen. He and I became acquainted through being associated with each other in the management of a Missionary Society. I saw him for the last time in London when he was about to leave his country and his friends forever, and was then informed of the circumstances which have afforded the material for this narrative."

BROTHER OWEN'S STORY

of

THE PARSON'S SCRUPLE.

CHAPTER I.

IF you had been in the far West of England about thirteen years since, and if you had happened to take up one of the Cornish newspapers on a certain day of the month, which need not be specially mentioned, you would have seen this notice of a marriage at the top of a column:

On the third instant, at the parish church, the Reverend Alfred Carling, Rector of Penliddy, to Emily Harriet, relict of the late Fergus Duncan, Esq., of Glendarn, N. B.

The rector's marriage did not produce a very favorable impression in the town, solely in consequence of the unaccountable private and unpretending manner in which the ceremony had been performed. The middle-aged bride and bridegroom had walked quietly to church one morning, had been married by the curate before any one was aware of it, and had embarked immediately afterward in the steamer for Tenby, where they proposed to pass their honeymoon. The bride being a stranger at Penliddy, all inquiries about her previous history were fruitless, and the townspeople had no alternative but to trust to their own investigations for enlightenment when the rector and his wife came home to settle among their friends.

After six weeks' absence Mr. and Mrs. Carling returned, and the simple story of the rector's courtship and marriage was gathered together in fragments, by inquisitive friends, from his own lips and from the lips of his wife.

Mr. Carling and Mrs. Duncan had met at Torquay. The rector, who had exchanged houses and duties for the season with a brother clergyman settled at Torquay, had called on Mrs. Duncan in his clerical capacity, and had come away from the interview deeply impressed and interested by the widow's manners and conversation. The visits were repeated; the acquaintance grew into friendship, and the friendship into love—ardent, devoted love on both sides.

Middle-aged man though he was, this was Mr. Carling's first attachment, and it was met by the same freshness of feeling on the lady's part. Her life with her first husband had not been a happy one. She had made the fatal mistake of marrying to please her parents rather than herself, and had repented it ever afterward. On her husband's death his family had not behaved well to her, and she had passed her widowhood, with her only child, a daughter, in the retirement of a small Scotch town many miles away from the home of her married life. After a time the little girl's health had begun to fail, and, by the doctor's advice, she had migrated southward to the mild climate of Torquay. The change had proved to be of no avail; and, rather more than a year since, the child had died. The place where her darling was buried was a sacred place to her and she remained a resident at Torquay. Her position in the world was now a lonely one. She was herself an only child; her father and mother were both dead; and, excepting cousins, her one near relation left alive was a maternal uncle living in London.

These particulars were all related simply and unaffectedly before Mr. Carling ventured on the confession of his attachment. When he made his proposal of marriage, Mrs. Duncan received it with an excess of agitation which astonished and almost alarmed the inexperienced clergyman. As soon as she could speak, she begged with extraordinary earnestness and anxiety for a week to consider her answer, and requested Mr. Carling not to visit her on any account until the week had expired.

The next morning she and her maid departed for London. They did not return until the week for consideration had expired. On the eighth day Mr. Carling called again and was accepted.

The proposal to make the marriage as private as possible came from the lady. She had been to London to consult her uncle (whose health, she regretted to say, would not allow him to travel to Cornwall to give his niece away at the altar), and he agreed with Mrs. Duncan that the wedding could not be too private and unpretending. If it was made public, the family of her first husband would expect cards to be sent to them, and a renewal of intercourse, which would be painful on both sides, might be the consequence. Other friends in Scotland, again, would resent her marrying a second time at her age, and would distress her and annoy her future husband in many ways. She was anxious to break altogether with her past existence, and to begin a new and happier life untrammeled by any connection with former times and troubles. She urged these points, as she had received the offer of marriage, with an agitation which was almost painful to see. This peculiarity in her conduct, however, which might have irritated some men, and rendered others distrustful, had no unfavorable effect on Mr. Carling. He set it down to an excess of sensitiveness and delicacy which charmed him. He was himself—though he never would confess it—a shy, nervous man by nature. Ostentation of any sort was something which he shrank from instinctively, even in the simplest affairs of daily life; and his future wife's proposal to avoid all the usual ceremony and publicity of a wedding was therefore more than agreeable to him—it was a positive relief.

The courtship was kept secret at Torquay, and the marriage was celebrated privately at Penliddy. It found its way into the local newspapers as a matter of course, but it was not, as usual in such cases, also advertised in the *Times*. Both husband and wife were equally happy in the enjoyment of their new life, and equally unsocial in taking no measures whatever to publish it to others.

Such was the story of the rector's marriage. Socially, Mr. Carling's position was but little affected either way by the change in his life. As a bachelor, his circle of friends had been a small one, and when he married he made no attempt to enlarge it. He had never been popular with the inhabitants of his parish generally. Essentially a weak man, he was, like other weak men, only capable of asserting himself positively in serious matters by running into extremes. As a consequence of this moral defect, he presented some singular anomalies in character. In the ordinary affairs of life he was the gentlest and most yielding of men, but in all that related to strictness of religious principle he was the sternest and the most aggressive of fanatics. In the pulpit he was a preacher of merciless sermons—an interpreter of the Bible by the letter rather than by the spirit, as pitiless and gloomy as one of the Puritans of old; while, on the other hand, by his own fireside he was considerate, forbearing, and humble almost to a fault. As a necessary result of this singular inconsistency of character, he was feared, and sometimes even disliked, by the members of his congregation who only knew him as their pastor, and he was prized and loved by the small circle of friends who also knew him as a man.

Those friends gathered round him more closely and more affectionately than ever after his marriage, not on his own account only, but influenced also by the attractions that they found in the society of his wife. Her refinement and gentleness of manner; her extraordinary accomplishments as a musician; her unvarying sweetness of temper, and her quick, winning, womanly intelligence in conversation, charmed every one who approached her. She was quoted as a model wife and woman by all her husband's friends, and she amply deserved the character that they gave her. Although no children came to cheer it, a happier and a more admirable married life has seldom been witnessed in this world than the life which was once to be seen in the rectory house at Penliddy.

With these necessary explanations, that preliminary part of my narrative of which the events may be massed together generally, for brevity's sake, comes to a close. What I have next to tell is of a deeper and a more serious interest, and must be carefully related in detail.

The rector and his wife had lived together without, as I honestly believe, a harsh word or an unkind look once passing between them for upward of two years, when Mr. Carling took his first step toward the fatal future that was awaiting him by devoting his leisure hours to the apparently simple a nd harmless occupation of writing a pamphlet.

He had been connected for many years with one of our great Missionary Societies, and had taken as active a part as a country clergyman could in the management of its affairs. At the period of which I speak, certain influential members of the society had proposed a plan for greatly extending the sphere of its operations, trusting to a proportionate increase in the annual subscriptions to defray the additional expenses of the new movement. The question was not now brought forward for the first time. It had been agitated eight years previously, and the settlement of it had been at that time deferred to a future opportunity. The revival of the project, as usual in such cases, split the working members of the society into two parties; one party cautiously objecting to run any risks, the other hopefully declaring that the venture was a safe one, and that success was sure to attend it. Mr. Carling sided enthusiastically with the members who espoused this latter side of the question, and the object of his pamphlet was to address the subscribers to the society on the subject, and so to interest them in it as to win their charitable support, on a larger scale than usual, to the new project.

He had worked hard at his pamphlet, and had got more than half way through it, when he found himself brought to a stand-still for want of certain facts which had been produced on the discussion of the question eight years since, and which were necessary to the full and fair statement of his case.

At first he thought of writing to the secretary of the society for information; but, remembering that he had not held his office more than two years, he had thought it little likely that this gentleman would be able to help him, and looked back to his own Diary of the period to see if he had made any notes in it relating to the original discussion of the affair. He found a note referring in general terms only to the matter in hand, but alluding at the end to a report in the *Times* of the proceedings of a deputation from the society which had waited on a member of the government of that day, and to certain letters to the editor which had followed the publication of the report. The note described these letters as "very important," and Mr. Carling felt, as he put his Diary away again, that the successful conclusion of his pamphlet now depended on his being able to get access to the back numbers of the *Times* of eight years since.

It was winter time when he was thus stopped in his work, and the prospect of a journey to London (the only place he knew of at which files of the paper were to be found) did not present many attractions; and yet he could see no other and easier means of effecting his object. After considering for a little while and arriving at no positive conclusion, he left the study, and went into the drawing-room to consult his wife.

He found her working industriously by the blazing fire. She looked so happy and comfortable—so gentle and charming in her pretty little lace cap, and her warm brown morning-dress, with its bright cherry-colored ribbons, and its delicate swan's down trimming circling round her neck and nestling over her bosom, that he stooped and kissed her with the tenderness of his bridegroom days before he spoke. When he told her of the cause that had suspended his literary occupation, she listened, with the sensation of the kiss still lingering in her downcast eyes and her smiling lips, until he came to the subject of his Diary and its reference to the newspaper.

As he mentioned the name of the *Times* she altered and looked him straight in the face gravely.

"Can you suggest any plan, love," he went on, "which may save me the necessity of a journey to London at this bleak time of the year? I must positively have this information, and, so far as I can see, London is the only place at which I can hope to meet with a file of the *Times*."

"A file of the *Times?*" she repeated.

"Yes—of eight years since," he said.

The instant the words passed his lips he saw her face overspread by a ghastly paleness; her eyes fixed on him with a strange mixture of rigidity and vacancy in their look; her hands, with her work held tight in them, dropped slowly on her lap, and a shiver ran through her from head to foot.

He sprang to his feet, and snatched the smelling-salts from her work-table, thinking she was going to faint. She put the bottle from her, when he offered it, with a hand that thrilled him with the deadly coldness of its touch, and said, in a whisper:

"A sudden chill, dear—let me go upstairs and lie down."

He took her to her room. As he laid her down on the bed, she caught his hand, and said, entreatingly:

"You won't go to London, darling, and leave me here ill?"

He promised that nothing should separate him from her until she was well again, and then ran downstairs to send for the doctor. The doctor came, and pronounced that Mrs. Carling was only suffering from a nervous attack; that there was not the least reason to be alarmed; and that, with proper care, she would be well again in a few days.

Both husband and wife had a dinner engagement in the town for that evening. Mr. Carling proposed to write an apology and to remain with his wife. But she would not hear of his abandoning the party on her account. The doctor also recommended that his patient should be left to her maid's care, to fall asleep under the influence of the quieting medicine which he meant to give her. Yielding to this advice, Mr. Carling did his best to suppress his own anxieties, and went to the dinner-party.

CHAPTER II.

AMONG the guests whom the rector met was a gentleman named Rambert, a single man of large fortune, well known in the neighborhood of Penliddy as the owner of a noble country-seat and the possessor of a magnificent library.

Mr. Rambert (with whom Mr. Carling was well acquainted) greeted him at the dinner-party with friendly expressions of regret at the time that had elapsed since they had last seen each other, and mentioned that he had recently been adding to his collection of books some rare old volumes of theology, which he thought the rector might find it useful to look over. Mr. Carling, with the necessity of finishing his pamphlet uppermost in his mind, replied, jestingly, that the species of literature which he was just then most interested in examining happened to be precisely of the sort which (excepting novels, perhaps) had least affinity to theological writing. The necessary explanation followed this avowal as a matter of course, and, to Mr. Carling's great delight, his friend turned on him gayly with the most surprising and satisfactory of answers:

"You don't know half the resources of my miles of bookshelves," he said, "or you would never have thought of going to London for what you can get from me. A whole side of one of my rooms upstairs is devoted to periodical literature. I have reviews, magazines, and three weekly newspapers, bound, in each case, from the first number; and, what is just now more to your purpose, I have the *Times* for the last fifteen years in huge half-yearly volumes. Give me the date to-night, and you shall have the volume you want by two o'clock to-morrow afternoon."

The necessary information was given at once, and, with a great sense of relief, so far as his literary anxieties were concerned, Mr. Carling went home early to see what the quieting medicine had done for his wife.

She had dozed a little, but had not slept. However, she was evidently better, for she was able to take an interest in the sayings and doings at the dinner-party, and questioned her husband about the guests and the conversation with all a woman's curiosity about the minutest matters. She lay with her face turned toward him and her eyes meeting his, until the course of her inquiries drew an answer from him, which informed her of his fortunate discovery in relation to Mr. Rambert's library, and of the prospect it afforded of his resuming his labors the next day.

When he mentioned this circumstance, she suddenly turned her head on the pillow so that her face was hidden from him, and he cou ld see through the counterpane that the shivering, which he had observed when her illness had seized her in the morning, had returned again.

"I am only cold," she said, in a hurried way, with her face under the clothes.

He rang for the maid, and had a fresh covering placed on the bed. Observing that she seemed unwilling to be disturbed, he did not remove the clothes from her face when he wished her goodnight, but pressed his lips on her head, and patted it gently with his hand. She shrank at the touch as if it hurt her, light as it was, and he went downstairs, resolved to send for the doctor again if she did not get to rest on being left quiet. In less than half an hour afterward the maid came down and relieved his anxiety by reporting that her mistress was asleep.

The next morning he found her in better spirits. Her eyes, she said, felt too weak to bear the light, so she kept the bedroom darkened. But in other respects she had little to complain of.

After answering her husband's first inquiries, she questioned him about his plans for the day. He had letters to write which would occupy him until twelve o'clock. At two o'clock he expected the volume of the *Times* to arrive, and he should then devote the rest of the afternoon to his work. After hearing what his plans were, Mrs. Carling suggested that he should ride out after he had done his letters, so as to get some exercise at the fine part of the day; and she then reminded him that a longer time than usual had elapsed since he had been to see a certain old pensioner of his, who had nursed him as a child, and who was now bedridden, in a village at some distance, called Tringweighton. Although the rector saw no immediate necessity for making this charitable visit, the more especially as the ride to the village and back, and the intermediate time devoted to gossip, would occupy at least two hours and a half, he assented to his wife's proposal, perceiving that she urged it with unusual earnestness, and being unwilling to thwart her, even in a trifle, at a time when she was ill.

Accordingly, his horse was at the door at twelve precisely. Impatient to get back to the precious volume of the *Times,* he rode so much faster than usual, and so shortened his visit to the old woman, that he was home again by a quarter past two. Ascertaining from the servant who opened the door that the volume had been left by Mr. Rambert's messenger punctually at two, he ran up to his wife's room to tell her about his visit before he secluded himself for the rest of the afternoon over his work. On entering the bedroom he found it still darkened, and he was struck by a smell of burned paper in it.

His wife (who was now dressed in her wrapper and lying on the sofa) accounted for the smell by telling him that she had fancied the room felt close, and that she had burned some paper—being afraid of the cold air if she opened the window—to fumigate it. Her eyes were evidently still weak, for she kept her hand over them while she spoke. After remaining with her long enough to relate the few trivial events of his ride, Mr. Carling descended to his study to occupy himself at last with the volume of the *Times.*

It lay on his table in the shape of a large flat brown paper package. On proceeding to undo the covering, he observed that it had been very carelessly tied up. The strings were crooked and loosely knotted, and the direction bearing his name and address, instead of being in the middle of the paper, was awkwardly folded over at the edge of the volume. However, his business was with the inside of the parcel; so he tossed away the covering and the string, and began at once to hunt through the volume for the particular number of the paper which he wished first to consult.

He soon found it, with the report of the speeches delivered by the members of the deputation, and the answer returned by the minister. After reading through the report, and putting a mark in the place where it occurred, he turned to the next day's number of the paper, to see what further hints on the subject the letters addressed to the editor might happen to contain.

To his inexpressible vexation and amazement, he found that one number of the paper was missing.

He bent the two sides of the volume back, looked closely between the leaves, and saw immediately that the missing number had been cut out.

A vague sense of something like alarm began to mingle with his first feeling of disappointment. He wrote at once to Mr. Rambert, mentioning the discovery he had just made, and sent the note off by his groom, with orders to the man to wait for an answer.

The reply with which the servant returned was almost insolent in the shortness and coolness of its tone. Mr. Rambert had no books in his library which were not in perfect condition. The volume of the *Times* had left his house perfect, and whatever blame might attach to the mutilation of it rested therefore on other shoulders than those of the owner.

Like many other weak men, Mr. Carling was secretly touchy on the subject of his dignity. After reading the note and questioning his servants, who were certain that the volume had not been touched till he had opened it, he resolved that the missing number of the *Times* should be procured at any expense and inserted in its place; that the volume should be sent back instantly without a word of comment; and that no more books from Mr. Rambert's library should enter his house.

He walked up and down the study considering what first step he should take to effect the purpose in view. Under the quickening influence of his irritation, an idea occurred to him, which, if it had only entered his mind the day before, might probably have proved the means of saving him from placing himself under an obligation to Mr. Rambert. He resolved to write immediately to his bookseller and publisher in London (who knew him well as an old and excellent customer), mentioning the date of the back number of the *Times* that was required, and authorizing the publisher to offer any reward he judged necessary to any person who might have the means of procuring it at the office of the paper or elsewhere. This letter he wrote and dispatched in good time for the London post, and then went upstairs to see his wife and to tell her what had happened. Her room was still darkened and she was still on the sofa. On the subject of the missing number she said nothing, but of Mr. Rambert and his note she spoke with the most sovereign contempt. Of course the pompous old fool was mistaken, and the proper thing to do was to send back the volume instantly and take no more notice of him.

"It shall be sent back," said Mr. Carling, "but not till the missing number is replaced." And he then told her what he had done.

The effect of that simple piece of information on Mrs. Carling was so extraordinary and so unaccountable that her husband fairly stood aghast. For the first time since their marriage he saw her temper suddenly in a flame. She started up from the sofa and walked about the room as if she had lost her senses, upbraiding him for making the weakest of concessions to Mr. Rambert's insolent assumption that the rector was to blame. If she could only have laid hands on that letter, she would have consulted her husband's dignity and independence by putting it in the fire! She hoped and prayed the number of the paper might not be found! In fact, it was certain that the number, after all these years, could not possibly be hunted up. The idea of his acknowledging himself to be in the wrong in that way, when he knew himself to be in the right! It was almost ridiculous— no, it was *quite* ridiculous! And she threw herself back on the sofa, and suddenly burst out laughing.

At the first word of remonstrance which fell from her husband's lips her mood changed again in an instant. She sprang up once more, kissed him passionately, with the tears streaming from her eyes, and implored him to leave her alone to recover herself. He quitted the room so seriously alarmed about her that he resolved to go to the doctor privately and question him on the spot. There was an unspeakable dread in his mind that the ner vous attack from which she had been pronounced to be suffering might be a mere phrase intended to prepare him for the future disclosure of something infinitely and indescribably worse.

The doctor, on hearing Mr. Carling's report, exhibited no surprise and held to his opinion. Her nervous system was out of order, and her husband had been needlessly frightened by a hysterical paroxysm. If she did not get better in a week, change of scene might then be tried. In the meantime, there was not the least cause for alarm.

On the next day she was quieter, but she hardly spoke at all. At night she slept well, and Mr. Carling's faith in the medical man revived again.

The morning after was the morning which would bring the answer from the publisher in London. The rector's study was on the ground floor, and when he heard the postman's knock, being especially anxious that morning about his correspondence, he went out into the hall to receive his letters the moment they were put on the table.

It was not the footman who had answered the door, as usual, but Mrs. Carling's maid. She had taken the letters from the postman, and she was going away with them upstairs.

He stopped her, and asked her why she did not put the letters on the hall table as usual. The maid, looking very much confused, said that her mistress had desired that whatever the postman had brought that morning should be carried up to her room. He took the letters abruptly from the girl, without asking any more questions, and went back into his study.

Up to this time no shadow of a suspicion had fallen on his mind. Hitherto there had been a simple obvious explanation for every unusual event that had occurred during the last three or four days; but this last circumstance in connection with the letters was not to be accounted for. Nevertheless, even now, it was not distrust of his wife that was busy at his mind—he was too fond of her and too proud of her to feel it—the sensation was more like uneasy surprise. He longed to go and question her, and get a satisfactory answer, and have done with it. But there was a voice speaking within him that had never made itself heard before—a voice with a persistent warning in it, that said, Wait; and look at your letters first.

He spread them out on the table with hands that trembled he knew not why. Among them was the back number of the *Times* for which he had written to London, with a letter from the publisher explaining the means by which the copy had been procured.

He opened the newspaper with a vague feeling of alarm at finding that those letters to the editor which he had been so eager to read, and that perfecting of the mutilated volume which he had been so anxious to accomplish, had become objects of secondary importance in his mind. An inexplicable curiosity about the general contents of the paper was now the one moving influence which asserted itself within him, he spread open the broad sheet on the table.

The first page on which his eye fell was the page on the right-hand side. It contained those very letters—three in number—which he had once been so anxious to see. He tried to read them, but no effort could fix his wandering attention. He looked aside to the opposite page, on the left hand. It was the page that contained the leading articles.

They were three in number. The first was on foreign politics; the second was a sarcastic commentary on a recent division in the House of Lords; the third was one of those articles on social subjects which have greatly and honorably helped to raise the reputation of the *Times* above all contest and all rivalry.

The lines of this third article which first caught his eye comprised the opening sentence of the second paragraph, and contained these words:

It appears, from the narrative which will be found in another part of our columns, that this unfortunate woman married, in the spring of the year 18—, one Mr. Fergus Duncan, of Glendarn, in the Highlands of Scotland. . .

The letters swam and mingled together under his eyes before he could go on to the next sentence. His wife exhibited as an object for public compassion in the *Times* newspaper! On the brink of the dreadful discovery that was advancing on him, his mind reeled back, and a deadly faintness came over him. There was water on a side-table—he drank a deep draught of it—roused himself—seized on the newspaper with both hands, as if it had been a living thing that could feel the desperate resolution of his grasp, and read the article through, sentence by sentence, word by word.

The subject was the Law of Divorce, and the example quoted was the example of his wife.

At that time England stood disgracefully alone as the one civilized country in the world having a divorce law for the husband which was not also a divorce law for the wife. The writer in the *Times* boldly and eloquently exposed this discreditable anomaly in the administration of justice; hinted delicately at the unutterable wrongs suffered by Mrs. Duncan; and plainly showed that she was indebted to the accident of having been married in Scotland, and to her consequent right of appeal to the Scotch tribunals, for a full and final release from the tie that bound her to the vilest of husbands, which the English law of that day would have mercilessly refused.

He read that. Other men might have gone on to the narrative extracted from the Scotch newspaper. But at the last word of the article *he* stopped.

The newspaper, and the unread details which it contained, lost all hold on his attention in an instant, and in their stead, living and burning on his mind, like the Letters of Doom on the walls of Belshazzar, there rose up in judgment against him the last words of a verse in the Gospel of Saint Luke—

"Whosoever marrieth her that is put away from her husband, committeth adultery."

He had preached from these words, he had warned his hearers, with the whole strength of the fanatical sincerity that was in him, to beware of prevaricating with the prohibition which that verse contained, and to accept it as literally, unreservedly, finally forbidding the marriage of a divorced woman. He had insisted on that plain interpretation of plain words in terms which had made his congregation tremble. And now he stood alone in the secrecy of his own chamber self-convicted of the deadly sin which he had denounced—he stood, as he had told the wicked among his hearers that they would stand at the Last Day, before the Judgment Seat.

He was unconscious of the lapse of time; he never knew whether it was many minutes or few before the door of his room was suddenly and softly opened. It did open, and his wife came in.

In her white dress, with a white shawl thrown over her shoulders; her dark hair, so neat and glossy at other times, hanging tangled about her colorless cheeks, and heightening the glassy brightness of terror in her eyes—so he saw her; the woman put away from her husband—the woman whose love had made his life happy and had stained his soul with a deadly sin.

She came on to within a few paces of him without a word or a tear, or a shadow of change passing over the dreadful rigidity of her face. She looked at him with a strange look; she pointed to the newspaper crumpled in his hand with a strange gesture; she spoke to him in a strange voice.

"You know it!" she said.

His eyes met hers—she shrank from them—turned—and laid her arms and her head heavily against the wall.

"Oh, Alfred," she said, "I was so lonely in the world, and I was so fond of you!"

The woman's delicacy, the woman's trembling tenderness welled up from her heart, and touched her voice with a tone of its old sweetness as she murmured those simple words.

She said no more. Her confession of her fault, her appeal to their past love for pardon, were both poured forth in that one sentence. She left it to his own heart to tell him the rest. How anxiously her vigilant love had followed his every word and treasured up his every opinion in the days when they first met; how weakly and falsely, and yet with how true an affection for him, she had shrunk from the disclosure which she knew but too well would have separated them even at the church door; how desperately she had fought against the coming discovery which threatened to tear her from the bosom she clung to, and to cast her out into the world with the shadow of her own shame to darken her life to the end—all this she left him to feel; for the moment which might part them forever was the moment when she knew best how truly, how passionately he had loved her.

His lips trembled as he stood looking at her in silence, and the slow, burning tears dropped heavily, one by one, down his cheeks. The natural human remembrance of the golden days of their companionship, of the nights and nights when that dear head—turned away from him now in unutterable misery and shame—had nestled itself so fondly and so happily on his breast, fought hard to silence his conscience, to root out his dreadful sense of guilt, to tear the words of Judgment from their ruthless hold on his mind, to claim him in the sweet names of Pity and of Love. If she had turned and looked at him at that moment, their next words would have been spoken in each other's arms. But the oppression of her despair under his silence was too heavy for her, and she never moved.

He forced himself to look away from her; he struggled hard to break the silence between them.

"God forgive you, Emily!" he said.

As her name passed his lips, his voice failed him, and the torture at his heart burst its way out in sobs. He hurried to the door to spare her the terrible reproof of the grief that had now mastered him. When he passed her she turned toward him with a faint cry.

He caught her as she sank forward, and saved her from dropping on the floor. For the last time his arms closed round her. For the last time his lips touched hers—cold and insensible to him now. He laid her on the sofa and went out.

One of the female servants was crossing the hall. The girl started as she met him, and turned pale at the sight of his face. He could not speak to her, but he pointed to the study door. He saw her go into the room, and then left the house.

He never entered it more, and he and his wife never met again.

Later on that last day, a sister of Mr. Carling's—a married woman living in the town—came to the rectory. She brought an open note with her, addressed to the unhappy mistress of the house. It contained these few lines, blotted and stained with tears:

May God grant us both the time for repentance! If I had loved you less, I might have trusted myself to see you again. Forgive me, and pity me, and remember me in your prayers, as I shall forgive, and pity, and remember you.

He had tried to write more, but the pen had dropped from his hand. His sister's entreaties had not moved him. After giving her the note to deliver, he had solemnly charged her to be gentle in communicating the tidings that she bore, and had departed alone for London. He heard all remonstrances with patience. He did not deny that the deception of which his wife had been guilty was the most pardonable of all concealments of the truth, because it sprang from her love for him; but he had the same hopeless answer for every one who tried to plead with him—the verse from the Gospel of Saint Luke.

His purpose in traveling to London was to make the necessary arrangements for his wife's future existence, and then to get employment which would separate him from his home and from all its associations. A missionary expedition to one of the Pacific Islands accepted him as a volunteer. Broken in body and spirit, his last look of England from the deck of the ship was his last look at land. A fortnight afterward, his brethren read the burial-service over him on a calm, cloudless evening at sea. Before he was committed to the deep, his little pocket Bible, which had been a present from his wife, was, in accordance with his dying wishes, placed open on his breast, so that the inscription, "To my dear Husband," might rest over his heart.

His unhappy wife still lives. When the farewell lines of her husband's writing reached her she was incapable of comprehending them. The mental prostration which had followed the parting scene was soon complicated by physical suffering—by fever on the brain. To the surprise of all who attended her, she lived through the shock, recovering with the complete loss of one faculty, which, in her situation, poor thing, was a mercy and a gain to her—the faculty of memory. From that time to this she has never had the slightest gleam of recollection of anything that happened before her illness. In her happy oblivion, the veriest trifles are as new and as interesting to her as if she was beginning her existence again. Under the tender care of the friends who now protect her, she lives contentedly the life of a child. When her last hour comes, may she die with nothing on her memory but the recollection of their kindness!

THE EIGHTH DAY.

THE wind that I saw in the sky yesterday has come. It sweeps down our little valley in angry howling gusts, and drives the heavy showers before it in great sheets of spray.

There are some people who find a strangely exciting effect produced on their spirits by the noise, and rush, and tumult of the elements on a stormy day. It has never been so with me, and it is less so than ever now. I can hardly bear to think of my son at sea in such a tempest as this. While I can still get no news of his ship, morbid fancies beset me which I vainly try to shake off. I see the trees through my window bending before the wind. Are the masts of the good ship bending like them at this moment? I hear the wash of the driving rain. Is *he* hearing the thunder of the raging waves? If he had only come back last night!—it is vain to dwell on it, but the thought will haunt me—if he had only come back last night!

I tried to speak cautiously about him again to Jessie, as Owen had advised me; but I am so old and feeble now that this ill-omened storm has upset me, and I could not feel sure enough of my own self-control to venture on matching myself to-day against a light-hearted, lively girl, with all her wits about her. It is so important that I should not betray George—it would be so inexcusable on my part if his interests suffered, even accidentally, in my hands.

This was a trying day for our guest. Her few trifling indoor resources had, as I could see, begun to lose their attractions for her at last. If we were not now getting to the end of the stories, and to the end, therefore, of the Ten Days also, our chance of keeping her much longer at the Glen Tower would be a very poor one.

It was, I think, a great relief for us all to be summoned together this evening for a definite purpose. The wind had fallen a little as it got on toward dusk. To hear it growing gradually fainter and fainter in the valley below added immeasurably to the comforting influence of the blazing fire and the cheerful lights when the shutters were closed for the night.

The number drawn happened to be the last of the series—Ten—and the last also of the stories which I had written. There were now but two numbers left in the bowl. Owen and Morgan had each one reading more to accomplish before our guest's stay came to an end, and the manuscripts in the Purple Volume were all exhausted.

"This new story of mine," I said, "is not, like the story I last read, a narrative of adventure happening to myself, but of adventures that happened to a lady of my acquaintance. I was brought into contact, in the first instance, with one of her male relatives, and, in the second instance, with the lady herself, by certain professional circumstances which I need not particularly describe. They involved a dry question of wills and title-deeds in no way connected with this story, but sufficiently important to interest me as a lawyer. The case came to trial at the Assizes on my circuit, and I won it in the face of some very strong points, very well put, on the other side. I was in poor health at the time, and my exertions so completely knocked me up that I was confined to bed in my lodgings for a week or more—"

"And the grateful lady came and nursed you, I suppose," said the Queen of Hearts, in her smart, off-h and way.

"The grateful lady did something much more natural in her position, and much more useful in mine," I answered—"she sent her servant to attend on me. He was an elderly man, who had been in her service since the time of her first marriage, and he was also one of the most sensible and well-informed persons whom I have ever met with in his station of life. From hints which he dropped while he was at my bedside, I discovered for the first time that his mistress had been unfortunate in her second marriage, and that the troubles of that period of her life had ended in one of the most singular events which had happened in that part of England for many a long day past. It is hardly necessary to say that, before I allowed the man to enter into any particulars, I stipulated that he should obtain his mistress's leave to communicate what he knew. Having gained this, and having further surprised me by mentioning that he had been himself connected with all the circumstances, he told me the whole story in the fullest detail. I have now tried to reproduce it as nearly as I could in his own language. Imagine, therefore, that I am just languidly recovering in bed, and that a respectable elderly man, in quiet black costume, is sitting at my pillow and speaking to me in these terms—"

Thus ending my little preface, I opened the manuscript and began my last story.

BROTHER GRIFFITH'S STORY

of

A PLOT IN PRIVATE LIFE.

CHAPTER I.

THE first place I got when I began going out to service was not a very profitable one. I certainly gained the advantage of learning my business thoroughly, but I never had my due in the matter of wages. My master was made a bankrupt, and his servants suffered with the rest of his creditors

My second situation, however, amply compensated me for my want of luck in the first. I had the good fortune to enter the service of Mr. and Mrs. Norcross. My master was a very rich gentleman. He had the Darrock house and lands in Cumberland, an estate also in Yorkshire, and a very large property in Jamaica, which produced, at that time and for some years afterward, a great income. Out in the West Indies he met with a pretty young lady, a governess in an English family, and, taking a violent fancy to her, married her, though she was a good five-and-twenty years younger than himself. After the wedding they came to England, and it was at this time that I was lucky enough to be engaged by them as a servant.

I lived with my new master and mistress three years. They had no children. At the end of that period Mr. Norcross died. He was sharp enough to foresee that his young widow would marry again, and he bequeathed his property so that it all went to Mrs. Norcross first, and then to any children she might have by a second marriage, and, failing that, to relations and friends of his own. I did not suffer by my master's death, for his widow kept me in her service. I had attended on Mr. Norcross all through his last illness, and had made myself useful enough to win my mistress's favor and gratitude. Besides me she also retained her maid in her service—a quadroon woman named Josephine, whom she brought with her from the West Indies. Even at that time I disliked the half-breed's wheedling manners, and her cruel, tawny face, and wondered how my mistress could be so fond of her as she was. Time showed that I was right in distrusting this woman. I shall have much more to say about her when I get further advanced with my story.

Meanwhile I have next to relate that my mistress broke up the rest of her establishment, and, taking me and the lady's maid with her, went to travel on the Continent.

Among other wonderful places we visited Paris, Genoa, Venice, Florence, Rome, and Naples, staying in some of those cities for months together. The fame of my mistress's riches followed her wherever she went; and there were plenty of gentlemen, foreigners as well as Englishmen, who were anxious enough to get into her good graces and to prevail on her to marry them. Nobody succeeded, however, in producing any very strong or lasting impression on her; and when we came back to England, after more than two years of absence, Mrs. Norcross was still a widow, and showed no signs of wanting to change her condition.

We went to the house on the Yorkshire estate first; but my mistress did not fancy some of the company round about, so we moved again to Darrock Hall, and made excursions from time to time in the lake district, some miles off. On one of these trips Mrs. Norcross met with some old friends, who introduced her to a gentleman of their party bearing the very common and very uninteresting name of Mr. James Smith.

He was a tall, fine young man enough, with black hair, which grew very long, and the biggest, bushiest pair of black whiskers I ever saw. Altogether he had a rakish, unsettled look, and a bounceable way of talking which made him the prominent person in company. He was poor enough himself, as I heard from his servant, but well connected—a gentleman by birth and education, though his manners were so free. What my mistress saw to like in him I don't know; but when she asked her friends to stay with her at Darrock, she included Mr. James Smith in the invitation. We had a fine, gay, noisy time of it at the Hall, the strange gentleman, in particular, making himself as much at home as if the place belonged to him. I was surprised at Mrs. Norcross putting up with him as she did, but I was fairly thunderstruck some months afterward when I heard that she and her free-and-easy visitor were actually going to be married! She had refused offers by dozens abroad, from higher, and richer, and better-behaved men. It seemed next to impossible that she could seriously think of throwing herself away upon such a hare-brained, headlong, penniless young gentleman as Mr. James Smith.

Married, nevertheless, they were, in due course of time; and, after spending the honeymoon abroad, they came back to Darrock Hall.

I soon found that my new master had a very variable temper. There were some days when he was as easy, and familiar, and pleasant with his servants as any gentleman need be. At other times some devil within him seemed to get possession of his whole nature. He flew into violent passions, and took wrong ideas into his head, which no reasoning or remonstrance could remove. It rather amazed me, considering how gay he was in his tastes, and how restless his habits were, that he should consent to live at such a quiet, dull place as Darrock. The reason for this, however, soon came out. Mr. James Smith was not much of a sportsman; he cared nothing for indoor amusements, such as reading, music, and so forth; and he had no ambition for representing the county in parliament. The one pursuit that he was really fond of was yachting. Darrock was within sixteen miles of a sea-port town, with an excellent harbor, and to this accident of position the Hall was entirely indebted for recommending itself as a place of residence to Mr. James Smith.

He had such an untiring enjoyment and delight in cruising about at sea, and all his ideas of pleasure seemed to be so closely connected with his remembrance of the sailing trips he had taken on board different yachts belonging to his friends, that I verily believe his chief object in marrying my mistress was to get the command of money enough to keep a vessel for himself. Be that as it may, it is certain that he prevailed on her, some time after their marriage, to make him a present of a fine schooner yacht, which was brought round from Cowes to our coast-town, and kept always waiting ready for him in the harbor.

His wife required some little persuasion before she could make up her mind to let him have the vessel. She suffered so much from sea-sickness that pleasure-sailing was out of the question for her; and, being very fond of her husband, she was naturally unwilling that he should engage in an amusement which took him away from her. However, Mr. James Smith used his influence over her cleverly, promising that he would never go away without first asking her leave, and engaging that his terms of absence at sea should never last for more than a week or ten days at a time. Accordingly, my mistress, who was the kindest and most unselfish woman in the world, put her own feelings aside, and made her husband happy in the possession of a vessel of his own.

While my master was away cruising, my mistress had a dull time of it at the Hall. The few gentlefolks there were in our part of the county lived at a distance, and could only come to Darrock when they were asked to stay there for some days together. As for the village near us, there was but one person living in it whom my mistress could think of asking to the Hall, and that person was the clergyman who did duty at the church.

This gentleman's name was Mr. Meeke. He was a single man, very young, and very lonely in his position. He had a mild, melancholy, pasty-looking face, and was as shy and soft-spoken as a little girl—altogether, what one may call, without being unjust or severe, a poor, weak creature, and, out of all sight, the very worst preacher I ever sat under in my life. The one thing he did, which, as I heard, he could really do well, was playing on the fiddle. He was uncommonly fond of music—so much so that he often took his instrument out with him when he went for a walk. This taste of his was his great recommendation to my mistress, who was a wonderfully fine player on the piano, and who was delighted to get such a performer as Mr. Meeke to play duets with her. Besides liking his society for this reason, she felt for him in his lonely position; naturally enough, I think, considering how often she was left in solitude herself. Mr. Meeke, on his side, when he got over his first shyness, was only too glad to leave his lonesome little parsonage for the fine music-room at the Hall, and for the company of a handsome, kind-hearted lady, who made much of him, and admired his fiddle-playing with all her heart. Thus it happened that, whenever my master was away at sea, my mistress and Mr. Meeke were always together, playing duets as if they had their living to get by it. A more harmless connection than the connection between those two never existed in this world; and yet, innocent as it was, it turned out to be the first cause of all the misfortunes that afterward happened.

My master's treatment of Mr. Meeke was, from the first, the very opposite of my mistress's. The restless, rackety, bounceable Mr. James Smith felt a contempt for the weak, womanish, fiddling little parson, and, what was more, did not care to conceal it. For this reason, Mr. Meeke (who was dreadfully frightened by my master's violent language and rough ways) very seldom visited at the Hall except when my mistress was alone there. Meaning no wrong, and therefore stooping to no concealment, she never thought of taking any measures to keep Mr. Meeke out of the way when he happened to be with her at the time of her husband's coming home, whether it was only from a riding excursion in the neighborhood or from a cruise in the schooner. In this way it so turned out that whenever my master came home, after a long or short absence, in nine cases out of ten he found the parson at the Hall.

At first he used to laugh at this circumstance, and to amuse himself with some coarse jokes at the expense of his wife and her companion. But, after a while, his variable temper changed, as usual. He grew sulky, rude, angry, and, at last, downright jealous of Mr. Meeke. Though too proud to confess it in so many words, he still showed the state of his mind clearly enough to my mistress to excite her indignation. She was a woman who could be led anywhere by any one for whom she had a regard, but there was a firm spirit within her that rose at the slightest show of injustice or oppression, and that resented tyrannical usage of any sort perhaps a little too warmly. The bare suspicion that her husband could feel any distrust of her set her all in a flame, and she took the most unfortunate, and yet, at the same time, the most natural way for a woman, of resenting it. The ruder her husband was to Mr. Meeke the more kindly she behaved to him. This led to serious disputes and dissensions, and thence, in time, to a violent quarrel. I could not avoid hearing the last part of the altercation between them, for it took place in the garden-walk, outside the dining-room window, while I was occupied in laying the table for lunch.

Without repeating their words—which I have no right to do, having heard by accident what I had no business to hear—I may say generally, to show how serious the quarrel was, that my mistress charged my master with having married from mercenary motives, with keeping out of her company as much as he could, and with insulting her by a suspicion which it would be hard ever to forgive, and impossible ever to forget. He replied by violent language directed against herself, and by commanding her never to open the doors again to Mr. Meeke; she, on her side, declaring that she would never consent to insult a clergyman and a gentleman in order to satisfy the whim of a tyrannical husband. Upon that, he called out, with a great oath, to have his horse saddled directly, declaring that he would not stop another instant under the same roof with a woman who had set him at defiance, and warning his wife that he would come back, if Mr. Meeke entered the house again, and horsewhip him, in spite of his black coat, all through the village.

With those words he left her, and rode away to the sea-port where his yacht was lying. My mistress kept up her spirit till he was out of sight, and then burst into a dreadful screaming passion of tears, which ended by leaving her so weak that she had to be carried to her bed like a woman who was at the point of death.

The same evening my master's horse was ridden back by a messenger, who brought a scrap of notepaper with him addressed to me. It only contained these lines:

"Pack up my clothes and deliver them immediately to the bearer. You may tell your mistress that I sail to-night at eleven o'clock for a cruise to Sweden. Forward my letters to the post-office, Stockholm."

I obeyed the orders given to me except that relating to my mistress. The doctor had been sent for, and was still in the house. I consulted him upon the propriety of my delivering the message. He positively forbade me to do so that night, and told me to give him the slip of paper, and leave it to his discretion to show it to her or not the next morning.

The messenger had hardly been gone an hour when Mr. Meeke's housekeeper came to the Hall with a roll of music for my mistress. I told the woman of my master's sudden departure, and of the doctor being in the house. This news brought Mr. Meeke himself to the Hall in a great flutter.

I felt so angry with him for being the cause—innocent as he might be—of the shocking scene which had taken place, that I exceeded the bounds of my duty, and told him the whole truth. The poor, weak, wavering, childish creature flushed up red in the face, then turned as pale as ashes, and dropped into one of the hall chairs crying—literally crying fit to break his heart. "Oh, William," says he, wringing his little frail, trembling white hands as helpless as a baby, "oh, William, what am I to do?"

"As you ask me that question, sir," says I, "you will excuse me, I hope, if, being a servant, I plainly speak my mind notwithstanding. I know my station well enough to be aware that, strictly speaking, I have done wrong, and far exceeded my duty, in telling you as much as I have told you already; but I would go through fire and water, sir," says I, feeling my own eyes getting moist, "for my mistress's sake. She has no relation here who can speak to you; and it is even better that a servant like me should risk being guilty of an impertinence, than that dreadful and lasting mischief should arise from the right remedy not being applied at the right time. This is what I should do, sir, in your place. Saving your presence, I should leave off crying; and go back home and write to Mr. James Smith, saying that I would not, as a clergyman, give him railing for railing, but would prove how unworthily he had suspected me by ceasing to visit at the Hall from thi s time forth, rather than be a cause of dissension between man and wife. If you will put that into proper language, sir, and will have the letter ready for me in half an hour's time, I will call for it on the fastest horse in our stables, and, at my own risk, will give it to my master before he sails to-night. I have nothing more to say, sir, except to ask your pardon for forgetting my proper place, and for making bold to speak on a very serious matter as equal to equal, and as man to man."

To do Mr. Meeke justice, he had a heart, though it was a very small one. He shook hands with me, and said he accepted my advice as the advice of a friend, and so went back to his parsonage to write the letter. In half an hour I called for it on horseback, but it was not ready for me. Mr. Meeke was ridiculously nice about how he should express himself when he got a pen into his hand. I found him with his desk littered with rough copies, in a perfect agony about how to turn his phrases delicately enough in referring to my mistress. Every minute being precious, I hurried him as much as I could, without standing on any ceremony. It took half an hour more, with all my efforts, before he could make up his mind that the letter would do. I started off with it at a gallop, and never drew rein till I got to the sea-port town.

The harbor-clock chimed the quarter past eleven as I rode by it, and when I got down to the jetty there was no yacht to be seen. She had been cast off from her moorings ten minutes before eleven, and as the clock struck she had sailed out of the harbor. I would have followed in a boat, but it was a fine starlight night, with a fresh wind blowing, and the sailors on the pier laughed at me when I spoke of rowing after a schooner yacht which had got a quarter of an hour's start of us, with the wind abeam and the tide in her favor.

I rode back with a heavy heart. All I could do now was to send the letter to the post-office, Stockholm.

The next day the doctor showed my mistress the scrap of paper with the message on it from my master, and an hour or two after that, a letter was sent to her in Mr. Meeke's handwriting, explaining the reason why she must not expect to see him at the Hall, and referring to me in terms of high praise as a sensible and faithful man who had spoken the right word at the right time. I am able to repeat the substance of the letter, because I heard all about it from my mistress, under very unpleasant circumstances so far as I was concerned.

The news of my master's departure did not affect her as the doctor had supposed it would. Instead of distressing her, it roused her spirit and made her angry; her pride, as I imagine, being wounded by the contemptuous manner in which her husband had notified his intention of sailing to Sweden at the end of a message to a servant about packing his clothes. Finding her in that temper of mind, the letter from Mr. Meeke only irritated her the more. She insisted on getting up, and as soon as she was dressed and downstairs, she vented her violent humor on me, reproaching me for impertinent interference in the affairs of my betters, and declaring that she had almost made up her mind to turn me out of my place for it. I did not defend myself, because I respected her sorrows and the irritation that came from them; also, because I knew the natural kindness of her nature well enough to be assured that she would make amends to me for her harshness the moment her mind was composed again. The result showed that I was right. That same evening she sent for me and begged me to forgive and forget the hasty words she had spoken in the morning with a grace and sweetness that would have won the heart of any man who listened to her.

Weeks passed after this, till it was more than a month since the day of my master's departure, and no letter in his handwriting came to Darrock Hall.

My mistress, taking this treatment more angrily than sorrowfully, went to London to consult her nearest relations, who lived there. On leaving home she stopped the carriage at the parsonage, and went in (as I thought, rather defiantly) to say good-by to Mr. Meeke. She had answered his letter, and received others from him, and had answered them likewise. She had also, of course, seen him every Sunday at church, and had always stopped to speak to him after the service; but this was the first occasion on which she had visited him at his house. As the carriage stopped, the little parson came out, in great hurry and agitation, to meet her at the garden gate.

"Don't look alarmed, Mr. Meeke," says my mistress, getting out. "Though you have engaged not to come near the Hall, I have made no promise to keep away from the parsonage." With those words she went into the house.

The quadroon maid, Josephine, was sitting with me in the rumble of the carriage, and I saw a smile on her tawny face as the parson and his visitor went into the house together. Harmless as Mr. Meeke was, and innocent of all wrong as I knew my mistress to be, I regretted that she should be so rash as to despise appearances, considering the situation she was placed in. She had already exposed herself to be thought of disrespectfully by her own maid, and it was hard to say what worse consequences might not happen after that.

Half an hour later we were away on our journey. My mistress stayed in London two months. Throughout all that long time no letter from my master was forwarded to her from the country house.

CHAPTER II.

WHEN the two months had passed we returned to Darrock Hall. Nobody there had received any news in our absence of the whereabouts of my master and his yacht.

Six more weary weeks elapsed, and in that time but one event happened at the Hall to vary the dismal monotony of the lives we now led in the solitary place. One morning Josephine came down after dressing my mistress with her face downright livid to look at, except on one check, where there was a mark as red as burning fire. I was in the kitchen at the time, and I asked what was the matter.

"The matter!" says she, in her shrill voice and her half-foreign English. "Use your own eyes, if you please, and look at this cheek of mine. What! have you lived so long a time with your mistress, and don't you know the mark of her hand yet?"

I was at a loss to understand what she meant, but she soon explained herself. My mistress, whose temper had been sadly altered for the worse by the trials and humiliations she had gone through, had got up that morning more out of humor than usual, and, in answer to her maid's inquiry as to how she had passed the night, had begun talking about her weary, miserable life in an unusually fretful and desperate way. Josephine, in trying to cheer her spirits, had ventured, most improperly, on making a light, jesting reference to Mr. Meeke, which had so enraged my mistress that she turned round sharp on the half-breed and gave her—to use the common phrase—a smart box on the ear. Josephine confessed that, the moment after she had done this, her better sense appeared to tell her that she had taken a most improper way of resenting undue familiarity. She had immediately expressed her regret for having forgotten herself, and had proved the sincerity of it by a gift of half a dozen cambric handkerchiefs, presented as a peace-offering on the spot. After that I thought it impossible that Josephine could bear any malice against a mistress whom she had served ever since she had been a girl, and I said as much to her when she had done telling me what had happened upstairs.

"I! Malice!" cries Miss Josephine, in her hard, sharp, snappish way. "And why, and wherefore, if you please? If my mistress smacks my cheek with one hand, she gives me handkerchiefs to wipe it with the other. My good mistress, my kind mistress, my pretty mistress! I, the servant, bear malice against her, the mistress! Ah! you bad man, even to think of such a thing! Ah! fie, fie! I am quite ashamed of you!"

She gave me one look—the wickedest look I ever saw, and burst out laughing—the harshest laugh I ever heard from a woman's lips. Turning away from me directly after, she said no more, and never referred to the subject again on any subsequent occasion.

From that time, however, I noticed an alteration in Miss Josephine; not in her way of doing her work, for she was just as sharp and careful about it as ever, but in her manners and habits. She grew amazingly quiet, and passed almost all her leisure time alone. I could bring no charge against her which authorized me to speak a word of warning; but, for all that, I could not help feeling that if I had been in my mistress's place, I would have followed up the present of the cambric handkerchiefs by paying her a month's wages in advance, and sending her away from the house the same evening.

With the exception of this little domestic matter, which appeared trifling enough at the time, hut which led to very serious consequences afterward, nothing happened at all out of the ordinary way during the six weary weeks to which I have referred. At the beginning of the seventh week, however, an event occurred at last.

One morning the postman brought a letter to the Hall addressed to my mistress. I took it upstairs, and looked at the direction as I put it on the salver. The handwriting was not my master's; was not, as it appeared to me, the handwriting of any well-educated person. The outside of the letter was also very dirty, and the seal a common office-seal of the usual lattice-work pattern. "This must be a begging-letter," I thought to myself as I entered the breakfast- room and advanced with it to my mistress.

She held up her hand before she opened it as a sign to me that she had some order to give, and that I was not to leave the room till I had received it. Then she broke the seal and began to read the letter.

Her eyes had hardly been on it a moment before her face turned as pale as death, and the paper began to tremble in her fingers. She read on to the end, and suddenly turned from pale to scarlet, started out of her chair, crumpled the letter up violently in her hand, and took several turns backward and forward in the room, without seeming to notice me as I stood by the door. "You villain! you villain! you villain!" I heard her whisper to herself many times over, in a quick, hissing, fierce way. Then she stopped, and said on a sudden, "Can it be true?" Then she looked up, and, seeing me standing at the door, started as if I had been a stranger, changed color again, and told me, in a stifled voice, to leave her and come back again in half an hour. I obeyed, feeling certain that she must have received some very bad news of her husband, and wondering, anxiously enough, what it might be.

When I returned to the breakfast-room her face was as much discomposed as ever. Without speaking a word she handed me two sealed letters: one, a note to be left for Mr. Meeke at the parsonage; the other, a letter marked "Immediate," and addressed to her solicitor in London, who was also, I should add, her nearest living relative.

I left one of these letters and posted the other. When I came back I heard that my mistress had taken to her room. She remained there for four days, keeping her new sorrow, whatever it was, strictly to herself. On the fifth day the lawyer from London arrived at the Hall. My mistress went down to him in the library, and was shut up there with him for nearly two hours. At the end of that time the bell rang for me.

"Sit down, William," said my mistress, when I came into the room. "I feel such entire confidence in your fidelity and attachment that I am about, with the full concurrence of this gentleman, who is my nearest relative and my legal adviser, to place a very serious secret in your keeping, and to employ your services on a matter which is as important to me as a matter of life and death."

Her poor eyes were very red, and her lips quivered as she spoke to me. I was so startled by what she had said that I hardly knew which chair to sit in. She pointed to one placed near herself at the table, and seemed about to speak to me again, when the lawyer interfered.

"Let me entreat you," he said, "not to agitate yourself unnecessarily. I will put this person in possession of the facts, and, if I omit anything, you shall stop me and set me right."

My mistress leaned back in her chair and covered her face with her handkerchief. The lawyer waited a moment, and then addressed himself to me.

"You are already aware," he said, "of the circumstances under which your master left this house, and you also know, I have no doubt, that no direct news of him has reached your mistress up to this time?"

I bowed to him and said I knew of the circumstances so far.

"Do you remember," he went on, "taking a letter to your mistress five days ago?"

"Yes, sir," I replied; "a letter which seemed to distress and alarm her very seriously."

"I will read you that letter before we say any more," continued the lawyer. "I warn you beforehand that it contains a terrible charge against your master, which, however, is not attested by the writer's signature. I have already told your mistress that she must not attach too much importance to an anonymous letter; and I now tell you the same thing."

Saying that, he took up a letter from the table and read it aloud. I had a copy of it given to me afterward, which I looked at often enough to fix the contents of the letter in my memory. I can now repeat them, I think, word for word.

"MADAM—I cannot reconcile it to my conscience to leave you in total ignorance of your husband 's atrocious conduct toward you. If you have ever been disposed to regret his absence do so no longer. Hope and pray, rather, that you and he may never meet face to face again in this world. I write in great haste and in great fear of being observed. Time fails me to prepare you as you ought to be prepared for what I have now to disclose. I must tell you plainly, with much respect for you and sorrow for your misfortune, that your husband *has married another wife*. I saw the ceremony performed, unknown to him. If I could not have spoken of this infamous act as an eye-witness, I would not have spoken of it at all.

"I dare not acknowledge who I am, for I believe Mr. James Smith would stick at no crime to revenge himself on me if he ever came to a knowledge of the step I am now taking, and of the means by which I got my information; neither have I time to enter into particulars. I simply warn you of what has happened, and leave you to act on that warning as you please. You may disbelieve this letter, because it is not signed by any name. In that case, if Mr. James Smith should ever venture into your presence, I recommend you to ask him suddenly what he has done with his *new wife,* and to see if his countenance does not immediately testify that the truth has been spoken by

"YOUR UNKNOWN FRIEND."

Poor as my opinion was of my master, I had never believed him to be capable of such villainy as this, and I could not believe it when the lawyer had done reading the letter.

"Oh, sir," I said, "surely that is some base imposition? Surely it cannot be true?"

"That is what I have told your mistress," he answered. "But she says in return—"

"That I feel it to be true," my mistress broke in, speaking behind the handkerchief in a faint, smothered voice.

"We need not debate the question," the lawyer went on. "Our business now is to prove the truth or falsehood of this letter. That must be done at once. I have written to one of my clerks, who is accustomed to conducting delicate investigations, to come to this house without loss of time. He is to be trusted with anything, and he will pursue the needful inquiries immediately.

It is absolutely necessary, to make sure of committing no mistakes, that he should be accompanied by some one who is well acquainted with Mr. James Smith's habits and personal appearance, and your mistress has fixed upon you to be that person. However well the inquiry is managed, it may be attended by much trouble and delay, may necessitate a long journey, and may involve some personal danger. Are you," said the lawyer, looking hard at me, "ready to suffer any inconvenience and to run any risk for your mistress's sake?"

"There is nothing I *can* do, sir," said I, "that I will not do. I am afraid I am not clever enough to be of much use; but, so far as troubles and risks are concerned, I am ready for anything from this moment."

My mistress took the handkerchief from her face, looked at me with her eyes full of tears, and held out her hand. How I came to do it I don't know, but I stooped down and kissed the hand she offered me, feeling half startled, half ashamed at my own boldness the moment after.

"You will do, my man," said the lawyer, nodding his head. "Don't trouble yourself about the cleverness or the cunning that may be wanted. My clerk has got head enough for two. I have only one word more to say before you go downstairs again. Remember that this investigation and the cause that leads to it must be kept a profound secret. Except us three, and the clergyman here (to whom your mistress has written word of what has happened), nobody knows anything about it. I will let my clerk into the secret when he joins us. As soon as you and he are away from the house, you may talk about it. Until then, you will close your lips on the subject."

The clerk did not keep us long waiting. He came as fast as the mail from London could bring him.

I had expected, from his master's description, to see a serious, sedate man, rather sly in his looks, and rather reserved in his manner. To my amazement, this practiced hand at delicate investigations was a brisk, plump, jolly little man, with a comfortable double chin, a pair of very bright black eyes, and a big bottle-nose of the true groggy red color. He wore a suit of black, and a limp, dingy white cravat; took snuff perpetually out of a very large box; walked with his hands crossed behind his back; and looked, upon the whole, much more like a parson of free-and-easy habits than a lawyer's clerk.

"How d'ye do?" says he, when I opened the door to him. "I'm the man you expect from the office in London. Just say Mr. Dark, will you? I'll sit down here till you come back; and, young man, if there is such a thing as a glass of ale in the house, I don't mind committing myself so far as to say that I'll drink it."

I got him the ale before I announced him. He winked at me as he put it to his lips.

"Your good health," says he. "I like you. Don't forget that the name's Dark; and just leave the jug and glass, will you, in case my master keeps me waiting."

I announced him at once, and was told to show him into the library.

When I got back to the hall the jug was empty, and Mr. Dark was comforting himself with a pinch of snuff, snorting over it like a perfect grampus. He had swallowed more than a pint of the strongest old ale in the house; and, for all the effect it seemed to have had on him, he might just as well have been drinking so much water.

As I led him along the passage to the library Josephine passed us. Mr. Dark winked at me again, and made her a low bow.

"Lady's maid," I heard him whisper to himself. "A fine woman to look at, but a damned bad one to deal with." I turned round on him, rather angry at his cool ways, and looked hard at him just before I opened the library door. Mr. Dark looked hard at me. "All right," says he. "I can show myself in." And he knocks at the door, and opens it, and goes in with another wicked wink, all in a moment.

Half an hour later the bell rang for me. Mr. Dark was sitting between my mistress (who was looking at him in amazement) and the lawyer (who was looking at him with approval). He had a map open on his knee, and a pen in his hand. Judging by his face, the communication of the secret about my master did not seem to have made the smallest impression on him.

"I've got leave to ask you a question," says he, the moment I appeared. "When you found your master's yacht gone, did you hear which way she had sailed? Was it northward toward Scotland? Speak up, young man, speak up!"

"Yes," I answered. "The boatmen told me that when I made inquiries at the harbor."

"Well, sir," says Mr. Dark, turning to the lawyer, "if he said he was going to Sweden, he seems to have started on the road to it, at all events. I think I have got my instructions now?"

The lawyer nodded, and looked at my mistress, who bowed her head to him. He then said, turning to me:

"Pack up your bag for traveling at once, and have a conveyance got ready to go to the nearest post-town. Look sharp, young man—look sharp!"

"And, whatever happens in the future," added my mistress, her kind voice trembling a little, "believe, William, that I shall never forget the proof you now show of your devotion to me. It is still some comfort to know that I have your fidelity to depend on in this dreadful trial—your fidelity and the extraordinary intelligence and experience of Mr. Dark."

Mr. Dark did not seem to hear the compliment. He was busy writing, with his paper upon the map on his knee.

A quarter of an hour later, when I had ordered the dog-cart, and had got down into the hall with my bag packed, I found him there waiting for me. He was sitting in the same chair which he had occupied when he first arrived, and he had another jug of the old ale on the table by his side.

"Got any fishing-rods in the house?" says he, when I put my bag down in the hall.

"Yes," I replied, astonished at the question. "What do you want with them?"

"Pack a couple in cases for traveling," says Mr. Dark, "with lines, and hooks, and fly-books all complete. Have a drop of the ale before you go—and don't stare, William, don't stare. I'll let the light in on you as soon as we are out of the house. Off with you for the rods! I want to be on the road in five minutes."

When I came back with the rods and tackle I found Mr. Dark in the dog-cart.

"Money, luggage, fishing-rods, papers of directions, copy of anonymous letter, guide-book, map," says he, running over in his mind the things wanted for the journey—"all right so far. Drive off."

I took the reins and started the horse. As we left the house I saw my mistress and Josephine looking after us from two of the windows on the second floor. The memory of those two attentive faces—one so fair and so good, the other so yellow and so wicked—haunted my mind perpetually for many days afterward.

"Now, William," says Mr. Dark, when we were clear of the lodge gates, "I'm going to begin by telling you that you must step out of your own character till further notice. You are a clerk in a bank, and I'm another. We have got our regular holiday, that comes, like Christmas, once a year, and we are taking a little tour in Scotland to see the curiosities, and to breathe the sea air, and to get some fishing whenever we can. I'm the fat cashier who digs holes in a drawerful of gold with a copper shovel, and you're the arithmetical young man who sits on a perch behind me and keeps the books. Scotland's a beautiful country, William. Can you make whisky-toddy? I can; and, what's more, unlikely as the thing may seem to you, I can actually drink it into the bargain."

"Scotland!" says I. "What are we going to Scotland for?"

"Question for question," says Mr. Dark. "What are we starting on a journey for?"

"To find my master," I answered, "and to make sure if the letter about him is true."

"Very good," says he. "How would you set about doing that, eh?"

"I should go and ask about him at Stockholm in Sweden, where he said his letters were to be sent."

"Should you, indeed?" says Mr. Dark. "If you were a shepherd, William, and had lost a sheep in Cumberland, would you begin looking for it at the Land's End, or would you try a little nearer home?"

"You're attempting to make a fool of me now," says I.

"No," says Mr. Dark, "I'm only letting the light in on you, as I said I would. Now listen to reason, William, and profit by it as much as you can. Mr. James Smith says he is going on a cruise to Sweden, and makes his word good, at the beginning, by starting northward toward the coast of Scotland. What does he go in? A yacht. Do yachts carry live beasts and a butcher on board? No. Will joints of meat keep fresh all the way from Cumberland to Sweden? No. Do gentlemen like living on salt provisions? No. What follows from these three Noes? That Mr. James Smith must have stopped somewhere on the way to S weden to supply his sea-larder with fresh provisions. Where, in that case, must he stop? Somewhere in Scotland, supposing he didn't alter his course when he was out of sight of your seaport. Where in Scotland? Northward on the main land, or westward at one of the islands? Most likely on the main land, where the seaside places are largest, and where he is sure of getting all the stores he wants. Next, what is our business? Not to risk losing a link in the chain of evidence by missing any place where he has put his foot on shore. Not to overshoot the mark when we want to hit it in the bull's-eye. Not to waste money and time by taking a long trip to Sweden till we know that we must absolutely go there. Where is our journey of discovery to take us to first, then? Clearly to the north of Scotland. What do you say to that, Mr. William? Is my catechism all correct, or has your strong ale muddled my head?"

It was evident by this time that no ale could do that, and I told him so. He chuckled, winked at me, and, taking another pinch of snuff, said he would now turn the whole case over in his mind again, and make sure that he had got all the bearings of it quite clear.

By the time we reached the post-town he had accomplished this mental effort to his own perfect satisfaction, and was quite ready to compare the ale at the inn with the ale at Darrock Hall. The dog-cart was left to be taken back the next morning by the hostler. A post-chaise and horses were ordered out. A loaf of bread, a Bologna sausage, and two bottles of sherry were put into the pockets of the carriage; we took our seats, and started briskly on our doubtful journey.

"One word more of friendly advice," says Mr. Dark, settling himself comfortably in his corner of the carriage. "Take your sleep, William, whenever you feel that you can get it. You won't find yourself in bed again till we get to Glasgow."

CHAPTER III.

ALTHOUGH the events that I am now relating happened many years ago, I shall still, for caution's sake, avoid mentioning by name the various places visited by Mr. Dark and myself for the purpose of making inquiries. It will be enough if I describe generally what we did, and if I mention in substance only the result at which we ultimately arrived.

On reaching Glasgow, Mr. Dark turned the whole case over in his mind once more. The result was that he altered his original intention of going straight to the north of Scotland, considering it safer to make sure, if possible, of the course the yacht had taken in her cruise along the western coast.

The carrying out of this new resolution involved the necessity of delaying our onward journey by perpetually diverging from the direct road. Three times we were sent uselessly to wild places in the Hebrides by false reports. Twice we wandered away inland, following gentlemen who answered generally to the description of Mr. James Smith, but who turned out to be the wrong men as soon as we set eyes on them. These vain excursions—especially the three to the western islands—consumed time terribly. It was more than two months from the day when we had left Darrock Hall before we found ourselves up at the very top of Scotland at last, driving into a considerable sea-side town, with a harbor attached to it. Thus far our journey had led to no results, and I began to despair of success. As for Mr. Dark, he never got to the end of his sweet temper and his wonderful patience.

"You don't know how to wait, William," was his constant remark whenever he heard me complaining. "I do."

We drove into the town toward evening in a modest little gig, and put up, according to our usual custom, at one of the inferior inns.

"We must begin at the bottom," Mr. Dark used to say. "High company in a coffee-room won't be familiar with us; low company in a tap-room will." And he certainly proved the truth of his own words. The like of him for making intimate friends of total strangers at the shortest notice I have never met with before or since. Cautious as the Scotch are, Mr. Dark seemed to have the knack of twisting them round his finger as he pleased. He varied his way artfully with different men, but there were three standing opinions of his which he made a point of expressing in all varieties of company while we were in Scotland. In the first place, he thought the view of Edinburgh from Arthur's Seat the finest in the world. In the second place, he considered whisky to be the most wholesome spirit in the world. In the third place, he believed his late beloved mother to be the best woman in the world. It may be worthy of note that, whenever he expressed this last opinion in Scotland, he invariably added that her maiden name was Macleod.

Well, we put up at a modest little inn near the harbor. I was dead tired with the journey, and lay down on my bed to get some rest. Mr. Dark, whom nothing ever fatigued, left me to take his toddy and pipe among the company in the taproom.

I don't know how long I had been asleep when I was roused by a shake on my shoulder. The room was pitch dark, and I felt a hand suddenly clapped over my mouth. Then a strong smell of whisky and tobacco saluted my nostrils, and a whisper stole into my ear—

"William, we have got to the end of our journey."

"Mr. Dark," I stammered out, "is that you? What, in Heaven's name, do you mean?"

"The yacht put in here," was the answer, still in a whisper, "and your blackguard of a master came ashore—"

"Oh, Mr. Dark," I broke in, "don't tell me that the letter is true!"

"Every word of it," says he. "He was married here, and was off again to the Mediterranean with Number Two a good three weeks before we left your mistress's house. Hush! don't say a word, Go to sleep again, or strike a light, if you like it better. Do anything but come downstairs with me. I'm going to find out all the particulars without seeming to want to know one of them. Yours is a very good-looking face, William, but it's so infernally honest that I can't trust it in the tap-room. I'm making friends with the Scotchmen already. They know my opinion of Arthur's Seat; they *see* what I think of whisky; and I rather think it won't be long before they hear that my mother's maiden name was Macleod."

With those words he slipped out of the room, and left me, as he had found me, in the dark.

I was far too much agitated by what I had heard to think of going to sleep again, so I struck a light, and tried to amuse myself as well as I could with an old newspaper that had been stuffed into my carpet bag. It was then nearly ten o'clock. Two hours later, when the house shut up, Mr. Dark came back to me again in high spirits.

"I have got the whole case here," says he, tapping his forehead—"the whole case, as neat and clean as if it was drawn in a brief. That master of yours doesn't stick at a trifle, William. It's my opinion that your mistress and you have not seen the last of him yet."

We were sleeping that night in a double-bedded room. As soon as Mr. Dark had secured the door and disposed himself comfortably in his bed, he entered on a detailed narrative of the particulars communicated to him in the tap-room. The substance of what he told me may be related as follows:

The yacht had had a wonderful run all the way to Cape Wrath. On rounding that headland she had met the wind nearly dead against her, and had beaten every inch of the way to the sea-port town, where she had put in to get a supply of provisions, and to wait for a change in the wind.

Mr. James Smith had gone ashore to look about him, and to see whether the principal hotel was the sort of house at which he would like to stop for a few days. In the course of his wandering about the town, his attention had been attracted to a decent house, where lodgings were to be let, by the sight of a very pretty girl sitting at work at the parlor window. He was so struck by her face that he came back twice to look at it, determining, the second time, to try if he could not make acquaintance with her by asking to see the lodgings. He was shown the rooms by the girl's mother, a very respectable woman, whom he discovered to be the wife of the master and part owner of a small coasting ves sel, then away at sea. With a little maneuvering he managed to get into the parlor where the daughter was at work, and to exchange a few words with her. Her voice and manner completed the attraction of her face. Mr. James Smith decided, in his headlong way, that he was violently in love with her, and, without hesitating another instant, he took the lodgings on the spot for a month certain.

It is unnecessary to say that his designs on the girl were of the most disgraceful kind, and that he represented himself to the mother and daughter as a single man. Helped by his advantages of money, position, and personal appearance, he had made sure that the ruin of the girl might be effected with very little difficulty; but he soon found that he had undertaken no easy conquest.

The mother's watchfulness never slept, and the daughter's presence of mind never failed her. She admired Mr. James Smith's tall figure and splendid whiskers; she showed the most encouraging partiality for his society; she smiled at his compliments, and blushed whenever he looked at her; but, whether it was cunning or whether it was innocence, she seemed incapable of understanding that his advances toward her were of any other than an honorable kind. At the slightest approach to undue familiarity, she drew back with a kind of contemptuous surprise in her face, which utterly perplexed Mr. James Smith. He had not calculated on that sort of resistance, and he could not see his way to overcoming it. The weeks passed; the month for which he had taken the lodgings expired. Time had strengthened the girl's hold on him till his admiration for her amounted to downright infatuation, and he had not advanced one step yet toward the fulfillment of the vicious purpose with which he had entered the house.

At this time he must have made some fresh attempt on the girl's virtue, which produced: a coolness between them; for, instead of taking the lodgings for another term, he removed to his yacht, in the harbor, and slept on board for two nights.

The wind was now fair, and the stores were on board, but he gave no orders to the sailing-master to weigh anchor. On the third day, the cause of the coolness, whatever it was, appears to have been removed, and he returned to his lodgings on shore. Some of the more inquisitive among the townspeople observed soon afterward, when they met him in the street, that he looked rather anxious and uneasy. The conclusion had probably forced itself upon his mind, by this time, that he must decide on pursuing one of two courses: either he must resolve to make the sacrifice of leaving the girl altogether, or he must commit the villainy of marrying her.

Scoundrel as he was, he hesitated at encountering the risk—perhaps, also, at being guilty of the crime—involved in this last alternative. While he was still in doubt, the father's coasting vessel sailed into the harbor, and the father's presence on the scene decided him at last. How this new influence acted it was impossible to find out from the imperfect evidence of persons who were not admitted to the family councils. The fact, however, was certain that the date of the father's return and the date of Mr. James Smith's first wicked resolution to marry the girl might both be fixed, as nearly as possible, at one and the same time.

Having once made up his mind to the commission of the crime, he proceeded with all possible coolness and cunning to provide against the chances of detection.

Returning on board his yacht he announced that he had given up his intention of cruising to Sweden and that he intended to amuse himself by a long fishing tour in Scotland. After this explanation, he ordered the vessel to be laid up in the harbor, gave the sailing-master leave of absence to return to his family at Cowes, and paid off the whole of the crew from the mate to the cabin-boy. By these means he cleared the scene, at one blow, of the only people in the town who knew of the existence of his unhappy wife. After that the news of his approaching marriage might be made public without risk of discovery, his own common name being of itself a sufficient protection in case the event was mentioned in the Scotch newspapers. All his friends, even his wife herself, might read a report of the marriage of Mr. James Smith without having the slightest suspicion of who the bridegroom really was.

A fortnight after the paying off of the crew he was married to the merchant-captain's daughter. The father of the girl was well known among his fellow-townsmen as a selfish, grasping man, who was too anxious to secure a rich son-in-law to object to any proposals for hastening the marriage. He and his wife, and a few intimate relations had been present at the ceremony; and after it had been performed the newly-married couple left the town at once for a honeymoon trip to the Highland lakes.

Two days later, however, they unexpectedly returned, announcing a complete change in their plans. The bridegroom (thinking, probably, that he would be safer out of England than in it) had been pleasing the bride's fancy by his descriptions of the climate and the scenery of southern parts. The new Mrs. James Smith was all curiosity to see Spain and Italy; and, having often proved herself an excellent sailor on board her father's vessel, was anxious to go to the Mediterranean in the easiest way by sea. Her affectionate husband, having now no other object in life than to gratify her wishes, had given up the Highland excursion, and had returned to have his yacht got ready for sea immediately. In this explanation there was nothing to awaken the suspicions of the lady's parents. The mother thought Mr. James Smith a model among bridegrooms. The father lent his assistance to man the yacht at the shortest notice with as smart a crew as could be picked up about the town. Principally through his exertions, the vessel was got ready for sea with extraordinary dispatch. The sails were bent, the provisions were put on board, and Mr. James Smith sailed for the Mediterranean with the unfortunate woman who believed herself to be his wife, before Mr. Dark and myself set forth to look after him from Darrock Hall.

Such was the true account of my master's infamous conduct in Scotland as it was related to me. On concluding, Mr. Dark hinted that he had something still left to tell me, but declared that he was too sleepy to talk any more that night. As soon as we were awake the next morning he returned to the subject.

"I didn't finish all I had to say last night, did I?" he began.

You unfortunately told me enough, and more than enough, to prove the truth of the statement in the anonymous letter," I answered.

"Yes," says Mr. Dark, "but did I tell you who wrote the anonymous letter?"

"You don't mean to say that you have found that out!" says I.

"I think I have," was the cool answer. "When I heard about your precious master paying off the regular crew of the yacht I put the circumstance by in my mind, to be brought out again and sifted a little as soon as the opportunity offered. It offered in about half an hour. Says I to the gauger, who was the principal talker in the room: 'How about those men that Mr. Smith paid off? Did they all go as soon as they got their money, or did they stop here till they had spent every farthing of it in the public-houses?' The gauger laughs. 'No such luck,' says he, in the broadest possible Scotch (which I translate into English, William, for your benefit); 'no such luck; they all went south, to spend their money among finer people than us—all, that is to say, with one exception. It was thought the steward of the yacht had gone along with the rest, when, the very day Mr. Smith sailed for the Mediterranean, who should turn up unexpectedly but the steward himself! Where he had been hiding, and why he had been hiding, nobody could tell.' 'Perhaps he had been imitating his master, and looking out for a wife,' says I. 'Likely enough,' says the gauger; 'he gave a very confused account of himself, and he cut all questions short by going away south in a violent hurry.' That was enough for me: I let the subject drop. Clear as daylight, isn't it, William? The steward suspected something wrong—the steward waited and watched—the steward wrote that anonymous letter to your mistress. We can find him, if we want him, by inquiring at Cowes; and we can send to the church for legal evidence of the marriage as soon as we are instructed to do so. All that we have got to do now is to go back to your mistress, and see what course she means to take under the circumstances. It's a pretty case, William, so far—an uncommonly pretty case, as it stands at present."

We returned to Darrock Hall as fast as coaches and post-horses could carry us.

Having from the first believed that the statement in the anonymous letter was true, my mistress received the bad news we brought calmly and resignedly—so far, at least, as outward appearances went. She astonished and disappointed Mr. Dark by declining to act in any way on the information that he had collected for her, and by insisting that the whole affair should still be buried in the profoundest secrecy. For the first time since I had known my traveling companion, he became depressed in spirits on hearing that nothing more was to be done, and, although he left the Hall with a handsome present, he left it discontentedly.

"Such a pretty case, William," says he, quite sorrowfully, as we shook hands— "such an uncommonly pretty case—it's a thousand pities to stop it, in this way, before it's half over!"

"You don't know what a proud lady and what a delicate lady my mistress is," I answered. "She would die rather than expose her forlorn situation in a public court for the sake of punishing her husband."

"Bless your simple heart!" says Mr. Dark, "do you really think, now, that such a case as this can be hushed up?"

"Why not," I asked, "if we all keep the secret?"

"That for the secret!" cries Mr. Dark, snapping his fingers. "Your master will let the cat out of the bag, if nobody else does."

"My master!" I repeated, in amazement.

"Yes, your master!" says Mr. Dark. "I have had some experience in my time, and I say you have not seen the last of him yet. Mark my words, William, Mr. James Smith will come back."

With that prophecy, Mr. Dark fretfully treated himself to a last pinch of snuff, and departed in dudgeon on his journey back to his master in London. His last words hung heavily on my mind for days after he had gone. It was some weeks before I got over a habit of starting whenever the bell was rung at the front door.

CHAPTER IV.

OUR life at the Hall soon returned to its old, dreary course. The lawyer in London wrote to my mistress to ask her to come and stay for a little while with his wife; but she declined the invitation, being averse to facing company after what had happened to her. Though she tried hard to keep the real state of her mind concealed from all about her, I, for one, could see plainly enough that she was pining under the bitter injury that had been inflicted on her. What effect continued solitude might have had on her spirits I tremble to think.

Fortunately for herself, it occurred to her, before long, to send and invite Mr. Meeke to resume his musical practicing with her at the Hall. She told him—and, as it seemed to me, with perfect truth—that any implied engagement which he had made with Mr. James Smith was now canceled, since the person so named had morally forfeited all his claims as a husband, first, by his desertion of her, and, secondly, by his criminal marriage with another woman. After stating this view of the matter, she left it to Mr. Meeke to decide whether the perfectly innocent connection between them should be resumed or not. The little parson, after hesitating and pondering in his helpless way, ended by agreeing with my mistress, and by coming back once more to the Hall with his fiddle under his arm. This renewal of their old habits might have been imprudent enough, as tending to weaken my mistress's case in the eyes of the world, but, for all that, it was the most sensible course she could take for her own sake. The harmless company of Mr. Meeke, and the relief of playing the old tunes again in the old way, saved her, I verily believe, from sinking altogether under the oppression of the shocking situation in which she was now placed.

So, with the assistance of Mr. Meeke and his fiddle, my mistress got though the weary time. The winter passed, the spring came, and no fresh tidings reached us of Mr. James Smith. It had been a long, hard winter that year, and the spring was backward and rainy. The first really fine day we had was the day that fell on the fourteenth of March.

I am particular in mentioning this date merely because it is fixed forever in my memory. As long as there is life in me I shall remember that fourteenth of March, and the smallest circumstances connected with it.

The day began ill, with what superstitious people would think a bad omen. My mistress remained late in her room in the morning, amusing herself by looking over her clothes, and by setting to rights some drawers in her cabinet which she had not opened for some time past. Just before luncheon we were startled by hearing the drawing-room bell rung violently. I ran up to see what was the matter, and the quadroon, Josephine, who had heard the bell in another part of the house, hastened to answer it also. She got into the drawing-room first, and I followed close on her heels. My mistress was standing alone on the hearth-rug, with an appearance of great discomposure in her face and manner.

"I have been robbed!" she said, vehemently, "I don't know when or how; but I miss a pair of bracelets, three rings, and a quantity of old-fashioned lace pocket-handkerchiefs."

"If you have any suspicions, ma'am," said Josephine, in a sharp, sudden way, "say who they point at. My boxes, for one, are quite at your disposal."

"Who asked about your boxes?" said my mistress, angrily. "Be a little less ready with your answer, if you please, the next time I speak."

She then turned to me, and began explaining the circumstances under which she had discovered her loss. I suggested that the missing things should be well searched for first, and then, if nothing came of that, that I should go for the constable, and place the matter under his direction.

My mistress agreed to this plan, and the search was undertaken immediately. It lasted till dinner-time, and led to no results. I then proposed going for the constable. But my mistress said it was too late to do anything that day, and told me to wait at table as usual, and to go on my errand the first thing the next morning. Mr. Meeke was coming with some new music in the evening, and I suspect she was not willing to be disturbed at her favorite occupation by the arrival of the constable.

When dinner was over the parson came, and the concert went on as usual through the evening. At ten o'clock I took up the tray, with the wine, and soda-water, and biscuits. Just as I was opening one of the bottles of soda-water, there was a sound of wheels on the drive outside, and a ring at the bell.

I had unfastened the wires of the cork, and could not put the bottle down to run at once to the door. One of the female servants answered it. I heard a sort of half scream—then the sound of a footstep that was familiar to me.

My mistress turned round from the piano, and looked me hard in the face.

"William," she said, "do you know that step?" Before I could answer the door was pushed open, and Mr. James Smith walked into the room.

He had his hat on. His long hair flowed down under it over the collar of his coat; his bright black eyes, after resting an instant on my mistress, turned to Mr. Meeke. His heavy eyebrows met together, and one of his hands went up to one of his bushy black whiskers, and pulled at it angrily.

"You here again!" he said, advancing a few steps toward the little parson, who sat trembling all over, with his fiddle hugged up in his arms as if it had been a child.

Seeing her villainous husband advance, my mistress moved, too, so as to face him. He turned round on her at the first step she took, as quick as lightning.

"You shameless woman!" he said. "Can you look me in the face in the presence of that man?" He pointed, as he spoke, to Mr. Meeke.

My mistress never shrank when he turned upon her. Not a sign of fear was in her face when they confronted each other. Not the faintest flush of anger came into her cheeks when he spoke. The sense of the insult and injury that he had inflicted on her, and the consciousness of knowing his guilty secret, gave her all her self-possession at that trying moment.

"I ask you again," he repeated, finding that she did not answer him, "how dare you look me in the face in the presence of that man?"

She raised her steady eyes to his hat, which he still kept on his head.

"Who has taught you to come into a room and speak to a lady with your hat on?" she asked, in quiet, contemptuous tones. "Is that a habit which is sanctioned by *your new wife?*"

My eyes were on him as she said those last words. His complexion, naturally dark and swarthy, changed instantly to a livid yellow white; his hand caught at the chair nearest to him, and he dropped into it heavily.

"I don't understand you," he said, after a moment of silence, looking about the room unsteadily while he spoke.

"You do," said my mistress. "Your tongue lies, but your face speaks the truth."

He called back his courage and audacity by a desperate effort, and started up from the chair again with an oath.

The instant before this happened I thought I heard the sound of a rustling dress in the passage outside, as if one of the women servants was stealing up to listen outside the door. I should have gone at once to see whether this was the case or not, but my master stopped me just after he had risen from the chair.

"Get the bed made in the Red Room, and light a fire there directly," he said, with his fiercest look and in his roughest tones. "When I ring the bell, bring me a kettle of boiling water and a bottle of brandy. As for you," he continued, turning toward Mr. Meeke, who still sat pale and speechless with his fiddle hugged up in his arms, "leave the house, or you won't find your cloth any protection to you."

At this insult the blood flew into my mistress's face. Before she could say anything, Mr. James Smith raised his voice loud enough to drown hers.

"I won't hear another word from you," he cried out, brutally. "You have been talking like a mad woman, and you look like a mad woman. You are out of your senses. As sure as you live, I'll have you examined by the doctors to-morrow. Why the devil do you stand there, you scoundrel?" he roared, wheeling round on his heel to me. "Why don't you obey my orders?"

I looked at my mistress. If she had directed me to knock Mr. James Smith down, big as he was, I think at that moment I could have done it.

"Do as he tells you, William," she said, squeezing one of her hands firmly over her bosom, as if she was trying to keep down the rising indignation in that way. "This is the last order of his giving that I shall ask you to obey."

"Do you threaten me, you mad—"

He finished the question by a word I shall not repeat.

"I tell you," she answered, in clear, ringing, resolute tones, "that you have outraged me past all forgiveness and all endurance, and that you shall never insult me again as you have insulted me to-night."

After saying those words she fixed one steady look on him, then turned away and walked slowly to the door.

A minute previously Mr. Meeke had summoned courage enough to get up and leave the room quietly. I noticed him walking demurely away, close to the wall, with his fiddle held under one tail of his long frock-coat, as if he was afraid that the savage passions of Mr. James Smith might be wreaked on that unoffending instrument. He got to the door before my mistress. As he softly pulled it open, I saw him start, and the rustling of the gown caught my ear again from the outside.

My mistress followed him into the passage, turning, however, in the opposite direction to that taken by the little parson, in order to reach the staircase that led to her own room. I went out next, leaving Mr. James Smith alone.

I overtook Mr. Meeke in the hall, and opened the door for him.

"I beg your pardon, sir," I said, "but did you come upon anybody listening outside the music-room when you left it just now?"

"Yes, William," said Mr. Meeke, in a faint voice, "I think it was Josephine; but I was so dreadfully agitated that I can't be quite certain about it."

Had she surprised our secret? That was the question I asked myself as I went away to light the fire in the Red Room. Calling to mind the exact time at which I had first detected the rustling outside the door, I came to the conclusion that she had only heard the last part of the quarrel between my mistress and her rascal of a husband. Those bold words about the "new wife" had been assuredly spoken before I heard Josephine stealing up to the door.

As soon as the fire was alight and the bed made, I went back to the music-room to announce that my orders had been obeyed. Mr. James Smith was walking up and down in a perturbed way, still keeping his hat on. He followed me to the Red Room without saying a word.

Ten minutes later he rang for the kettle and the bottle of brandy. When I took them in I found him unpacking a small carpet-bag, which was the only luggage he had brought with him. He still kept silence, and did not appear to take any notice of me. I left him immediately without our having so much as exchanged a single word.

So far as I could tell, the night passed quietly. The next morning I heard that my mistress was suffering so severely from a nervous attack that she was unable to rise from her bed. It was no surprise to me to be told that, knowing as I did what she had gone through the night before.

About nine o'clock I went with the hot water to the Red Room. After knocking twice I tried the door, and, finding it not locked, went in with the jug in my hand.

I looked at the bed—I looked all round the room. Not a sign of Mr. James Smith was to be seen anywhere.

Judging by appearances, the bed had certainly been occupied. Thrown across the counterpane lay the nightgown he had worn. I took it up and saw some spots on it. I looked at them a little closer. They were spots of blood.

CHAPTER V.

THE first amazement and alarm produced by this discovery deprived me of my presence of mind. Without stopping to think what I ought to do first, I ran back to the servants' hall, calling out that something had happened to my master.

All the household hurried directly into the Red Room, Josephine among the rest. I was first brought to my senses, as it were, by observing the strange expression of her countenance when she saw the bed-gown and the empty room. All the other servants were bewildered and frightened. She alone, after giving a little start, recovered herself directly. A look of devilish satisfaction broke out on her face, and she left the room quickly and quietly, without exchanging a word with any of us. I saw this, and it aroused my suspicions. There is no need to mention what they were, for, as events soon showed, they were entirely wide of the mark.

Having come to myself a little, I sent them all out of the room except the coachman. We two then examined the place.

The Red Room was usually occupied by visitors. It was on the ground floor, and looked out into the garden. We found the window-shutters, which I had barred overnight, open, but the window itself was down. The fire had been out long enough for the grate to be quite cold. Half the bottle of brandy had been drunk. The carpet-bag was gone. There were no marks of violence or struggling anywhere about the bed or the room. We examined every corner carefully, but made no other discoveries than these.

When I returned to the servants' hall, bad news of my mistress was awaiting me there. The unusual noise and confusion in the house had reached her ears, and she had been told what had happened without sufficient caution being exercised in preparing her to hear it. In her weak, nervous state, the shock of the intelligence had quite prostrated her. She had fallen into a swoon, and had been brought back to her senses with the greatest difficulty. As to giving me or anybody else directions what to do under the e mbarrassing circumstances which had now occurred, she was totally incapable of the effort.

I waited till the middle of the day, in the hope that she might get strong enough to give her orders; but no message came from her. At last I resolved to send and ask her what she thought it best to do. Josephine was the proper person to go on this errand; but when I asked for Josephine, she was nowhere to be found. The housemaid, who had searched for her ineffectually, brought word that her bonnet and shawl were not hanging in their usual places. The parlor-maid, who had been in attendance in my mistress's room, came down while we were all aghast at this new disappearance. She could only tell us that Josephine had begged her to do lady's-maid's duty that morning, as she was not well. Not well! And the first result of her illness appeared to be that she had left the house!

I cautioned the servants on no account to mention this circumstance to my mistress, and then went upstairs myself to knock at her door. My object was to ask if I might count on her approval if I wrote in her name to the lawyer in London, and if I afterward went and gave information of what had occurred to the nearest justice of the peace. I might have sent to make this inquiry through one of the female servants; but by this time, though not naturally suspicious, I had got to distrust everybody in the house, whether they deserved it or not.

So I asked the question myself, standing outside the door. My mistress thanked me in a faint voice, and begged me to do what I had proposed immediately.

I went into my own bedroom and wrote to the lawyer, merely telling him that Mr. James Smith had appeared unexpectedly at the Hall, and that events had occurred in consequence which required his immediate presence. I made the letter up like a parcel, and sent the coachman with it to catch the mail on its way through to London.

The next thing was to go to the justice of the peace. The nearest lived about five miles off, and was well acquainted with my mistress. He was an old bachelor, and he kept house with his brother, who was a widower. The two were much respected and beloved in the county, being kind, unaffected gentlemen, who did a great deal of good among the poor. The justice was Mr. Robert Nicholson, and his brother, the widower, was Mr. Philip.

I had got my hat on, and was asking the groom which horse I had better take, when an open carriage drove up to the house. It contained Mr. Philip Nicholson and two persons in plain clothes, not exactly servants and not exactly gentlemen, as far as I could judge. Mr. Philip looked at me, when I touched my hat to him, in a very grave, downcast way, and asked for my mistress. I told him she was ill in bed. He shook his head at hearing that, and said he wished to speak to me in private. I showed him into the library. One of the men in plain clothes followed us, and sat in the hall. The other waited with the carriage.

"I was just going out, sir," I said, as I set a chair for him, "to speak to Mr. Robert Nicholson about a very extraordinary circumstance—"

"I know what you refer to," said Mr. Philip, cutting me short rather abruptly; "and I must beg, for reasons which will presently appear, that you will make no statement of any sort to me until you have first heard what I have to say. I am here on a very serious and a very shocking errand, which deeply concerns your mistress and you."

His face suggested something worse than his words expressed. My heart began to beat fast, and I felt that I was turning pale.

"Your master, Mr. James Smith," he went on, "came here unexpectedly yesterday evening, and slept in this house last night. Before he retired to rest he and your mistress had high words together, which ended, I am sorry to hear, in a threat of a serious nature addressed by Mrs. James Smith to her husband. They slept in separate rooms. This morning you went into your master's room and saw no sign of him there. You only found his nightgown on the bed, spotted with blood."

"Yes, sir," I said, in as steady a voice as I could command. "Quite true."

"I am not examining you," said Mr. Philip. "I am only making a certain statement, the truth of which you can admit or deny before my brother."

"Before your brother, sir!" I repeated. "Am I suspected of anything wrong?"

"There is a suspicion that Mr. James Smith has been murdered," was the answer I received to that question.

My flesh began to creep all over from head to foot.

"I am shocked—I am horrified to say," Mr. Philip went on, "that the suspicion affects your mistress in the first place, and you in the second."

I shall not attempt to describe what I felt when he said that. No words of mine, no words of anybody's, could give an idea of it. What other men would have done in my situation I don't know. I stood before Mr. Philip, staring straight at him, without speaking, without moving, almost without breathing. If he or any other man had struck me at that moment, I do not believe I should have felt the blow.

"Both my brother and myself," said Mr. Philip, "have such unfeigned respect for your mistress, such sympathy for her under these frightful circumstances, and such an implicit belief in her capability of proving her innocence, that we are desirous of sparing her in this dreadful emergency as much as possible. For those reasons, I have undertaken to come here with the persons appointed to execute my brother's warrant—"

"Warrant, sir!" I said, getting command of my voice as he pronounced that word—"a warrant against my mistress!"

"Against her and against you," said Mr. Philip. "The suspicious circumstances have been sworn to by a competent witness, who has declared on oath that your mistress is guilty, and that you are an accomplice."

"What witness, sir?"

"Your mistress's quadroon maid, who came to my brother this morning, and who has made her deposition in due form."

"And who is as false as hell," I cried out passionately, "in every word she says against my mistress and against me."

"I hope—no, I will go further, and say I believe she is false," said Mr. Philip. "But her perjury must he proved, and the necessary examination must take place. My carriage is going back to my brother's, and you will go in it, in charge of one of my men, who has the warrant to take you in custody. I shall remain here with the man who is waiting in the hall; and before any steps are taken to execute the other warrant, I shall send for the doctor to ascertain when your mistress can be removed."

"Oh, my poor mistress!" I said, "this will be the death of her, sir."

"I will take care that the shock shall strike her as tenderly as possible," said Mr. Philip. "I am here for that express purpose. She has my deepest sympathy and respect, and shall have every help and alleviation that I can afford her."

The hearing him say that, and the seeing how sincerely he meant what he said, was the first gleam of comfort in the dreadful affliction that had befallen us. I felt this; I felt a burning anger against the wretch who had done her best to ruin my mistress's fair name and mine, but in every other respect I was like a man who had been stunned, and whose faculties had not perfectly recovered from the shock. Mr. Philip was obliged to remind me that time was of importance, and that I had better give myself up immediately, on the merciful terms which his kindness offered to me. I acknowledged that, and wished him good morning. But a mist seemed to come over my eyes as I turned round to go away—a mist that prevented me from finding my way to the door. Mr. Philip opened it for me, and said a friendly word or two which I could hardly hear. The man waiting outside took me to his companion in the carriage at the door, and I was driven away, a prisoner for the first time in my life.

On our way to the justice's, what little thinking faculty I had left in me was all occupied in the attempt to trace a motive for the inconceivable treachery and falsehood of which Josephine had been guilty.

Her words, her looks, and her manner, on that unfortunate day when my mistress so far forget herself as to strike, her, came back diml y to my memory, and led to the inference that part of the motive, at least, of which I was in search, might be referred to what had happened on that occasion. But was this the only reason for her devilish vengeance against my mistress? And, even if it were so, what fancied injuries had I done her? Why should I be included in the false accusation? In the dazed state of my faculties at that time, I was quite incapable of seeking the answer to these questions. My mind was clouded all over, and I gave up the attempt to clear it in despair.

I was brought before Mr. Robert Nicholson that day, and the fiend of a quadroon was examined in my presence. The first sight of her face, with its wicked self-possession, with its smooth leering triumph, so sickened me that I turned my head away and never looked at her a second time throughout the proceedings. The answers she gave amounted to a mere repetition of the deposition to which she had already sworn. I listened to her with the most breathless attention, and was thunderstruck at the inconceivable artfulness with which she had mixed up truth and falsehood in her charge against my mistress and me.

This was, in substance, what she now stated in my presence:

After describing the manner of Mr. James Smith's arrival at the Hall, the witness, Josephine Durand, confessed that she had been led to listen at the music-room door by hearing angry voices inside, and she then described, truly enough, the latter part of the altercation between husband and wife. Fearing, after this, that something serious might happen, she had kept watch in her room, which was on the same floor as her mistress's. She had heard her mistress's door open softly between one and two in the morning—had followed her mistress, who carried a small lamp, along the passage and down the stairs into the hall—had hidden herself in the porter's chair—had seen her mistress take a dagger in a green sheath from a collection of Eastern curiosities kept in the hall—had followed her again, and seen her softly enter the Red Room—had heard the heavy breathing of Mr. James Smith, which gave token that he was asleep—had slipped into an empty room, next door to the Red Roam, and had waited there about a quarter of an hour, when her mistress came out again with the dagger in her hand—had followed her mistress again into the hall, where she had put the dagger back into its place—had seen her mistress turn into a side passage that led to my room—had heard her knock at my door, and heard me answer and open it—had hidden again in the porter's chair—had, after a while, seen me and my mistress pass together into the passage that led to the Red Room—had watched us both into the Red Room—and had then, through fear of being discovered and murdered herself, if she risked detection any longer, stolen back to her own room for the rest of the night.

After deposing on oath to the truth of these atrocious falsehoods, and declaring, in conclusion, that Mr. James Smith had been murdered by my mistress, and that I was an accomplice, the quadroon had further asserted, in order to show a motive for the crime, that Mr. Meeke was my mistress's lover; that he had been forbidden the house by her husband, and that he was found in the house, and alone with her, on the evening of Mr. James Smith's return. Here again there were some grains of truth cunningly mixed up with a revolting lie, and they had their effect in giving to the falsehood a look of probability.

I was cautioned in the usual manner and asked if I had anything to say.

I replied that I was innocent, but that I would wait for legal assistance before I defended myself. The justice remanded me and the examination was over. Three days later my unhappy mistress was subjected to the same trial. I was not allowed to communicate with her. All I knew was that the lawyer had arrived from London to help her. Toward the evening he was admitted to see me. He shook his head sorrowfully when I asked after my mistress.

"I am afraid," he said, "that she has sunk under the horror of the situation in which that vile woman has placed her. Weakened by her previous agitation, she seems to have given way under this last shock, tenderly and carefully as Mr. Philip Nicholson broke the bad news to her. All her feelings appeared to be strangely blunted at the examination to-day. She answered the questions put to her quite correctly, but at the same time quite mechanically, with no change in her complexion, or in her tone of voice, or in her manner, from beginning to end. It is a sad thing, William, when women cannot get their natural vent of weeping, and your mistress has not shed a tear since she left Darrock Hall."

"But surely, sir," I said, "if my examination has not proved Josephine's perjury, my mistress's examination must have exposed it?"

"Nothing will expose it," answered the lawyer, "but producing Mr. James Smith, or, at least, legally proving that he is alive. Morally speaking, I have no doubt that the justice before whom you have been examined is as firmly convinced as we can be that the quadroon has perjured herself. Morally speaking, he believes that those threats which your mistress unfortunately used referred (as she said they did to-day) to her intention of leaving the Hall early in the morning, with you for her attendant, and coming to me, if she had been well enough to travel, to seek effectual legal protection from her husband for the future. Mr. Nicholson believes that; and I, who know more of the circumstances than he does, believe also that Mr. James Smith stole away from Darrock Hall in the night under fear of being indicted for bigamy. But if I can't find him—if I can't prove him to be alive—if I can't account for those spots of blood on the night-gown, the accidental circumstances of the case remain unexplained—your mistress's rash language, the bad terms on which she has lived with her husband, and her unlucky disregard of appearances in keeping up her intercourse with Mr. Meeke, all tell dead against us—and the justice has no alternative, in a legal point of view, but to remand you both, as he has now done, for the production of further evidence."

"But how, then, in Heaven's name, is our innocence to be proved, sir?" I asked.

"In the first place," said the lawyer, "by finding Mr. James Smith; and, in the second place, by persuading him, when he is found, to come forward and declare himself."

"Do you really believe, sir," said I, "that he would hesitate to do that, when he knows the horrible charge to which his disappearance has exposed his wife? He is a heartless villain, I know; but surely—"

"I don't suppose," said the lawyer, cutting me short, "that he is quite scoundrel enough to decline coming forward, supposing he ran no risk by doing so. But remember that he has placed himself in a position to be tried for bigamy, and that he believes your mistress will put the law in force against him."

I had forgotten that circumstance. My heart sank within me when it was recalled to my memory, and I could say nothing more.

"It is a very serious thing," the lawyer went on—"it is a downright offense against the law of the land to make any private offer of a compromise to this man. Knowing what we know, our duty as good citizens is to give such information as may bring him to trial. I tell you plainly that, if I did not stand toward your mistress in the position of a relation as well as a legal adviser, I should think twice about running the risk—the very serious risk—on which I am now about to venture for her sake. As it is, I have taken the right measures to assure Mr. James Smith that he will not be treated according to his deserts. When he knows what the circumstances are, he will trust us—supposing always that we can find him. The search about this neighborhood has been quite useless. I have sent private instructions by to-day's post to Mr. Dark in London, and with them a carefully-worded form of advertisement for the public newspapers. You may rest assured that every human means of tracing him will be tried forthwith. In the meantime, I have an important question to put to you about Josep hine. She may know more than we think she does; she may have surprised the secret of the second marriage, and may be keeping it in reserve to use against us. If this should turn out to be the case, I shall want some other chance against her besides the chance of indicting her for perjury. As to her motive now for making this horrible accusation, what can you tell me about that, William?"

"Her motive against me, sir?"

"No, no, not against you. I can see plainly enough that she accuses you because it is necessary to do so to add to the probability of her story, which, of course, assumes that you helped your mistress to dispose of the dead body. You are coolly sacrificed to some devilish vengeance against her mistress. Let us get at that first.

Has there ever been a quarrel between them?"

I told him of the quarrel, and of how Josephine had looked and talked when she showed me her cheek.

"Yes," he said, "that is a strong motive for revenge with a naturally pitiless, vindictive woman. But is that all? Had your mistress any hold over her? Is there any self-interest mixed up along with this motive of vengeance? Think a little, William. Has anything ever happened in the house to compromise this woman, or to make her fancy herself compromised?"

The remembrance of my mistress's lost trinkets and handkerchiefs, which later and greater troubles had put out of my mind, flashed back into my memory while he spoke. I told him immediately of the alarm in the house when the loss was discovered.

"Did your mistress suspect Josephine and question her?" he asked, eagerly.

"No, sir," I replied. "Before she could say a word, Josephine impudently asked who she suspected, and boldly offered her own boxes to be searched."

The lawyer's face turned red as scarlet. He jumped out of his chair, and hit me such a smack on the shoulder that I thought he had gone mad.

"By Jupiter!" he cried out, "we have got the whip-hand of that she-devil at last."

I looked at him in astonishment.

"Why, man alive," he said, "don't you see how it is? Josephine's the thief! I am as sure of it as that you and I are talking together. This vile accusation against your mistress answers another purpose besides the vindictive one —it is the very best screen that the wretch could possibly set up to hide herself from detection. It has stopped your mistress and you from moving in the matter; it exhibits her in the false character of an honest witness against a couple of criminals; it gives her time to dispose of the goods, or to hide them, or to do anything she likes with them. Stop! let me be quite sure that I know what the lost things are. A pair of bracelets, three rings, and a lot of lace pocket-handkerchiefs—is that what you said?"

"Yes, sir."

"Your mistress will describe them particularly, and I will take the right steps the first thing to-morrow morning. Good-evening, William, and keep up your spirits. It shan't be my fault if you don't soon see the quadroon in the right place for her—at the prisoner's bar."

With that farewell he went out.

The days passed, and I did not see him again until the period of my remand had expired. On this occasion, when I once more appeared before the justice, my mistress appeared with me. The first sight of her absolutely startled me, she was so sadly altered. Her face looked so pinched and thin that it was like the face of an old woman. The dull, vacant resignation of her expression was something shocking to see. It changed a little when her eyes first turned heavily toward me, and she whispered, with a faint smile, "I am sorry for you, William—I am very, very sorry for you." But as soon as she had said those words the blank look returned, and she sat with her head drooping forward, quiet, and inattentive, and hopeless—so changed a being that her oldest friends would hardly have known her.

Our examination was a mere formality. There was no additional evidence either for or against us, and we were remanded again for another week.

I asked the lawyer, privately, if any chance had offered itself of tracing Mr. James Smith. He looked mysterious, and only said in answer, "Hope for the best." I inquired next if any progress had been made toward fixing the guilt of the robbery on Josephine.

"I never boast," he replied. "But, cunning as she is, I should not be surprised if Mr. Dark and I, together, turned out to be more than a match for her."

Mr. Dark! There was something in the mere mention of his name that gave me confidence in the future. If I could only have got my poor mistress's sad, dazed face out of my mind, I should not have had much depression of spirits to complain of during the interval of time that elapsed between the second examination and the third.

CHAPTER VI.

ON the third appearance of my mistress and myself before the justice, I noticed some faces in the room which I had not seen there before. Greatly to my astonishment—for the previous examinations had been conducted as privately as possible—I remarked the presence of two of the servants from the Hall, and of three or four of the tenants on the Darrock estate, who lived nearest to the house. They all sat together on one side of the justice-room. Opposite to them and close at the side of a door, stood my old acquaintance, Mr. Dark, with his big snuff-box, his jolly face, and his winking eye. He nodded to me, when I looked at him, as jauntily as if we were meeting at a party of pleasure. The quadroon woman, who had been summoned to the examination, had a chair placed opposite to the witness-box, and in a line with the seat occupied by my poor mistress, whose looks, as I was grieved to see, were not altered for the better. The lawyer from London was with her, and I stood behind her chair.

We were all quietly disposed in the room in this way, when the justice, Mr. Robert Nicholson, came in with his brother. It might have been only fancy, but I thought I could see in both their faces that something remarkable had happened since we had met at the last examination.

The deposition of Josephine Durand was read over by the clerk, and she was asked if she had anything to add to it. She replied in the negative. The justice then appealed to my mistress's relation, the lawyer, to know if he could produce any evidence relating to the charge against his clients.

"I have evidence," answered the lawyer, getting briskly on his legs, "which I believe, sir, will justify me in asking for their discharge."

"Where are your witnesses?" inquired the justice, looking hard at Josephine while he spoke.

"One of them is in waiting, your worship," said Mr. Dark, opening the door near which he was standing.

He went out of the room, remained away about a minute, and returned with his witness at his heels.

My heart gave a bound as if it would jump out of my body. There, with his long hair cut short, and his bushy whiskers shaved off—there, in his own proper person, safe and sound as ever, was Mr. James Smith!

The quadroon's iron nature resisted the shock of his unexpected presence on the scene with a steadiness that was nothing short of marvelous. Her thin lips closed together convulsively, and there was a slight movement in the muscles of her throat. But not a word, not a sign betrayed her. Even the yellow tinge of her complexion remained unchanged.

"It is not necessary, sir, that I should waste time and words in referring to the wicked and preposterous charge against my clients," said the lawyer, addressing Mr. Robert Nicholson. "The one sufficient justification for discharging them immediately is before you at this moment in the person of that gentleman. There, sir, stands the murdered Mr. James Smith, of Darrock Hall, alive and well, to answer for himself."

"That is not the man!" cried Josephine, her shrill voice just as high, clear, and steady as ever, "I denounce that man as an impostor. Of my own knowledge, I deny that he is Mr. James Smith."

"No doubt you do," said the lawyer; "but we will prove his identity for all that."

The first witness called was Mr. Philip Nicholson. He could swear that he had seen Mr. James Smith, and spoken to him at least a dozen times. The person now before h im was Mr. James Smith, altered as to personal appearance by having his hair cut short and his whiskers shaved off, but still unmistakably the man he assumed to be.

"Conspiracy!" interrupted the prisoner, hissing the word out viciously between her teeth.

"If you are not silent," said Mr. Robert Nicholson, "you will be removed from the room. It will sooner meet the ends of justice," he went on, addressing the lawyer, "if you prove the question of identity by witnesses who have been in habits of daily communication with Mr. James Smith."

Upon this, one of the servants from the Hall was placed in the box.

The alteration in his master's appearance evidently puzzled the man. Besides the perplexing change already adverted to, there was also a change in Mr. James Smith's expression and manner. Rascal as he was, I must do him the justice to say that he looked startled and ashamed when he first caught sight of his unfortunate wife. The servant, who was used to be eyed tyrannically by him, and ordered about roughly, seeing him now for the first time abashed and silent, stammered and hesitated on being asked to swear to his identity.

"I can hardly say for certain, sir," said the man, addressing the justice in a bewildered manner. "He is like my master, and yet he isn't. If he wore whiskers and had his hair long, and if he was, saying your presence, sir, a little more rough and ready in his way, I could swear to him anywhere with a safe conscience."

Fortunately for us, at this moment Mr. James Smith's feeling of uneasiness at the situation in which he was placed changed to a feeling of irritation at being coolly surveyed and then stupidly doubted in the matter of his identity by one of his own servants.

"Can't you say in plain words, you idiot, whether you know me or whether you don't?" he called out, angrily.

"That's his voice!" cried the servant, starting in the box. "Whiskers or no whiskers, that's him!"

"If there's any difficulty, your worship, about the gentleman's hair," said Mr. Dark, coming forward with a grin, "here's a small parcel which, I may make so bold as to say, will remove it." Saying that, he opened the parcel, took some locks of hair out of it, and held them up close to Mr. James Smith's head. "A pretty good match, your worship," continued Mr. Dark. "I have no doubt the gentleman's head feels cooler now it's off. We can't put the whiskers on, I'm afraid, but they match the hair; and they are in the paper (if one may say such a thing of whiskers) to speak for themselves."

"Lies! lies! lies!" screamed Josephine, losing her wicked self-control at this stage of the proceedings.

The justice made a sign to two of the constables present as she burst out with those exclamations, and the men removed her to an adjoining room.

The second servant from the Hall was then put in the box, and was followed by one of the tenants. After what they had heard and seen, neither of these men had any hesitation in swearing positively to their master's identity.

"It is quite unnecessary," said the justice, as soon as the box was empty again, "to examine any more witnesses as to the question of identity. All the legal formalities are accomplished, and the charge against the prisoners falls to the ground. I have great pleasure in ordering the immediate discharge of both the accused persons, and in declaring from this place that they leave the court without the slightest stain on their characters."

He bowed low to my mistress as he said that, paused a moment, and then looked inquiringly at Mr. James Smith.

"I have hitherto abstained from making any remark unconnected with the immediate matter in hand," he went on. "But, now that my duty is done, I cannot leave this chair without expressing my strong sense of disapprobation of the conduct of Mr. James Smith—conduct which, whatever may be the motives that occasioned it, has given a false color of probability to a most horrible charge against a lady of unspotted reputation, and against a person in a lower rank of life whose good character ought not to have been imperiled even for a moment. Mr. Smith may or may not choose to explain his mysterious disappearance from Darrock Hall, and the equally unaccountable change which he has chosen to make in his personal appearance. There is no legal charge against him; but, speaking morally, I should be unworthy of the place I hold if I hesitated to declare my present conviction that his conduct has been deceitful, inconsiderate, and unfeeling in the highest degree."

To this sharp reprimand Mr. James Smith (evidently tutored beforehand as to what he was to say) replied that, in attending before the justice, he wished to perform a plain duty and to keep himself strictly within the letter of the law. He apprehended that the only legal obligation laid on him was to attend in that court to declare himself, and to enable competent witnesses to prove his identity. This duty accomplished, he had merely to add that he preferred submitting to a reprimand from the bench to entering into explanations which would involve the disclosure of domestic circumstances of a very unhappy nature. After that brief reply he had nothing further to say, and he would respectfully request the justice's permission to withdraw.

The permission was accorded. As he crossed the room he stopped near his wife, and said, confusedly, in a very low tone:

"I have done you many injuries, but I never intended this. I am sorry for it. Have you anything to say to me before I go?"

My mistress shuddered and hid her face. He waited a moment, and, finding that she did not answer him, bowed his head politely and went out. I did not know it then, but I had seen him for the last time.

After he had gone, the lawyer, addressing Mr. Robert Nicholson, said that he had an application to make in reference to the woman Josephine Durand.

At the mention of that name my mistress hurriedly whispered a few words into her relation's ear. He looked toward Mr. Philip Nicholson, who immediately advanced, offered his arm to my mistress, and led her out. I was about to follow, when Mr. Dark stopped me, and begged that I would wait a few minutes longer, in order to give myself the pleasure of seeing "the end of the case."

In the meantime, the justice had pronounced the necessary order to have the quadroon brought back. She came in, as bold and confident as ever. Mr. Robert Nicholson looked away from her in disgust and said to the lawyer:

"Your application is to have her committed for perjury, of course?"

"For perjury?" said Josephine, with her wicked smile. "Very good. I shall explain some little matters that I have not explained before. You think I am quite at your mercy now? Bah! I shall make myself a thorn in your sides yet."

"She has got scent of the second marriage," whispered Mr. Dark to me.

There could be no doubt of it. She had evidently been listening at the door on the night when my master came back longer than I had supposed. She must have heard those words about "the new wife"—she might even have seen the effect of them on Mr. James Smith.

"We do not at present propose to charge Josephine Durand with perjury," said the lawyer, "but with another offense, for which it is important to try her immediately, in order to effect the restoration of property that has been stolen. I charge her with stealing from her mistress, while in her service at Darrock Hall, a pair of bracelets, three rings, and a dozen and a half of lace pocket-handkerchiefs. The articles in question were taken this morning from between the mattresses of her bed; and a letter was found in the same place which clearly proves that she had represented the property as belonging to herself, and that she had tried to dispose of it to a purchaser in London." While he was speaking, Mr. Dark produced the jewelry, the handkerchiefs and the letter, and laid them before the justice.

Even Josephine's extraordinary powers of self-control now gave way at last. At the first words of the unexpected charge against her she struck her hands together violently, gnashed her sharp white teeth, and burst out with a torrent of fierce-sounding words in some foreig n language, the meaning of which I did not understand then and cannot explain now.

"I think that's checkmate for marmzelle," whispered Mr. Dark, with his invariable wink. "Suppose you go back to the Hall, now, William, and draw a jug of that very remarkable old ale of yours? I'll be after you in five minutes, as soon as the charge is made out."

I could hardly realize it when I found myself walking back to Darrock a free man again.

In a quarter of an hour's time Mr. Dark joined me, and drank to my health, happiness and prosperity in three separate tumblers. After performing this ceremony, he wagged his head and chuckled with an appearance of such excessive enjoyment that I could not avoid remarking on his high spirits.

"It's the case, William—it's the beautiful neatness of the case that quite intoxicates me. Oh, Lord, what a happiness it is to be concerned in such a job as this!" cries Mr. Dark, slapping his stumpy hands on his fat knees in a sort of ecstasy.

I had a very different opinion of the case for my own part, but I did not venture on expressing it. I was too anxious to know how Mr. James Smith had been discovered and produced at the examination to enter into any arguments. Mr. Dark guessed what was passing in my mind, and, telling me to sit down and make myself comfortable, volunteered of his own accord to inform me of all that I wanted to know.

"When I got my instructions and my statement of particulars," he began, "I was not at all surprised to hear that Mr. James Smith had come back. (I prophesied that, if you remember, William, the last time we met?) But I was a good deal astonished, nevertheless, at the turn things had taken, and I can't say I felt very hopeful about finding our man. However, I followed my master's directions, and put the advertisement in the papers. It addressed Mr. James Smith by name, but it was very carefully worded as to what was wanted of him. Two days after it appeared, a letter came to our office in a woman's handwriting. It was my business to open the letters, and I opened that. The writer was short and mysterious. She requested that somebody would call from our office at a certain address, between the hours of two and four that afternoon, in reference to the advertisement which we had inserted in the newspapers. Of course, I was the somebody who went. I kept myself from building up hopes by the way, knowing what a lot of Mr. James Smiths there were in London. On getting to the house, I was shown into the drawing-room, and there, dressed in a wrapper and lying on a sofa, was an uncommonly pretty woman, who looked as if she was just recovering from an illness. She had a newspaper by her side, and came to the point at once: 'My husband's name is James Smith,' she says, 'and I have my reasons for wanting to know if he is the person you are in search of.' I described our man as Mr. James Smith, of Darrock Hall, Cumberland. 'I know no such person,' says she—"

"What! was it not the second wife, after all?" I broke out.

"Wait a bit," says Mr. Dark. "I mentioned the name of the yacht next, and she started up on the sofa as if she had been shot. 'I think you were married in Scotland, ma'am,' says I. She turns as pale as ashes, and drops back on the sofa, and says, faintly: 'It is my husband. Oh, sir, what has happened? What do you want with him? Is he in debt?' I took a minute to think, and then made up my mind to tell her everything, feeling that she would keep her husband (as she called him) out of the way if I frightened her by any mysteries. A nice job I had, William, as you may suppose, when she knew about the bigamy business. What with screaming, fainting, crying, and blowing me up (as if I was to blame!), she kept me by that sofa of hers the best part of an hour—kept me there, in short, till Mr. James Smith himself came back. I leave you to judge if that mended matters. He found me mopping the poor woman's temples with scent and water; and he would have pitched me out of the window, as sure as I sit here, if I had not met him and staggered him at once with the charge of murder against his wife. That stopped him when he was in full cry, I can promise you. 'Go and wait in the next room,' says he, 'and I'll come in and speak to you directly.' "

"And did you go?" I asked.

"Of course I did," said Mr. Dark. "I knew he couldn't get out by the drawing-room windows, and I knew I could watch the door; so away I went, leaving him alone with the lady, who didn't spare him by any manner of means, as I could easily hear in the next room. However, all rows in this world come to an end sooner or later, and a man with any brains in his head may do what he pleases with a woman who is fond of him. Before long I heard her crying and kissing him. 'I can't go home,' she says, after this. 'You have behaved like a villain and a monster to me—but oh, Jemmy, I can't give you up to anybody! Don't go back to your wife! Oh, don't, don't go back to your wife!' 'No fear of that,' says he. 'My wife wouldn't have me if I did go back to her.' After that I heard the door open, and went out to meet him on the landing. He began swearing the moment he saw me, as if that was any good. 'Business first, if you please, sir,' says I, 'and any pleasure you like, in the way of swearing, afterward.' With that beginning, I mentioned our terms to him, and asked the pleasure of his company to Cumberland in return, he was uncommonly suspicious at first, but I promised to draw out a legal document (mere waste paper, of no earthly use except to pacify him), engaging to hold him harmless throughout the proceedings; and what with that, and telling him of the frightful danger his wife was in, I managed, at last, to carry my point."

"But did the second wife make no objection to his going away with you?" I inquired.

"Not she," said Mr. Dark. "I stated the case to her just as it stood, and soon satisfied her that there was no danger of Mr. James Smith's first wife laying any claim to him. After hearing that, she joined me in persuading him to do his duty, and said she pitied your mistress from the bottom of her heart. With her influence to back me, I had no great fear of our man changing his mind. I had the door watched that night, however, so as to make quite sure of him. The next morning he was ready to time when I called, and a quarter of an hour after that we were off together for the north road. We made the journey with post-horses, being afraid of chance passengers, you know, in public conveyances. On the way down, Mr. James Smith and I got on as comfortably together as if we had been a pair of old friends. I told the story of our tracing him to the north of Scotland, and he gave me the particulars, in return, of his bolting from Darrock Hall. They are rather amusing, William; would you like to hear them?"

I told Mr. Dark that he had anticipated the very question I was about to ask him.

"Well," he said, "this is how it was: To begin at the beginning, our man really took Mrs. Smith, Number Two, to the Mediterranean, as we heard. He sailed up the Spanish coast, and, after short trips ashore, stopped at a seaside place in France called Cannes. There he saw a house and grounds to be sold which took his fancy as a nice retired place to keep Number Two in. Nothing particular was wanted but the money to buy it; and, not having the little amount in his own possession, Mr. James Smith makes a virtue of necessity, and goes back overland to his wife with private designs on her purse-strings. Number Two, who objects to be left behind, goes with him as far as London. There he trumps up the first story that comes into his head about rents in the country, and a house in Lincolnshire that is too damp for her to trust herself in; and so, leaving her for a few days in London, starts boldly for Darrock Hall. His notion was to wheedle your mistress out of the money by good behavior; but it seems he started badly by quarreling with her about a fiddle-playing parson—"

"Yes, yes, I know all about that part of the story," I broke in, seeing by Mr. Dark's manner that he was likely to speak both ignorantly and impertinently of my mistress's unlucky friend ship for Mr. Meeke. "Go on to the time when I left my master alone in the Red Room, and tell me what he did between midnight and nine the next morning."

"Did?" said Mr. Dark. "Why, he went to bed with the unpleasant conviction on his mind that your mistress had found him out, and with no comfort to speak of except what he could get out of the brandy bottle. He couldn't sleep; and the more he tossed and tumbled, the more certain he felt that his wife intended to have him tried for bigamy. At last, toward the gray of the morning, he could stand it no longer, and he made up his mind to give the law the slip while he had the chance. As soon as he was dressed, it struck him that there might be a reward offered for catching him, and he determined to make that slight change in his personal appearance which puzzled the witnesses so much before the magistrate to-day. So he opens his dressing-case and crops his hair in no time, and takes off his whiskers next. The fire was out, and he had to shave in cold water. What with that, and what with the flurry of his mind, naturally enough he cut himself—"

"And dried the blood with his nightgown?" says I.

"With his nightgown," repeated Mr. Dark. "It was the first thing that lay handy, and he snatched it up. Wait a bit, though; the cream of the thing is to come. When he had done being his own barber, he couldn't for the life of him hit on a way of getting rid of the loose hair. The fire was out, and he had no matches; so he couldn't burn it. As for throwing it away, he didn't dare do that in the house or about the house, for fear of its being found, and betraying what he had done. So he wraps it all up in paper, crams it into his pocket to be disposed of when he is at a safe distance from the Hall, takes his bag, gets out at the window, shuts it softly after him, and makes for the road as fast as his long legs will carry him. There he walks on till a coach overtakes him, and so travels back to London to find himself in a fresh scrape as soon as be gets there. An interesting situation, William, and hard traveling from one end of France to the other, had not agreed together in the case of Number Two. Mr. James Smith found her in bed, with doctor's orders that she was not to be moved. There was nothing for it after that but to lie by in London till the lady got better. Luckily for us, she didn't hurry herself; so that, after all, your mistress has to thank the very woman who supplanted her for clearing her character by helping us to find Mr. James Smith."

"And, pray, how did you come by that loose hair of his which you showed before the justice to-day?" I asked.

"Thank Number Two again," says Mr. Dark. "I was put up to asking after it by what she told me. While we were talking about the advertisement, I made so bold as to inquire what first set her thinking that her husband and the Mr. James Smith whom we wanted might be one and the same man. 'Nothing,' says she, 'but seeing him come home with his hair cut short and his whiskers shaved off, and finding that he could not give me any good reason for disfiguring himself in that way. I had my suspicions that something was wrong, and the sight of your advertisement strengthened them directly.' The hearing her say that suggested to my mind that there might be a difficulty in identifying him after the change in his looks, and I asked him what he had done with the loose hair before we left London. It was found in the pocket of his traveling coat just as he had huddled it up there on leaving the Hall, worry, and fright, and vexation, having caused him to forget all about it. Of course I took charge of the parcel, and you know what good it did as well as I do. So to speak, William, it just completed this beautifully neat case. Looking at the matter in a professional point of view, I don't hesitate to say that we have managed our business with Mr. James Smith to perfection. We have produced him at the right time, and we are going to get rid of him at the right time. By to-night he will be on his way to foreign parts with Number Two, and he won't show his nose in England again if he lives to the age of Methuselah."

It was a relief to hear that and it was almost as great a comfort to find, from what Mr. Dark said next, that my mistress need fear nothing that Josephine could do for the future.

The charge of theft, on which she was about to be tried, did not afford the shadow of an excuse in law any more than in logic for alluding to the crime which her master had committed. If she meant to talk about it she might do so in her place of transportation, but she would not have the slightest chance of being listened to previously in a court of law.

"In short," said Mr. Dark, rising to take his leave, "as I have told you already, William, it's checkmate for marmzelle. She didn't manage the business of the robbery half as sharply as I should have expected. She certainly began well enough by staying modestly at a lodging in the village to give her attendance at the examinations, as it might be required; nothing could look more innocent and respectable so far; but her hiding the property between the mattresses of her bed—the very first place that any experienced man would think of looking in— was such an amazingly stupid thing to do, that I really can't account for it, unless her mind had more weighing on it than it was able to bear, which, considering the heavy stakes she played for, is likely enough. Anyhow, her hands are tied now, and her tongue too, for the matter of that. Give my respects to your mistress, and tell her that her runaway husband and her lying maid will never either of them harm her again as long as they live. She has nothing to do now but to pluck up her spirits and live happy. Here's long life to her and to you, William, in the last glass of ale; and here's the same toast to myself in the bottom of the jug."

With those words Mr. Dark pocketed his large snuff-box, gave a last wink with his bright eye, and walked rapidly away, whistling, to catch the London coach. From that time to this he and I have never met again.

A few last words relating to my mistress and to the other persons chiefly concerned in this narrative will conclude all that it is now necessary for me to say.

For some months the relatives and friends, and I myself, felt sad misgivings on my poor mistress's account. We doubted if it was possible, with such a quick, sensitive nature as hers, that she could support the shock which had been inflicted on her. But our powers of endurance are, as I have learned to believe, more often equal to the burdens laid upon us than we are apt to imagine. I have seen many surprising recoveries from illness after all hope had been lost, and I have lived to see my mistress recover from the grief and terror which we once thought would prove fatal to her. It was long before she began to hold up her head again; but care and kindness, and time and change wrought their effect on her at last. She is not now, and never will be again, the woman she was once; her manner is altered, and she looks older by many a year than she really is. But her health causes us no anxiety now; her spirits are calm and equal, and I have good hope that many quiet years of service in her house are left for me still. I myself have married during the long interval of time which I am now passing over in a few words. This change in my life is, perhaps, not worth mentioning, but I am reminded of my two little children when I speak of my mistress in her present position. I really think they make the great happiness, and interest, and amusement of her life, and prevent her from feeling lonely and dried up at heart. It is a pleasant reflection to me to remember this, and perhaps it may be the same to you, for which reason only I speak of it.

As for the other persons connected with the troubles at Darrock Hall, I may mention the vile woman Josephine first, so as to have the sooner done with her. Mr. Dark's guess, when he tried to account for her want of cunning in hiding the stolen property, by saying that her mind might have had more weighing on it than she was able to bear, turned out to b e nothing less than the plain and awful truth. After she had been found guilty of the robbery, and had been condemned to seven years' transportation, a worse sentence fell upon her from a higher tribunal than any in this world. While she was still in the county jail, previous to her removal, her mind gave way, the madness breaking out in an attempt to set fire to the prison. Her case was pronounced to be hopeless from the first. The lawful asylum received her, and the lawful asylum will keep her to the end of her days.

Mr. James Smith, who, in my humble opinion, deserved hanging by law, or drowning by accident at least, lived quietly abroad with his Scotch wife (or no wife) for two years, and then died in the most quiet and customary manner, in his bed, after a short illness. His end was described to me as a "highly edifying one." But as he was also reported to have sent his forgiveness to his wife—which was as much as to say that *he* was the injured person of the two—I take leave to consider that he was the same impudent vagabond in his last moments that he had been all his life. His Scotch widow has married again, and is now settled in London. I hope her husband is all her own property this time.

Mr. Meeke must not be forgotten, although he has dropped out of the latter part of my story because he had nothing to do with the serious events which followed Josephine's perjury. In the confusion and wretchedness of that time, he was treated with very little ceremony, and was quite passed over when we left the neighborhood. After pining and fretting some time, as we afterward heard, in his lonely parsonage, he resigned his living at the first chance he got, and took a sort of under-chaplain's place in an English chapel abroad. He writes to my mistress once or twice a year to ask after her health and well-being, and she writes back to him. That is all the communication they are ever likely to have with each other. The music they once played together will never sound again. Its last notes have long since faded away and the last words of this story, trembling on the lips of the teller, may now fade with them.

THE NINTH DAY.

A LITTLE change in the weather. The rain still continues, but the wind is not quite so high. Have I any reason to believe, because it is calmer on land, that it is also calmer at sea? Perhaps not. But my mind is scarcely so uneasy to-day, nevertheless.

I had looked over the newspaper with the usual result, and had laid it down with the customary sense of disappointment, when Jessie handed me a letter which she had received that morning. It was written by her aunt, and it upbraided her in the highly exaggerated terms which ladies love to employ, where any tender interests of their own are concerned, for her long silence and her long absence from home. Home! I thought of my poor boy and of the one hope on which all his happiness rested, and I felt jealous of the word when I saw it used persuasively in a letter to our guest. What right had any one to mention "home" to her until George had spoken first?

"I must answer it by return of post," said Jessie, with a tone of sorrow in her voice for which my heart warmed to her. "You have been very kind to me; you have taken more pains to interest and amuse me than I am worth. I can laugh about most things, but I can't laugh about going away. I am honestly and sincerely too grateful for that."

She paused, came round to where I was sitting, perched herself on the end of the table, and, resting her hands on my shoulders, added gently:

"It must be the day after to-morrow, must it not?"

I could not trust myself to answer. If I had spoken, I should have betrayed George's secret in spite of myself.

"To-morrow is the tenth day," she went on, softly. "It looks so selfish and so ungrateful to go the moment I have heard the last of the stories, that I am quite distressed at being obliged to enter on the subject at all. And yet, what choice is left me? what can I do when my aunt writes to me in that way?"

She took up the letter again, and looked at it so ruefully that I drew her head a little nearer to me, and gratefully kissed the smooth white forehead.

"If your aunt is only half as anxious to see you again, my love, as I am to see my son, I must forgive her for taking you away from us." The words came from me without premeditation. It was not calculation this time, but sheer instinct that impelled me to test her in this way, once more, by a direct reference to George. She was so close to me that I felt her breath quiver on my cheek. Her eyes had been fixed on my face a moment before, but they now wandered away from it constrainedly. One of her hands trembled a little on my shoulder, and she took it off.

"Thank you for trying to make our parting easier to me," she said, quickly, and in a lower tone than she had spoken in yet. I made no answer, but still looked her anxiously in the face. For a few seconds her nimble delicate fingers nervously folded and refolded the letter from her aunt, then she abruptly changed her position.

"The sooner I write, the sooner it will be over," she said, and hurriedly turned away to the paper-case on the side-table.

How was the change in her manner to be rightly interpreted? Was she hurt by what I had said, or was she secretly so much affected by it, in the impressionable state of her mind at that moment, as to be incapable of exerting a young girl's customary self-control? Her looks, actions, and language might bear either interpretation. One striking omission had marked her conduct when I had referred to George's return. She had not inquired when I expected him back. Was this indifference? Surely not. Surely indifference would have led her to ask the conventionally civil question which ninety-nine persons out of a hundred would have addressed to me as a matter of course. Was she, on her side, afraid to trust herself to speak of George at a time when an unusual tenderness was aroused in her by the near prospect of saying farewell? It might be—it might not be—it might be. My feeble reason took the side of my inclination; and, after vibrating between Yes and No, I stopped where I had begun—at Yes.

She finished the letter in a few minutes, and dropped it into the post-bag the moment it was done.

"Not a word more," she said, returning to me with a sigh of relief—"not a word about my aunt or my going away till the time comes. We have two more days; let us make the most of them."

Two more days! Eight-and-forty hours still to pass; sixty minutes in each of those hours; and every minute long enough to bring with it an event fatal to George's future! The bare thought kept my mind in a fever. For the remainder of the day I was as desultory and as restless as our Queen of Hearts herself. Owen affectionately did his best to quiet me, but in vain. Even Morgan, who whiled away the time by smoking incessantly, was struck by the wretched spectacle of nervous anxiety that I presented to him, and pitied me openly for being unable to compose myself with a pipe. Wearily and uselessly the hours wore on till the sun set. The clouds in the western heaven wore wild and tortured shapes when I looked out at them; and, as the gathering darkness fell on us, the fatal fearful wind rose once more.

When we assembled at eight, the drawing of the lots had no longer any interest or suspense, so far as I was concerned. I had read my last story, and it now only remained for chance to decide the question of precedency between Owen and Morgan. Of the two numbers left in the bowl, the one drawn was Nine. This made it Morgan's turn to read, and left it appropriately to Owen, as our eldest brother, to close the proceedings on the next night.

Morgan looked round the table when he had spread out his manuscript, and seemed half inclined to open fire, as usual, with a little preliminary sarcasm; but his eyes met mine; he saw the anxiety I was suffering; and his natural kindness, perversely as he might strive to hide it, got the better of him. He looked down on his paper; growled out briefly, "No need for a preface; my little bit of writing explains itself; let's go on and have don e with it," and so began to read without another word from himself or from any of us.

BROTHER MORGAN'S STORY

of

FAUNTLEROY.

CHAPTER I.

IT was certainly a dull little dinner-party. Of the four guests, two of us were men between fifty and sixty, and two of us were youths between eighteen and twenty, and we had no subjects in common. We were all intimate with our host, but were only slightly acquainted with each other. Perhaps we should have got on better if there had been some ladies among us; but the master of the house was a bachelor, and, except the parlor-maids who assisted in waiting on us at dinner, no daughter of Eve was present to brighten the dreary scene.

We tried all sorts of subjects, but they dropped one after the other. The elder gentlemen seemed to be afraid of committing themselves by talking too freely within hearing of us juniors, and we, on our side, restrained our youthful flow of spirits and youthful freedom of conversation out of deference to our host, who seemed once or twice to be feeling a little nervous about the continued propriety of our behavior in the presence of his respectable guests. To make matters worse, we had dined at a sensible hour. When the bottles made their first round at dessert, the clock on the mantel-piece only struck eight. I counted the strokes, and felt certain, from the expression of his face, that the other junior guest, who sat on one side of me at the round table, was counting them also. When we came to the final eight, we exchanged looks of despair. "Two hours more of this! What on earth is to become of us?" In the language of the eyes, that was exactly what we said to each other.

The wine was excellent, and I think we all came separately and secretly to the same conclusion—that our chance of getting through the evening was intimately connected with our resolution in getting through the bottles.

As a matter of course, we talked wine. No company of Englishmen can assemble together for an evening without doing that. Every man in this country who is rich enough to pay income-tax has at one time or other in his life effected a very remarkable transaction in wine. Sometimes he has made such a bargain as he never expects to make again. Sometimes he is the only man in England, not a peer of the realm, who has got a single drop of a certain famous vintage which has perished from the face of the earth. Sometimes he has purchased, with a friend, a few last left dozens from the cellar of a deceased potentate, at a price so exorbitant that he can only wag his head and decline mentioning it; and, if you ask his friend, that friend will wag his head, and decline mentioning it also. Sometimes he has been at an out-of-the-way country inn; has found the sherry not drinkable; has asked if there is no other wine in the house; has been informed that there is some "sourish foreign stuff that nobody ever drinks"; has called for a bottle of it; has found it Burgundy, such as all France cannot now produce, has cunningly kept his own counsel with the widowed landlady, and has bought the whole stock for "an old song." Sometimes he knows the proprietor of a famous tavern in London, and he recommends his one or two particular friends, the next time they are passing that way, to go in and dine, and give his compliments to the landlord, and ask for a bottle of the brown sherry, with the light blue—as distinguished from the dark blue—seal. Thousands of people dine there every year, and think they have got the famous sherry when they get the dark blue seal; but the real wine, the famous wine, is the light blue seal, and nobody in England knows it but the landlord and his friends. In all these wine-conversations, whatever variety there may be in the various experiences related, one of two great first principles is invariably assumed by each speaker in succession. Either he knows more about it than any one else, or he has got better wine of his own even than the excellent wine he is now drinking. Men can get together sometimes without talking of women, without talking of horses, without talking of politics, but they cannot assemble to eat a meal together without talking of wine, and they cannot talk of wine without assuming to each one of themselves an absolute infallibility in connection with that single subject which they would shrink from asserting in relation to any other topic under the sun.

How long the inevitable wine-talk lasted on the particular social occasion of which I am now writing is more than I can undertake to say. I had heard so many other conversations of the same sort at so many other tables that my attention wandered away wearily, and I began to forget all about the dull little dinner-party and the badly-assorted company of guests of whom I formed one. How long I remained in this not over-courteous condition of mental oblivion is more than I can tell; but when my attention was recalled, in due course of time, to the little world around me, I found that the good wine had begun to do its good office.

The stream of talk on either side of the host's chair was now beginning to flow cheerfully and continuously; the wine-conversation had worn itself out; and one of the elder guests—Mr. Wendell—was occupied in telling the other guest—Mr. Trowbridge—of a small fraud which had lately been committed on him by a clerk in his employment. The first part of the story I missed altogether. The last part, which alone caught my attention, followed the career of the clerk to the dock of the Old Bailey.

"So, as I was telling you," continued Mr. Wendell, "I made up my mind to prosecute, and I did prosecute. Thoughtless people blamed me for sending the young man to prison, and said I might just as well have forgiven him, seeing that the trifling sum of money I had lost by his breach of trust was barely as much as ten pounds. Of course, personally speaking, I would much rather not have gone into court; but I considered that my duty to society in general, and to my brother merchants in particular, absolutely compelled me to prosecute for the sake of example. I acted on that principle, and I don't regret that I did so. The circumstances under which the man robbed me were particularly disgraceful. He was a hardened reprobate, sir, if ever there was one yet; and I believe, in my conscience, that he wanted nothing but the opportunity to be as great a villain as Fauntleroy himself."

At the moment when Mr. Wendell personified his idea of consummate villainy by quoting the example of Fauntleroy, I saw the other middle-aged gentleman—Mr. Trowbridge—color up on a sudden, and begin to fidget in his chair.

"The next time you want to produce an instance of a villain, sir," said Mr. Trowbridge, "I wish you could contrive to quote some other example than Fauntleroy."

Mr. Wendell naturally enough looked excessively astonished when he heard these words, which were very firmly and, at the same time, very politely addressed to him.

"May I inquire why you object to my example?" he asked.

"I object to it, sir," said Mr. Trowbridge, "because it makes me very uncomfortable to hear Fauntleroy called a villain."

"Good heavens above!" exclaimed Mr. Wendell, utterly bewildered. "Uncomfortable!—you, a mercantile man like myself—you, whose character stands so high everywhere—you uncomfortable when you hear a man who was hanged for forgery called a villain! In the name of wonder, why?"

"Because," answered Mr. Trowbridge, with perfect composure, "Fauntleroy was a friend of mine."

"Excuse me, my dear sir," retorted Mr. Wendell, in as polished a tone of sarcasm as he could command; "but of all the friends whom you have made in the course of your useful and honorable career, I should have thought the friend you have just mentioned would have been the very last to whom you were likely to refer in respectable society, at least by name."

"Fauntleroy committed an unpardonable crime, and died a disgraceful death," said Mr. Trowbridge. "But, for all that, Fauntleroy was a friend of mine, and in that character I shall always acknowledge him boldly to my dying day. I have a tenderness for his memory, though he violated a sacred trust, and die d for it on the gallows. Don't look shocked, Mr. Wendell. I will tell you, and our other friends here, if they will let me, why I feel that tenderness, which looks so strange and so discreditable in your eyes. It is rather a curious anecdote, sir, and has an interest, I think, for all observers of human nature quite apart from its connection with the unhappy man of whom we have been talking. You young gentlemen," continued Mr. Trowbridge, addressing himself to us juniors, "have heard of Fauntleroy, though he sinned and suffered, and shocked all England long before your time?"

We answered that we had certainly heard of him as one of the famous criminals of his day. We knew that he had been a partner in a great London banking-house; that he had not led a very virtuous life; that he had possessed himself, by forgery, of trust-moneys which he was doubly bound to respect; and that he had been hanged for his offense, in the year eighteen hundred and twenty-four, when the gallows was still set up for other crimes than murder, and when Jack Ketch was in fashion as one of the hard-working reformers of the age.

"Very good," said Mr. Trowbridge. "You both of you know quite enough of Fauntleroy to be interested in what I am going to tell you. When the bottles have been round the table, I will start with my story."

The bottles went round—claret for the degenerate youngsters; port for the sterling, steady-headed, middle-aged gentlemen. Mr. Trowbridge sipped his wine—meditated a little—sipped again—and started with the promised anecdote in these terms:

CHAPTER II.

WHAT I am going to tell you, gentlemen, happened when I was a very young man, and when I was just setting up in business on my own account.

My father had been well acquainted for many years with Mr. Fauntleroy, of the famous London banking firm of Marsh, Stracey, Fauntleroy & Graham. Thinking it might be of some future service to me to make my position known to a great man in the commercial world, my father mentioned to his highly-respected friend that I was about to start in business for myself in a very small way, and with very little money. Mr. Fauntleroy received the intimation with a kind appearance of interest, and said that he would have his eye on me. I expected from this that he would wait to see if I could keep on my legs at starting, and that, if he found I succeeded pretty well, he would then help me forward if it lay in his power. As events turned out, he proved to be a far better friend than that, and he soon showed me that I had very much underrated the hearty and generous interest which he had felt in my welfare from the first.

While I was still fighting with the difficulties of setting up my office, and recommending myself to my connection, and so forth, I got a message from Mr. Fauntleroy telling me to call on him, at the banking-house, the first time I was passing that way. As you may easily imagine, I contrived to be passing that way on a particularly early occasion, and, on presenting myself at the bank, I was shown at once into Mr. Fauntleroy's private room.

He was as pleasant a man to speak to as ever I met with—bright, and gay, and companionable in his manner—with a sort of easy, hearty, jovial bluntness about him that attracted everybody. The clerks all liked him—and that is something to say of a partner in a banking-house, I can tell you!

"Well, young Trowbridge," says he, giving his papers on the table a brisk push away from him, "so you are going to set up in business for yourself, are you? I have a great regard for your father, and a great wish to see you succeed. Have you started yet? No? Just on the point of beginning, eh? Very good. You will have your difficulties, my friend, and I mean to smooth one of them away for you at the outset. A word of advice for your private ear—Bank with us."

"You are very kind, sir," I answered, "and I should ask nothing better than to profit by your suggestion, if I could. But my expenses are heavy at starting, and when they are all paid I am afraid I shall have very little left to put by for the first year. I doubt if I shall be able to muster much more than three hundred pounds of surplus cash in the world after paying what I must pay before I set up my office, and I should be ashamed to trouble your house, sir, to open an account for such a trifle as that."

"Stuff and nonsense!" says Mr. Fauntleroy. "Are *you* a banker? What business have you to offer an opinion on the matter? Do as I tell you—leave it to me— bank with us—and draw for what you like. Stop! I haven't done yet. When you open the account, speak to the head cashier. Perhaps you may find he has got something to tell you. There! there! go away—don't interrupt me—good-by— God bless you!"

That was his way—ah! poor fellow, that was his way.

I went to the head cashier the next morning when I opened my little modicum of an account. He had received orders to pay my drafts without reference to my balance. My checks, when I had overdrawn, were to be privately shown to Mr. Fauntleroy. Do many young men who start in business find their prosperous superiors ready to help them in that way?

Well, I got on—got on very fairly and steadily, being careful not to venture out of my depth, and not to forget that small beginnings may lead in time to great ends. A prospect of one of those great ends—great, I mean, to such a small trader as I was at that period—showed itself to me when I had been some little time in business. In plain terms, I had a chance of joining in a first-rate transaction, which would give me profit, and position, and everything I wanted, provided I could qualify myself for engaging in it by getting good security beforehand for a very large amount.

In this emergency, I thought of my kind friend, Mr. Fauntleroy, and went to the bank, and saw him once more in his private room.

There he was at the same table, with the same heaps of papers about him, and the same hearty, easy way of speaking his mind to you at once, in the fewest possible words. I explained the business I came upon with some little hesitation and nervousness, for I was afraid he might think I was taking an unfair advantage of his former kindness to me. When I had done, he just nodded his head, snatched up a blank sheet of paper, scribbled a few lines on it in his rapid way, handed the writing to me, and pushed me out of the room by the two shoulders before I could say a single word. I looked at the paper in the outer office. It was my security from the great banking-house for the whole amount, and for more, if more was wanted.

I could not express my gratitude then, and I don't know that I can describe it now. I can only say that it has outlived the crime, the disgrace, and the awful death on the scaffold. I am grieved to speak of that death at all; but I have no other alternative. The course of my story must now lead me straight on to the later time, and to the terrible discovery which exposed my benefactor and my friend to all England as the forger Fauntleroy.

I must ask you to suppose a lapse of some time after the occurrence of the events that I have just been relating. During this interval, thanks to the kind assistance I had received at the outset, my position as a man of business had greatly improved. Imagine me now, if you please, on the high road to prosperity, with good large offices and a respectable staff of clerks, and picture me to yourselves sitting alone in my private room between four and five o'clock on a certain Saturday afternoon.

All my letters had been written, all the people who had appointments with me had been received. I was looking carelessly over the newspaper, and thinking about going home, when one of my clerks came in, and said that a stranger wished to see me immediately on very important business.

"Did he mention his name?" I inquired.

"No, sir."

"Did you not ask him for it?"

"Yes, sir. And he said you would be none the wiser if he told me what it was."

"Does he look like a begging-letter writer?"

"He looks a little shabby, sir, but he doesn't talk at all like a begging-letter writer. He spoke sharp and decided, sir, and said it was in your interests that he came, and that you would deeply regret it afterward if you refused to see him."

"He said that, did he? Show him in at once, then."

He was shown in immediately: a middling-sized man, with a sharp, unwholesome-looking face, and with a flippant, reckless manner, dressed in a style of shabby smartness, eying me with a bold look, and not so overburdened with politeness as to trouble himself about taking off his hat when he came in. I had never seen him before in my life, and I could not form the slightest conjecture from his appearance to guide me toward guessing his position in the world. He was not a gentleman, evidently; but as to fixing his whereabouts in the infinite downward gradations of vagabond existence in London, that was a mystery which I was totally incompetent to solve.

"Is your name Trowbridge?" he began.

"Yes," I answered, dryly enough.

"Do you bank with Marsh, Stracey, Fauntleroy & Graham?"

"Why do you ask?"

"Answer my question, and you will know."

"Very well, I *do* bank with Marsh, Stracey, Fauntleroy & Graham—and what then?"

"Draw out every farthing of balance you have got before the bank closes at five to-day."

I stared at him in speechless amazement. The words, for an instant, absolutely petrified me.

"Stare as much as you like," he proceeded, coolly, "I mean what I say. Look at your clock there. In twenty minutes it will strike five, and the bank will be shut. Draw out every farthing, I tell you again, and look sharp about it."

"Draw out my money!" I exclaimed, partially recovering myself. "Are you in your right senses? Do you know that the firm I bank with represents one of the first houses in the world? What do you mean—you, who are a total stranger to me—by taking this extraordinary interest in my affairs? If you want me to act on your advice, why don't you explain yourself?"

"I have explained myself. Act on my advice or not, just as you like. It doesn't matter to me. I have done what I promised, and there's an end of it."

He turned to the door. The minute-hand of the clock was getting on from the twenty minutes to the quarter.

"Done what you promised?" I repeated, getting up to stop him.

"Yes," he said, with his hand on the lock. "I have given my message. Whatever happens, remember that. Good-afternoon."

He was gone before I could speak again.

I tried to call after him, but my speech suddenly failed me. It was very foolish, it was very unaccountable, but there was something in the man's last words which had more than half frightened me.

I looked at the clock. The minute-hand was on the quarter.

My office was just far enough from the bank to make it necessary for me to decide on the instant. If I had had time to think, I am perfectly certain that I should not have profited by the extraordinary warning that had just been addressed to me. The suspicious appearance and manners of the stranger; the outrageous improbability of the inference against the credit of the bank toward which his words pointed; the chance that some underhand attempt was being made, by some enemy of mine, to frighten me into embroiling myself with one of my best friends, through showing an ignorant distrust of the firm with which he was associated as partner—all these considerations would unquestionably have occurred to me if I could have found time for reflection; and, as a necessary consequence, not one farthing of my balance would have been taken from the keeping of the bank on that memorable day.

As it was, I had just time enough to act, and not a spare moment for thinking. Some heavy payments made at the beginning of the week had so far decreased my balance that the sum to my credit in the banking-book barely reached fifteen hundred pounds. I snatched up my check-book, wrote a draft for the whole amount, and ordered one of my clerks to run to the bank and get it cashed before the doors closed. What impulse urged me on, except the blind impulse of hurry and bewilderment, I can't say. I acted mechanically, under the influence of the vague inexplicable fear which the man's extraordinary parting words had aroused in me, without stopping to analyze my own sensations—almost without knowing what I was about. In three minutes from the time when the stranger had closed my door the clerk had started for the bank, and I was alone again in my room, with my hands as cold as ice and my head all in a whirl.

I did not recover my control over myself until the clerk came back with the notes in his hand. He had just got to the bank in the nick of time. As the cash for my draft was handed to him over the counter, the clock struck five, and he heard the order given to close the doors.

When I had counted the bank-notes and had locked them up in the safe, my better sense seemed to come back to me on a sudden. Never have I reproached myself before or since as I reproached myself at that moment. What sort of return had I made for Mr. Fauntleroy's fatherly kindness to me? I had insulted him by the meanest, the grossest distrust of the honor and the credit of his house, and that on the word of an absolute stranger, of a vagabond, if ever there was one yet. It was madness—downright madness in any man to have acted as I had done. I could not account for my own inconceivably thoughtless proceeding. I could hardly believe in it myself. I opened the safe and looked at the bank-notes again. I locked it once more, and flung the key down on the table in a fury of vexation against myself. There the money was, upbraiding me with my own inconceivable folly, telling me in the plainest terms that I had risked depriving myself of my best and kindest friend henceforth and forever.

It was necessary to do something at once toward making all the atonement that lay in my power. I felt that, as soon as I began to cool down a little. There was but one plain, straight-forward way left now out of the scrape in which I had been mad enough to involve myself. I took my hat, and, without stopping an instant to hesitate, hurried off to the bank to make a clean breast of it to Mr. Fauntleroy.

When I knocked at the private door and asked for him, I was told that he had not been at the bank for the last two days. One of the other partners was there, however, and was working at that moment in his own room.

I sent in my name at once, and asked to see him. He and I were little better than strangers to each other, and the interview was likely to be, on that account, unspeakably embarrassing and humiliating on my side. Still, I could not go home. I could not endure the inaction of the next day, the Sunday, without having done my best on the spot to repair the error into which my own folly had led me. Uncomfortable as I felt at the prospect of the approaching interview, I should have been far more uneasy in my mind if the partner had declined to see me.

To my relief, the bank porter returned with a message requesting me to walk in.

What particular form my explanations and apologies took when I tried to offer them is more than I can tell now. I was so confused and distressed that I hardly knew what I was talking about at the time. The one circumstance which I remember clearly is that I was ashamed to refer to my interview with the strange man, and that I tried to account for my sudden withdrawal of my balance by referring it to some inexplicable panic, caused by mischievous reports which I was unable to trace to their source, and which, for anything I knew to the contrary, might, after all, have been only started in jest. Greatly to my surprise, the partner did not seem to notice the lamentable lameness of my excuses, and did not additionally confuse me by asking any questions. A weary, absent look, which I had observed on his face when I came in, remained on it while I was speaking. It seemed to be an effort to him even to keep up the appearance of listening to me; and when, at last, I fairly broke down in the middle of a sentence, and gave up the hope of getting any further, all the answer he gave me was comprised in these few civil commonplace words:

"Never mind, Mr. Trowbridge; pray don't think of apologizing. We are all liable to make mista kes. Say nothing more about it, and bring the money back on Monday if you still honor us with your confidence."

He looked down at his papers as if he was anxious to be alone again, and I had no alternative, of course, but to take my leave immediately. I went home, feeling a little easier in my mind now that I had paved the way for making the best practical atonement in my power by bringing my balance back the first thing on Monday morning. Still, I passed a weary day on Sunday, reflecting, sadly enough, that I had not yet made my peace with Mr. Fauntleroy. My anxiety to set myself right with my generous friend was so intense that I risked intruding myself on his privacy by calling at his town residence on the Sunday. He was not there, and his servant could tell me nothing of his whereabouts. There was no help for it now but to wait till his weekday duties brought him back to the bank.

I went to business on Monday morning half an hour earlier than usual, so great was my impatience to restore the amount of that unlucky draft to my account as soon as possible after the bank opened.

On entering my office, I stopped with a startled feeling just inside the door. Something serious had happened. The clerks, instead of being at their desks as usual, were all huddled together in a group, talking to each other with blank faces. When they saw me, they fell back behind my managing man, who stepped forward with a circular in his hand.

"Have you heard the news, sir?" he said.

"No. What is it?"

He handed me the circular. My heart gave one violent throb the instant I looked at it. I felt myself turn pale; I felt my knees trembling under me.

Marsh, Stracey, Fauntleroy & Graham had stopped payment.

"The circular has not been issued more than half an hour," continued my managing clerk. "I have just come from the bank, sir. The doors are shut; there is no doubt about it. Marsh & Company have stopped this morning."

I hardly heard him; I hardly knew who was talking to me. My strange visitor of the Saturday had taken instant possession of all my thoughts, and his words of warning seemed to be sounding once more in my ears. This man had known the true condition of the bank when not another soul outside the doors was aware of it! The last draft paid across the counter of that ruined house, when the doors closed on Saturday, was the draft that I had so bitterly reproached myself for drawing; the one balance saved from the wreck was my balance. Where had the stranger got the information that had saved me? and why had he brought it to my ears?

I was still groping, like a man in the dark, for an answer to those two questions—I was still bewildered by the unfathomable mystery of doubt into which they had plunged me—when the discovery of the stopping of the bank was followed almost immediately by a second shock, far more dreadful, far heavier to bear, so far as I was concerned, than the first.

While I and my clerks were still discussing the failure of the firm, two mercantile men, who were friends of mine, ran into the office, and overwhelmed us with the news that one of the partners had been arrested for forgery. Never shall I forget the terrible Monday morning when those tidings reached me, and when I knew that the partner was Mr. Fauntleroy.

I was true to him—I can honestly say I was true to my belief in my generous friend—when that fearful news reached me. My fellow-merchants had got all the particulars of the arrest. They told me that two of Mr. Fauntleroy's fellow-trustees had come up to London to make arrangements about selling out some stock. On inquiring for Mr. Fauntleroy at the banking-house, they had been informed that he was not there; and, after leaving a message for him, they had gone into the City to make an appointment with their stockbroker for a future day, when their fellow-trustee might be able to attend. The stock-broker volunteered to make certain business inquiries on the spot, with a view to saving as much time as possible, and left them at his office to await his return. He came back, looking very much amazed, with the information that the stock had been sold out down to the last five hundred pounds. The affair was instantly investigated; the document authorizing the selling out was produced; and the two trustees saw on it, side by side with Mr. Fauntleroy's signature, the forged signatures of their own names. This happened on the Friday, and the trustees, without losing a moment, sent the officers of justice in pursuit of Mr. Fauntleroy. He was arrested, brought up before the magistrate, and remanded on the Saturday. On the Monday I heard from my friends the particulars which I have just narrated.

But the events of that one morning were not destined to end even yet. I had discovered the failure of the bank and the arrest of Mr. Fauntleroy. I was next to be enlightened, in the strangest and the saddest manner, on the difficult question of his innocence or his guilt.

Before my friends had left my office—before I had exhausted the arguments which my gratitude rather than my reason suggested to me in favor of the unhappy prisoner—a note, marked immediate, was placed in my hands, which silenced me the instant I looked at it. It was written from the prison by Mr. Fauntleroy, and it contained two lines only, entreating me to apply for the necessary order, and to go and see him immediately.

I shall not attempt to describe the flutter of expectation, the strange mixture of dread and hope that agitated me when I recognized his handwriting, and discovered what it was that he desired me to do. I obtained the order and went to the prison. The authorities, knowing the dreadful situation in which he stood, were afraid of his attempting to destroy himself, and had set two men to watch him. One came out as they opened his cell door. The other, who was bound not to leave him, very delicately and considerately affected to be looking out of window the moment I was shown in.

He was sitting on the side of his bed, with his head drooping and his hands hanging listlessly over his knees when I first caught sight of him. At the sound of my approach he started to his feet, and, without speaking a word, flung both his arms round my neck

My heart swelled up.

"Tell me it's not true, sir! For God's sake, tell me it's not true!" was all I could say to him.

He never answered—oh me! he never answered, and he turned away his face.

There was one dreadful moment of silence. He still held his arms round my neck, and on a sudden he put his lips close to my ear.

"Did you get your money out?" he whispered. "Were you in time on Saturday afternoon?"

I broke free from him in the astonishment of hearing those words.

"What!" I cried out loud, forgetting the third person at the window. "That man who brought the message—"

"Hush!" he said, putting his hand on my lips. "There was no better man to be found, after the officers had taken me—I know no more about him than you do—I paid him well as a chance messenger, and risked his cheating me of his errand."

"*You* sent him, then!"

"I sent him."

My story is over, gentlemen. There is no need for me to tell you that Mr. Fauntleroy was found guilty, and that he died by the hangman's hand. It was in my power to soothe his last moments in this world by taking on myself the arrangement of some of his private affairs, which, while they remained unsettled, weighed heavily on his mind. They had no connection with the crimes he had committed, so I could do him the last little service he was ever to accept at my hands with a clear conscience.

I say nothing in defense of his character—nothing in palliation of the offense for which he suffered. But I cannot forget that in the time of his most fearful extremity, when the strong arm of the law had already seized him, he thought of the young man whose humble fortunes he had helped to build; whose heartfelt gratitude he had fairly won; whose simple faith he was resolved never to betray. I leave it to greater intellects than mine to reconcile the anomaly of his reckless falsehood toward others and his steadfast truth toward me. It is as certain as that we sit here that one of Fauntleroy's last efforts in this world was the effort he made to preserve me from being a loser by the trust that I had placed in him. There is the secret of my strange tenderness for the memory of a felon; that is why the word villain does somehow still grate on my heart when I hear it associated with the name—the disgraced name, I grant you—of the forger Fauntleroy. Pass the bottles, young gentlemen, and pardon a man of the old school for having so long interrupted your conversation with a story of the old time.

THE TENTH DAY.

THE storm has burst on us in its full fury. Last night the stout old tower rocked on its foundations.

I hardly ventured to hope that the messenger who brings us our letters from the village—the postman, as we call him—would make his appearance this morning; but he came bravely through rain, hail and wind. The old pony which he usually rides had refused to face the storm, and, sooner than disappoint us, our faithful postman had boldly started for The Glen Tower on foot. All his early life had been passed on board ship, and, at sixty years of age, he had battled his way that morning through the storm on shore as steadily and as resolutely as ever he had battled it in his youth through the storm at sea.

I opened the post-bag eagerly. There were two letters for Jessie from young lady friends; a letter for Owen from a charitable society; a letter to me upon business; and—on this last day, of all others—no newspaper!

I sent directly to the kitchen (where the drenched and weary postman was receiving the hospitable attentions of the servants) to make inquiries. The disheartening answer returned was that the newspaper could not have arrived as usual by the morning's post, or it must have been put into the bag along with the letters. No such accident as this had occurred, except on one former occasion, since the beginning of the year. And now, on the very day when I might have looked confidently for news of George's ship, when the state of the weather made the finding of that news of the last importance to my peace of mind, the paper, by some inconceivable fatality, had failed to reach me! If there had been the slightest chance of borrowing a copy in the village, I should have gone there myself through the tempest to get it. If there had been the faintest possibility of communicating, in that frightful weather, with the distant county town, I should have sent there or gone there myself. I even went the length of speaking to the groom, an old servant whom I knew I could trust. The man stared at me in astonishment, and then pointed through the window to the blinding hail and the writhing trees.

"No horse that ever was foaled, sir," he said, "would face *that* for long. It's a'most a miracle that the postman got here alive. He says himself that he dursn't go back again. I'll try it, sir, if you order me; but if an accident happens, please to remember, whatever becomes of *me*, that I warned you beforehand."

It was only too plain that the servant was right, and I dismissed him. What I suffered from that one accident of the missing newspaper I am ashamed to tell. No educated man can conceive how little his acquired mental advantages will avail him against his natural human inheritance of superstition, under certain circumstances of fear and suspense, until he has passed the ordeal in his own proper person. We most of us soon arrive at a knowledge of the extent of our strength, but we may pass a lifetime and be still ignorant of the extent of our weakness.

Up to this time I had preserved self-control enough to hide the real state of my feelings from our guest; but the arrival of the tenth day, and the unexpected trial it had brought with it, found me at the end of my resources. Jessie's acute observation soon showed her that something had gone wrong, and she questioned me on the subject directly. My mind was in such a state of confusion that no excuse occurred to me. I left her precipitately, and entreated Owen and Morgan to keep her in their company, and out of mine, for the rest of the day. My strength to preserve my son's secret had failed me, and my only chance of resisting the betrayal of it lay in the childish resource of keeping out of the way. I shut myself into my room till I could bear it no longer. I watched my opportunity, and paid stolen visits over and over again to the barometer in the hall. I mounted to Morgan's rooms at the top of the tower, and looked out hopelessly through rain-mist and scud for signs of a carriage on the flooded valley-road below us. I stole down again to the servants' hall, and questioned the old postman (half-tipsy by this time with restorative mulled ale) about his past experience of storms at sea; drew him into telling long, rambling, wearisome stories, not one-tenth part of which I heard; and left him with my nervous irritability increased tenfold by his useless attempts to interest and inform me. Hour by hour, all through that miserable day, I opened doors and windows to feel for myself the capricious changes of the storm from worse to better, and from better to worse again. Now I sent once more for the groom, when it looked lighter; and now I followed him hurriedly to the stables, to countermand my own rash orders. My thoughts seemed to drive over my mind as the rain drove over the earth; the confusion within me was the image in little of the mightier turmoil that raged outside.

Before we assembled at the dinner-table, Owen whispered to me that he had made my excuses to our guest, and that I need dread nothing more than a few friendly inquiries about my health when I saw her again. The meal was dispatched hastily and quietly. Toward dusk the storm began to lessen, and for a moment the idea of sending to the town occurred to me once more. But, now that the obstacle of weather had been removed, the obstacle of darkness was set up in its place. I felt this; I felt that a few more hours would decide the doubt about George, so far as this last day was concerned, and I determined to wait a little longer, having already waited so long. My resolution was the more speedily taken in this matter, as I had now made up my mind, in sheer despair, to tell my son's secret to Jessie if he failed to return before she left us. My reason warned me that I should put myself and my guest in a false position by taking this step, but something stronger than my reason forbade me to let her go back to the gay world and its temptations without first speaking to her of George in the lamentable event of George not being present to speak for himself.

We were a sad and silent little company when the clock struck eight that night, and when we met for the last time to hear the last story. The shadow of the approaching farewell—itself the shade of the long farewell—rested heavily on our guest's spirits. The gay dresses which she had hitherto put on to honor our little ceremony were all packed up, and the plain gown she wore kept the journey of the morrow cruelly before her eyes and ours. A quiet melancholy shed its tenderness over her bright young face as she drew the last number, for form's sake, out of the bowl, and handed it to Owen with a faint smile. Even our positions at the table were altered now. Under the pretense that the light hurt my eyes, I moved back into a dim corner, to keep my anxious face out of view. Morgan, looking at me hard, and muttering under his breath, "Thank Heaven, I never married!" stole his chair by degrees, with rough, silent kindness, nearer and nearer to mine. Jessie, after a moment's hesitation, vacated her place next, and, saying that she wanted to sit close to one of us on the farewell night, took a chair at Owen's side. Sad! sad! we had instinctively broken up already, so far as our places at the table were concerned, before the reading of the last story had so much as begun.

It was a relief when Owen's quiet voice stole over the weary silence, and pleaded for our attention to the occupation of the night.

"Number Six," he said, "is the number that chance has left to remain till the last. The manuscript to which it refers is not, as you may see, in my handw riting. It consists entirely of passages from the Diary of a poor hard-working girl— passages which tell an artless story of love and friendship in humble life. When that story has come to an end, I may inform you how I became possessed of it. If I did so now, I should only forestall one important part of the interest of the narrative. I have made no attempt to find a striking title for it. It is called, simply and plainly, after the name of the writer of the Diary—the Story of Anne Rodway."

In the short pause that Owen made before he began to read, I listened anxiously for the sound of a traveler's approach outside. At short intervals, all through the story, I listened and listened again. Still, nothing caught my ear but the trickle of the rain and the rush of the sweeping wind through the valley, sinking gradually lower and lower as the night advanced.

BROTHER OWEN'S STORY

of

ANNE RODWAY.

[TAKEN FROM HER DIARY.]

* * * MARCH 3d, 1840. A long letter today from Robert, which surprised and vexed me so that I have been sadly behindhand with my work ever since. He writes in worse spirits than last time, and absolutely declares that he is poorer even than when he went to America, and that he has made up his mind to come home to London.

How happy I should be at this news, if he only returned to me a prosperous man! As it is, though I love him dearly, I cannot look forward to the meeting him again, disappointed and broken down, and poorer than ever, without a feeling almost of dread for both of us. I was twenty-six last birthday and he was thirty-three, and there seems less chance now than ever of our being married. It is all I can do to keep myself by my needle; and his prospects, since he failed in the small stationery business three years ago, are worse, if possible, than mine.

Not that I mind so much for myself; women, in all ways of life, and especially in my dressmaking way, learn, I think, to be more patient than men. What I dread is Robert's despondency, and the hard struggle he will have in this cruel city to get his bread, let alone making money enough to marry me. So little as poor people want to set up in housekeeping and be happy together, it seems hard that they can't get it when they are honest and hearty, and willing to work. The clergyman said in his sermon last Sunday evening that all things were ordered for the best, and we are all put into the stations in life that are properest for us. I suppose he was right, being a very clever gentleman who fills the church to crowding; but I think I should have understood him better if I had not been very hungry at the time, in consequence of my own station in life being nothing but plain needlewoman.

March 4th. Mary Mallinson came down to my room to take a cup of tea with me. I read her bits of Robert's letter, to show her that, if she has her troubles, I have mine too; but I could not succeed in cheering her. She says she is born to misfortune, and that, as long back as she can remember, she has never had the least morsel of luck to be thankful for. I told her to go and look in my glass, and to say if she had nothing to be thankful for then; for Mary is a very pretty girl, and would look still prettier if she could be more cheerful and dress neater. However, my compliment did no good. She rattled her spoon impatiently in her tea-cup, and said, "If I was only as good a hand at needle-work as you are, Anne, I would change faces with the ugliest girl in London." "Not you!" says I, laughing. She looked at me for a moment, and shook her head, and was out of the room before I could get up and stop her. She always runs off in that way when she is going to cry, having a kind of pride about letting other people see her in tears.

March 5th. A fright about Mary. I had not seen her all day, as she does not work at the same place where I do; and in the evening she never came down to have tea with me, or sent me word to go to her; so, just before I went to bed, I ran upstairs to say good-night.

She did not answer when I knocked; and when I stepped softly in the room I saw her in bed, asleep, with her work not half done, lying about the room in the untidiest way. There was nothing remarkable in that, and I was just going away on tiptoe, when a tiny bottle and wine-glass on the chair by her bedside caught my eye. I thought she was ill and had been taking physic, and looked at the bottle. It was marked in large letters, "Laudanum—Poison."

My heart gave a jump as if it was going to fly out of me. I laid hold of her with both hands, and shook her with all my might. She was sleeping heavily, and woke slowly, as it seemed to me—but still she did wake. I tried to pull her out of bed, having heard that people ought to be always walked up and down when they have taken laudanum but she resisted, and pushed me away violently.

"Anne!" says she, in a fright. "For gracious sake, what's come to you! Are you out of your senses?"

"Oh, Mary! Mary!" says I, holding up the bottle before her, "if I hadn't come in when I did—" And I laid hold of her to shake her again.

She looked puzzled at me for a moment—then smiled (the first time I had seen her do so for many a long day)—then put her arms round my neck.

"Don't be frightened about me, Anne," she says; "I am not worth it, and there is no need."

"No need!" says I, out of breath—"no need, when the bottle has got Poison marked on it!"

"Poison, dear, if you take it all," says Mary, looking at me very tenderly, "and a night's rest if you only take a little."

I watched her for a moment, doubtful whether I ought to believe what she said or to alarm the house. But there was no sleepiness now in her eyes, and nothing drowsy in her voice; and she sat up in bed quite easily, without anything to support her.

"You have given me a dreadful fright, Mary," says I, sitting down by her in the chair, and beginning by this time to feel rather faint after being startled so.

She jumped out of bed to get me a drop of water, and kissed me, and said how sorry she was, and how undeserving of so much interest being taken in her. At the same time, she tried to possess herself of the laudanum bottle which I still kept cuddled up tight in my own hands.

"No," says I. "You have got into a low-spirited, despairing way. I won't trust you with it."

"I am afraid I can't do without it," says Mary, in her usual quiet, hopeless voice. "What with work that I can't get through as I ought, and troubles that I can't help thinking of, sleep won't come to me unless I take a few drops out of that bottle. Don't keep it away from me, Anne; it's the only thing in the world that makes me forget myself."

"Forget yourself!" says I. "You have no right to talk in that way, at your age. There's something horrible in the notion of a girl of eighteen sleeping with a bottle of laudanum by her bedside every night. We all of us have our troubles. Haven't I got mine?"

"You can do twice the work I can, twice as well as me," says Mary. "You are never scolded and rated at for awkwardness with your needle, and I always am. You can pay for your room every week, and I am three weeks in debt for mine."

"A little more practice," says I, "and a little more courage, and you will soon do better. You have got all your life before you—"

"I wish I was at the end of it," says she, breaking in. "I am alone in the world, and my life's no good to me."

"You ought to be ashamed of yourself for saying so," says I. "Haven't you got me for a friend? Didn't I take a fancy to you when first you left your step-mother and came to lodge in this house? And haven't I been sisters with you ever since? Suppose you are alone in the world, am I much better off? I'm an orphan like you. I've almost as many things in pawn as you; and, if your pockets are empty, mine have only got ninepence in them, to last me for all the rest of the week."

"Your father and mother were honest people," says Mary, obstinately. "My mother ran away from home, and died in a hospital. My father was always drunk, and always beating me. My step-mother is as good as dead, for all she cares about me. My only brother is thousands of miles away in fore ign parts, and never writes to me, and never helps me with a farthing. My sweetheart—"

She stopped, and the red flew into her face. I knew, if she went on that way, she would only get to the saddest part of her sad story, and give both herself and me unnecessary pain.

"*My* sweetheart is too poor to marry me, Mary," I said, "so I'm not so much to be envied even there. But let's give over disputing which is worst off. Lie down in bed, and let me tuck you up. I'll put a stitch or two into that work of yours while you go to sleep."

Instead of doing what I told her, she burst out crying (being very like a child in some of her ways), and hugged me so tight round the neck that she quite hurt me. I let her go on till she had worn herself out, and was obliged to lie down. Even then, her last few words before she dropped off to sleep were such as I was half sorry, half frightened to hear.

"I won't plague you long, Anne," she said. "I haven't courage to go out of the world as you seem to fear I shall; but I began my life wretchedly, and wretchedly I am sentenced to end it."

It was of no use lecturing her again, for she closed her eyes.

I tucked her up as neatly as I could, and put her petticoat over her, for the bedclothes were scanty, and her hands felt cold. She looked so pretty and delicate as she fell asleep that it quite made my heart ache to see her, after such talk as we had held together. I just waited long enough to be quite sure that she was in the land of dreams, then emptied the horrible laudanum bottle into the grate, took up her half-done work, and, going out softly, left her for that night.

March 6th. Sent off a long letter to Robert, begging and entreating him not to be so down-hearted, and not to leave America without making another effort. I told him I could bear any trial except the wretchedness of seeing him come back a helpless, broken-down man, trying uselessly to begin life again when too old for a change.

It was not till after I had posted my own letter, and read over part of Robert's again, that the suspicion suddenly floated across me, for the first time, that he might have sailed for England immediately after writing to me. There were expressions in the letter which seemed to indicate that he had some such headlong project in his mind. And yet, surely, if it were so, I ought to have noticed them at the first reading. I can only hope I am wrong in my present interpretation of much of what he has written to me—hope it earnestly for both our sakes.

This has been a doleful day for me. I have been uneasy about Robert and uneasy about Mary. My mind is haunted by those last words of hers: "I began my life wretchedly, and wretchedly I am sentenced to end it." Her usual melancholy way of talking never produced the same impression on me that I feel now. Perhaps the discovery of the laudanum-bottle is the cause of this. I would give many a hard day's work to know what to do for Mary's good. My heart warmed to her when we first met in the same lodging-house two years ago, and, although I am not one of the over-affectionate sort myself, I feel as if I could go to the world's end to serve that girl. Yet, strange to say, if I was asked why I was so fond of her, I don't think I should know how to answer the question.

March 7th. I am almost ashamed to write it down, even in this journal, which no eyes but mine ever look on; yet I must honestly confess to myself that here I am, at nearly one in the morning, sitting up in a state of serious uneasiness because Mary has not yet come home.

I walked with her this morning to the place where she works, and tried to lead her into talking of the relations she has got who are still alive. My motive in doing this was to see if she dropped anything in the course of conversation which might suggest a way of helping her interests with those who are bound to give her all reasonable assistance. But the little I could get her to say to me led to nothing. Instead of answering my questions about her step-mother and her brother, she persisted at first, in the strangest way, in talking of her father, who was dead and gone, and of one Noah Truscott, who had been the worst of all the bad friends he had, and had taught him to drink and game. When I did get her to speak of her brother, she only knew that he had gone out to a place called Assam, where they grew tea. How he was doing, or whether he was there still, she did not seem to know, never having heard a word from him for years and years past.

As for her step-mother, Mary not unnaturally flew into a passion the moment I spoke of her. She keeps an eating-house at Hammersmith, and could have given Mary good employment in it; but she seems always to have hated her, and to have made her life so wretched with abuse and ill usage that she had no refuge left but to go away from home, and do her best to make a living for herself. Her husband (Mary's father) appears to have behaved badly to her, and, after his death, she took the wicked course of revenging herself on her step-daughter. I felt, after this, that it was impossible Mary could go back, and that it was the hard necessity of her position, as it is of mine, that she should struggle on to make a decent livelihood without assistance from any of her relations. I confessed as much as this to her; but I added that I would try to get her employment with the persons for whom I work, who pay higher wages, and show a little more indulgence to those under them than the people to whom she is now obliged to look for support.

I spoke much more confidently than I felt about being able to do this, and left her, as I thought, in better spirits than usual. She promised to be back to-night to tea at nine o'clock, and now it is nearly one in the morning, and she is not home yet. If it was any other girl I should not feel uneasy, for I should make up my mind that there was extra work to be done in a hurry, and that they were keeping her late, and I should go to bed. But Mary is so unfortunate in everything that happens to her, and her own melancholy talk about herself keeps hanging on my mind so, that I have fears on her account which would not distress me about any one else. It seems inexcusably silly to think such a thing, much more to write it down; but I have a kind of nervous dread upon me that some accident—

What does that loud knocking at the street door mean? And those voices and heavy footsteps outside? Some lodger who has lost his key, I suppose. And yet, my heart— What a coward I have become all of a sudden!

More knocking and louder voices. I must run to the door and see what it is. Oh, Mary! Mary! I hope I am not going to have another fright about you, but I feel sadly like it.

March 8th.

March 9th.

March 10th.

March 11th. Oh me! all the troubles I have ever had in my life are as nothing to the trouble I am in now. For three days I have not been able to write a single line in this journal, which I have kept so regularly ever since I was a girl. For three days I have not once thought of Robert—I, who am always thinking of him at other times.

My poor, dear, unhappy Mary! the worst I feared for you on that night when I sat up alone was far below the dreadful calamity that has really happened. How can I write about it, with my eyes full of tears and my hand all of a tremble? I don't even know why I am sitting down at my desk now, unless it is habit that keeps me to my old every-day task, in spite of all the grief and fear which seem to unfit me entirely for performing it.

The people of the house were asleep and lazy on that dreadful night, and I was the first to open the door. Never, never could I describe in writing, or even say in plain talk, though it is so much easier, what I felt when I saw two policemen come in, carrying between them what seemed to me to be a dead girl, and that girl Mary! I caught hold of her, and gave a scream that must have alarmed the whole house; for frightened people came crowding downstairs in their night-dresses. There was a dreadful confusion and noise of loud talking, but

I heard nothing and saw nothing till I had got her into my room and laid on my bed . I stooped down, frantic-like, to kiss her, and saw an awful mark of a blow on the left temple, and felt, at the same time, a feeble flutter of her breath on my cheek. The discovery that she was not dead seemed to give me back my senses again. I told one of the policemen where the nearest doctor was to be found, and sat down by the bedside while he was gone, and bathed her poor head with cold water. She never opened her eyes, or moved, or spoke; but she breathed, and that was enough for me, because it was enough for life.

The policeman left in the room was a big, thick-voiced, pompous man, with a horrible unfeeling pleasure in hearing himself talk before an assembly of frightened, silent people. He told us how he had found her, as if he had been telling a story in a tap-room, and began with saying: "I don't think the young woman was drunk."

Drunk! My Mary, who might have been a born lady for all the spirits she ever touched—drunk! I could have struck the man for uttering the word, with her lying—poor suffering angel—so white, and still, and helpless before him. As it was, I gave him a look, but he was too stupid to understand it, and went droning on, saying the same thing over and over again in the same words. And yet the story of how they found her was, like all the sad stories I have ever heard told in real life, so very, very short. They had just seen her lying along on the curbstone a few streets off, and had taken her to the station-house. There she had been searched, and one of my cards, that I gave to ladies who promise me employment, had been found in her pocket, and so they had brought her to our house. This was all the man really had to tell. There was nobody near her when she was found, and no evidence to show how the blow on her temple had been inflicted.

What a time it was before the doctor came, and how dreadful to hear him say, after he had looked at her, that he was afraid all the medical men in the world could be of no use here! He could not get her to swallow anything; and the more he tried to bring her back to her senses the less chance there seemed of his succeeding. He examined the blow on her temple, and said he thought she must have fallen down in a fit of some sort, and struck her head against the pavement, and so have given her brain what he was afraid was a fatal shake. I asked what was to be done if she showed any return to sense in the night. He said: "Send for me directly"; and stopped for a little while afterward stroking her head gently with his hand, and whispering to himself: "Poor girl, so young and so pretty!" I had felt, some minutes before, as if I could have struck the policeman, and I felt now as if I could have thrown my arms round the doctor's neck and kissed him. I did put out my hand when he took up his hat, and he shook it in the friendliest way. "Don't hope, my dear," he said, and went out.

The rest of the lodgers followed him, all silent and shocked, except the inhuman wretch who owns the house and lives in idleness on the high rents he wrings from poor people like us.

"She's three weeks in my debt," says he, with a frown and an oath. "Where the devil is my money to come from now?" Brute! brute!

I had a long cry alone with her that seemed to ease my heart a little. She was not the least changed for the better when I had wiped away the tears and could see her clearly again. I took up her right hand, which lay nearest to me. It was tight clinched. I tried to unclasp the fingers, and succeeded after a little time. Something dark fell out of the palm of her hand as I straightened it.

I picked the thing up, and smoothed it out, and saw that it was an end of a man's cravat.

A very old, rotten, dingy strip of black silk, with thin lilac lines, all blurred and deadened with dirt, running across and across the stuff in a sort of trellis-work pattern. The small end of the cravat was hemmed in the usual way, but the other end was all jagged, as if the morsel then in my hands had been torn off violently from the rest of the stuff. A chill ran all over me as I looked at it; for that poor, stained, crumpled end of a cravat seemed to be saying to me, as though it had been in plain words: "If she dies, she has come to her death by foul means, and I am the witness of it."

I had been frightened enough before, lest she should die suddenly and quietly without my knowing it, while we were alone together; but I got into a perfect agony now, for fear this last worst affliction should take me by surprise. I don't suppose five minutes passed all that woful night through without my getting up and putting my cheek close to her mouth, to feel if the faint breaths still fluttered out of it. They came and went just the same as at first, though the fright I was in often made me fancy they were stilled forever.

Just as the church clocks were striking four I was startled by seeing the room door open. It was only Dusty Sal (as they call her in the house), the maid-of-all-work. She was wrapped up in the blanket off her bed; her hair was all tumbled over her face, and her eyes were heavy with sleep as she came up to the bedside where I was sitting.

"I've two hours good before I begin to work," says she, in her hoarse, drowsy voice, "and I've come to sit up and take my turn at watching her. You lay down and get some sleep on the rug. Here's my blanket for you. I don't mind the cold—it will keep me awake."

"You are very kind—very, very kind and thoughtful, Sally," says I, "but I am too wretched in my mind to want sleep, or rest, or to do anything but wait where I am, and try and hope for the best."

"Then I'll wait, too," says Sally. "I must do something; if there's nothing to do but waiting, I'll wait."

And she sat down opposite me at the foot of the bed, and drew the blanket close round her with a shiver.

"After working so hard as you do, I'm sure you must want all the little rest you can get," says I.

"Excepting only you," says Sally, putting her heavy arm very clumsily, but very gently at the same time, round Mary's feet, and looking hard at the pale, still face on the pillow. "Excepting you, she's the only soul in this house as never swore at me, or give me a hard word that I can remember. When you made puddings on Sundays, and give her half, she always give me a bit. The rest of 'em calls me Dusty Sal. Excepting only you, again, she always called me Sally, as if she knowed me in a friendly way. I ain't no good here, but I ain't no harm, neither; and I shall take my turn at the sitting up—that's what I shall do!"

She nestled her head down close at Mary's feet as she spoke those words, and said no more. I once or twice thought she had fallen asleep, but whenever I looked at her her heavy eyes were always wide open. She never changed her position an inch till the church clocks struck six; then she gave one little squeeze to Mary's feet with her arm, and shuffled out of the room without a word. A minute or two after, I heard her down below, lighting the kitchen fire just as usual.

A little later the doctor stepped over before his breakfast-time to see if there had been any change in the night. He only shook his head when he looked at her as if there was no hope. Having nobody else to consult that I could put trust in, I showed him the end of the cravat, and told him of the dreadful suspicion that had arisen in my mind when I found it in her hand.

"You must keep it carefully, and produce it at the inquest," he said. "I don't know, though, that it is likely to lead to anything. The bit of stuff may have been lying on the pavement near her, and her hand may have unconsciously clutched it when she fell. Was she subject to fainting-fits?"

"Not more so, sir, than other young girls who are hard-worked and anxious, and weakly from poor living," I answered.

"I can't say that she may not have got that blow from a fall," the doctor went on, locking at her temple again. "I can't say that it presents any positive appearance of having been inflicted by another person. It will be important, however, to ascertain what state of health she was in last night. Have you any idea where she was yesterday evening?"

I told him where she was employed at work, and said I imagined she must have been kept there later than usual.

"I shall pass the place this morning" said the doctor, "in going my rounds among my patients, and I'll just step in and make some inquiries."

I thanked him, and we parted. Just as he was closing the door he looked in again.

"Was she your sister?" he asked.

"No, sir, only my dear friend."

He said nothing more, but I heard him sigh as he shut the door softly. Perhaps he once had a sister of his own, and lost her? Perhaps she was like Mary in the face?

The doctor was hours gone away. I began to feel unspeakably forlorn and helpless, so much so as even to wish selfishly that Robert might really have sailed from America, and might get to London in time to assist and console me.

No living creature came into the room but Sally. The first time she brought me some tea; the second and third times she only looked in to see if there was any change, and glanced her eye toward the bed. I had never known her so silent before; it seemed almost as if this dreadful accident had struck her dumb. I ought to have spoken to her, perhaps, but there was something in her face that daunted me; and, besides, the fever of anxiety I was in began to dry up my lips, as if they would never be able to shape any words again. I was still tormented by that frightful apprehension of the past night, that she would die without my knowing it—die without saying one word to clear up the awful mystery of this blow, and set the suspicions at rest forever which I still felt whenever my eyes fell on the end of the old cravat.

At last the doctor came back.

"I think you may safely clear your mind of any doubts to which that bit of stuff may have given rise," he said. "She was, as you supposed, detained late by her employers, and she fainted in the work-room. They most unwisely and unkindly let her go home alone, without giving her any stimulant, as soon as she came to her senses again. Nothing is more probable, under these circumstances, than that she should faint a second time on her way here. A fall on the pavement, without any friendly arm to break it, might have produced even a worse injury than the injury we see. I believe that the only ill usage to which the poor girl was exposed was the neglect she met with in the work-room."

"You speak very reasonably, I own, sir," said I, not yet quite convinced. "Still, perhaps she may—"

"My poor girl, I told you not to hope," said the doctor, interrupting me. He went to Mary, and lifted up her eyelids, and looked at her eyes while he spoke; then added, "If you still doubt how she came by that blow, do not encourage the idea that any words of hers will ever enlighten you. She will never speak again."

"Not dead! Oh, sir, don't say she's dead!"

"She is dead to pain and sorrow—dead to speech and recognition. There is more animation in the life of the feeblest insect that flies than in the life that is left in her. When you look at her now, try to think that she is in heaven. That is the best comfort I can give you, after telling the hard truth."

I did not believe him. I could not believe him. So long as she breathed at all, so long I was resolved to hope. Soon after the doctor was gone, Sally came in again, and found me listening (if I may call it so) at Mary's lips. She went to where my little hand-glass hangs against the wall, took it down, and gave it to me.

"See if the breath marks it," she said.

Yes; her breath did mark it, but very faintly. Sally cleaned the glass with her apron, and gave it back to me. As she did so, she half stretched out her hand to Mary's face, but drew it in again suddenly, as if she was afraid of soiling Mary's delicate skin with her hard, horny fingers. Going out, she stopped at the foot of the bed, and scraped away a little patch of mud that was on one of Mary's shoes.

"I always used to clean 'em for her," said Sally, "to save her hands from getting blacked. May I take 'em off now, and clean 'em again?"

I nodded my head, for my heart was too heavy to speak. Sally took the shoes off with a slow, awkward tenderness, and went out.

An hour or more must have passed, when, putting the glass over her lips again, I saw no mark on it. I held it closer and closer. I dulled it accidentally with my own breath, and cleaned it. I held it over her again. Oh, Mary, Mary, the doctor was right! I ought to have only thought of you in heaven!

Dead, without a word, without a sign—without even a look to tell the true story of the blow that killed her! I could not call to anybody, I could not cry, I could not so much as put the glass down and give her a kiss for the last time. I don't know how long I had sat there with my eyes burning, and my hands deadly cold, when Sally came in with the shoes cleaned, and carried carefully in her apron for fear of a soil touching them. At the sight of that—

I can write no more. My tears drop so fast on the paper that I can see nothing.

March 12th. She died on the afternoon of the eighth. On the morning of the ninth, I wrote, as in duty bound, to her stepmother at Hammersmith. There was no answer. I wrote again; my letter was returned to me this morning unopened. For all that woman cares, Mary might be buried with a pauper's funeral; but this shall never be, if I pawn everything about me, down to the very gown that is on my back. The bare thought of Mary being buried by the workhouse gave me the spirit to dry my eyes, and go to the undertaker's, and tell him how I was placed. I said if he would get me an estimate of all that would have to be paid, from first to last, for the cheapest decent funeral that could be had, I would undertake to raise the money. He gave me the estimate, written in this way, like a common bill:

A walking funeral complete............**Pounds 1 13 8**	
Vestry...0 4 4	
Rector...0 4 4	
Clerk...0 1 0	
Sexton...0 1 0	
Beadle...0 1 0	
Bell..0 1 0	
Six feet of ground....................................0 2 0	
	————
Total	**Pounds 2 8 4**

If I had the heart to give any thought to it, I should be inclined to wish that the Church could afford to do without so many small charges for burying poor people, to whose friends even shillings are of consequence. But it is useless to complain; the money must be raised at once. The charitable doctor—a poor man himself, or he would not be living in our neighborhood—has subscribed ten shillings toward the expenses; and the coroner, when the inquest was over, added five more. Perhaps others may assist me. If not, I have fortunately clothes and furniture of my own to pawn. And I must set about parting with them without delay, for the funeral is to be to-morrow, the thirteenth.

The funeral—Mary's funeral! It is well that the straits and difficulties I am in keep my mind on the stretch. If I had leisure to grieve, where should I find the courage to face to-morrow?

Thank God they did not want me at the inquest. The verdict given, with the doctor, the policeman, and two persons from the place where she worked, for witnesses, was Accidental Death. The end of the cravat was produced, and the coroner said that it was certainly enough to suggest suspicion; but the jury, in the absence of any positive evidence, held to the doctor's notion that she had fainted and fallen down, and so got the blow on her temple. They reproved the people where Mary worked for letting her go home alone, without so much as a drop of brandy to support her, after she had fallen into a swoon from exhaustion before their eyes. The coroner added, on his own account, that he thought the reproof was thoroughly deserved. After that, the cravat-end was given back to me by my own desire, the police saying that they could make no investigations with such a slight clew to guide them. They may think so, and the coroner, and doctor, and jury may think so; but, in spite of all that has passed, I am now more firmly persuaded than ever that there is some dreadful mystery in connection with that blow on my poor lost Mary's temple which has yet to be revealed, and which may come to be discovered through this very fragment of a cravat that I found in her hand. I cannot give any good reason for why I think so, but I know that if I had been one of the jury at the inquest, nothing should have induced me to consent to such a verdict as Accidental Death.

After I had pawned my things, and had begged a small advance of wages at the place where I work to make up what was still wanting to pay for Mary's funeral, I thought I might have had a little quiet time to prepare myself as I best could for to-morrow. But this was not to be. When I got home the landlord met me in the passage. He was in liquor, and more brutal and pitiless in his way of looking and speaking than ever I saw him before.

"So you're going to be fool enough to pay for her funeral, are you?" were his first words to me.

I was too weary and heart-sick to answer; I only tried to get by him to my own door.

"If you can pay for burying her," he went on, putting himself in front of me, "you can pay her lawful debts. She owes me three weeks' rent. Suppose you raise the money for that next, and hand it over to me? I'm not joking, I can promise you. I mean to have my rent; and, if somebody don't pay it, I'll have her body seized and sent to the workhouse!"

Between terror and disgust, I thought I should have dropped to the floor at his feet. But I determined not to let him see how he had horrified me, if I could possibly control myself. So I mustered resolution enough to answer that I did not believe the law gave him any such wicked power over the dead.

"I'll teach you what the law is!" he broke in; "you'll raise money to bury her like a born lady, when she's died in my debt, will you? And you think I'll let my rights be trampled upon like that, do you? See if I do! I'll give you till to-night to think about it. If I don't have the three weeks she owes before to-morrow, dead or alive, she shall go to the workhouse!"

This time I managed to push by him, and get to my own room, and lock the door in his face. As soon as I was alone I fell into a breathless, suffocating fit of crying that seemed to be shaking me to pieces. But there was no good and no help in tears; I did my best to calm myself after a little while, and tried to think who I should run to for help and protection.

The doctor was the first friend I thought of; but I knew he was always out seeing his patients of an afternoon. The beadle was the next person who came into my head. He had the look of being a very dignified, unapproachable kind of man when he came about the inquest; but he talked to me a little then, and said I was a good girl, and seemed, I really thought, to pity me. So to him I determined to apply in my great danger and distress.

Most fortunately, I found him at home. When I told him of the landlord's infamous threats, and of the misery I was suffering in consequence of them, he rose up with a stamp of his foot, and sent for his gold-laced cocked hat that he wears on Sundays, and his long cane with the ivory top to it.

"I'll give it to him," said the beadle. "Come along with me, my dear. I think I told you you were a good girl at the inquest—if I didn't, I tell you so now. I'll give it to him! Come along with me."

And he went out, striding on with his cocked hat and his great cane, and I followed him.

"Landlord!" he cries, the moment he gets into the passage, with a thump of his cane on the floor, "landlord!" with a look all round him as if he was King of England calling to a beast, "come out!"

The moment the landlord came out and saw who it was, his eye fixed on the cocked hat, and he turned as pale as ashes.

"How dare you frighten this poor girl?" says the beadle. "How dare you bully her at this sorrowful time with threatening to do what you know you can't do? How dare you be a cowardly, bullying, braggadocio of an unmanly landlord? Don't talk to me: I won't hear you. I'll pull you up, sir. If you say another word to the young woman, I'll pull you up before the authorities of this metropolitan parish. I've had my eye on you, and the authorities have had their eye on you, and the rector has had his eye on you. We don't like the look of your small shop round the corner; we don't like the look of some of the customers who deal at it; we don't like disorderly characters; and we don't by any manner of means like you. Go away. Leave the young woman alone. Hold your tongue, or I'll pull you up. If he says another word, or interferes with you again, my dear, come and tell me; and, as sure as he's a bullying, unmanly, braggadocio of a landlord, I'll pull him up."

With those words the beadle gave a loud cough to clear his throat, and another thump of his cane on the floor, and so went striding out again before I could open my lips to thank him. The landlord slunk back into his room without a word. I was left alone and unmolested at last, to strengthen myself for the hard trial of my poor love's funeral to-morrow.

March 13th. It is all over. A week ago her head rested on my bosom. It is laid in the churchyard now; the fresh earth lies heavy over her grave. I and my dearest friend, the sister of my love, are parted in this world forever.

I followed her funeral alone through the cruel, hustling streets. Sally, I thought, might have offered to go with me, but she never so much as came into my room. I did not like to think badly of her for this, and I am glad I restrained myself; for, when we got into the churchyard, among the two or three people who were standing by the open grave I saw Sally, in her ragged gray shawl and her patched black bonnet. She did not seem to notice me till the last words of the service had been read and the clergyman had gone away; then she came up and spoke to me.

"I couldn't follow along with you," she said, looking at her ragged shawl, "for I haven't a decent suit of clothes to walk in. I wish I could get vent in crying for her like you, but I can't; all the crying's been drudged and starved out of me long ago. Don't you think about lighting your fire when you get home. I'll do that, and get you a drop of tea to comfort you."

She seemed on the point of saying a kind word or two more, when, seeing the beadle coming toward me, she drew back, as if she was afraid of him, and left the churchyard.

"Here's my subscription toward the funeral," said the beadle, giving me back his shilling fee. "Don't say anything about it, for it mightn't be approved of in a business point of view, if it came to some people's ears. Has the landlord said anything more to you? no, I thought not. He's too polite a man to give me the trouble of pulling him up. Don't stop crying here, my dear. Take the advice of a man familiar with funerals, and go home."

I tried to take his advice, but it seemed like deserting Mary to go away when all the rest forsook her.

I waited about till the earth was thrown in and the man had left the place, then I returned to the grave. Oh, how bare and cruel it was, without so much as a bit of green turf to soften it! Oh, how much harder it seemed to live than to die, when I stood alone looking at the heavy piled-up lumps of clay, and thinking of what was hidden beneath them!

I was driven home by my own despairing thoughts. The sight of Sally lighting the fire in my room eased my heart a little. When she was gone, I took up Robert's letter again to keep my mind employed on the only subject in the world that has any interest for it now.

This fresh reading increased the doubts I had already felt relative to his having remained in America after writing to me. My grief and forlornness have made a strange alteration in my former feelings about his coming back. I seem to have lost all my prudence and self-denial, and to care so little about his poverty, and so much about himself, that the prospect of his return is really the only comforting thought I have now to support me. I know this is weak in me, and that his coming back can l ead to no good result for either of us; but he is the only living being left me to love; and—I can't explain it—but I want to put my arms round his neck and tell him about Mary.

March 14th. I locked up the end of the cravat in my writing-desk. No change in the dreadful suspicions that the bare sight of it rouses in me. I tremble if I so much as touch it.

March 15th, 16th, 17th. Work, work, work. If I don't knock up, I shall be able to pay back the advance in another week; and then, with a little more pinching in my daily expenses, I may succeed in saving a shilling or two to get some turf to put over Mary's grave, and perhaps even a few flowers besides to grow round it.

March 18th. Thinking of Robert all day long. Does this mean that he is really coming back? If it does, reckoning the distance he is at from New York, and the time ships take to get to England, I might see him by the end of April or the beginning of May.

March 19th. I don't remember my mind running once on the end of the cravat yesterday, and I am certain I never looked at it; yet I had the strangest dream concerning it at night. I thought it was lengthened into a long clew, like the silken thread that led to Rosamond's Bower. I thought I took hold of it, and followed it a little way, and then got frightened and tried to go back, but found that I was obliged, in spite of myself, to go on. It led me through a place like the Valley of the Shadow of Death, in an old print I remember in my mother's copy of the Pilgrim's Progress. I seemed to be months and months following it without any respite, till at last it brought me, on a sudden, face to face with an angel whose eyes were like Mary's. He said to me, "Go on, still; the truth is at the end, waiting for you to find it." I burst out crying, for the angel had Mary's voice as well as Mary's eyes, and woke with my heart throbbing and my cheeks all wet. What is the meaning of this? Is it always superstitious, I wonder, to believe that dreams may come true?

April 30th. I have found it! God knows to what results it may lead; but it is as certain as that I am sitting here before my journal that I have found the cravat from which the end in Mary's hand was torn. I discovered it last night; but the flutter I was in, and the nervousness and uncertainty I felt, prevented me from noting down this most extraordinary and unexpected event at the time when it happened. Let me try if I can preserve the memory of it in writing now.

I was going home rather late from where I work, when I suddenly remembered that I had forgotten to buy myself any candles the evening before, and that I should be left in the dark if I did not manage to rectify this mistake in some way. The shop close to me, at which I usually deal, would be shut up, I knew, before I could get to it; so I determined to go into the first place I passed where candles were sold. This turned out to be a small shop with two counters, which did business on one side in the general grocery way, and on the other in the rag and bottle and old iron line.

There were several customers on the grocery side when I went in, so I waited on the empty rag side till I could be served. Glancing about me here at the worthless-looking things by which I was surrounded, my eye was caught by a bundle of rags lying on the counter, as if they had just been brought in and left there. From mere idle curiosity, I looked close at the rags, and saw among them something like an old cravat. I took it up directly and held it under a gaslight. The pattern was blurred lilac lines running across and across the dingy black ground in a trellis-work form. I looked at the ends: one of them was torn off.

How I managed to hide the breathless surprise into which this discovery threw me I cannot say, but I certainly contrived to steady my voice somehow, and to ask for my candles calmly when the man and woman serving in the shop, having disposed of their other customers, inquired of me what I wanted.

As the man took down the candles, my brain was all in a whirl with trying to think how I could get possession of the old cravat without exciting any suspicion. Chance, and a little quickness on my part in taking advantage of it, put the object within my reach in a moment. The man, having counted out the candles, asked the woman for some paper to wrap them in. She produced a piece much too small and flimsy for the purpose, and declared, when he called for something better, that the day's supply of stout paper was all exhausted. He flew into a rage with her for managing so badly. Just as they were beginning to quarrel violently, I stepped back to the rag-counter, took the old cravat carelessly out of the bundle, and said, in as light a tone as I could possibly assume:

"Come, come, don't let my candles be the cause of hard words between you. Tie this ragged old thing round them with a bit of string, and I shall carry them home quite comfortably."

The man seemed disposed to insist on the stout paper being produced; but the woman, as if she was glad of an opportunity of spiting him, snatched the candles away, and tied them up in a moment in the torn old cravat. I was afraid he would have struck her before my face, he seemed in such a fury; but, fortunately, another customer came in, and obliged him to put his hands to peaceable and proper use.Ê

"Quite a bundle of all-sorts on the opposite counter there," I said to the woman, as I paid her for the candles.

"Yes, and all hoarded up for sale by a poor creature with a lazy brute of a husband, who lets his wife do all the work while he spends all the money," answered the woman, with a malicious look at the man by her side.

"He can't surely have much money to spend, if his wife has no better work to do than picking up rags," said I.

"It isn't her fault if she hasn't got no better," says the woman, rather angrily. "She's ready to turn her hand to anything. Charing, washing, laying-out, keeping empty houses—nothing comes amiss to her. She's my half-sister, and I think I ought to know."

"Did you say she went out charing?" I asked, making believe as if I knew of somebody who might employ her.

"Yes, of course I did," answered the woman; "and if you can put a job into her hands, you'll be doing a good turn to a poor hard-working creature as wants it. She lives down the Mews here to the right—name of Horlick, and as honest a woman as ever stood in shoe-leather. Now, then, ma'am, what for you?"

Another customer came in just then, and occupied her attention. I left the shop, passed the turning that led down to the Mews, looked up at the name of the street, so as to know how to find it again, and then ran home as fast as I could. Perhaps it was the remembrance of my strange dream striking me on a sudden, or perhaps it was the shock of the discovery I had just made, but I began to feel frightened without knowing why, and anxious to be under shelter in my own room.

It Robert should come back! Oh, what a relief and help it would be now if Robert should come back!

May 1st. On getting indoors last night, the first thing I did, after striking a light, was to take the ragged cravat off the candles, and smooth it out on the table. I then took the end that had been in poor Mary's hand out of my writing-desk, and smoothed that out too. It matched the torn side of the cravat exactly. I put them together, and satisfied myself that there was not a doubt of it.

Not once did I close my eyes that night. A kind of fever got possession of me—a vehement yearning to go on from this first discovery and find out more, no matter what the risk might be. The cravat now really became, to my mind, the clew that I thought I saw in my dream—the clew that I was resolved to follow. I determined to go to Mrs. Horlick this evening on my return from work.

I found the Mews easily. A crook-backed dwarf of a man was lounging at the corner of it smoking his pipe. Not liking his looks, I did not inquire of him where Mrs. Horlick lived, but went down the Mews till I met with a woman, and asked her. She directed me to the right number. I knocked at the door, and Mrs. Horlick herself—a lean, ill-tempered, miserable-looking woman—answered it. I told her at once that I had come to ask what her terms were for charing. She stared at me for a moment, then answered my question civilly enough.

"You look surprised at a stranger like me finding you out," I said. "I first came to hear of you last night, from a relation of yours, in rather an odd way."

And I told her all that had happened in the chandler's shop, bringing in the bundle of rags, and the circumstance of my carrying home the candles in the old torn cravat, as often as possible.

"It's the first time I've heard of anything belonging to him turning out any use," said Mrs. Horlick, bitterly.

"What! the spoiled old neck-handkerchief belonged to your husband, did it?" said I, at a venture.

"Yes; I pitched his rotten rag of a neck-'andkercher into the bundle along with the rest, and I wish I could have pitched him in after it," said Mrs. Horlick. "I'd sell him cheap at any ragshop. There he stands, smoking his pipe at the end of the Mews, out of work for weeks past, the idlest humpbacked pig in all London!"

She pointed to the man whom I had passed on entering the Mews. My cheeks began to burn and my knees to tremble, for I knew that in tracing the cravat to its owner I was advancing a step toward a fresh discovery. I wished Mrs. Horlick good evening, and said I would write and mention the day on which I wanted her.

What I had just been told put a thought into my mind that I was afraid to follow out. I have heard people talk of being light-headed, and I felt as I have heard them say they felt when I retraced my steps up the Mews. My head got giddy, and my eyes seemed able to see nothing but the figure of the little crook-backed man, still smoking his pipe in his former place. I could see nothing but that; I could think of nothing but the mark of the blow on my poor lost Mary's temple. I know that I must have been light-headed, for as I came close to the crook-backed man I stopped without meaning it. The minute before, there had been no idea in me of speaking to him. I did not know how to speak, or in what way it would be safest to begin; and yet, the moment I came face to face with him, something out of myself seemed to stop me, and to make me speak without considering beforehand, without thinking of consequences, without knowing, I may almost say, what words I was uttering till the instant when they rose to my lips.

"When your old neck-tie was torn, did you know that one end of it went to the rag-shop, and the other fell into my hands?"

I said these bold words to him suddenly, and, as it seemed, without my own will taking any part in them.

He started, stared, changed color. He was too much amazed by my sudden speaking to find an answer for me. When he did open his lips, it was to say rather to himself than me:

"You're not the girl."

"No," I said, with a strange choking at my heart, "I'm her friend."

By this time he had recovered his surprise, and he seemed to be aware that he had let out more than he ought.

"You may be anybody's friend you like," he said, brutally, "so long as you don't come jabbering nonsense here. I don't know you, and I don't understand your jokes."

He turned quickly away from me when he had said the last words. He had never once looked fairly at me since I first spoke to him.

Was it his hand that had struck the blow? I had only sixpence in my pocket, but I took it out and followed him. If it had been a five-pound note I should have done the same in the state I was in then.

"Would a pot of beer help you to understand me?" I said, and offered him the sixpence.

"A pot ain't no great things," he answered, taking the sixpence doubtfully.

"It may lead to something better," I said. His eyes began to twinkle, and he came close to me. Oh, how my legs trembled—how my head swam!

"This is all in a friendly way, is it?" he asked, in a whisper.

I nodded my head. At that moment I could not have spoken for worlds.

"Friendly, of course," he went on to himself, "or there would have been a policeman in it. She told you, I suppose, that I wasn't the man?"

I nodded my head again. It was all I could do to keep myself standing upright.

"I suppose it's a case of threatening to have him up, and make him settle it quietly for a pound or two? How much for me if you lay hold of him?"

"Half."

I began to be afraid that he would suspect something if I was still silent. The wretch's eyes twinkled again and he came yet closer.

"I drove him to the Red Lion, corner of Dodd Street and Rudgely Street. The house was shut up, but he was let in at the jug and bottle door, like a man who was known to the landlord. That's as much as I can tell you, and I'm certain I'm right. He was the last fare I took up at night. The next morning master gave me the sack—said I cribbed his corn and his fares. I wish I had."

I gathered from this that the crook-backed man had been a cab-driver.

"Why don't you speak?" he asked, suspiciously. "Has she been telling you a pack of lies about me? What did she say when she came home?"

"What ought she to have said?"

"She ought to have said my fare was drunk, and she came in the way as he was going to get into the cab. That's what she ought to have said to begin with."

"But after?"

"Well, after, my fare, by way of larking with her, puts out his leg for to trip her up, and she stumbles and catches at me for to save herself, and tears off one of the limp ends of my rotten old tie. 'What do you mean by that, you brute?' says she, turning round as soon as she was steady on her legs, to my fare. Says my fare to her: 'I means to teach you to keep a civil tongue in your head.' And he ups with his fist, and—what's come to you, now? What are you looking at me like that for? How do you think a man of my size was to take her part against a man big enough to have eaten me up? Look as much as you like, in my place you would have done what I done—drew off when he shook his fist at you, and swore he'd be the death of you if you didn't start your horse in no time."

I saw he was working himself up into a rage; but I could not, if my life had depended on it, have stood near him or looked at him any longer. I just managed to stammer out that I had been walking a long way, and that, not being used to much exercise, I felt faint and giddy with fatigue. He only changed from angry to sulky when I made that excuse. I got a little further away from him, and then added that if he would be at the Mews entrance the next evening I should have something more to say and something more to give him. He grumbled a few suspicious words in answer about doubting whether he should trust me to come back. Fortunately, at that moment, a policeman passed on the opposite side of the way. He slunk down the Mews immediately, and I was free to make my escape.

How I got home I can't say, except that I think I ran the greater part of the way. Sally opened the door, and asked if anything was the matter the moment she saw my face. I answered: "Nothing—nothing." She stopped me as I was going into my room, and said:

"Smooth your hair a bit, and put your collar straight. There's a gentleman in there waiting for you."

My heart gave one great bound: I knew who it was in an instant, and rushed into the room like a mad woman.

"Oh, Robert, Robert!"

All my heart went out to him in those two little words.

"Good God, Anne, has anything happened? Are you ill?"

"Mary! my poor, lost, murdered, dear, dear Mary!"

That was all I could say before I fell on his breast.

May 2d. Misfortunes and disappointments have saddened him a little, but toward me he is unaltered. He is as good, as kind, as gently and truly affectionate as ever. I believe no other man in the world could have listened to the story of Mary's death with such tenderness and pity as he. Instead of cutting me short anywhere, he drew me on to tell more than I had intended; and his first generous words when I had done were to assure me that he would see himself to the grass being laid and the flowers planted on Mary's grave. I could almost have gone on my knees and worshiped him when he made me that promise.

Surely this best, and kindest, and noblest of men cannot always be unfortunate! My cheeks burn when I think that he has come back with only a few pounds in his pocket, after all his hard and honest struggles to do well in America. They must be bad people there when such a man as Robert cannot get on among them. He now talks calmly and resignedly of trying for any one of the lowest employments by which a man can earn his bread honestly in this great city—he who knows French, who can write so beautifully! Oh, if the people who have places to give away only knew Robert as well as I do, what a salary he would have, what a post he would be chosen to occupy!

I am writing these lines alone while he has gone to the Mews to treat with the dastardly, heartless wretch with whom I spoke yesterday.

Robert says the creature—I won't call him a man—must be humored and kept deceived about poor Mary's end, in order that we may discover and bring to justice the monster whose drunken blow was the death of her. I shall know no ease of mind till her murderer is secured, and till I am certain that he will be made to suffer for his crimes. I wanted to go with Robert to the Mews, but he said it was best that he should carry out the rest of the investigation alone, for my strength and resolution had been too hardly taxed already. He said more words in praise of me for what I have been able to do up to this time, which I am almost ashamed to write down with my own pen. Besides, there is no need; praise from his lips is one of the things that I can trust my memory to preserve to the latest day of my life.

May 3d. Robert was very long last night before he came back to tell me what he had done. He easily recognized the hunchback at the corner of the Mews by my description of him; but he found it a hard matter, even with the help of money, to overcome the cowardly wretch's distrust of him as a stranger and a man. However, when this had been accomplished, the main difficulty was conquered. The hunchback, excited by the promise of more money, went at once to the Red Lion to inquire about the person whom he had driven there in his cab. Robert followed him, and waited at the corner of the street. The tidings brought by the cabman were of the most unexpected kind. The murderer—I can write of him by no other name—had fallen ill on the very night when he was driven to the Red Lion, had taken to his bed there and then, and was still confined to it at that very moment. His disease was of a kind that is brought on by excessive drinking, and that affects the mind as well as the body. The people at the public house call it the Horrors.

Hearing these things, Robert determined to see if he could not find out something more for himself by going and inquiring at the public house, in the character of one of the friends of the sick man in bed upstairs. He made two important discoveries. First, he found out the name and address of the doctor in attendance. Secondly, he entrapped the barman into mentioning the murderous wretch by his name. This last discovery adds an unspeakably fearful interest to the dreadful misfortune of Mary's death. Noah Truscott, as she told me herself in the last conversation I ever had with her, was the name of the man whose drunken example ruined her father, and Noah Truscott is also the name of the man whose drunken fury killed her. There is something that makes one shudder, something supernatural in this awful fact. Robert agrees with me that the hand of Providence must have guided my steps to that shop from which all the discoveries since made took their rise. He says he believes we are the instruments of effecting a righteous retribution; and, if he spends his last farthing, he will have the investigation brought to its full end in a court of justice.

May 4th. Robert went to-day to consult a lawyer whom he knew in former times The lawyer was much interested, though not so seriously impressed as he ought to have been by the story of Mary's death and of the events that have followed it. He gave Robert a confidential letter to take to the doctor in attendance on the double-dyed villain at the Red Lion. Robert left the letter, and called again and saw the doctor, who said his patient was getting better, and would most likely be up again in ten days or a fortnight. This statement Robert communicated to the lawyer, and the lawyer has undertaken to have the public house properly watched, and the hunchback (who is the most important witness) sharply looked after for the next fortnight, or longer if necessary. Here, then, the progress of this dreadful business stops for a while.

May 5th. Robert has got a little temporary employment in copying for his friend the lawyer. I am working harder than ever at my needle, to make up for the time that has been lost lately.

May 6th. To-day was Sunday, and Robert proposed that we should go and look at Mary's grave. He, who forgets nothing where a kindness is to be done, has found time to perform the promise he made to me on the night when we first met. The grave is already, by his orders, covered with turf, and planted round with shrubs. Some flowers, and a low headstone, are to be added, to make the place look worthier of my poor lost darling who is beneath it. Oh, I hope I shall live long after I am married to Robert! I want so much time to show him all my gratitude!

May 20th. A hard trial to my courage to-day. I have given evidence at the police-office, and have seen the monster who murdered her.

I could only look at him once. I could just see that he was a giant in size, and that he kept his dull, lowering, bestial face turned toward the witness-box, and his bloodshot, vacant eyes staring on me. For an instant I tried to confront that look; for an instant I kept my attention fixed on him—on his blotched face—on the short, grizzled hair above it—on his knotty, murderous right hand, hanging loose over the bar in front of him, like the paw of a wild beast over the edge of its den. Then the horror of him—the double horror of confronting him, in the first place, and afterward of seeing that he was an old man—overcame me, and I turned away, faint, sick, and shuddering. I never faced him again; and, at the end of my evidence, Robert considerately took me out.

When we met once more at the end of the examination, Robert told me that the prisoner never spoke and never changed his position. He was either fortified by the cruel composure of a savage, or his faculties had not yet thoroughly recovered from the disease that had so lately shaken them. The magistrate seemed to doubt if he was in his right mind; but the evidence of the medical man relieved this uncertainty, and the prisoner was committed for trial on a charge of manslaughter.

Why not on a charge of murder? Robert explained the law to me when I asked that question. I accepted the explanation, but it did not satisfy me. Mary Mallinson was killed by a blow from the hand of Noah Truscott. That is murder in the sight of God. Why not murder in the sight of the law also?

June 18th. To-morrow is the day appointed for the trial at the Old Bailey.

Before sunset this evening I went to look at Mary's grave. The turf has grown so green since I saw it last, and the flowers are springing up so prettily. A bird was perched dressing his feathers on the low white headstone that bears the inscription of her name and age. I did not go near enough to disturb the little creature. He looked innocent and pretty on the grave, as Mary herself was in her lifetime. When he flew away I went and sat for a little by the headstone, and read the mournful lines on it. Oh, my love! my love! what harm or wrong had you ever done in this world, that you should die at eighteen by a blow from a drunkard's hand?

June 19th. The trial. My experience of what happened at it is limited, like my experience of the examination at the police-office, to the time occupied in giving my own evidence. They made me say much more than I said before the magistrate. Between examination and cross-examination, I had to go into almost all the particulars about poor Mary and her funeral that I have written i n this journal; the jury listening to every word I spoke with the most anxious attention. At the end, the judge said a few words to me approving of my conduct, and then there was a clapping of hands among the people in court. I was so agitated and excited that I trembled all over when they let me go out into the air again.

I looked at the prisoner both when I entered the witness-box and when I left it. The lowering brutality of his face was unchanged, but his faculties seemed to be more alive and observant than they were at the police-office. A frightful blue change passed over his face, and he drew his breath so heavily that the gasps were distinctly audible while I mentioned Mary by name and described the mark or the blow on her temple. When they asked me if I knew anything of the prisoner, and I answered that I only knew what Mary herself had told me about his having been her father's ruin, he gave a kind of groan, and struck both his hands heavily on the dock. And when I passed beneath him on my way out of court, he leaned over suddenly, whether to speak to me or to strike me I can't say, for he was immediately made to stand upright again by the turnkeys on either side of him. While the evidence proceeded (as Robert described it to me), the signs that he was suffering under superstitious terror became more and more apparent; until, at last, just as the lawyer appointed to defend him was rising to speak, he suddenly cried out, in a voice that startled every one, up to the very judge on the bench: "Stop!"

There was a pause, and all eyes looked at him. The perspiration was pouring over his face like water, and he made strange, uncouth signs with his hands to the judge opposite. "Stop all this!" he cried again; "I've been the ruin of the father and the death of the child. Hang me before I do more harm! Hang me, for God's sake, out of the way!" As soon as the shock produced by this extraordinary interruption had subsided, he was removed, and there followed a long discussion about whether he was of sound mind or not. The matter was left to the jury to decide by their verdict. They found him guilty of the charge of manslaughter, without the excuse of insanity. He was brought up again, and condemned to transportation for life. All he did, on hearing the dreadful sentence, was to reiterate his desperate words: "Hang me before I do more harm! Hang me, for God's sake, out of the way!"

.June 20th. I made yesterday's entry in sadness of heart, and I have not been better in my spirits to-day. It is something to have brought the murderer to the punishment that he deserves. But the knowledge that this most righteous act of retribution is accomplished brings no consolation with it. The law does indeed punish Noah Truscott for his crime, but can it raise up Mary Mallinson from her last resting-place in the churchyard?

While writing of the law, I ought to record that the heartless wretch who allowed Mary to be struck down in his presence without making an attempt to defend her is not likely to escape with perfect impunity. The policeman who looked after him to insure his attendance at the trial discovered that he had committed past offenses, for which the law can make him answer. A summons was executed upon him, and he was taken before the magistrate the moment he left the court after giving his evidence.

I had just written these few lines, and was closing my journal, when there came a knock at the door. I answered it, thinking that Robert had called on his way home to say good-night, and found myself face to face with a strange gentleman, who immediately asked for Anne Rodway. On hearing that I was the person inquired for, he requested five minutes' conversation with me. I showed him into the little empty room at the back of the house, and waited, rather surprised and fluttered, to hear what he had to say.

He was a dark man, with a serious manner, and a short, stern way of speaking I was certain that he was a stranger, and yet there seemed something in his face not unfamiliar to me. He began by taking a newspaper from his pocket, and asking me if I was the person who had given evidence at the trial of Noah Truscott on a charge of manslaughter. I answered immediately that I was.

"I have been for nearly two years in London seeking Mary Mallinson, and always seeking her in vain," he said. "The first and only news I have had of her I found in the newspaper report of the trial yesterday."

He still spoke calmly, but there was something in the look of his eyes which showed me that he was suffering in spirit. A sudden nervousness overcame me, and I was obliged to sit down.

"You knew Mary Mallinson, sir?" I asked, as quietly as I could.

"I am her brother."

I clasped my hands and hid my face in despair. Oh, the bitterness of heart with which I heard him say those simple words!

"You were very kind to her," said the calm, tearless man. "In her name and for her sake, I thank you."

"Oh, sir," I said, "why did you never write to her when you were in foreign parts?"

"I wrote often," he answered; "but each of my letters contained a remittance of money. Did Mary tell you she had a stepmother? If she did, you may guess why none of my letters were allowed to reach her. I now know that this woman robbed my sister. Has she lied in telling me that she was never informed of Mary's place of abode?"

I remembered that Mary had never communicated with her stepmother after the separation, and could therefore assure him that the woman had spoken the truth.

He paused for a moment after that, and sighed. Then he took out a pocket-book, and said:

"I have already arranged for the payment of any legal expenses that may have been incurred by the trial, but I have still to reimburse you for the funeral charges which you so generously defrayed. Excuse my speaking bluntly on this subject; I am accustomed to look on all matters where money is concerned purely as matters of business."

I saw that he was taking several bank-notes out of the pocket-book, and stopped him.

"I will gratefully receive back the little money I actually paid, sir, because I am not well off, and it would be an ungracious act of pride in me to refuse it from you," I said; "but I see you handling bank-notes, any one of which is far beyond the amount you have to repay me. Pray put them back, sir. What I did for your poor lost sister I did from my love and fondness for her. You have thanked me for that, and your thanks are all I can receive."

He had hitherto concealed his feelings, but I saw them now begin to get the better of him. His eyes softened, and he took my hand and squeezed it hard.

"I beg your pardon," he said; "I beg your pardon, with all my heart."

There was silence between us, for I was crying, and I believe, at heart, he was crying too. At last he dropped my hand, and seemed to change back, by an effort, to his former calmness.

"Is there no one belonging to you to whom I can be of service?" he asked. "I see among the witnesses on the trial the name of a young man who appears to have assisted you in the inquiries which led to the prisoner's conviction. Is he a relation?"

"No, sir—at least, not now—but I hope—"

"What?"

"I hope that he may, one day, be the nearest and dearest relation to me that a woman can have." I said those words boldly, because I was afraid of his otherwise taking some wrong view of the connection between Robert and me

"One day?" he repeated. "One day may be a long time hence."

"We are neither of us well off, sir," I said. "One day means the day when we are a little richer than we are now."

"Is the young man educated? Can he produce testimonials to his character? Oblige me by writing his name and address down on the back of that card."

When I had obeyed, in a handwriting which I am afraid did me no credit, he took out another card and gave it to me.

"I shall leave England to-morrow," he said. "There is nothing now to keep me in my own country. If you are ever in any difficulty or distress (which I pray God you may never be), apply to my London agent, whose address you have there."

He stopped, and looked at me attentively, then took my hand again.

"Wher e is she buried?" he said, suddenly, in a quick whisper, turning his head away.

I told him, and added that we had made the grave as beautiful as we could with grass and flowers. I saw his lips whiten and tremble.

"God bless and reward you!" he said, and drew me toward him quickly and kissed my forehead. I was quite overcome, and sank down and hid my face on the table. When I looked up again he was gone.

June 25th, 1841. I write these lines on my wedding morning, when little more than a year has passed since Robert returned to England.

His salary was increased yesterday to one hundred and fifty pounds a year. If I only knew where Mr. Mallinson was, I would write and tell him of our present happiness. But for the situation which his kindness procured for Robert, we might still have been waiting vainly for the day that has now come.

I am to work at home for the future, and Sally is to help us in our new abode. If Mary could have lived to see this day! I am not ungrateful for my blessings; but oh, how I miss that sweet face on this morning of all others!

I got up to-day early enough to go alone to the grave, and to gather the nosegay that now lies before me from the flowers that grow round it. I shall put it in my bosom when Robert comes to fetch me to the church. Mary would have been my bridesmaid if she had lived; and I can't forget Mary, even on my wedding-day. . . .

THE NIGHT.

THE last words of the last story fell low and trembling from Owen's lips. He waited for a moment while Jessie dried the tears which Anne Rodway's simple diary had drawn from her warm young heart, then closed the manuscript, and taking her hand patted it in his gentle, fatherly way.

"You will be glad to hear, my love," he said, "that I can speak from personal experience of Anne Rodway's happiness. She came to live in my parish soon after the trial at which she appeared as chief witness, and I was the clergyman who married her. Months before that I knew her story, and had read those portions of her diary which you have just heard. When I made her my little present on her wedding day, and when she gratefully entreated me to tell her what she could do for me in return, I asked for a copy of her diary to keep among the papers that I treasured most. 'The reading of it now and then,' I said, 'will encourage that faith in the brighter and better part of human nature which I hope, by God's help, to preserve pure to my dying day.' In that way I became possessed of the manuscript: it was Anne's husband who made the copy for me. You have noticed a few withered leaves scattered here and there between the pages. They were put there, years since, by the bride's own hand: they are all that now remain of the flowers that Anne Rodway gathered on her marriage morning from Mary Mallinson's grave."

Jessie tried to answer, but the words failed on her lips. Between the effect of the story, and the anticipation of the parting now so near at hand, the good, impulsive, affectionate creature was fairly overcome. She laid her head on Owen's shoulder, and kept tight hold of his hand, and let her heart speak simply for itself, without attempting to help it by a single word.

The silence that followed was broken harshly by the tower clock. The heavy hammer slowly rang out ten strokes through the gloomy night-time and the dying storm.

I waited till the last humming echo of the clock fainted into dead stillness. I listened once more attentively, and again listened in vain. Then I rose, and proposed to my brothers that we should leave our guest to compose herself for the night.

When Owen and Morgan were ready to quit the room, I took her by the hand, and drew her a little aside.

"You leave us early, my dear," I said; "but, before you go to-morrow morning—"

I stopped to listen for the last time, before the words were spoken which committed me to the desperate experiment of pleading George's cause in defiance of his own request. Nothing caught my ear but the sweep of the weary weakened wind and the melancholy surging of the shaken trees.

"But, before you go to-morrow morning," I resumed, "I want to speak to you in private. We shall breakfast at eight o'clock. Is it asking too much to beg you to come and see me alone in my study at half past seven?"

Just as her lips opened to answer me I saw a change pass over her face. I had kept her hand in mine while I was speaking, and I must have pressed it unconsciously so hard as almost to hurt her. She may even have uttered a few words of remonstrance; but they never reached me: my whole hearing sense was seized, absorbed, petrified. At the very instant when I had ceased speaking, I, and I alone, heard a faint sound—a sound that was new to me—fly past the Glen Tower on the wings of the wind.

"Open the window, for God's sake!" I cried.

My hand mechanically held hers tighter and tighter. She struggled to free it, looking hard at me with pale cheeks and frightened eyes. Owen hastened up and released her, and put his arms round me.

"Griffith, Griffith!" he whispered, "control yourself, for George's sake."

Morgan hurried to the window and threw it wide open.

The wind and rain rushed in fiercely. Welcome, welcome wind! They all heard it now. "Oh, Father in heaven, so merciful to fathers on earth—my son, my son!"

It came in, louder and louder with every gust of wind—the joyous, rapid gathering roll of wheels. My eyes fastened on her as if they could see to her heart, while she stood there with her sweet face turned on me all pale and startled. I tried to speak to her; I tried to break away from Owen's arms, to throw my own arms round her, to keep her on my bosom, till *he* came to take her from me. But all my strength had gone in the long waiting and the long suspense. My head sank on Owen's breast—but I still heard the wheels. Morgan loosened my cravat, and sprinkled water over my face—I still heard the wheels. The poor terrified girl ran into her room, and came back with her smelling-salts—I heard the carriage stop at the house. The room whirled round and round with me; but I heard the eager hurry of footsteps in the hall, and the opening of the door. In another moment my son's voice rose clear and cheerful from below, greeting the old servants who loved him. The dear, familiar tones just poured into my ear, and then, the moment they filled it, hushed me suddenly to rest.

When I came to myself again my eyes opened upon George. I was lying on the sofa, still in the same room; the lights we had read by in the evening were burning on the table; my son was kneeling at my pillow, and we two were alone.

THE MORNING.

THE wind is fainter, but there is still no calm. The rain is ceasing, but there is still no sunshine. The view from my window shows me the mist heavy on the earth, and a dim gray veil drawn darkly over the sky. Less than twelve hours since, such a prospect would have saddened me for the day. I look out at it this morning, through the bright medium of my own happiness, and not the shadow of a shade falls across the steady inner sunshine that is poring over my heart.

The pen lingers fondly in my hand, and yet it is little, very little, that I have left to say. The Purple Volume lies open by my side, with the stories ranged together in it in the order in which they were read. My son has learned to prize them already as the faithful friends who served him at his utmost need. I have only to wind off the little thread of narrative on which they are all strung together before the volume is closed and our anxious literary experiment fairly ended.

My son and I had a quiet hour together on that happy night before we retired to rest. The little love-plot invented in George's interests now required one last stroke of diplomacy to complete it before we all threw off our masks and assumed our true characters for the future. When my son and I parted for the night, we had planned the necessary stratagem for taking our lovely guest by surprise as soon as she was out of her bed in the morning.

Shortly after seven o'clock I sent a message to Jessie by her maid, informing her that a good night's rest had done wonders for me, and that I expected to see her in my study at half past seven, as we had arranged the evening before. As soon as her answer, promising to be punctual to the appointment, had reached me, I took George into my study—left him in my place to plead his own cause—and stole away, five minutes before the half hour, to join my brothers in the breakfast-room.

Although the sense of my own happiness disposed me to take the brightest view of my son's chances, I must nevertheless acknowledge that some nervous anxieties still fluttered about my heart while the slow minutes of suspense were counting themselves out in the breakfast-room. I had as little attention to spare for Owen's quiet prognostications of success as for Morgan's pitiless sarcasms on love, courtship, and matrimony. A quarter of an hour elapsed—then twenty minutes. The hand moved on, and the clock pointed to five minutes to eight, before I heard the study door open, and before the sound of rapidly-advancing footsteps warned me that George was coming into the room.

His beaming face told the good news before a word could be spoken on either side. The excess of his happiness literally and truly deprived him of speech. He stood eagerly looking at us all three, with outstretched hands and glistening eyes.

"Have I folded up my surplice forever," asked Owen, "or am I to wear it once again, George, in your service?"

"Answer this question first," interposed Morgan, with a look of grim anxiety. "Have you actually taken your young woman off my hands, or have you not?"

No direct answer followed either question. George's feelings had been too deeply stirred to allow him to return jest for jest at a moment's notice.

"Oh, father, how can I thank you!" he said. "And you! and you!" he added, looking at Owen and Morgan gratefully.

"You must thank Chance as well as thank us," I replied, speaking as lightly as my heart would let me, to encourage him. "The advantage of numbers in our little love-plot was all on our side. Remember, George, we were three to one."

While I was speaking the breakfast-room door opened noiselessly, and showed us Jessie standing on the threshold, uncertain whether to join us or to run back to her own room. Her bright complexion heightened to a deep glow; the tears just rising in her eyes, and not yet falling from them; her delicate lips trembling a little, as if they were still shyly conscious of other lips that had pressed them but a few minutes since; her attitude irresolutely graceful; her hair just disturbed enough over her forehead and her cheeks to add to the charm of them—she stood before us, the loveliest living picture of youth, and tenderness, and virgin love that eyes ever looked on. George and I both advanced together to meet her at the door. But the good, grateful girl had heard from my son the true story of all that I had done, and hoped, and suffered for the last ten days, and showed charmingly how she felt it by turning at once to *me*.

"May I stop at the Glen Tower a little longer?" she asked, simply.

"If you think you can get through your evenings, my love," I answered. "'But surely you forget that the Purple Volume is closed, and that the stories have all come to an end?"

She clasped her arms round my neck, and laid her cheek fondly against mine.

"How you must have suffered yesterday!" she whispered, softly.

"And how happy I am to-day!"

The tears gathered in her eyes and dropped over her cheeks as she raised her head to look at me affectionately when I said those words. I gently unclasped her arms and led her to George.

"So you really did love him, then, after all," I whispered, "though you were too sly to let me discover it?"

A smile broke out among the tears as her eyes wandered away from mine and stole a look at my son. The clock struck the hour, and the servant came in with breakfast. A little domestic interruption of this kind was all that was wanted to put us at our ease. We drew round the table cheerfully, and set the Queen of Hearts at the head of it, in the character of mistress of the house already.

Lightning Source UK Ltd.
Milton Keynes UK
24 August 2010

158943UK00001B/107/A